D1355731

9030 00007 8179 8

TRAITOR
IN THE
ICE

By K. J. Maitland

Daniel Pursglove novels
The Drowned City
Traitor in the Ice

As Karen Maitland
The White Room
Company of Liars
The Owl Killers
The Gallows Curse
The Falcons of Fire and Ice
The Vanishing Witch
The Raven's Head
The Plague Charmer
A Gathering of Ghosts

Digital short stories
Liars and Thieves
The Dangerous Art of Alchemy
Wicked Children: Murderous Tales from History

K. J. MAITLAND

TRAITOR
IN THE
ICE

REVIEW

First published in 2022 by Headline Review
An imprint of HEADLINE PUBLISHING GROUP

1

Cataloguing in Publication Data is available from the British Library

Hardback ISBN 978 1 4722 7545 5
Trade paperback ISBN 978 1 4722 7546 2

Typeset by EM&EN

Printed and bound in Great Britain by Clays Ltd, Elcograf S.p.A.

www.headline.co.uk
www.hachette.co.uk

'Many malignant and devilish Papists, Jesuits, and Seminary Priests, much envying and fearing, conspired most horribly, when the King's most excellent Majesty, the Queen, the Prince, and the Lords Spiritual and Temporal, and Commons, should have been assembled in the Upper House of Parliament upon the Fifth Day of November in the Year of our Lord One thousand six hundred and five, suddenly to have blown up the said whole House with Gunpowder: an invention so inhuman, barbarous and cruel, as the like was never before heard of . . . which would have turned to the utter ruin of this whole kingdom, had it not pleased Almighty God, by inspiring the King's most excellent Majesty with a Divine Spirit, to interpret some dark phrases of a letter showed to his Majesty, above and beyond ordinary construction, thereby miraculously discovering this hidden treason not many hours before the appointed time for the execution thereof . . .'

The introduction to the 'Thanksgiving Act' or 'The Observance of 5th November 1605' which required that 'Ministers in every Cathedral and Parish Church, or other usual Place for Common Prayer . . . shall always upon the fifth day of November say Morning Prayer, and give unto Almighty God thanks for this most happy deliverance'. During this service the minister was ordered to 'publickly, distinctly and plainly' read out the text of the Act and 'all persons to diligently and faithfully resort to the Parish Church or Chapel accustomed' on 5 November and 'to abide orderly and soberly during the time of said prayers'.

Prologue

BATTLE ABBEY, SUSSEX

HE SHOULD HAVE turned back before the blood-red sun began to sink. He should have hurried away before the rooks descended like ragged witches upon their night roost. He'd been a fool to walk all the way out there to the holy spring at that hour and he would live long enough to curse himself for it . . . *just* long enough. We fret and sweat over the choices that seem certain to tip the balance of our fortunes, but in truth it's not the crossroads of our lives that determine their lengths. It is the unseen thorn which poisons our finger, the forgotten key we turn back for, the single careless step. It is these tiny pismires in our fragile lives that will ultimately cut them dead.

The bitter cold had savaged every field and forest, byre and barn. The wolf's bite they called it, for the beast had sunk its sharp teeth deep into the heart of the land and nothing would make it relinquish its prey. As the cold sun sank behind the black bones of leafless trees, the man could feel the breath of the ice wolf on his skin. He stamped his feet as he trudged over the frozen leaf mould, trying to force feeling back into numbed toes. He had stuffed his boots with raw sheep's wool, torn from the hedges, but the frosted air sucked every last drop of heat from his limbs.

A crack echoed through the wood. He spun round, but nothing was stirring, not even the withered brown bracken, each frond encased in its own ice coffin. Sense told him he should be holding his staff at the ready, for darkness was closing in and with it the foul creatures of the night, both animal and human. But he had tied his staff to the pack on his back for it was more of a hindrance than a help on the iron-hard ground. Now he was too weary and stiff to wrestle the pack to the ground. Besides, all he wanted to do was to reach the blessed heat of a warm room and a blazing fire as quickly as his frozen legs would carry him.

With clumsy fingers, he pushed the scarf he'd tied around his face higher up his nose, breathing hard through the cloth, though that was now stiff with ice from his breath. He quickened his pace. For the second time that evening, he cursed himself for not having started back an hour since. If he had, he'd already be warming his numb feet at the hearth, his belly full of hot mutton stew, his fingers wrapped around a steaming beaker of mulled ale. He slipped in one of the ice-filled ruts on the path and his shoulder crashed into a tree trunk. He growled in pain and annoyance.

He stood for a moment, trying to regain his breath. It was almost dark now. Only a faint grey breath of light ghosted between the black trunks. The first stars glittered in the devil-dark sky. No animals scuttled through the crust of fallen leaves; not even the owls called to one another. The only sounds in the stillness were the crackles, like ice popping in water; the branches were splintering in the cold.

He strode forward again, suddenly aware now of the echo of his own footfalls as his thick boots crunched over the frozen ground. He had never heard an echo in woods. The icy air must be playing tricks on his ears, just as it was on his eyes, making the stars seem to creep between the tangled branches. He stopped, but the echo did not. It quickened. It was no longer an echo of his footsteps, for his own feet had taken root in the earth. He sensed, rather than saw, the movement behind him, felt, but did not hear, the great crack on his skull. He fell to his knees and was already insensible before his face crashed down on to the glass-sharp leaves.

*

He thought he was lying in a deep well, fighting up through the heavy, back water, struggling to reach the light and air above. Only the sudden explosion of pain in his head convinced him that he wasn't trapped in a dream. He tried to open his eyes and thought for a moment that his lids had frozen shut, until he painfully twisted his head and glimpsed three needlepoints of silver light that he realised must be stars far above him and by their faint light he saw the jagged spars of a broken roof.

It was only as he tried to move that he understood that his numb and gloveless hands were bound tightly behind him. His legs . . . did he have legs? The searing pain in his bare feet told him they must still be attached to him. The throbbing of his head and limbs was so all-consuming that it was only as he tried to cry out that he found he could barely draw breath. The cloth which he had used to mask his face from the cold had been tied tightly across his mouth, smothering any sound. He was cold, so cold. His coat was gone. He lay on the icy earth, clad only in his shirt and breeches.

He heard footsteps crunching over the leaves, ponderous, heavy, coming closer and closer. He turned his head. Someone was standing over him, staring down. Relief flooded through him. He wriggled and mewed through the gag, trying to show his rescuer he was alive but bound. It was too dark to see the figure's face, only a shadowy mass, a smudged outline, the whites of eyes shining in the starlight that pierced the broken roof. He caught the smell of tobacco and a sickly, fetid stench. He knew that foul odour. He had smelled it before. But his head was aching so much, the cold gnawing so deep into his thoughts, that he was struggling to put a name to it.

The figure heaved up something large and heavy, holding it in both hands, seeming to take aim at the helpless man lying trussed beneath him. Relief turned instantly to terror. The man tried frantically to roll away. He was pleading, praying, calling out to Christ to save him, but his desperate words were smothered by the thick gag. A shock of icy water cascaded down on his head

3

and back, snatching the breath from his lungs and momentarily arresting his heart so that he feared it might never beat again. He lay shaking violently, jerking back and forth, as if he was in the grip of the falling sickness.

For a long moment, the figure stood over him, watching him silently, then it turned and trudged away without word. The man on the ground was dimly aware of the footsteps fading away into silence in the woods beyond the hut. They did not return.

He had gone beyond shivering. His sodden shirt had frozen to his skin and to the hard earth beneath him, but the agony in his hands and feet had melted away. He felt hot now. He was at home, sitting far too close to the fire. The air was stifling. He couldn't breathe. He was burning up. He was dragging off his clothes, running out through the door, trying to reach the pump or the river, desperate for cold water.

But as quickly as he'd grown hot, he was suddenly chilled to the marrow of his bones again. It was dark, so dark. Where was he? What was he doing out here? How had he got there? He was sure he could remember if he tried, but he was too tired to think now. He was sinking down and down into the soft oozing mud of sleep. Briefly he turned his face towards the jagged hole above. Three eyes were peering down at him, glittering like little fish in a brook, or were they candles? Had they come to light his way home?

The pale pink light of dawn washed through the trees, sending sparks of light shivering across the frost that lay thick on the broken spars of the old hut. A spider's web hung from the corner, each hair-thin thread gilded in silver and spangled with a thousand tiny diamonds. The black spider who had spun this exquisitely lethal trap lay as dead as the husks of the flies beneath it.

A hungry rat, driven by desperation from its hole beneath the ruined hut, gnawed on a blackened fingertip of the corpse. Why should worms feast while rats starve? The trees beyond did not hear the scrabble of sharp claws on the man's frozen skin or the rasp of yellow teeth on bone. They stood peering down in wonder at the rust-red puddles and the scarlet pools frozen at their feet, red as the blood of the ten thousand men once slaughtered in this place. Proof, they say, that the earth rejects the blood of the innocents, as water rejects the bones of a witch. Our corpse will not want for company among that great army of the dead.

Chapter One

OUT OF THE DARKNESS, cannon fire roared across the river, reverberating off the buildings around Charing Cross. Shutters and doors rattled, and an old barrel set on top of the teetering pile of firewood, towering almost as high as the Eleanor Cross itself, crashed to the ground, exploding into a shower of splinters and dust. But the crowd gathered around only roared with merriment when those close by fell over their own feet as they scrambled aside. Another round of cannon fire answered the first, and the night sky was suddenly lit by a red and orange glow as bonfires all along the banks of the Thames, and in every patch of open ground in the city, burst into flames. In Charing Cross, two men dashed forward to the heap of wood, brandishing burning torches, trails of smoke and fire streaming behind them in the chill breeze. They thrust the torches deep into the base of the bonfire. The rush and crackle of flames as they swept up through the pyre was drowned out by the roar of the crowd.

'Traitors! Traitors! Death to all traitors!'

Two small boys ran up, their arms full of broken wooden panels that looked as if they had been newly torn from the shutters of a house. Whooping, they hurled them on to the fire, their gleeful, dirty faces aglow in the flames. Judging by the assortment of wooden clothesline poles, stools and pails, many goodwives in London would be cursing the gunpowder plotters anew as their tenements and yards were ransacked for anything that passing lads could carry off to burn on the bonfires.

A man, squeezing between the houses and the back of the crowd, found himself momentarily trapped as the mass of people drew back from the stinging smoke pouring from tar-covered timbers and green wood that had been heaped on the pyre. A volley of shots rattled across the river, as men in the boats fired their pieces at the squibs exploding in the night sky, as if they were shooting at firebirds. Everyone seemed determined that this year's celebrations should be even wilder than the last.

Church bells had been ringing out across London for most of the day, and the regular congregations had been swollen to bursting by those crowding in to listen to the thanksgiving sermons and the prayers of deliverance from the Jesuit plot two years earlier, which had threatened to blow the King, his family and every member of Parliament and the House of Lords into millions of bloody pieces. Attendance at church on this day was compulsory and few men or women, Protestant, Catholic or Puritan, would dare to absent themselves from the services when the Act of the Observance was read out from every pulpit in the land. There were eyes and spies on every street and any man's neighbour or goodwife's maid might be willing to report such an absence to prove their own loyalty, or for the temptation of a fat purse.

But the man trying now to extract himself from the press of people was one of the few exceptions, though you would not have guessed as much merely by observing him. He was clad in plain brown and olive-green riding clothes and leather boots. He had left his heavy riding cloak at the inn where he had taken lodgings for the night and replaced it with a short half-cloak fastened across one shoulder, which left his dagger arm free for swift defence, should it prove necessary. His dark hair, neatly cut, grazed his shoulders, but he sported no curled lovelock, and his beard, which had also been newly trimmed, was unfashionably full and long. Together with the high white collar of the shirt, they mostly concealed the scarlet firemark that encircled his neck like a noose from all but the keenest stare.

Daniel Pursglove, which was not, of course, his real name, but the most recent of many he had adopted over his thirty years, had not attended church that day, nor had he any intention of doing so. He had ridden into London late that afternoon, and now he had only two things on his mind: food, and the message he had received three days before, summoning him to the tiny hamlet of Rotherhithe on the banks of the Thames the following morning.

Obliged to spend the night in London, he had avoided the cheap taverns of Southwark; not that he had money to waste, but he had frequented those places when he had worked the streets entertaining the crowds with his tricks of legerdemain, before those same conjuring tricks had got him arrested on charges of sorcery, and he could not risk running into old friends – or enemies.

Daniel extracted himself from the crowd and started up the street away from the bonfire, but before he could turn the corner, he heard shouts and boots pounding up the street behind him. He whirled round, his back pressed against the solid wall of a house, his knife already in his hand. A dozen or so youths were running towards him, stout sticks and iron bars in their fists. Daniel braced himself, but they didn't give him a second glance as they rushed by, slowing only when they reached some houses further ahead. The group had divided, so that they were now running along each side of the street, beating on doors and shutters with their cudgels, and gouging the plaster on the walls of the houses as they passed. A woman foolishly opened a window in one of the upper rooms, shouting at them in broad Scottish accent to 'leave folks be'.

'We'll leave you be, when you leave London,' one yelled up at her. Another started a familiar chant and the others joined in high-pitched parody of the woman's voice:

'Hark, hark, the dogs do bark,
The beggars have come to town,
Some in rags and some in jags
And one in a velvet gown.'

It was a dangerous mockery of King James and his Scottish courtiers, for no one in the city could mistake who the last line of the verse referred to, but it was one that Daniel had heard chanted with increasing boldness over these past months. Resentment of the Scots was growing by the day and rumours swilled through every street and village that all of the money raised by the fines on the English Catholics was being sent north of the border or lavished on the King's Scottish favourites, the latest of which, if the broadsides were to be believed, was the dashing young horseman Robert Carr.

The woman in the upper window vanished for a moment, then reappeared with a pail, which she emptied on the men standing below. They leaped back as vegetable peelings, mutton bones and chicken guts slithered out and tumbled down. Their clothes were splashed as the soggy mess plopped into the mud, but they only laughed and jeered, scooping up handfuls of it from the street and hurling it back, splattering the walls as they tried to lob it through the open casement. The woman hastily slammed the window. The men beat on her stout front door with their iron bars, denting and splintering the wood.

They seemed hell-bent on staving it in and would probably have continued until they had succeeded, had not a young man turned into the street ahead of them. With a howl like a pack of wolves, the 'Swaggerers' ran at him, their cudgels and iron bars raised high. The man stared at them in a moment of frozen alarm, then turned and fled. Daniel knew if they caught him, he would be lucky if he could crawl home. Many Scots had taken up residence in Charing Cross and Holborn, banding together for protection and support from their hostile English neighbours. The Swaggerers knew their hunting grounds well and they seemed to have developed an instinct for spotting a Scot even at a distance.

A boom from the cannons rang across the city, probably from a ship making its own loyal salute to God and King. It was followed by another wild burst of shot as men fired their own pieces with reckless abandon. It was to be hoped that no one got killed this year as the ships' crews tried to outdo each other by producing ever-louder explosions, determined to make as great a bang as the gunpowder plotters had intended.

As the sound of the cannon died away, a blast of pipe, lute, cymbals and drums rolled out from the archway ahead, with cheers and good-natured yells. The music, if you could call it that, was coming from the courtyard of a tenement inn where a play – a comedy, judging by the shrieks of laughter – had just ended. Men and women hung over the balconies tossing coins down upon the motley group of players below who, between deep bows, scrambled to scoop them up and make their escape, darting anxious glances at any new faces that appeared through the archway. Either they were not licensed to perform by the Lord Chamberlain, Daniel thought, or the play was one that might land its authors in the Tower for sedition, as the authors of *Eastward Hoe* had discovered to their cost. And the players had good reason to be nervous, for every informer and intelligencer in the pay of Robert Cecil or the King would be abroad among the crowds this night, listening for talk of plots, unrest or treason.

Now that the play was concluded, trestle tables were being dragged forward and those who had been in the balcony were already clattering down the wooden staircases, drawn by the smell of roasting pig and crab apple sauce that wafted out tantalisingly from the kitchens. Daniel's belly growled. But he marched on passed the inn and drew back into the recesses of a dark doorway, from where he could watch the street without being seen. Behind him, a broad shaft of light spilled out right across the road from the lanterns and torches that had been lit in the courtyard of the inn to illuminate the players. Anyone walking past would have to pass through that cone of light and would, for a few moments, be clearly visible.

Daniel had been on his guard ever since the message from Charles FitzAlan had arrived, sure that his journey into London was being tracked and that FitzAlan would already know where he was lodging and would have someone trailing his every step. But none of those who strolled through the shaft of light seemed to be following him. No one quickened their pace as if they had lost sight of their quarry or pulled hoods lower over their faces as the light struck them.

He forced himself to wait a little longer, then made his way back to the courtyard, seating himself in the corner beneath the overhang of balcony above, from where he could watch all who came and went through the archway. The pork proved to be every bit as succulent as it smelled, the skin crisp, honey-sweet and spicy, glistening red-gold in the lamplight. The musicians continued to play bawdy songs on fiddle, lute and pipe which a few customers joined in singing, but most were occupied with the serious task of eating and drinking, while others wagered on games of Maw or Hazard, their muttered conversations punctuated by shouts of triumph or groans as they won or lost on the roll of the dice or the card in their hands.

The inn was evidently a popular one, especially on this night when every man and woman in London seemed to be abroad, determined to make the most of the revels. No table or bench remained empty for long, as those pushing out through the archway were quickly replaced by those shoving in, seduced by the savour of sweet roasting meat and the familiar tunes of the musicians. Those who could not find places to sit had gathered close to burning braziers, for though the courtyard was sheltered on three sides by the buildings, with the coming of darkness the air had taken on a sharp winter chill and a snide wind from the river made even those highborn enough to be wrapped in fur cloaks draw them tighter.

A furious yell made Daniel glance across to the far side. Two men had risen from a dicing table and now appeared to be confronting four others who had just entered the courtyard. Both the men who'd been gambling were clearly of some wealth, if not standing. Their hair was long and curled over stiff lace ruffs, plumes were fastened to their hats by jewelled broches, and by the weighty hang of their velvet cloaks, they were fur-lined. The shorter of the two men sported a long drop earing in his left ear, which gleamed red like a clot of fresh blood in the lamplight, swinging and dancing with the smallest movement of his head.

The four men who'd entered were more plainly clad, their hair shorter, their beards spade-cut, and wore long collars of soft linen in place of stiffened ruffs. As they advanced, they flicked back their woollen cloaks, three of them revealing long daggers on their belts, the other a wickedly slender stiletto, the assassin's weapon. Although they had not drawn their blades, the threatening gestures were unmistakable. Customers began to back away. Those who had been playing with the two men swept up their dice and coins, and rapidly vacated the benches. Those seated at nearby tables also scrambled up, some slipping out through the archway, others lingering to watch. The innkeeper, alerted, perhaps, by one of the serving girls, came hurrying across the yard, frantically signalling to the musicians to play louder, as if the music might sooth the inflamed tempers. But though it drowned out the words, it was evident to all it had not calmed the men, for judging by the obscene and threatening gestures, taunts and insults were flying freely on the chill wind. All the time, the two parties were edging closer to each other.

One of the four newcomers lunged towards the pair, grabbing the earing that had been winking and flashing so provocatively in the light and tearing it from the man's lobe, ripping the flesh away with it. The man yelped, pressing his hand to the wound. Blood ran from between his ringed fingers, splashing down on to the white lace ruff. The musicians' notes faltered and died as they retreated. The assailant brandished the jewel aloft in a clenched fist, whooping in triumph and punching the night sky with it, while his three companions rocked with exaggerated guffaws of laughter.

'Whoreson Scots!' a man close to Daniel snarled. 'Been snatching earrings all over London. Some've had their whole ear slashed off.'

'Aye.' His neighbour shook his head 'So, you'd think those popinjays would have more brains than to walk around wearing them if they're not looking for trouble.'

'And why should any true Englishman be forced to change what he wears in his own city by those foreign barbarians?' his wife retorted.

Her husband opened his mouth to argue but was cut off by a screech of rage. All craned to see what was happening. One of the serving girls came flying out from the kitchens like an avenging fury, yelling curses at the Scots. She pulled the wounded man down on to a bench, cradling his head against her breasts, and attempted to staunch the copious flow of blood with the stained and grubby cloth she used to wipe the spills from the table.

His companion unfastened his cloak clasp with one hand as he drew his rapier with the other. The cloak fell to ground and he advanced on the Scotsman, who had his back to him and was still waving his prize aloft, jeering and laughing. His fellow country-men, catching sight of the weapon, yelled a warning and pulled out their own daggers. The ringleader whirled round and tried to unsheathe his stiletto, but he was not swift enough. The rapier flashed as the Englishman thrust it forward in a deadly strike. The Scotsman swerved aside, but though it missed his heart, the blade went right through his shoulder with such force that the steel, glistening with scarlet blood, protruded a good three or four inches out the other side. The Englishman twisted it, trying to drag it out, while the Scot, his face contorted in agony, kicked out at his stomach, attempting to knock him backwards and wrench the weapon from his hand. After a moment's hesita-tion, the other three Scotsmen darted into the fray, their daggers drawn, while another man vaulted across a table and savagely struck the Englishman's sword arm with an iron ladle, so that he lost his grip on the rapier hilt. But the crowd around were not standing for that. Brandishing stools, knives and even wooden trenchers, men and women alike charged at the Scots.

For a moment, little could be seen or heard except for shrieks and yells, the crash of overturning benches, and the clatter of falling pots and jugs as the knot of people pushed and shoved. Then, with a howl of fury, the gang of Swaggerers that Daniel had seen earlier came running into the courtyard. At the sight of them, two of the Scotsmen tore themselves free from the fight and, unable to escape through the archway, charged towards the doorway of the inn, slashing out wildly with their daggers as they ran. The man who had snatched the earring staggered after them. He had evidently managed to wrench the rapier from his shoulder, but blood was streaming down his arm, leaving a wet glistening trail on the flagstones behind him. The fourth man lay slumped on the ground, his face battered and bleeding. The Swaggerers charged after the fleeing men. The Englishman, pausing only to snatch up his rapier, sprinted after them. As they hurtled towards the parlour door of the inn, they came within touching distance of Daniel.

Up to then, the face of the man wielding the rapier had been largely in the shadows, but now Daniel saw him clearly. He was in his thirties, tawny blond hair, his cheeks clean-shaven and a beard trimmed into a short, sharp point. Those eyes, pale and green as spring grass, were only too familiar to Daniel. In fact, he knew them better than he knew his own, for he'd spent most of the first fifteen years of his life studying, sleeping and eating in this man's company. Together, they had learned to ride, to duel, to fight. Together they had grown from boys to men. They had been raised as if they were brothers, but they were not and never could be. Richard Fairfax!

He had already reached the door, charging straight past Daniel, so intent on hunting down his quarry that he hadn't even looked in his direction, still dismissing all those around him as not even worthy of a glance. Daniel's dagger was in his hand before he was even aware of it, the blade pointing straight between those shoulder blades framed in the doorway. One swift thrust, that was all it would take. He had done it before. Killing a man was easy; forcing himself to lower the dagger was not. Daniel pressed himself back into the shadows, as more men crowded through the open doorway behind Richard. Then he turned and walked out through the archway, his fist still gripping the knife.

Chapter Two

ROTHERHITHE, NEAR LONDON

CHARLES FITZALAN was already seated in a high-backed wooden chair at the far end of the long narrow galley, his twisted foot hidden beneath a draped table. Daniel bowed low as the door was closed softly behind him and he waited, listening to the sound of the servant's heavy footsteps retreating down the wooden stairs behind it. FitzAlan flicked his hand, gesturing for Daniel to come closer. Woven-reed mats stretching the length of the gallery deadened the sound of Daniel's riding boots on the boards as he took that slow, silent walk, but he found himself acutely conscious of the empty dagger sheath swinging against his hip. The burly servant had demanded he surrender the blade down in the hall below. He had expected as much. You did not enter this man's presence armed. All the same, he felt naked and defenceless.

The oak-panelled gallery to which he had been conducted was on the second floor of the house and ran the full length of the wing. The outer wall was blind, but from the casements on the inner wall you could look down into an enclosed knot garden below and beyond it to the slug-grey waters of the Thames. The oriel windows had been designed to make it impossible for anyone walking on the paths below to glimpse the occupants of the gallery, unless they were standing directly in one of the casement alcoves above. But it scarcely mattered on that leaden November afternoon: the garden was deserted save for a black-bird pecking at the sodden earth beneath the stark skeletons of the rosebushes.

The family who owned the house was evidently absent, for Daniel had seen no signs of life as he was led through the hall and up the stairs except for the hulk of a servant who had admitted him. The fire in the soot-black cavernous hearth had been laid, but not lit, in spite of the winter chill. Smoke rising from the chimney would send up a signal for miles that the house was being used, and FitzAlan clearly did not intend for that to be known.

Rotherhithe, which lay between Greenwich and the city of London, was a tiny hamlet, boasting few attractions except a church and a cluster of cottages. The wherryman who had rowed him there had looked at Daniel curiously, as if wondering what business any man might have in such a piddling village. Was this the only clandestine meeting FitzAlan had attended here? Who else had he summoned to this dismal house? But at least it *was* a house and not a prison, which is where Daniel had last been ordered to wait upon FitzAlan's pleasure; this time Daniel was a freeman, not a prisoner, but that could change with a single word.

FitzAlan watched him approach down the gallery in silence, his fingers restlessly plucking at the hilt of his sword, as if to remind Daniel that he was armed and Daniel was not. In front of the table, Daniel bowed again.

'Battle Abbey, do ye know it?' FitzAlan demanded in his thick Scots accent before Daniel had even fully straightened up. 'The late Viscount Montague's residence, have you visited it?' He pressed the tips of his black-rimmed fingernails together, leaning forward and studying Daniel as if he could read the answer in his face without him needing to utter a word.

'No, sir, I have not. Though my former employer, Viscount Rowe, spoke of Anthony Montague. He was once a member of the Privy Council, I believe.'

'Aye, he had that honour until he tried to thwart the wishes of Parliament and Queen Bess by publicly opposing the Act of Supremacy. Refused to swear the oath that the Sovereign was head of the Church of England and not the Pope. Montague

18

should have faced the block for that treason.' His fist clenched on the table. His tone had grown strident, but when he spoke again, his voice was brisk and light, almost as if, moments before, a demon had taken possession of him and was speaking through his mouth. 'Are you quite certain, Master Pursglove, that you've not been to Battle? But you've been to one of Montague's other houses, I've nay doubt, Cowdray Park or their London house?' His eyes narrowed and the bulging bags beneath them seemed to flick upwards, reminding Daniel of a lizard. 'Speak up, mon, but speak the truth. I'll not hold against ye if you tell me the Viscount or his widow, Magdalen, called on Lord Fairfax when you were a boy. I know these recusants cleave to each other like flies to shit. There's no blame would attach to you.'

Daniel kept his expression blank. *So, you have finally admitted to knowing I was raised by Lord Fairfax. And you would most certainly hold it against me if you thought I was one of those flies. I know who you are, FitzAlan. And I know only too well the fate that awaits those you blame.*

'I do not recall ever meeting the Viscount or his wife, sir.'

FitzAlan gave a mirthless bark. 'Lord Salisbury would say that sounds like a Jesuit equivocation, but I'll take your words as plainly meant. After all, if you're deceiving me and Magdalen recognises you, you'll be paying for it with a knife in your ribs. The last man the King sent to Battle to gather evidence against her is dead, mouldering in a roadside grave. And she'd not hesitate to have another dug for you alongside him. She may be in her seventieth year, but the wits and cunning that have kept her from the block these past decades are still sharper than an executioner's axe.'

'Am I to meet the lady, then?'

'Meet?' FitzAlan gave another bark. 'Who do you think you are, upstart!' You may once have moved in those circles as Secretary to Viscount Rowe, but I doubt the lady in question has ever bandied words with a common trickster.'

Beneath his short cloak, Daniel's fists clenched,

'I don't doubt you heard your master Rowe speak of "Little Rome". It's what they call Magdalen's household at Court. Half the locals in Battle town attend Mass in that old besom's chapel, along with all the recusant nobles in Sussex and beyond. They say as many as a hundred and twenty people have gathered there at some services, in brazen defiance of the law. The King has it on good report that there is even a holy well in Battle Abbey grounds to which she and other women make regular pilgrimage. That old woman's houses are crammed to the rafters with retired Marion priests, whom she now passes off as her servants. All of them lawfully ordained in England before Elizabeth took the throne, or so the old dowager claims.' FitzAlan threw himself back in the chair and snorted. 'If that's so, they must have been ordained before their beardless fathers even plucked their virgin mothers, else her entire staff would now be so old they could scarcely dress themselves, much less her table.'

Still leaning back, he stabbed a finger savagely towards Daniel. 'Mark me well, those priests she shelters now were not ordained in this realm. They're men who stole away to France to be trained in the ways of the Devil and now they have crept back, like rats into a barn of wheat, to make mischief and gnaw away at the very foundations of this kingdom. Battle Abbey, where Lady Magdalen has taken up permanent residence, is close to the coast, and it is certain that these priest and foreign spies are being smuggled in through Battle. The pursuivant, Richard Topcliffe, informed the King that she has even allowed a Catholic printing press to be set up in one of houses, so that their poison may be spread throughout England and beyond.'

And what method of torture did Topcliffe employ to extract that information? Daniel wondered. Starvation? Whipping? Gauntlets were said to be Topcliffe's favoured method. Topcliffe, one of several men commissioned by the Privy Council to hunt down and arrest known Catholic priests and traitors, had even endured a brief spell in prison himself when his zeal for inflicting pain had caused the Jesuit poet Robert Southwell to die under torture. Topcliffe's crime, though, had not been Southwell's murder, but that Topcliffe had let him die before he talked.

'If this much is known against Lady Magdalen . . .' Daniel began cautiously. He paused, considering how to phrase the question. It would be dangerous to ask if a warrant for her arrest had been signed. FitzAlan had already suggested Daniel had known the Montagues as a boy. He could be baiting a trap, convinced that Daniel would try to warn her.

'Known, yes, but *knowing* it seems is not sufficient proof for those beef-witted bladders who call themselves the Privy Council.' FitzAlan brought his fist down like a hammer upon the table, the bang echoing down the long empty gallery. 'Lady Magdalen believes herself so invincible that she openly flouts the law of the land and her liege King by refusing to attend the Protestant services. What's more, she encourages the villagers to ape her. And those blatherskites on the Privy Council claim she is a frail old woman of delicate breeding, so they will not sentence her for recusancy.'

She must have a powerful protector on the Privy Council, Daniel thought. Old age and high rank had certainly not saved others from the Tower or the block. Did she have information that someone on the Privy Council feared she could reveal if she was questioned, information which might implicate them in treason?

'Sir, if the Privy Council refuse to have her arrested by reason of her age and a man with Richard Topcliffe's reputation could not uncover sufficient evidence to convince them of her guilt, then what would you have me do?'

'Do?' FitzAlan snapped, glaring at Daniel as if he thought he was being deliberately obtuse. 'I thought I had made that plain enough. Master Benet, the King's pursuivant, is dead, in all likelihood murdered as he was leaving Battle to deliver his report. You appear to have a liking for digging into murders. You uncovered the truth behind those at Bristol, even though that was not your mission. Well, then, this time it is. If Benet was silenced, then it was because he had unearthed something far more dangerous to those at the Abbey than mere recusancy. Spero Pettingar has still not been run to ground. But someone knows who he is and where he is, and Lady Magdalen sits at the very heart of the Catholic network.'

Not that spectre again. Daniel's jaw clenched beneath his beard, but he tried to keep his expression blank. FitzAlan's obsession with the traitor had plainly not diminished over these few months. Doubtless the accursed star that had been hovering over England all through the autumn was to thank for that.

In the days that followed Guy Fawkes' arrest, an intelligencer had reported that on the final occasion when the gunpowder conspirators had all met together in the Mitre Tavern, there was a man among them who he knew only as Spero Pettingar. After that meeting, Pettingar disappeared as mysteriously as a gold ring vanishing from a conjurer's magic box. Even under torture, none of the conspirators admitted to knowing his real identity, but that had only served to convince King James that Pettingar was the fifth priest involved in that Jesuit plot and the most dangerous of all of the conspirators, maybe even their ringleader.

And the King could hardly have failed to notice the bearded star with a tail of fire that had been nightly blazing over England since September. The pamphleteers had taken a malicious delight in pointing out that such stars foretold the death of kings and kingdoms, no doubt fuelling James's fear that Pettingar would again try to murder him and that this time he would succeed.

'You believe Pettingar is at Battle, sir?'

FitzAlan frowned, then waved his hand as if swatting away an irritating fly. 'That foul traitor has gone to ground. He might even now be in hiding in Battle, or she may have smuggled him out to the Low Countries or to Spain. But the priests and spies she shelters swarm all over England and far beyond her shores. One of them at least must know the true identity of Pettingar and where he is. It is the King's wish that you go to Battle Abbey and get yourself taken into her household. You were raised a Catholic; you can win their confidence.'

Did this man have any idea what he was demanding? Did he imagine you could simply stroll up to the door, announce that you were a Catholic and be gathered in like a lost lamb? He was expecting Daniel to inveigle his way into this household, which half the pursuivants and intelligencers in England had tried to infiltrate without apparent success, and start interrogating the priests in hiding there about Spero Pettingar without arousing anyone's suspicions. FitzAlan really must believe him to be a sorcerer and magician. Besides, the last thing Daniel wanted was to find himself back in a house of priests and piety; he'd spent half his youth trying to escape that.

'Sir, there are many recusant houses throughout England which Pettingar might have taken refuge in. Has His Majesty any reason to believe—'

'He has every reason,' FitzAlan snapped. 'The dowager's late husband, Viscount Montague, his son-in-law the Earl of Southampton and Magdalen's own brother, were all implicated in the plot to depose their lawful queen in the Rising of the North, but Elizabeth was always too inclined to mercy where justice would have better served her, and they all contrived to escape their well-deserved punishment.'

Daniel recalled hearing talk of that rebellion among some of the older commanders when he had served as a field messenger in the Irish uprising. But the Rising of the North had been nearly forty years ago, and half the recusant nobles in England had at some time or other been accused of plotting against Elizabeth. That was not reason enough to suspect the dowager now, surely?

FitzAlan eye's narrowed as he examined Daniel's face. He grunted. 'Always sceptical, eh, Master Pursglove? I suppose that's to be expected from a man who once earned his living by convincing simpletons and gowks that gold coins can appear in empty dishes and kittens be transformed into mice with the wave of a hand. Very well, I'll tell you something more, if it will convince you. When he was little more than a boy, the man who was to set the match to the kegs of gunpowder, the very devil-of-the-vault himself, entered the service of Magdalen's late husband as a footman on his estate at Cowdray. Fawkes was born into a wealthy and godly Protestant family, but such was the corrupting influence of the Montagues that in the short time he was with them he was turned into the fiend who tried to foully murder the King, the Queen and hundreds of innocents in Parliament, and drag England and Scotland, both, back under the heel of the Pope. It was not only Magdalen's late husband Fawkes served, but his grandson too, when he in turn became the second Viscount Montague, for he also took this would-be assassin into his service and fed his vile nature.'

And the second Viscount was arrested and imprisoned in the Tower for that association, Daniel remembered, but even the little ferret Robert Cecil could not find enough evidence to prove that he knew about the plot to hold him, much less put him on trial.

But Daniel was grudgingly forced to admit that *if* Spero Pettingar had ever existed, he could probably find no better hiding place than one of Montague's houses. If the old dowager was hiding even a handful of priests, her houses would be riddled with priest's holes. And those hiding places must have been very well constructed, if they not yet yielded their secrets. There was only one man whom such a family as the Montague's would have trusted to construct those hidden chambers upon which the lives of dozens of priests depended, and that was the Jesuit hunchback Nicholas Owen who, according to the official version of his death had sliced his own guts open in the Tower rather than betray a single man. Tavern gossip had it that his belly had burst open under merciless torture while he was suspended by his wrists in iron manacles. But whatever the truth, all were agreed that Owen, whom Daniel's old tutor Father Waldegrave had always referred to as 'Little John', had refused to divulge the whereabouts of even one of the scores of hiding places he had constructed throughout the length and breadth of England.

Had this house in which he was now standing been one of them, Daniel wondered, seized by the Crown in penalty of *praemunire*, for the owners' refusal to take the Oath of Allegiance? If it had, the long gallery would probably even now be concealing at least one hidden chamber – a secret room behind that oak panelling, or beneath the fireplace or the stairs. Owen had always ensured that every refuge was unique, so that if the secret of one was unlocked, it could not be used to crack another. But even now, Daniel did not allow his gaze to stray to the wooden panels. Waldegrave had instilled in both him and Richard that guarding your eyes was as vital as guarding your tongue. Boys, like servants, would be watched closely by the searchers. Many a fugitive had been unwittingly betrayed and seized because a child or terrified maid had glanced towards a hiding place.

'Sir, it will not be easy to gain admittance to Battle Abbey. They will be on their guard against any who try to infiltrate the network.'

'They will indeed.' FitzAlan's tone was so cheerful, Daniel half expected to see him rubbing his hands in relish at the prospect. 'Robert Cecil has his network of turncoats and informers who pass themselves off as priests and travel with those being smuggled into this realm. And even they have failed to penetrate that stronghold.'

'And Benet? Was his death investigated?'

'It was not,' FitzAlan said. 'He was found dead in a pit on the outskirts of Battle on the road to London. But the local coroner and jury, all of whom are, no doubt, in league with that old besom, returned a verdict of *felo de se*.'

Daniel grimaced. 'Self-murder? Casting yourself into a pit doesn't seem the most reliable way for a sane man to take his own life, even if he wished to make it appear an accident . . . unless it was a very deep pit, deep enough to smash his skull?'

'On the contrary, the reports say it was a shallow one. I'm told that someone would be unlucky to break so much as his ankle if he jumped in, much less his neck. He was returning to London to make report, I am certain of that. Whatever he had uncovered was something so important he'd not risk committing it to the hand of a messenger.' FitzAlan's frown had deepened and his foot was drumming rapidly against the table leg, but he didn't seem aware of it. 'At least, not a messenger he sent to his King,' he added almost under his breath.

So, he suspects a message was sent, but to whom? Robert Cecil? If he did intercept it, the King's beagle has plainly not shared that juicy bone with his master. But if not him, then Benet may have double-crossed them both.

FitzAlan suddenly jerked from his revery with a shake of his head, as if he was trying to banish the lingering image of a bad dream. 'You must learn the truth about Benet's death, Master Pursglove, discover what secret he had unearthed. But you'll have to be on your guard, my wee sparrow. Outfox the old vixen and those *vulpes* that surround her. The fox and the Devil share the same nature. The fox besmirches himself in blood-red mud, then lays still upon the ground, feigning death until the foolish carrion crow comes ambling close, thinking it has found itself a meal. Then it is the crow that is devoured. The Devil can fool us into thinking he is dead until we have strayed into his path. The Devil and Spero Pettingar, they are neither of them vanquished, Master Pursglove. Some of the plotters ended their days on the quartering block, but they were merely the limbs of the beast; the plot was conceived in the head and the head still lives. As King Solomon himself charged his servants – "Catch us the little foxes that destroy the vines." Catch them, Master Pursglove, and the King will see them hanged higher than vermin on a gamekeeper's gibbet, for every crow to peck at.'

Chapter Three

OUTSKIRTS OF BATTLE TOWN

DANIEL PURSGLOVE

I SPOTTED THE MEN riding towards me through the bare trees before they noticed me, but I knew better than to urge my gelding, Diligence, to the gallop to try to outdistance them. The winter sun was low in the sky and I'd been riding since daybreak over tracks that were nothing but bog and water-filled holes. The horse had no burst of speed left in him.

I dragged on the rein and turned Diligence towards the riders, waving as if I was anxious to speak with them. As soon as they caught sight of me, they spurred their mounts towards me and in moments I was surrounded by five men, armed with swords and muskets.

'Good sirs,' I blurted out eagerly, 'tell me you've seen a stray hawk in these parts. I've been searching since noon and she's not returned.'

The men frowned. They'd not been expecting me to question them.

'Assure me you have heard her bells, at least,' I babbled. 'The sound carries so far at this season. That way, was it?' I gestured innocently in the direction from which they'd been riding. They glanced at one another and shrugged or shook their heads. They were clad in stout leather jerkins, mud-splattered and stained like their battered steel helmets, which glinted only dully in the pale sunshine. Their faces, like their clothes, showed the grim, weather-beaten weariness of men who had been riding for days.

Seeing that one was about to speak, I swiftly interrupted. 'Are you sure you've not heard my hawk scream?' When they again shook their heads, I feigned an expression of grave disappointment. 'My thanks, sirs, but in that case, I'd best make haste with my search. It'll be dark soon and then I fear I may lose her entirely.' I dug my heels into Diligence and urged him between two of them. But at that moment the two horses in front swung their flanks around, trapping us once more. I could have forced my horse through, but the trees were too widely spaced here to provide cover and Diligence could not carry me out of range of those muskets swiftly enough.

'Never mind your hawk. Have you seen two men on foot pass this way?' the rider nearest to me demanded.

'A few. Mostly pedlars or stockmen. How long since?'

The man grimaced. 'We reckoned to be half a day behind them when we started tracking from Winchelsea. Came up river as far as Brede, they did. Be making for the road to London.'

'I told ye, 'em's doubled back and gone to ground,' another said, glaring at him. 'Else we'd have overtaken 'em long since.'

'You best hope they haven't, because if they slip through, you'll be going to ground yourself. I'll bury you up to your neck in the salts to wait for the tide to roll in.'

'Tracking felons, are you?' I asked. 'Dangerous, are they? What crimes are they wanted for? Murder?'

The sheriff's officer grunted. 'Sedition, treason, spying for the King's enemies. Some such, I reckon. We won't rightly know what they'll hang for till we catch them. Boat brought them off a French ship in the dead of night, before she sailed on into port. Someone saw two men being dropped ashore on a quiet stretch of beach in the dark, and the pinnace was rowed straight back to ship.'

'Priests or spies, it makes no mind,' another added sourly. 'They'll die either way, but I want a turn with them first, after the merry dance they've led us.'

So, unless this *someone* was a smuggler-turned-informer to save his own skin, it seemed the authorities were now paying local men to watch the remote beaches as well as the ports.

I nodded affably to the men. 'Hope you catch the traitors, brothers.' I pointedly glanced up at the grey sky above the bare trees. 'Best make haste, though, you've only an hour of light left at most.' I dug my heels sharply into Diligence's flanks, so that he bounded forward, pushing aside the horses that blocked our path, and trotted rapidly away. I raised my hand in farewell without turning round.

'Hold hard!' the leader called out. 'We've still some questions for you!'

Pretending I hadn't heard him, I swiftly turned Diligence off the track and pulled him sideways, ensuring that the trunk of an ancient oak tree was between me and the men, for I knew I was still within range of a musket ball, and my back was too broad a target. I urged Diligence on as swiftly as the crowd of trees would allow, gambling that the men would not waste time pursing me if they thought their quarry was heading towards London.

As I heard the creaking of the leathers and the hooves fading behind me, I allowed my horse to slow his pace. Searching for a lost hawk was a trick I had learned from the master deceivers. So, it was as well for me the sheriff's men had never been schooled in the writings of the Jesuits. Pursuivants like Richard Topcliffe were not so ignorant though. They had studied them thoroughly – *Learn the ways of your enemy, as a huntsman learns the ways of the wild boar, that both may be brought to bay.* But was I to be huntsman or the hunted here?

I had obtained two sets of papers before setting out from London. It had taken a few days, for I could not go to the same forgers for both. The first set of documents I carried were letters of introduction and bills of sale. The papers were written in various hands and the gall inks of different shades of black. They would pass an inspection on the road or satisfy an innkeeper who'd been paid to inform on any suspicious customers travelling through, though if anyone checked with those who were supposed to have written them, they would soon discover they were as real as unicorn eggs. But that would take someone a deal of time and many days in the saddle, by which time, unless I'd been arrested, I would be long gone.

The other two documents I carried were intended for other eyes and these I had slipped between the leather binding and wooden cover of the book written by King James himself, *Daemonologie*. It was my own private jest, but a pragmatic one. It was not a book any Catholic priest would favour and so would not arouse suspicions if found by the King's men. I gambled that they would be reluctant to tear apart a book that their Sovereign had written and the hidden papers would escape detection until I reached Battle. But I hoped I wouldn't need to use them even then. The Catholic network depended on caution and secrecy. I knew they would not be content with simply examining those letters; they would check them thoroughly. Their lives depended on it, and so would mine, if they discovered them to be false.

'ADDLEPATED CLOTPOLE! That's what you are, ape, lubber!' The stream of insults was followed by thumps, as if someone was being kicked or beaten, and then a wail of misery.

I cautiously edged Diligence towards the sound. Twilight had crept between the trees and a thin white mist snaked silently a foot or two above the rotting leaves. The birds of the day had fallen silent. Those of the night had not yet roused themselves and the bitter words and blows sounded even more jarring in the stillness.

A sledge lay on its side. Beside it, a sack of turnips and skirrets, the roots looking like bundles of dead men's fingers, spilled out over a scattered heap of wood and kindling. A man was kicking viciously at something on the ground and cursing. His cheeks were flushed with anger and frustration, his hands clenched into fists. I thought he must be venting his rage on some small lad lying curled in the leaves, but then I realised he was lashing out at an old tree stump half buried under the withered brown fronds of a fern. He was shouting and raging too loudly to hear my approach through the wet leaf litter.

'What's amiss?' I called out, though I could see for myself plainly enough.

He wheeled round and stared at me, his mouth hanging open. Then he grabbed one of the branches that had tumbled from the sledge and held it across himself, as if he wanted me to know that he would defend his woodpile and vegetables from any who might have designs on them. But he was visibly cringing and I suspected that if I came any closer he'd throw down the make-shift weapon and run.

'Easy, brother. I only want to help.' I swung down from the saddle and tethered Diligence to the nearest tree. The young man watched me warily, raising the branch defensively as I took a few paces towards him. It was hard to make out any of his features in the fading light, but as I came closer, I saw that he wasn't a man at all. For all his great height and large frame, he was little more than a boy. He was almost as tall as me, with shoulders like an ox, but there was not even the wisp of a beard on his chin and his eyes were those of a frightened child, though his face already bore several white scars.

'Waste of good shoe leather, kicking that stump. It'll not beg your pardon and we'd both get a fright if it did.'

He gaped at me, then giggled, and pressed his fingers to his mouth as if afraid of the sound escaping.

I nodded towards the overturned sledge. 'Come on, between us we can right that and get it reloaded.'

We worked in silence at first. What he lacked in dexterity and speed, he made up for in strength, but several times I had to reposition an awkward branch for him so that the pile did not become unbalanced.

'You live close by?'

'In vert yonder.' He gestured towards the edge of the wood, a mass of twisted branches dark against the pale, silvery glow of the setting sun. Anxiety creased his features. 'She'll be wanting these for the bacon. She'll be waiting.'

'Then we'd best get them to her. Would she be willing to let me sleep in your barn for the night?'

Again, the boy stared doubtfully. 'We've no barn. Only a hog pound.'

I had bedded with horses, hounds and all manner of men, but I drew the line at pigs. They were apt to regard any human who slept with them as a juicy meal.

I tied the neck of the sack of vegetables with a piece of cord from my own bags; the boy's cord, if it had ever existed, seemed to have been lost. He heaved it on top of the wood. 'Ma's cooking bacon,' he repeated, 'and she'll have some to spare.'

Me eating the pig, now that sounded more like it. I untethered Diligence and prepared to follow the lad. He heaved the rope attached to the front of the sledge over his shoulder and began to drag the heavy load over the muddy ground. Runners were more practical than wheels when the ground was this soft, especially if they were well greased with lard, but in the fading light the boy kept stumbling and jolting the sledge over raised tree roots and stones half buried in the leaf mould, causing it to leap and yawl at alarming angles. Several times, the whole thing almost capsized again. I began to wonder if the lad had weak eyes.

It was a relief to both of us when we finally reached the cottage. It stood alone, its back to the forest, in the corner of a marshy expanse of pasture. A little fenced garden squatted on one side of it, with the stone hog pound at the far end. A small woman was coaxing a few scrawny chickens into a coop for the night with a handful of grain. As she heard us approach, she glanced round with the same anxious expression as her son, but there the resemblance ended. She fastened the door of the coop and hurried towards us, rubbing her red-raw hands on the sacking apron which covered the coarse woollen gown. She was a good head shorter than the lad and, in contrast to him, so slight she looked as if a gust of wind might topple her. Everything about her, from her pale blue eyes to her dry, blanched lips and her dun-coloured skirts, seemed cracked and faded.

'Brought them, Ma. Fetched everything you said.'

'It's late. I've been worried. Your father will be back soon wanting his supper.' But all the time she was speaking, she didn't take her eyes from me. Her fingers repeatedly bunched and kneaded the fabric of her apron, betraying her agitation.

'God grant you a good evening, mistress. I met your son in the woods and he thought you might be able to spare a little of your supper and perhaps a place at your fireside as the hour grows late . . .' A look of consternation darted across her face. 'I would pay, of course.'

'We can't . . . my husband will be back soon,' she repeated, as if he was a giant who might devour any man who ventured into his tower. *Fy, fa, fum! I smell the blood of an Englishman!* 'Young Sam speaks afore he thinks, that's his trouble.' She darted a look at her son, but it was more worried than scolding.

I was about to remount Diligence when Sam lumbered across and grabbed the reins. 'He's not a King's man, Ma. They'd not dirty their hands. Stone-boat canted and he helped right it and load it again.'

So, she was afraid that I was a pursuivant or intelligencer. Given the task FitzAlan had forced on to me, it wasn't far from the truth.

The woman glanced over her shoulder, as if she feared someone might even now be watching us. Then she gave a half-smile and a nod. 'If you've done my lad a kindness, I'll not repay it with coldness. You're welcome to share what we have. We don't feast like those at the Abbey, but we don't starve.'

My senses prickled at the mention of the Abbey, but I knew better than to press her. When a horse is wary, you stand still and let it approach you.

The cottage consisted of two rooms. The first was simply furnished with a rough table, single chair and bench, several small chests and a loom. An iron pot simmered over the fire in an open heath. The smoke curled around the flitches of bacon, bunches of dried herbs and fat golden onions which hung from the beams, before filtering out through a hole high in the wall beneath the thatch. Chimneys, it seemed, had not yet reached these parts. A salt box hung on the wall close to the fire and a few sacks and flour barrels stood along the opposite wall. The open door beyond revealed a glimpse of a smaller room which appeared to serve both as bedchamber and storeroom, for in addition to the bedstead and linen chest, the walls were festooned with ropes, traps, billhooks and axes.

The woman motioned me to the only chair. 'Sam'll see to your horse. He has a way with beasts.' She gave a sad smile. 'I think it might have suited him more if the bailiff could have found him work with the shepherd or in the stables at the Abbey, but my husband, Matthew, wouldn't hear of it. Says it would shame him to have his only son taken on by another man to be taught their trade. Be different, perhaps, if we'd been blessed with more sons. But the eldest lad must rightly follow the trade of his father, that's the way of it, he says, always has been. But Sam don't seem to take to the skills of a woodward.'

All the time she was talking, her hands were busy scrubbing and chopping the bunches of thin white skirret roots, dropping each handful as they were prepared straight into the cauldron seething over the fire. Already it was, as Sam had promised, giving off a tantalising aroma of bacon and onions, and I found my belly growling in answer to its call.

'Has your husband been long employed by Viscount Montague?'

Her fingers paused for a moment and she darted me a sharp glance at the mention of the name. 'Man and boy, and his father and grandfather were woodward before him, 'course the first Viscount was just plain Sir Anthony back when Matthew's grandfather came to Battle as a lad to work for him. Old Samuel Crowhurst, Matthew's father, was born in this very cottage, like Matthew himself and young Sam here.'

'So, you know the dowager widow too? I hear she lives here all year round now, dare say that's made more work for Matthew and the household, hasn't it? I warrant there have been a fair few changes since his father's time.' I kept my tone light, as if I was simply passing the time in idle chatter. But again, her hands froze. This time she avoided my eyes.

'Matthew has his duties in the woods same as always. No matter who's living at the house, ponds still got to be cleaned, fences checked, dead trees cleared. He doesn't go up to the Abbey. When the bailiff wants to talk to him, he comes here, so as he can do his rounds at the same time, make his inspections and see everything is in order . . . which it always is and always will be. Waste of both their time for Matthew to go traipsing up there, when what the bailiff wants to see is here. I don't go up to the house either, don't have any cause to. My work's here, same as his.'

Her voice had grown guarded, her expression sullen. She wanted to make quite sure I understood that she and her husband knew nothing about what went on at Battle Abbey, which meant she did know, or at the very least suspected. I wondered if all of the dowager's servants had learned that safety lay in being blind, deaf and dumb.

The door crashed open and Sam lumbered in, his broad face flushed but beaming. 'Horse been watered and fed. I've tethered him behind the wall where the wind don't blow too much this time of year. He's a fine beast, middlin' fine.' He added in a tone of such undisguised enthusiasm that I took it to be the highest compliment he could bestow.

He slid on to the bench and gazed at the steaming pot as if he could summon it to walk across to him. His mother wasted no time in ladling the pottage into two wooden bowls and setting one before each of us, with a hunk of bread. There was,

35

surprisingly, more wheat in the loaf than rye, and it was fresh. Lady Magdalen was not beggarly with her servants: a wise course, when so much rested on their loyalty

'Will you not eat with us, Goodwife Crowhurst?' For a moment, I wondered if I was consuming her portion, but a glance into the pot told me she could have fed a half-dozen men with what remained.

'I don't eat till my husband's been served,' she said firmly. 'He's master.'

It was growing dark outside and she bustled about restlessly, lighting the single tallow candle, and sweeping the skirret peelings into the pig pail. She swung the cauldron away from the fire on the iron arm, so that it would not burn, then minutes later pushed it back, seemingly afraid it would cool too much. In all my travels throughout the years, I've seldom come across anyone in a village or remote farm who on meeting a stranger has not at once asked their business, where they've come and where they are bound, as greedy as seagulls for news from outside. But this woman and her son asked me nothing, though from their repeated glances I knew they were curious.

Like a dog that suddenly lifts it head at an approaching sound, the woman straightened herself and scrubbed her raw hands in the coarse sacking apron. Moments later, I too heard the sound of approaching boots. The door opened and a man ducked inside. Dragging off his coat, he thrust it at his wife. She hung it from a peg by the door, then hurried across to the fire to fill a wooden bowl which had been warming by the hearth.

Matthew Crowhurst stopped in mid-stride, only now catching sight of someone sitting in his chair. I rose.

'Goodman Crowhurst? God grant this house peace. Your wife was kind enough to offer me a place at your table.'

He scowled at me. He was no taller than his son, but just as stocky. Steel muscles corded his neck and his arms bulged almost as thick as his legs. He was as dark as the boy was fair, with a black beard, dense as a bear's pelt, hacked short around his face, accentuating the sideways bend of his nose. He had clearly broken it at some time and it had mended crookedly. If I had not known his trade, I would have easily guessed it, for his skin was tanned to oak brown by wind and rain, and his eyes, even in the dim light of the cottage, seemed to be squinting against some invisible sun.

'Fortune has favoured you, brother,' I said, smiling as affably as I could, in spite of his churlish refusal to return my greeting. 'I've seldom tasted such excellent pottage. You must count yourself blessed to come home to such good fare each night.'

His gaze had turned from me to his wife, who laid the brimming bowl on the table. Even without looking at her husband, she seemed to understand some explanation was required.

'Gentleman did our Sam a good turn. Helped him right and reload the stone-boat after it canted. Only right we offered him a bite and a bed seeing as he'd have likely reached the town in daylight if he hadn't stopped to help . . . He rides a fine horse.'

Crowhurst stared at her in silence for a moment, then without warning his arm lashed out, swift as a viper's tongue, slapping the boy so hard across his head he was knocked backwards over the bench and crashed into the wall behind. Crowhurst took a pace or two so that he was standing over the boy, who balled himself up on the floor, his arms wrapped across his head.

'Clotpole! Ape!' he yelled down at Sam. 'How many times have I told you to watch where you're dragging that boat? You got to think, boy, think about how wide it is, not go smashing it into rocks. Even a dumb ox can pull a cart without sending it arse-over. You can't even do that, you clumsy lubber.' He rounded on his wife. 'And you still swear on your life, that boy is of my getting. Everything he does makes a liar of you, Alys Crowhurst.'

'It wasn't the lad's fault,' I said quietly. 'The sledge hit a stump hidden under old undergrowth. No one could have seen it, especially in the fading light.'

Crowhurst's head jerked round and he glowered at me with such ferocity and loathing, I braced myself ready to parry the blow that I was sure was coming.

'And there's no harm done,' I said. 'Sam didn't lose a single stick of wood or skirret either and they taste like honey in that pottage, I can tell you. I'm certain even her ladyship up at the Abbey won't be eating better fare.'

His wife lifted the bowl of pottage. 'I'll warm it for you again, husband. You must be starving.'

'Don't you tell me what I must be, woman,' Crowhurst growled. But the aroma of bacon and onions rising from the pot made his stomach rumble so loudly we could hear it. He pulled the bowl from her hand, snatched the remaining half-loaf from the table and strode towards the back chamber. 'I'll do my eating in peace. Then I'm to my bed, so I'll thank you all to be silent.' He gave me a curt nod. 'You can use the boy's truckle bed.'

'No need for that, I'll make shift on the floor. A warm fire is comfort enough.'

'You'll take the boy's bed. He'll be tethered outside tonight. Maybe a night in the cold will teach him to mind what he's doing next time.' He set the bowl and bread down again and lumbered across the room to lift a chain with a rusty iron collar from the wall. Clutching it in his great fist, he advanced towards the boy.

Sam let out a howl like a wounded dog and Alys ran towards her husband, her face stricken. She reached out as if she would catch hold of him, but let her arm drop.

'No, husband, please, you know he's terrified of Wild Tom. It might fright him into another of his fits.'

Crowhurst glanced over her shoulder at Sam, who was visibly shaking, his eyes wide and rolling back in his head, so that I could only see the whites of them in the candlelight. Crowhurst watched in disgust. Then he let the chain and collar crash to the floor.

'Only because I don't want to listen to him howling like a mad dog all night and you keeping me awake with your tossing and turning.' Retrieving his supper, he vanished into the back room, kicking the door shut behind him with a crash.

As soon as the door was closed, Alys returned to her son and taking both his great hands in her small ones, she gently shook him. 'Look at me, Sam, look . . . Your father says you may sleep by the hearth, but not a peep out of you, mind, whatever you hear. Else he might change his mind. He needs his rest and we mustn't vex him.'

The straw mattress on the narrow bed that Alys and Sam pulled out for me was so thin that I ceased to pity the lad for being ordered to sleep on the floor. Curled in a blanket in front of the fire, his sleeping place was probably more comfortable than mine, and judging by his snores, neither that nor his father's threats had kept him awake for long. Perhaps he was well used to both.

Like his wife, Crowhurst had not asked me anything about what I was doing in those parts, not even my name. But I suspected asking any stranger his name in Battle would be a waste of words, since neither the hunters nor the hunted would offer the name that birth and family had bestowed upon them. And I was one of them. I didn't even know the year of my birth, much less the name my father had given me, if indeed any man had ever owned to being my father.

Had Crowhurst retreated into the second room and ordered his family not to speak so that they could truthfully answer they knew nothing about me if they were questioned, or was it more that he feared what I might discover about them? I glanced over at Sam lying curled in front of the fire, his broad shoulders silhouetted against the ruby glow. He seemed a good-hearted lad, but a simple one, just the sort of boy that a pursuivant would seek out in his hunt for priests, for he'd innocently blurt out the truth that would condemn a man to the gallows. Perhaps Crowhurst was wiser than his wife realised in deciding to keep the lad close by in this isolated cottage.

A CLATTER JERKED ME from sleep. I rolled over, thinking the wind had toppled something. But the noise continued, rapid and persistent, the loud hollow clack, clack of wood against wood moving around the cottage, coming first from behind it and then in front. It wasn't rain rattling against shutter, nor was it the wind in the trees. Then came a long high-pitched shriek, shriller than any vixen.

The room was dark, but by the faint red glow from the banked-down fire, I could see a shape like a dog moving across the floor. It took a moment or two before I realised it was Sam crawling on all fours towards the furthest corner, still wrapped in his blanket. He pressed himself into a space between the chest and the wall, drawing the covering over his head. I heaved myself up out of the low bed and went to kneel beside him. Unable to stop the whimpers escaping him, he stuffed the blanket into his mouth with clenched fists to smother the sound.

'Sam,' I whispered, for it was plain he'd taken his father's threat seriously. 'Sam, what is making that racket outside, do you know?'

He mumbled something through the cloth, but I couldn't distinguish the words. I tugged it away from his face. 'What's making that noise?' It was odd that Crowhurst had not come out to investigate. He might be sleeping through it, but I suspected Alys wasn't. She was probably lying rigid and wide awake, too afraid to move in case she angered him.

'Wild Tom . . . It's Wild Tom . . . trying to get in. He's coming to drown me!'

A bogeyman invented to frighten a child into behaving. The story had certainly had the desired effect on Sam, but whatever was causing that din was no fable. I pulled on my boots, colliding with the chair as I stumbled towards the door, but if the clatter outside hadn't woken my surly host by now, then I could have cantered Diligence across the floor and not disturbed him.

Diligence! It wouldn't be the first time someone had tried to steal him. He was, as young Sam had said, a fine and valuable beast. I turned back to the bed, groped beneath the straw pillow for my dagger and pulled it from its sheath. Then I eased open the door, stepped out and pulled it shut behind me.

Outside, the night was as dark as the Devil's armpit. Clouds raced across the moon and the wind hissed through the bare branches of the trees behind the cottage. In the little garden, bushes rustled and stirred in the breeze, but the rapid clacking and shrieking had stopped abruptly, as if whatever had been making the noise had sensed or heard the door opening.

I thought I could see something moving beyond the low fence up by the hog pound. Holding my dagger ready, I crept towards it, but before I had taken more than a pace or two away from the wall of the cottage, something flew over my head. I heard a dull thump as it hit the thatch, then it tumbled down the steep roof and fell with a loud crack on the flagstones, missing me by inches. In a brief shaft of moonlight, I could see a stone on the ground, the size of a goose egg, still rocking from the momentum of the fall. Not even a violent gust of wind could have cast that up there. I whipped round, and glimpsed something or someone scuttling across the meadow, but the clouds swarmed across the moon once more and the darkness closed around the creature before I could even get a sense of whether it was a man or a beast.

I stooped and picked up the stone. It was large enough to kill a man, heavy as iron and as cold. Was it simply meant to torment young Sam and his parents or was it intended as a welcome for me? I was here to solve the murder of Master Benet, but it seemed FitzAlan had been right: I could all too easily find myself lying in a grave beside him.

Chapter Four

As I left the cottage the next morning, the rising sun, pale and pearly through the thin mist, was just creeping over the low hills. White ribbons of thicker fog wound between the trees and hung two or three foot above the meadow, so that Diligence seemed to be surging through a milky lake. Alys and Crowhurst had said nothing about the night's disturbance and in the morning light only young Sam's drawn face and fearful glances convinced me that I had not dreamt it. The woodward and his wife were anxious for me to be gone, and though Alys took the coins I handed her willingly enough, she neither looked at me nor spoke, as if even a word of farewell might be dangerous.

I reached the far end of the meadow and began to weave through the edge of a woodland, heading back in the direction of the track I had left the previous day. Diligence suddenly reared up and gave an explosive snort of alarm. I steadied him, but he skipped sideways, eyes rolling, and continued to snort like a baleful dragon at something on the ground hidden beneath the blanket of mist. It couldn't be an adder at this season of the year, but whatever it was, Diligence would not pass it.

I turned him, looking for another way through the dense thicket of trees, but then I caught a faint sound. The mist was swirling, stirred like a boiling cauldron by the horse's legs. As it briefly parted, I glimpsed something large and dark slithering through the fallen leaves. I guided Diligence a few paces off, dismounted and tethered him securely to a tree. Then, drawing my dagger, I edged towards the place where I had seen the creature. I crouched, waving my arm, trying to part the mist again. A man was sprawled on his back in the wet undergrowth, trying desperately to drag himself away from me. The edge of his cloak was clamped between his jaws to muffle his groans, and then I saw why. His foot was held fast in a heavy iron trap. The metal teeth had bitten savagely through the leather of his boot and into his flesh. The jaws of the trap were wet with blood.

He jerked in fear as I bent towards him.

He pulled the cloth from his mouth. 'Get back . . . have a knife.' The words were forced out through gritted teeth and the hand that held the weapon was shaking.

'Aye, so I see, brother, but I doubt you could fend off a pigeon with that. Set it down, before you do yourself more mischief.'

The blade of his knife was broken and bent, the bone handle splintered. He had evidently been trying to prise the jaws of the trap apart with it and, judging by the fragments that lay around him, he had also tried to use a rotten branch and a stone, but to no effect. He was a young man, perhaps in his early twenties, though his face was so pinched and drawn with pain and cold that it was hard to gauge. Dressed plainly in dark green and brown, he might have blended well into a forest in summer, but not at this season. Gouges in the muddy leaf litter marked where he had tried to crawl into the shelter of a thicket but had been pulled short by the stout chain on the trap, which was locked around a tree trunk.

'How long have you lain here?'

'Dark . . . when I trod on it . . . maybe an hour after sunset . . .' His voice was weak, punctuated by sharp gasps of breath and it was hard to place his accent, though it was English, and well schooled.

If he was speaking the truth, he hadn't caused the disturbance at the woodward's cottage. However, if he had been trying to frighten the family, he'd have every reason to lie about it. Maybe Crowhurst had set the trap in order to catch the perpetrator. But if this man had innocently stumbled into it, then what had he been doing in the woods after dark? He certainly wasn't a poacher. His clothes, though damp and streaked with mud, were too well cut and the weave of the cloth too fine to have come from any cottager's loom.

But an innocent man finding himself accidently caught like this would have tried to drag himself on to open ground where he might be seen by hunters or someone collecting wood who could have come to his aid. This man hadn't even called for help when he'd heard my horse approach; on the contrary, he'd tried to hide himself and to stifle his groans. I suspected he had far more reason to fear being caught than any poacher, and so would I, if I was found helping him. But I wouldn't leave a stray cat to suffer like this.

I examined the trap, looking for the means to release the jaws. Every blacksmith prides himself on his own design and no two are quite the same.

'I'm going to pull you over, so that you're beneath that branch. You'll need something to steady yourself on as I free you. It'll hurt, brother. There's no help for it. Best bite on that cloak again.'

I dragged him over the ground as swiftly as I could, though the pain made beads of sweat pop on his ashen face. But as I positioned his sound leg so that I could haul him upright, I noticed something else about his clothes. I hadn't seen it at first beneath the mud and leaf mould which clung to them, but now I saw a white stain in a line around his breeches and all along the bottom of his travelling cloak. It was the mark that saltwater leaves on dark cloth.

I was certain now that he was one of the fugitives the sheriff's men-at-arms had been tracking from the ship. He'd probably split from his companion, hoping that this would make it harder for their pursuers. The officer should have listened to his subordinate: at least one of their quarries had doubled back.

I hauled him to his feet and steadied him until he had grasped the low branch above him. 'When the jaws open, pull your leg out as swiftly as you can. The trap might snap shut again without warning if I cannot open it all the way.'

44

I trod down with as much weight as I could muster on the lever and the jaws slowly widened, dragging the vicious iron teeth out of the wounds in his flesh. I could feel his body juddering in pain, but that would be nothing to the agony he would taste if he was caught by those men who were hunting him. As soon as his foot was clear, I let the jaws spring shut again and heaved the trap up against the tree, where it could do no more harm to man or beast, at least for now. I was certain it had been intended to catch a man, for I couldn't imagine there were any wild creatures large enough to warrant a trap of that size in this shire. Had the sheriff's men set it to catch their quarry, or were they themselves the intended prey? . . . They or a pursuivant, like Benet, who might be spying on the Abbey?

He was swaying as if he was about to pass out and I helped him to sit again, propped up against a trunk, while I fetched a flask of wine from my bags and held it to his lips. He drank greedily. Gradually, his pain began to ebb a little and his breathing steadied. He reached for his boot, trying to pull it off, but I grabbed his wrist and stopped him.

'You'll do yourself greater injury if you remove it here. You were fortunate that the leather of your boot is stout. Your bones may be broken and the flesh pierced, but with luck and rest, you might yet keep your leg.'

'I am in your debt, sir.' He struggled to get to his feet, but crumpled to the ground. He stared at me, a look of helplessness and fear dawning in his eyes.

'I wonder that you did not seek shelter in Battle last night. Were you bound for the Abbey? You must have passed it as you journeyed from Winchelsea.'

His eyes flashed wide, but he tried to recover himself. 'I am returning to London.'

'On foot?'

'My horse shied and threw me . . . It bolted this way and I followed, hoping to find it grazing . . . Have you seen a riderless horse?' he added belatedly.

Another man schooled in the art of looking for a lost animal, I thought wryly. I must invent a new tale for myself: even the most beef-witted of the sheriff's men would eventually grow suspicious if too many more invisible animals started roaming these woods.

'I've heard that this shire is plagued by a demon horse that carries its riders into deep pools to drown them, unless they can jump off. Perhaps you were riding such a wraith, brother, in which case it would be fruitless to look for such a beast.'

I untethered Diligence and led him close. 'My horse is a creature of flesh and blood, and if we can get you up on it, I'll take you to the Abbey. I think you will be welcomed there, if you are not already expected.'

He lowered his eyes and said nothing, as if he thought further denial was futile. Perhaps it was as well he'd be obliged to rest there for the weeks or months it would take his leg to mend. Even if he'd been in possession of two sound legs, I wagered he was about as well equipped to survive on the road as a lamb sent out among the wolves. That mantrap had been a blessing in disguise for him and with luck it might prove to be the same for me.

Chapter Five

I HAD BEEN KICKING MY HEELS in the Abbey gatehouse for most of the day, ever since I'd delivered the injured man into their care. After servants had been summoned with a bier to carry him into the house where his wounds could be tended, the steward had ordered that a breakfast be served to me in the gatehouse for my trouble. A yeoman waiter had brought me a loaf of good wheaten bread, baked herring and small ale, before withdrawing to the porter's room next door to share the porter's morning ale and a pipe. Delivering a dole of food to a stranger at the gate was an oddly menial task for a servant of his standing, but I had already noticed the tracery in the wall: it probably concealed a squint, enabling the porter or anyone in his office to observe those waiting in the chamber I occupied. So before eating, I made the sign of the cross over the loaf with a small movement of my thumb, pressing it fleetingly to my lips, as if the gesture was habitual. I was sure from the studied glance the servant gave me as he collected the empty dish and trencher that he had seen it.

After breakfast, I took my time watering and feeding Diligence, and as I hoped, the yeoman waiter returned, asking me to wait a while, for his mistress wished to speak with me and would send word when she was ready to receive me. But dinner came and went at ten of the clock and I had still not been summoned. Around noon, I thought I heard the muffled ringing of a distant bell and I wondered if the psalms for Sext were being recited. Leaden clouds started to gather and though it was still only early afternoon, the sky above the Abbey began to darken.

Finally, the black-robed porter emerged and gestured for me to follow. Wordlessly, he led the way up the vaulted staircase in one of the turrets to a chamber on the first floor of the gatehouse. Candlelight from the lanterns that illuminated the dark steps in the tower flickered over the two black murder holes as we passed, constructed to allow those inside to rain terror on to the heads of any attempting to breach the staircase below. It was a sinister defence for the holy monks of old to have constructed and, in the end, it had not protected them from King Henry's men. I wondered when those holes had last been used to deliver death.

All the shutters had been closed in the large square room into which I emerged and it was in near-darkness save for a single candle which burned above a door. I could make out little in the chamber except for the smudge of a long table, and humps that might have been benches and chests. But the chamber through the door beyond was brightly lit. A fire blazed in the hearth and candles burned in sconces on the walls and in prickets set on the carved table and on the chests. Several large rugs warmed the floor and a finely executed tapestry of Judith holding up the freshly severed head of Holofernes hung from a wooden partition that probably screened the door to a chamber beyond. I suspected that much of what passed in this room could be heard by anyone listening on the other side of that wooden panel. Just who was standing in those shadows?

The two occupants of the room were seated on either side of the hearth: a stately old woman, her wrinkled hands folded gracefully in her lap, and a younger man, who gripped the arms of the high-backed chair as if it were a recalcitrant beast he was obliged to hold in check.

'Come closer, Goodman Pursglove, into the light where the Viscountess may clearly see you.' My back stiffened at the title goodman, which he pronounced with distain, as if he was spitting out an eel bone.

I advanced towards them into the bright circle cast by the candles, which I realised had been deliberately arranged for that purpose. Ignoring the man, I made a deep and courtly bow to the dowager.

'God keep and prosper your house, my lady.'

Magdalen briefly inclined her head, but her bright eyes never left my face. Even though she was seated, I could see she was uncommonly tall for a woman and that the hair, plucked back deep from her forehead, was white. Her face, though lined, was still strikingly handsome. She must have been a rare beauty in her youth, but now there were dark circles beneath those eyes that betrayed troubled nights. She was dressed entirely in widow's black, relieved only by pearl earrings and a pearl necklace, though even the necklace had at its centre a large square black stone that glistened like liquid tar in the candlelight.

She gestured towards the man opposite her with a natural grace that had none of the studied affectation of many women of her rank. Unusually for a wealthy woman, there were no jewelled rings on her hands, except for a single ring on her third finger studied with tiny stones of different hues. It wasn't a marriage band, but a rosary ring, and one so subtly designed that no one unless they had been raised among Catholics would have recognised it as that.

'This is my good friend and adviser, Richard Smith.'

Her chaplain, then. One of those priests smuggled in from France. I kept my face expressionless, acutely conscious of the light that would reveal the slightest twitch of eye or mouth.

I bowed, but only as deep as common courtesy demanded from a gentleman to an equal. I would not grovel to a priest. 'God grant you long life, Mr Smith.'

The gesture and the words were not wasted on him. The fingers tightened on the arms of the chair.

'The man you brought here this morning tells me you rescued him from a trap like the Good Samaritan. That was an act of charity for which you are to be commended,' Smith said. 'And then you brought him here?'

'His wounds needed attention; I thought it likely that those in this manor would be able to give him what he needed.'

'And what do you believe he needs, *Goodman* Pursglove?'

I fought to keep my face impassive. I did not like this man. 'It is evident, Mr Smith, that he will not be able to travel for weeks, perhaps months. He needs a place to rest.'

'Then why not take him straight to the town?' Smith said. 'It is well supplied with inns, and as a merchant it would be far more convenient for him, since he would be able to conduct his business while resting. This house may be titled Battle Abbey, but I assure you it is no longer the custom here to give shelter to every passing traveller as the old monks once did. You presumed too much on the Viscountess's hospitality.'

I inclined my head to Magdalen, addressing her instead of Smith. 'I would not presume upon your time and patience, my lady. But it was a place of *safety* for the man I sought, a place where those hunting him will not find him.'

The dowager's gaze flicked momentarily towards her chaplain, but he was careful to betray nothing.

I saw no reason for prolonging this game. I had to persuade them to trust me. But I knew I was wagering with my life. If they even suspected I was one of Cecil's or the King's agents trying to infiltrate this stronghold, there might yet be another corpse discovered in that convenient hole.

'I encountered a band of the sheriff's men on the road yesterday. They were hunting two men who came ashore under cover of darkness from a French ship near Winchelsea. One of the men-at-arms thought they might have doubled back, but fortunately for our friend, his officer was intent on pressing on, though this man's good fortune might yet prove the undoing of the second if he was ahead.'

I searched Smith's face for any sign that he knew of the fate of the second man, but it was hard to read, for he had positioned himself so that light from neither fire nor candle fell on him.

'If you suspected the injured man was a fugitive, even an enemy of England, did you not consider it your duty to hand him to the watch? You could easily have done so, for he could not resist, unless . . .' He leaned forward, his hands pressed flat together, the tips of his fingers touching his lips as if he were pondering upon some great matter. 'Unless,' he repeated 'you are also a wanted man.'

That was the question I'd been waiting for. 'Some duties are greater than others, are they not? And where they conflict, the secular must be sacrificed to the sacred.'

'That reasoning has led some to the gallows.'

'Which some have called their cross and thanked God for it.' I was certain he would recognise the allusion to Garnet's words before he mounted the scaffold. The London streets had been littered with broadsides detailing every detail of Henry Garnet's execution, but only a Catholic would still recall the old Jesuit's words now, for there had been many executions since and enough final words to fill a library.

He nodded and I thought I detected a faint smile, though there was no warmth in it. 'But you have adroitly evaded my question, Goodman Pursglove. So, I will ask you another. Master Cobbe says he could tell you were not familiar with the path to Battle Abbey, and all who come from Battle town or any of the villages around know the roads which lead here. So, as a stranger newly come to this place, what business is it that brings you to these parts?'

'This.' I had removed the two forged documents from their hiding place in the book *Daemonologie* while I was waiting below. I stepped forward and handed the first to him. He unfolded it and read it swiftly. 'This is a summons for recusancy,' he said, without the slightest flicker of interest, passing it to the old dowager.

'It's not the first time I've been summoned for refusing to attend the Protestant service. I couldn't pay the fine. The first fine had taken all I had, so I would have been thrown into Marshalsea prison.'

When I'd commissioned the document, my forger had said suspiciously that it was only the time he'd ever been asked to fake a summons by the man upon whom it was to be served. I'd told him I wanted it to show to my wife, to persuade her I had to vanish, so that she would not pursue me and discover me in the arms of a second bride, who was far sweeter of face and tongue. He'd chuckled over that and set to work with a will.

'I am told you have a fine horse,' Magdalen said. She was holding the summons between thumb and forefinger, but she had not even glanced down it. She was studying me. 'It is . . . *unusual* that you were permitted to keep that, when others have had their last chicken snatched from them.'

'I have a good friend who gave me his, so that I could flee.'

'Flee? To Battle?' Smith pounced on the word. 'I am given to understand that most recusants trying to evade the authorities make for the Ridings of Yorkshire, where they think they can more easily escape detection.'

It was true, yet the mention of Yorkshire, where I'd grown up, made me momentarily uneasy. I didn't answer, but drew out the second paper I'd hidden in the book and offered it to Magdalen. 'I was told that if I ever needed help, I would find it here.'

She took the paper and, lifting a reading glass which hung from her waist, she studied it. I concentrated on keeping my breathing level. Newgate gaol is a strange meeting place. Thieves and murderers find themselves sharing the same stinking cell as priests and Puritans. I'd had no desire to join in the prayers and services of either, but in the darkness, when most men are trying to escape their misery in a few hours of tormented sleep, whispered conversations are easily overheard. And by day, not that we ever saw daylight, rumours and stories are spread among the inmates and all they have to gossip about in that hellhole is each other. I had told FitzAlan I had never met Magdalen or her husband and that was the truth. What I did not say was that, thanks to my incarceration, I had already learned all that he was telling me about the Viscountess and Little Rome. In truth, I could probably have told him a thing or two he didn't know, like the name of the priest on the letter which Magdalen was reading now with such a sorrowful expression.

The priest had passed through Battle Abbey on his way back from France, but had been arrested some months later, when a safe house in London was raided, and had been cast into Newgate. Now he was commending me to her, as a good and faithful Catholic, or rather, that is what I had dictated to the forger of that carefully worn and stained letter, along with a couple of minor details I had gleaned about his time in Battle to authenticate it. I hoped that Magdalen would not know the priest's handwriting. But if she did, then the pursuivants had handed me the perfect explanation. Suspend a man by his hands in manacles for long enough, and you maim those hands for life, or whatever life remains to him before he mounts the gallows.

For a few moments, the old dowager sat in silence, her head bowed, her fingers twisting the little rosary ring, before she finally lifted her head.

'You also suffered in Newgate, then, Master Pursglove. Many have done so for their faith.'

'Not as harshly as the priests, my lady. My scars have healed well.' I glanced pointedly down at my ankles to make it clear I was prepared to show them the marks of the iron fetters, which were still visible, although of course in my case they were certainly not the marks of piety. Smith opened his mouth as if he was going to probe deeper, but for the first time Magdalen silenced him with a wave of her hand.

'But it has not turned you from the faith, Master Pursglove. It seems it has only served to strengthen your resolve.' She tapped the summons for recusancy, which still lay in her lap.

I seized the opportunity. 'Now I must find work quickly, if I am not to spend the winter in a ditch, for what little I have will not buy me more than a night or two even in the meanest inn. If I have done Father Cobbe or this house a good service, Father Smith, I would deem it more than repaid if you might recommend me to any master or mistress in the district who is in need of a servant.'

The request seemed not to be quite what Smith was expecting, but it was the dowager's expression which had changed the most. She was glaring at the summons through her reading glass.

'They will bring this land to bloody war with these fines. Livelihoods ripped from the hands of the honest and hard-working, and bread from their children's mouths. Old men who can scarcely draw breath cast into fever-ridden prisons; their families thrown on to the streets to beg, for no crime save faith. What does it profit them to force people to pretend to a Church they do not acknowledge in their hearts? It does nothing except reward liars, deceivers and hypocrites.'

'And by those three demons is their Church built, Lady Magdalen,' Smith said evenly, with none of the passion or fury that had been in the Viscountess's voice.

But she was not attending to her chaplain. 'If it is work as a servant you seek, Pursglove, you need search no more. A position will be found for you in this household immediately. My steward will speak with you and decide where you may best be of service, but you need have no fear of sleeping in a ditch, nor will you have to hide your faith. You will once more be able to take consolation in the Mass and the sacraments of our Holy Church.'

Smith had been staring at her with growing alarm. 'No, Lady Magdalen, I do not advise it. We know nothing about this man and there are many lives at stake, including your own. Checks must first be made. We only have his word—'

'We have these,' the dowager said, flapping the papers. 'And we have this man's deeds too. Did he not risk arrest himself by bringing Master Cobbe to us? I could not turn away one of our own brethren to perish of cold or hunger. I would not have the stain of that sin upon my soul. My mind is quite settled, Father Smith. I will have him in my household.'

Chapter Six

ROTHERHITHE, NEAR LONDON

A THICK, MUSTARD-YELLOW FOG hung heavy over the Thames, acrid with the smoke of the coal fires from the city tenements and the slightly sweeter smell of wood smoke from the country cottages which collided over the tiny hamlet. From out of the darkness came the muffled sound of oars rhythmically dipping in and out of the twisting black water and with it the hoarse cries of the wherryman, warning of his approach. Not that he expected to run into any other boats at this late hour, so far from the city, unless some despairing wretch was being rowed to the Tower. But as his old grandfather had always warned, on nights such as this the ghost-boat rode the river, collecting the souls of the dead who had fallen, jumped or been thrown – with throats cut or heads bludgeoned – into that relentless surge. Hungry ghosts, they were, who steered the demon wherry, and if they couldn't find the dead, they took the living for their oarsmen.

Only the offer of double the fare the wherryman could normally command convinced him to make this the final trip of a long day. Winter was setting in and a man of his advancing years couldn't afford to turn down such a sum, for you never knew what misfortune might lie ahead. There were some days now when the rain and cold made his joints ache so badly he could barely clamber into his boat.

He heard an answering call from the bank, and then glimpsed the smudge of a lantern glow appearing and vanishing through the swirling mist. It would have been impossible even for men who had lived all their lives on the land in those parts to tell where exactly they were on the Thames in this fog, but the wherryman could read every eddy and swirl created by each mooring post and fishing jetty along the bank better than a sea-captain could read a chart. He could feel his way through the currents' pressure on the oars as if the great river was woven from the twisted skeins of little streams, each flowing along at its own pace. And it was as well that he could, for there were always ruffians lying in wait on such nights to lure a naive man to the side with a lantern, only to rob him of his takings, his boat and often his life too.

Answering a call from the bank, the solitary passenger in the wherry leaned forward. 'Moor up here.'

The wherryman grunted, expertly steering the boat out of the current and bringing it alongside the small wooden jetty. A burly man stood ready on the boards. He set down the lantern and caught the rope thrown to him, then steadied the craft as the passenger stepped out.

'How long am I to wait?' the wherryman asked. He could see no lights, but knew there was a large house close by, conjuring visions of a warm kitchen fire, a beaker or two of ale and maybe a bowl of mutton stew if there was a pot simmering, although he'd heard rumours the house had been seized and the owners had fled before they could be arrested. But nowhere remained vacant for long. If half of what they said of him in the taverns was true, the King would already have bestowed this house on some newly knighted Scot, or one of those comely lads who'd taken his fancy.

> 'Hark, hark, the dogs do bark,
> The beggars have come to town,
> Some in rags and some in jags
> And one in a velvet gown.'

The wherryman grinned to himself: you only had to murmur that taunt in the hearing of a Scot to start a brawl in any tavern in London. They were easier to bait than the old blind bear on Bankside.

But his smirk quickly faded when the man on the jetty growled. 'You'll bide your time here until your passenger returns, unless you want to find yourself floating at the bottom of the river instead of rowing over it.' Something in the man's voice told the wherrymen this was no jest.

'You will not lose by it if you wait,' his passenger assured him, clinking the coins in a weighty purse. The wherryman grunted again and settled down in the boat, trying to persuade himself that on a night like this only a fool would leave his livelihood unattended anyway, even for the promise of supper and a roaring fire.

The burly servant lifted the lantern and led the visitor towards a gate in the high wall. 'This way, if you please. He's already waiting and that don't sweeten his temper none.'

The anti-chamber into which Cimex was ushered was a small, square room on the ground floor, the oak-panel walls lined with chairs and the floor covered with multiple carpets laid over one another so that only sections of those beneath could be seen. Low tables and high carved chests filled the spaces between the chairs, but they were bare, with no ornaments, gleaming candle prickets or colourful dishes upon them with which any owner of such a great house would want to impress a visitor.

FitzAlan was sitting hunched over the small fire that burned in the hearth. In this fog, chimney smoke would not be seen. The miserable yellow light that trickled from the few candles burning on the wall opposite did not illuminate FitzAlan's face, but his visitor could see the tension in his frame, the twitching and agitation of his limbs. In the fire's red glow, he resembled a large black spider which might, without warning, scuttle up one of the walls.

FitzAlan jerked his arm towards a small chair, placed further from the fire. A low table stood beside it, on which a glass of blood-red liquid glistened. FitzAlan could throw back three or four glasses of the strong, oversweet wine he favoured without the slightest effect. But it was not a wine his visitor enjoyed and FitzAlan knew it.

'You have news of your wee prodigy, Cimex. I trust you've nae wasted my time fetching me here only to tell me that he's in Battle.'

It was FitzAlan who had summoned Cimex, but that was not a point it was worth risking his wrath to make.

Cimex bowed before sliding into the chair. 'We both have our sources, sir, and I've no doubt you know what Daniel has for supper before he's even seated at table.'

A snorting bark which might have been a chuckle escaped FitzAlan. 'Come, then, drink up and speak out.'

'My information concerns where Daniel spent the night in London before he came to see you,' Cimex said cautiously. You had to be careful how you delivered such news. FitzAlan was apt to take umbrage if he thought you knew something he didn't, and Cimex would have wagered a heavy purse on FitzAlan not knowing this. The man trailing Daniel that evening had been waylaid, deliberately so, and lost track of his quarry, but Cimex was hardly likely to have admitted as much to FitzAlan.

FitzAlan was silent, but his nails scratched repeatedly against the carving on the armrest, like the rats in the walls.

'Daniel was seen at one of the inns in Southwark, the Three Pigeons. A play was being performed there, a play that was not licensed.'

The scratching stopped. The grip had tightened. 'By those same playwrights who penned that scurrilous filth *Eastward Hoe*?'

'The authors of this particular play have not yet been discovered, but certainly there were again references to thirty-pound knights and to . . .' Cimex hesitated. 'To a magic ring which, if put through the nose of a Scottish bull, would drag him back to his highland pasture, his bullocks following him.'

'That is incitement to uprising,' FitzAlan's voice had sunk

dangerously low, almost to the hissing of a snake. 'And what is the nature of this ring?'

'It may be nothing more than a feeble jest to amuse the drunken rabble who attend such illegal plays.'

'The play was performed on the very night when England was giving thanks for her Sovereign's deliverance from a murderous plot, and you think that a jest?'

'My source is even now trying to discover the author of the play and, when he is found, no doubt he can be persuaded to confess whether those lines he penned about a magic ring mean anything beyond a cheap joke. It was but a few days before the performance that a man was hanged at Cheapside for selling rings that he claimed would conjure demons who could be sent to do a man's bidding and bring him buried treasure. There was a great crowd at his execution and huge merriment as they watched him dance on the rope, joking about whether the demons would fly down and carry him off the scaffold. That may be all that the playwright—'

FitzAlan dismissed this with a flick of his hand. 'So, your wee sparrow is entertained by the execution of his fellow crossbiters. I hope he is still laughing when he finds himself on the scaffold.'

'Sir, Daniel did not witness the play,' Cimex said hastily. 'I am informed he arrived only when it had ended.'

'To meet with the author of this sedition or one of these unlicensed players?'

'The actors melted away as soon as the play was concluded and if Daniel had arranged to meet anyone, he did not get that chance. A fight broke out between a group of Scotsmen who also entered after the entertainment was over. But some nobles who were already there dicing had, it seemed, watched this play without instructing the innkeeper to halt it.'

Cimex had expected an outburst of fury, but instead FitzAlan lifted his goblet, holding it for his visitor to refill, even though the ewer of wine sat on the table next to his own elbow. His eyes seemed to glaze as he stared at the twisting rivulet of ruby wine pouring down in the firelight, like blood flowing from the block. 'The names of these nobles?'

Cimex placed the ewer back on the table, handed him the goblet and sat down again before answering. 'The name of one is known . . . Lord Richard Fairfax. It seems that the Scots took exception to the earring worn by one of the men he was dicing with and, after bandying insults, tore it off. Lord Fairfax drew a rapier to avenge the insult to his companion and wounded one of the Scots, though not mortally. A skirmish ensued, and the Scots . . .' Cimex hesitated, realising it might not be politic to use the word *fled* to a fellow countryman. 'The two parties lost each other in the crowd.'

'Scots can't walk the streets without being set on. These English fops flaunting their earrings like Southwark whores, it's like dangling a scrap of meat in front of a pack of hounds. Is it any wonder they rise to the sport? But by the same token, you canna blame Fairfax for drawing his weapon if a fellow Englishman was insulted.' He studied his visitor thoughtfully. 'Some wee brawl between men in their cups, there's a dozen of those a day in every street in the city. Even the marketplace cronies wouldn't waste words gossiping about that. So, what is it, Cimex? Speak out – you'll not get paid more for leaving me dangling.'

'Then I'll come to the point. The man who Lord Fairfax was defending, the man with whom he was dicing, was *not* English, sir. His name is Luis de Camargo and he is in the employ of the Spanish Ambassador. And there is something else you might wish to know about him – I am told he was a former lover of Catherine Howard, Countess of Suffolk.'

FitzAlan had slumped down in the chair, but at the mention of this woman he shot bolt upright and leaned forward, his eyes blazing almost as brightly as the flames in the hearth.

'If that's what you've been told then your intelligence is worth no more than fishwives' gossip.'

'It is court gossip that not all of her fourteen children are of her husband's getting,' Cimex retorted. 'She is a great beauty and only has to glance at most men for them to fall at her pretty little feet. Since Queen Anne gave her charge of Her Majesty's chambers in Greenwich, she has acquired the irresistible alchemy of both beauty and influence, a golden net that lures every gudgeon into it.'

'I ken well she has lovers. Do ye take me for a blind fool? She's a courtful of them, but they are the English who paw at her. Her Majesty knows her own ladies-in-waiting and who she may trust. God's cods, the Countess was even to have been made goddaughter to Princess Sophia, if the wee bairn had lived! Had Her Majesty heard a whisper that Catherine had taken a Spaniard to her bed, she'd have been appointed to a chamber in the Tower, not the Queen's bedchamber.' FitzAlan leaned back in his chair. The words had been delivered like a violent hailstorm, seemingly without drawing breath or swallowing, and saliva trickled down the corner of his sparse beard. He wiped his mouth with the back of his hand and took a great gulp of wine.

Cimex was reluctant to provoke another outburst, but was still smarting over FitzAlan's jibe about fishwife gossip. However, there was more at stake than injured pride. For when traitors were finally unmasked, and gossip was made truth, the conspirators had an unfortunate habit of dragging all those around them into the Tower. The crime of misprision of treason carried no less a penalty than that of treason itself, as Father Garnet and many others had discovered to their cost in the quartering block.

'As you say, sir, the English Court is full of her lovers, and Lord Salisbury is rumoured to be one of them. If what passes between them reaches the Spanish Ambassador . . .'

FitzAlan let out a bark of what might have been laughter, but he was not smiling. 'Robert Cecil? I heard the rumour bandied at one time that he and Catherine had an affair, but even the most addlepated clatterfart in Court knows that to be a jest. Your own words, Cimex, prove that to be so. She only has to glance at a man to have him fall at her feet. Why would she look twice at a little hunchbacked runt like Robert Cecil? I don't doubt he lusts for her; he has been ten years a widower. But a beggar may pine day and night for a queen, while the queen scarcely even notices him in the crowd.'

'But Lord Salisbury is no beggar, sir, and there are women who would gladly fondle a leper, if that leper has power or gold enough. My information is that Lord Salisbury is still much enamoured of this Catholic beauty and that she is still much enamoured of Spain.'

Chapter Seven

DANIEL PURSGLOVE

'I WILL TURN THE MATTRESSES. You must empty the easement chairs and the urinals.' The young man gestured towards the glass flasks on the chests beside each bed. Erasmus, or so he called himself, was a head shorter than me, and was forced to raise his chin as he tried to stare me down. He'd adopted a childishly imperious tone, as if he was unused to commanding others and feared he would not be obeyed. 'The men are all in good health,' he announced, 'so the urine does not need to be kept for the physician.'

'Does Lady Magdalen keep her own physician here, then?' I wondered if that was who had attended to Cobbe's broken leg.

His gaze darted away and he swallowed hard, his prominent Adam's apple rising and falling in his skinny throat, as if he'd swallowed a live toad that was endeavouring to crawl back out. He looked no more than seventeen, but was probably a year or so older, and his beard was so downy and sparse it only accentuated his youth.

'Not here . . . but there is one who can be fetched . . .' he added weakly.

Evidently one who can be trusted.

Erasmus seemed to remember he was supposed to be giving me instructions and lifted his head, peering at me down his long thin nose, which made him look even less like a man in authority and more like an anxious greyhound. 'You must be sure to scrub the pans and urinals well, and sweeten them before you bring them back.'

Real servants would call them pisspots when speaking among themselves. Erasmus would have to learn how to talk like a servant if he was to pass for one. But I knew many of the household here were not what they purported to be.

I would have wagered, however, that the steward, Master Brathwayt, was a genuine servant – a loyal Catholic, yes, but not a priest. I'd judged him to be in his early sixties. In contrast to his large, rotund belly, the dull, yellowish skin of his face sagged loose upon his bones and the lank grey hair that hung beneath his black cap to his shoulders was moulting. But his eyes had that sly, greedy look of a man who had spent most of his life scheming and plotting his way up through the ranks to this lofty position as head of the household.

He had constantly fondled the polished bloodstone seal dangling from a silver chain about his neck, while he apparently considered where he should place me, as if he wanted me to be in no doubt that my livelihood and safety lay in his stubby hands. But I knew Richard Smith had already intervened, even before Brathwayt had spoken to me, and told him that I was to be placed where I could be watched and kept well away from the dowager.

'A Yeoman of the Chambers,' the steward had finally pronounced. 'A very *junior* yeoman, naturally, until we see how well you perform your duties. You will not be required to wait upon Lady Magdalen or her ward, Lady Katheryne, or on Master Smith, but on some other gentlemen who are guests in the house.'

Not being able to get close to the dowager was annoying, but I could immediately see how I could use that to my advantage. It would give me much more free time to explore the Abbey and the little town beyond, and to gain the confidence of the lowlier servants, who would not be as guarded as the more senior men and might easily let something slip.

I lifted the padded seat of the easement chair to remove the pan of shit, and collected the glass flasks of piss from beside each of the narrow beds, stacking them in a pail. I did not know *who* these gentlemen were, but I was in little doubt as to *what* they were. While there were few outward symbols of their faith in the room except for plain wooden crosses above each bed, there was also little that might be expected to provide comfort and luxury in the chamber of a gentlemen of leisure. No jars of sweet-smelling unguents, silver brushes or mirrors, no soft cushions or portraits of court beauties. It was as austere a chamber as any priest might require.

Outside, the courtyard was bustling with activity, such as you would find in any large household in the early morning: men and women fetching water, wood and provisions for the kitchen, and milk for the dairy; lads stirring steaming vats of scraps for hounds, hogs and fowls over the fires, and girls carrying bundles of linens to the laundry. Across the far side of the yard was a long wooden shed built against one of the stone walls. Several of the servants nodded their heads or touched their hats as they passed its open doorway, calling a greeting to whoever was inside.

'Good morrow, Bailiff.'

'Flocks in fine fettle this morning, Master Yaxley.'

And as I drew level, I peered in, curious to see the man who the woodward, Crowhurst, answered to. I was sure that, like the steward, the bailiff of husbandry, who carried the huge responsibility of all the farmland, livestock, woods, ponds and mills on this great estate, would not be a priest in disguise. And I was not wrong, for the man I saw sitting behind a long narrow table had the muscular shoulders and bull-neck of a blacksmith, not a cleric. Nevertheless, quills, ink and several ledgers sat on the table, together with a small wooden chest from which protruded a large key. Though the sun had risen, the sky was so heavy with clouds it might have been twilight, and Master Yaxley had been forced to light a lantern to see his work.

A boy stood at one end of the table. Reaching into the sack at his feet, he drew out the decapitated heads of several animals and birds that he then lined up for the bailiff's inspection. Two hedgehog heads, their severed stumps still scarlet, were joined by the heads of three crows, a pair of magpies, and a stoat which, unlike the other vermin, seemed to have been killed some time ago, for the eye sockets were empty and the flesh was rotting from the skull. Even from the doorway, the stench of rotting meat almost overpowered the stink of the shit pail I was carrying.

The bailiff touched the candle from the lantern to the bowl of his long-stemmed pipe and sucked heartily, presumably hoping the smoke would mask the smell. He looked to be in his fifties, with a dense, fox-coloured beard and weather-beaten face, scarred and pitted like his hands, as if over the years many beasts and bushes had bitten and scratched away pieces of his flesh. He glanced up and caught sight of me. I set the pail down and stepped into the doorway, introducing myself.

'Aye, Pursglove,' he nodded, his eyes narrowing suspiciously. 'Was it you who brought that man in yesterday who'd got himself caught in a trap?'

'One of your traps, Master Yaxley?' I asked.

'None of my husbandmen use traps that size – no cause to, not even for the wild cats. Townsfolk mostly use snares for the vermin.' He jabbed the stem of his pipe towards the row of severed heads.

'Catch them all yourself, did you, lad?' I asked.

The boy looked uncertainly at Master Yaxley and for a moment I wondered if he was simple.

'Giles works hard,' the bailiff answered for him. 'Earned himself good bounty today.'

He pulled one of the ledgers towards him and, dipping his quill in the ink, began to record the tally of heads and how much the lad would be paid for each, muttering the entries aloud as he inscribed them. 'Two urchins, four pence apiece. Three crows, penny apiece.'

Both had now turned their attention to the count of corpses and I left them to it. I still had the delightful task of cleaning the pisspots to look forward to, and if I knew anything about young men who have just been elevated from junior servant to being in charge of one, that little maggot Erasmus would not merely offload on to me all the tasks he most disliked, but would be looking for any opportunity to lecture me about taking too long over them, eager to make up for the many times he had been the victim of a tongue-lashing from the man above him. The sooner I could solve the riddle of Benet's death and leave this place, the happier I'd be.

I SPUN ROUND as I felt the draught from the library door opening quietly behind me. On the floors below, the doors of the storerooms, kitchens and servants' quarters creaked and groaned on their hinges as most do in winter. But I'd discovered that the doors to some of the upper chambers had recently been oiled and rubbed down so that even on the wettest day, someone could slip in or out without making a sound, should it prove necessary.

'Been looking for you everywhere! What you doing in here?' The speaker was leaning against the open doorway of the chamber, his arms folded and his bandy legs crossed. I recognised him from the servants' hall earlier in the day. He'd sat two places down from me at the second sitting of dinner that morning, where he'd come to eat having waited on Lady Magdalen and her household in the Great Hall.

Before setting out to explore the house, I had armed myself with two new candles, which I'd removed from a sconce in the one of the bedchambers. I held them up. 'Someone said more candles were wanted in here.'

He glanced about him. It was well past five of the clock in the evening and the candles in the sconces on either side of the door had already been lit, for it was dark outside. A fire was blazing in the hearth, though only a small one, set in an iron basket. Its heat did not extend far down the long room. Magdalen, her chaplain, the steward, all of the guests and most of the servants were occupied with supper in the Great Hall, and those who weren't were hard at work in the kitchen or were eating their own meals. With

most of the rooms empty, it had seemed like the perfect opportunity to begin looking for some answers. And I had decided to
begin on the top floor of the guest wing.

This room had a polished and handsomely carved table running down the centre, with two long benches on either side, and
smaller tables and wooden chairs arranged in the corners. A fresh
sheaf of blank paper, quills and newly wetted inks were set at one
end of the table, more than any one man could use in an evening.
A room intended for study. Several shelves of books lined one
wall and I'd begun to examine the titles, half expecting them to
be Catholic theology. I was sure there would be many works
of that kind in the house. But it seemed the dowager was just
as astute as FitzAlan believed, for so far, I had only discovered
books such as *Palladis Tamia: Wits Treasury*, *Basilikon Doron*
and *The True Law of Free Monarchy*, these last two written
by our own industrious King. They had, no doubt, been left
prominently displayed to prove to any searchers that this was
a loyal household. As well these, there were herbals, tomes on
household management and Protestant theology, discourses on
animals, and books about the wonders and peoples to be found
in faraway lands – nothing that even the most zealous pursuivant
could use as evidence.

'Someone'll get himself strung up by his cods if Master Brathwayt finds out this room wasn't ready and checked over long
before supper. Master Smith and the other gentlemen come here
straight from the Great Hall.'

'For a glass of wine and a pipe of tobacco?' I suggested innocently.

A broad grin spread across the waiter's misshapen features.
'Oh aye, that's what they're up to, of course. They have some rare
old fun and games in here, I can tell you. Dancing and dicing, all
the vices. You should see Father Smith and her ladyship leaping
and cavorting together when they're doing the galliard.'

His smile suddenly froze and he stuck his head out into the
passageway, then turned quickly back. 'If you've finished setting

the candles, we need to get out of here. The likes of thee and me are not supposed to be on up this floor after supper. Look sharp.'

I followed him out into the passageway. I caught a smell of the baked gammon which had been served in the Great Hall earlier, but this was a long way from either there or the kitchens. Someone had passed along here with a dish of hot food, only minutes before. My belly growled, reminding me that I had missed my own supper. They were probably taking food to poor Cobbe. He must be laid up somewhere in one of the rooms, nursing his mangled leg. I was about to ask which room he was in, but my new watchdog was already herding me down a narrow wooden staircase behind one of the doors.

He informed me that his name was Arthur and that Master Brathwayt had instructed him to take me to one of the taverns in Battle for the evening. His duties were finished for the day and I would not be required again until the gentlemen retired for the night.

'There's a fair few alehouses in the town, but there's only one we're supposed to use. Can go there whenever we're free, but you have to be sure to be back afore the clock chimes ten of the hour, when the great door to the gatehouse is locked. We've all to lodge within the house every night.'

'But I bet there's another way in and out of the manor without going through that gatehouse,' I said, giving him a nudge.

We were halfway down the road that led through the centre of the town by then and he cocked his head, grinning up at me in the light cast by a lantern swaying over a door.

'And there's me thinking you were another of those pious saints her ladyship collects, who says the rosary each night afore tucking himself up in his cot without a naughty thought in his innocent little head.'

'Like you?' I returned his grin.

He laughed. 'There's always another door in Battle for those who know where to look.' He tapped the side of his nose. 'I might show you one day, if I reckon I can trust you.'

'And how do I win your trust?' I asked.

He turned down a narrow alley between two houses, pushing open a door and waving me in. 'You can start by buying me a beer. If you're not from these parts, you'll not have tasted our brew. Knucker's Milk, they call it. Much finer than the Mad Dog they serve at the alehouse old Brathwayt wants us to use.'

So, this wasn't the approved inn. I briefly wondered if Arthur was deliberately trying to make trouble for me. But as soon as we entered, I could tell he was a regular drinker in here. He probably knew that the steward or even the chaplain had a spy in the other alehouse, someone who reported back not only on how the manor servants behaved, but what they said and who they said it to. Or maybe Knucker's Milk really was the better brew.

A few people glanced up curiously as I followed him into the smoke-filled parlour. Arthur was clearly well known, and two men good-naturedly shuffled along on the bench by the single long table to make room for us.

One man stared pointedly at Arthur and gave a small jerk of his head towards me, plainly wanting to know the identity of the stranger he'd brought in.

'Him?' Arthur jabbed a thumb in my direction. 'Taken on as a Yeoman of Chambers, started today. Gets the privilege of emptying pisspots, if he behaves.' The laughter that rippled down the table was friendly enough.

I rose and made a mock bow. 'Daniel Pursglove, piss-pagger, at your service.'

'At least they don't ask you to taste it,' an old man said with a lopsided grin. 'Not like our pissprophet. Spends half his life with his nose in other men's water. If that's where book reading gets you, I'm glad my father never sent me to school.'

'I hear they fetched the pissprophet yesterday, to tend a man's leg up at the Abbey,' said another. He looked eagerly at my companion, as if expecting to be told more.

'Daniel, here, was the one that brought the injured man to the house. Had to free him from a mantrap, isn't that right, Dannet?'

he asked, but ploughed on without waiting for an answer. He plainly ruled as the news-bringer here. 'Poor bastard's bones had snapped like dry twigs and his flesh been mangled. He'll not be taking another stroll anytime soon.'

'Or running,' someone muttered darkly.

'If his leg was broke yesterday, stands to reason it couldn't have been him last night, could it?' the alewife said from the doorway. 'The wrong man got caught in that trap.'

'Who was it intended to catch?' I asked. Everyone fell silent, but I saw the sidelong glances flicking between the men on the benches. They knew.

'Poachers?' I suggested, to try to coax an answer. Though if the bailiff was speaking the truth, that trap hadn't been set on his orders.

'Been a bit of trouble in the town,' a man growled. He looked to be a stonemason from the badge on his jerkin. He lifted a pipe from the hand of the man next to him and drank down a long draught of smoke before handing it back. The smoke curled out of his mouth and nose as he considered his next words. 'We've a night-creeper at work. These past three weeks, folks have been woken by clattering and banging on their doors and shutters, stones thrown on to roofs to come crashing down on the flags. And this creature wailing and shrieking, like a soul in torment. Sets all the dogs off barking and howling, and all the babes crying and screaming. But before anyone manages to clamber out of their beds and unfasten the door, the creature's vanished again.'

That must have been what I'd heard the night before last at Crowhurst's cottage. 'Wild Tom', young Sam had called his bogeyman, but it seemed the Crowhursts weren't the only ones being terrorised.

'There's chickens go missing too. Not every night, but often enough. I found my Biddy gone last week, and she was a feisty bird,' the alewife said, leaning over as she set a flagon and two tankards down on the table in front of Arthur. 'First night it happened my old father reckon it to be a pack of foxes or wild

cats, for they can make a din worse than a hoard of demons . . .
Foxes you said it was, didn't you, Father?' she added, shouting to
a withered old man in the corner of the alehouse, sitting as close
to the fire as he could get without climbing in.

He looked up. 'Winter of the deep snow.' He pulled a patched
cloak tighter around his bowed shoulders, as if he could still feel
the cold of it in his bones. 'Skulk of foxes came out of the woods,
must have been nearly a score of them. Starving, they were. Made
a terrible din, they did, searching for food, leaping on to barrels
. . . knocking over everything that wasn't nailed down.' His chest
heaved with the effort of speaking. 'Killed all the fowls in the
town, cats too . . .' He paused to catch his breath, holding up a
trembling hand to show he was not done talking yet. 'One night
. . . one night they got into the cobbler's house, mauled his son
in his cradle, chewed his face and hands right off. Terrible it was.
His poor mother, she couldn't fight them off . . . Too many of
them, see . . . all as bold as lions,' he wheezed.

The stonemason rolled his eyes at the others. 'We've all heard
the old tales, Amor, but I keep telling you, this isn't foxes. Foxes
don't open the latched doors of chicken coops and fasten them
again afore they leave. Besides, if a dog or fox gets among chickens, they chase them all round and send them into a flurry of
squawking and flapping. A fox'll kill a whole flock for the sport
of it before he's done.'

But the old man was staring back into the heart of the flames
and gave no sign he had heard.

The man with the lopsided grin waggled the stem of his pipe.
'Jacob's right, it's no fox. I saw the heels of it vanishing round
the corner. It was a demon, near eight foot tall, with great black
wings in place of arms.'

'You saw a shadow, you old fool,' Arthur said. 'Even a dwarf
can cast a shadow as tall as a giant if the sun's right.'

'What sun, addlepate? It was the dark of the night.'

The alewife moved swiftly to refill his empty tankard, as if she
was well practised in distracting her customers before arguments

escalated into fights. 'Whatever this beast is, something will have to be done to put an end to it. Bad enough for those that have got menfolk in the house, but what of the likes of Widow Goody, who's all alone? Sudden banging or shrieking coming out of nowhere is enough to fright her to death. She says she daren't close her eyes at night for fear the night-creeper will break in. The terror of it will put her in her early grave if this goes on.'

'I reckon it's a *grave* that's the cause of all this,' the stonemason said. 'I don't know what old Walter saw, but he's right about one thing – that creature is a demon. It's my belief this night-creeper of ours is one of the walking dead. A corpse raised from the earth by the Devil to torment the living.'

This was an old tale; one I'd only ever heard the elderly sewing maids or old men tell when I was a boy. But ever since King James had come to the English throne, the broadsides had been printing such stories with increasing frequency. In the inns of Southwark, it was a joke often repeated by the English to bait the Scots, that half the Scottish courtiers were revenants raised from their graves, for they dressed like mouldering corpses, gabbled in strange tongues like the possessed and behaved like rampaging demons.

But the King was convinced that revenants were not merely legends or the stuff of idle jokes. My former master, Gentleman Pensioner Viscount Rowe, had returned home one morning chuckling about an argument he'd heard between the King and a bishop while my master was standing guard. The bishop had mildly remarked that a corpse could only be animated and possessed by an evil spirit if that person had led a wicked life or had not been given a Christian burial. The King had leaped in, recounting half a dozen cases which had been presented to him in Scotland to prove that even the corpse of a good Protestant or the bishop's own cadaver could become possessed after death, for the Christian soul, having departed to heaven, left only the corrupt body behind it, with no soul to guard it from the Devil. A cup that had been filled with sweet wine, once emptied, could be filled with foul poison, and so it was with any corpse. The King had become so vehement on this point that eventually the bishop had capitulated, which was just as well, Rowe said, because he was beginning to think that the King might decide to conduct one of his experiments and have the bishop killed to see if a demon would indeed animate his corpse.

In the light of that, I wryly reflected it might be wise to leave this alehouse discussion about revenants out of any report I made to FitzAlan. But that thought began to gnaw at me. FitzAlan had had me watched in Bristol. He'd known all I'd done before I'd even reached London. He would certainly be having me watched here too. His words from our very first meeting still echoed in my head – *Remember, the King has spies everywhere.* I glanced at the faces around me. Arthur? No, he wasn't the kind of man anyone would employ as a spy. But what about the others in the house? Magdalen had taken me in and I wasn't the only person who'd come seeking her protection. Had the King or Robert Cecil already succeeded in planting someone here before I'd even arrived?

The men around the table were still arguing about night-creepers and revenants. I took a swig of the Knucker's Milk. It was better and stronger than most beers served in London, as Arthur had said; a good, flavoursome brew, if you ignored the scum of husks floating in it.

'Well, think on it,' someone was saying. 'The night-creeping started barely a week after that coffin was brought from the Abbey and buried in our parish churchyard. There was no proper service, and not even a wooden cross or lump of stone to mark the grave or give the soul a name. And with Dean Wythines never setting foot in Battle to take services from one year's end to the next, for all that he draws a fat stipend from St Mary's, there's none to ask who was in that coffin or how they died. But it's as plain as a pikestaff, there was something nasty inside, for Lady Magdalen didn't want it in her chapel, else she would have had them laid to rest there and saved herself the bother.'

All eyes turned to Arthur, the fount of all news from the Abbey.

But he shrugged. 'Told you then and I'm telling you now, I don't know who they put in that grave. There was no talk of a death in the manor. A vagabond they found dead along the roadside maybe.'

'Did Master Brathwayt speak on it?'

'Not a word. If you ask me, he knows no more than the rest of us, not that he'd admit it. He likes you to think he knows everything that goes on in the Abbey.' Arthur gave a sly grin. 'But he doesn't, not the half of it.'

Chapter Eight

HORSES AND THEIR RIDERS had been arriving at Battle Abbey in twos and threes since dusk. The stable boys and grooms had run to catch the reins and, as soon as their riders had been helped to dismount, the lads had swiftly vaulted into the vacated saddles and trotted away into the gathering darkness. The stables were already occupied by horses belonging to the Abbey, their leathers always kept close at hand, ready to be put on at a moment's notice if it became necessary for Richard Smith and the other 'guests' to depart in haste. Although there were enough stalls to have accommodated most of the newly arrived horses, they were being dispersed to various outbuildings throughout the Abbey grounds, so that their riders would not all be crowded together in one place if swift flight became vital.

Not that I had time to watch where the beasts were being hidden, for the steward and the gentlemen of the chambers were barking orders at me and all the other house servants, even before we'd finished the tasks we were already engaged upon – 'Light the fires in the bedchambers!', 'Prepare the beds!', 'Fetch ewers of hot water!', 'Bring flagons of wine!', 'Carry up the travel bags!' All the while the visitors, like their horses, were arriving splattered with mud from the roads and exhausted from the tension of their journey, which had put most of them in a worse temper even than the steward.

As I laid the bellows to the fire I'd just kindled in one of the as yet unoccupied guest chambers, Erasmus crossed to the casement and peered out into the gloom. He had paused halfway through folding the linen towels and was now absently twisting one in his fists, creasing it badly.

'Will Lady Magdalen's guests stay for many days?' I asked. I already suspected what the answer would be, but I wanted to see how much I could coax out of him.

He didn't tear his gaze from the window. 'They are only here for supper tonight. Most will leave tomorrow, but at different times.'

'Supper and then Mass tomorrow.'

This time he did briefly glance at me and gave a slight nod, his prominent Adam's apple sliding up and down beneath the skin of his scraggy throat.

I expected that the guests would slip away in twos and threes after the service, to avoid drawing attention to themselves by forming a large group on the road. Seeing that Erasmus's attention was once again riveted on the scene outside, curiosity drove me to the casement. It was almost dark now, but there were very few lanterns lit below us and they were being carried low down, illuminating little more than the ground, which had been strewn with straw, not just to keep men and horses from slipping on the muddy stones, but to muffle sound and mask footprints. Breeches and skirts were briefly caught in the pools of light as the guests hurried passed, making the figures appear headless, as if they were already victims of the executioner's axe.

I thought at first that it was this sight that was distracting Erasmus, but he was not staring down at the courtyard below; his gaze was fastened on the darkness outside the Abbey grounds. Beyond the walls, scattered pinpricks of yellow or red light glimmered like tiny jewels on a mourning gown.

'You think that there are watchers out there?' I asked him.

'There are always watchers. The manor has people posted to look out for strangers on the road, but all they can do is give warning of their approach, try to stall them to buy us a few minutes of time to hide the instruments of Mass and the priests. They cannot stop the leopards bursting in, tearing the house apart and dragging out . . .' His jaw clenched and he twisted the linen towel fiercely, as if it were a garotte he was tightening around a man's neck.

Most Catholics called them the leopards: the men trained to search every inch of a house to uncover the priest holes, measuring walls inside and out, tapping the plaster, ripping off panelling, tearing down ceilings, prising up floorboards and stairs to expose the secret hiding places whenever a pursuivant gave them the word his quarry was hidden somewhere inside. Those selected as leopards were as ruthless and bloodthirsty as their namesake, but they did not attack until someone gave the order for their leashes to be slipped. It is the master not the beast who gives the order to kill.

A bell sounded somewhere below. Erasmus stared down at the crumpled cloth, as if he couldn't remember how he came to be holding it. He thrust it towards me.

'This is soiled. You cannot lay this out for one of Lady Magdalen's guests. Take it away at once, before it is seen,' he commanded, snatching up another towel from the pile of ironed linens and laying it carefully on the chest.

My fingers were itching to knot it round his own scrawny neck, so it was as well that at that moment the bell rang again, silencing us both: five of the clock, the summons for household and guests to come to the Great Hall for supper. The little maggot pushed past me and stalked out of the door, as if he thought he was already a cardinal.

I took my place with the other servants lining the passageway. This being Saturday, there was no meat served, but a great array of herrings, eels, salmon, pike and all manner of salt- and fresh-water fish were carried ceremonially into the hall, with no servant permitted to turn their backs on the procession of dishes destined for the high table, but everyone having to remove their hats and stand as if we were watching a great lord walk by. That rule I remembered well enough from my time as Secretary to Viscount Rowe, except that when I held that lofty post, I had been dining in the hall with Rowe and his guests. This time when the command rang out – 'Gentlemen and yeomen, wait upon the sewer for my lady' – the doors of the Great Hall were firmly shut against me and against all of those who were not required to wait at table. We hurried away to stuff down our own more modest suppers, before we would once more be sent upstairs to mend fires, trim wicks and see all was ready for the Lady Magdalen and her guests when they retired from their meal.

But before we could even take a bite of oyster pie or spear a slice of pickled eel, Steward Brathwayt strode into the long room. A shocked silence descended instantly upon the servants' hall. It was almost unheard of for a steward to leave his master's or mistress's table, especially when they were entertaining visitors. Several of the younger men scrambled to their feet, one knocking over his full beaker, spilling a pool of dark beer across the table. The clumsy young man turned scarlet to the tips of his ears, as the steward glowered at him. From beneath his cloaked arm Brathwayt extracted a leather-bound, oil-stained ledger, which he handed wordlessly to the bailiff. Then his gaze ranged up and down the long table, resting for a moment on the face of each man, woman, boy and girl, as if memorising who was there and who was missing.

Finally, he spoke, his fingers twisting the bloodstone seal on its silver chain, which glinted in the red glow of the fire. 'You all know what's to take place here on the morrow before sunrise. All those who were expected have now arrived, so if any comes knocking on the door this night, you must assume that they are here to do her ladyship harm. There are presently no known pursuivants biding in the town, nor have any been seen in the woods or on the roads hereabouts this day, but that doesn't mean to say there are no local watchers in the town, and there may even be traitors or spies inside this Abbey.'

It was hard to see any man's expression clearly in the dim candlelight, but I thought, just for a moment, his eyes turned in my direction.

'Justices of the Peace could even now be riding towards us. Should any man arrive demanding admittance, yeomen and grooms of the chambers, you are to make haste at once to the rooms you prepared for the guests today and make sure that nothing has been left lying in sight that would endanger them – no books or papers, no rosaries hung over the beds, no crucifixes or medals. Same for those of you who work in the kitchens: check to see the wafer irons have been hidden away and there are no robes in the sewing rooms or laundry. Meanwhile, Methuselah will be dispatched to open the great door. You all know he did not get his nickname for his youth.'

A few laughed. 'That old codger can move faster than a grey-hound chasing a hare if someone dangles a bottle of sack in front of him,' one man said, with a grin.

'Aye,' another countered, 'but slower than a month-dead corpse when there's work to be done. They'll be kicking their heels till Christmas if they're waiting for him to unlock that door.'

There was more laughter, but the steward remained grim-faced. 'But if they do come, let me remind you boiled brains that there are to be no weapons drawn, no resistance, else it won't just be you that'll suffer. Bad enough that Lady Magdalen will have to pay the ruffians for the privilege of being searched out of her own purse, without her being arrested for refusing to co-operate. So, you'll be obliging . . . *so* obliging and *so* helpful you'll have them crawling up their own backsides. Make sure they see everything they don't want to see and nothing they do. Understand?' He fixed each one of us in turn with his gaze.

'One thing more. The leopards usually pounce just before dawn, while everyone's still abed, or when they think the Mass has begun. See you tidy the beds which are occupied by those gentlemen who will need to vanish swiftly. And be sure you turn their mattresses and pillows over so that the heat from their bodies doesn't reveal that their beds were slept in. The searchers aren't fools; they will feel for that and they will count all those present. Keep your heads clear this night and your wits freshly sharpened. None is be permitted to go out to the inns in the town on this eve. The great door is locked.'

A few of the men exchanged sly glances. Like Arthur, they clearly knew there were other ways in and out of the Abbey. It was to be hoped the pursuivants hadn't discovered their secret. The steward plainly misread their glances, for he added. 'And don't think to get bowsy here instead. Mind you sup only small ale. I want no one fuddled by drink if the knock should come.'

They were silent until the door closed behind him; then came an explosion of chuckles and chatter.

'What's put the wind up old Brathwayt?'

'He's as twitchy as a heifer in a herd of bulls.'

'Here, do you reckon this means he's had warning of a raid?' someone asked.

The grins instantly gave way to anxious frowns. Voices dropped into low murmurs.

I pushed the oyster pie towards the man seated next to me. 'The steward seems to have worked out what needs to be done,' I said. 'I assume the leopards have searched this house before.'

'Not this one in Battle. I hear tell there were a couple of raids on the Viscountess's home in Southwark, but that was back when Queen Bess was on the throne. Didn't find who they were looking for, though. Sharp as a butcher's knife, her ladyship is. She knows how to handle them.' He grinned. 'Then someone told the local justices she was storing kegs of gunpowder in Southwark, but they never found that either. 'Course, they wouldn't. The whole tale was nothing but tilly-fally, or else a piece of pure malice. I mean, who in their right mind would keep a stash of gunpowder in the cellars or attic, knowing it could blow them to minced meat at any hour?' He suddenly seemed to realise what he'd said and glanced around nervously, but everyone was occupied, muttering to their neighbours. 'But that was six, seven years before the great treason, you understand. Neither Lady Magdalen nor none of the Montagues would ever countenance such wickedness.'

And yet according to FitzAlan, Guy Fawkes had been employed both by Lady Magdalen's husband and his grandson, and indeed the latter had even been incarcerated in the Tower for a spell after the plot was uncovered, in the belief that he was implicated by that very association.

The oyster pie commanded my neighbour's full attention as he made a pointed attempt to end this dangerous conversation, but I was determined to press further. 'I take it that Master Brathwayt doesn't usually make such a grave speech before a Mass.'

'Oh, he makes enough grave speeches to keep a dozen sextons busy.' He made a weak attempt at a grin.

'But not usually when the house is full of visitors, I warrant. Most stewards would be far too busy with the guests on an evening like this. '

He nodded glumly, then leaned towards me, lowering his voice still further. 'We've had Masses aplenty here, and the ladies coming for the pilgrimages the Viscountess leads to the holy well in the grounds, and we all know what to do for the special gentlemen if they have to disappear, but we've never had cause to do it. I reckon Salisbury's men have always left us alone, because it'd be too hard to surround the place and stop people slipping through.'

Or FitzAlan's suspicions were correct and Lady Magdalen was being protected by the Privy Council.

'But if old Brathwayt feels a chill, we all shiver,' my neighbour said. He lifted a bread sop dipped in fish broth to his mouth, but lowered it again without tasting it, and looked at me earnestly, seeking reassurance.

'You came lately to these parts. Did you hear any rumours on the road . . . any threats?'

'Nothing on the road.' *God's arse, I was beginning to talk like a priest; that was just the sort of equivocal answer my old tutor, Waldegrave, would have offered.* 'But I did hear there was a pursuivant hanging around here a couple of months back.'

He shrugged. 'They turn up in the town from time to time in the hope of sniffing out something. Always leave with their tails between their legs.'

'I heard this one didn't leave.'

My neighbour grinned. 'He left alright, but not for London. Went to a much hotter place.' He jerked his thumb down towards the floor. 'You'd have passed his grave on the roadside, a mile or so beyond the town, if you came that way. I dare say he was too afeared to go back to his masters and tell them he'd found nothing, so he turned himself into crows' pudding to save the hangman the trouble. Only report he'll be making now is to the Devil.'

The door opened for the second time and a kitchen girl hurried in, panting a little, her cheeks flushed from the heat of the fires. Sooty grease was smeared across her forehead and strands of hair were snaking down from beneath her cap. She stared around, then her gaze alighted on the bailiff, Yaxley, and, with evident relief, she scurried over, bobbed a little curtsey and bent low to whisper some message. Silence had fallen once more. Yaxley heaved himself out of his chair, but noticing the anxious eyes of the servants all fixed on him, he lifted his hand in reassurance.

'A doe found with her guts torn out. It'll be poachers' dogs or wild cats.' He winked at the kitchen girl and patted her backside. 'But don't you go fretting, my little heifer, it's not the leopards; they like to roast their meat.'

Some round the table laughed, but a few of the younger ones looked almost sick. The bailiff followed the girl towards the kitchen; as she held the door for him to pass through, he gave her breast a sharp squeeze. She squealed, and her cheeks flushed deeper.

'Have you ever been in a house when it was being searched?' a lad opposite me whispered. 'I've heard they look for the servants that they know will be the most easily broken. They can see the signs in your face. And if you refuse to talk, they use—'

'To your duties, yeomen and grooms!' barked Goodenouth, the senior Gentleman of the Chambers, as he clambered to his feet. 'Some of the guests may wish to retire as soon as they leave the Great Hall. They've ridden far today and will rise early.'

There were groans as men looked longingly at the unfinished meals on their trenchers, but they all scrambled up, some still hastily draining a tankard of ale or stuffing a last bite of bread or fish into their mouths. The rest of the evening was spent by us lowly servants flying up and down the stairs like rabid squirrels. The senior staff waited in the chambers, while those of lesser rank, like me, were sent to fetch hot, scented water for bathing, take boots and cloaks outside to brush clean from dried mud, or trudge up the stairs with spiced hippocras, steaming possets and liveries for guests to fortify themselves with before the midnight hour, when the fast for Mass would begin. I saw only glimpses of the Abbey's visitors, through doors that opened briefly for the senior servants to take from me whatever I had brought. Some chambers were occupied by three or four ladies, from women who could be no older than twenty to those aged enough to be their grandmothers. The men were similarly ranged in age. Even if they were married, husbands and wives slept apart with their own sex, for there was to be no temptation to lust the night before receiving the sacrament.

One by one the fires were banked down, candles snuffed out and halls and passageways plunged into near-darkness. Only single lanterns were left burning at intervals on hooks or windows, ready to be snatched up if light was needed quickly. The lesser servants withdrew to the servants' hall, leaving only a few who settled at intervals along the passageways, wrapping themselves in cloaks and preparing to spend a cold, uncomfortable night, snatching what sleep they could, but always ready to leap up, instantly awake, should a guest require any service or should that dread knock come thundering on the door.

I made my way towards the kitchens with a voiding basket full of dirty glasses and platters collected from the guests' chambers. In the darkened passageway a glint like burnished steel caught my eye, somewhere above my head. I set the basket down and, gripping my dagger hilt, inched forward. But the eye is the master conjurer and as I drew closer, I realised that what I had glimpsed was nothing more threatening than a dead king-fisher, a halcyon, hanging from a beam above me, its iridescent blue feathers gleaming in the faint light from the distant lantern. It was a common enough sight in many households, and indeed on many ships: suspended by the legs, it would turn as the wind changed, its beak pointing out the direction from which the wind would blow. A west wind was coming, it seemed to be telling me. That meant a wet journey home for our travellers on the morrow, but then again, it would mire the sheriff's men too, so Lady Magdalen's guests might yet have cause to bless the halcyon bird.

The kingfisher spun around above my head, caught in a draught as the door leading to the kitchens was flung open. A tall, skinny woman came bustling towards me, holding a covered tray.

'At least some of you idlers are still working. The Holy Ghost alone knows where all the rest have vanished to. Young Erasmus said a strong broth was wanted for Master Cobbe, but he's not come back down to fetch it. That's mashed brains of capons in almond milk, best thing I know for an ailing man, but it'll be as cold as a corpse in winter if it waits much longer and it must be supped hot if it's to do him any good. Can't heat again, else the cream will curdle.'

That was the floor Arthur had told me we were not permitted to be on after supper, which made it irresistible to me. 'I'll take it up for you,' I offered. 'I expect you've been running round all day. You're exhausted.'

She hesitated, gnawing her lip and glancing anxiously up at the ceiling above.

'It must have taken you a great deal of trouble to make it. It would be a sin to see it go to waste, especially if Master Cobbe's in need of it.'

'I suppose it can't do any harm if you were just to take it to the door. Come straight down, mind. They'll be hell to pay if Master Brathwayt catches you up there.'

I took the tray from her hands before she could change her mind and made for the small staircase Arthur had shown me. I paused outside the room I had started searching the day before. The wooden door was stout and the lock seemed formidable enough, but I knew from experience that it could easily be *charmed*. My skill would not be put to the test tonight, however, for behind the door I could hear the rumble of voices. I knocked and, without waiting, marched in.

Cobbe sat closest to the fire, huddled in a padded chair mounted on two stout poles, which must have been used to carry him into the room. His heavily bandaged leg was propped up on a stool. He was pale and drawn, his eyes sunk into dark hollows. Beads of sweat glistened on his face, though he pulled the blanket tighter around him. The dowager's chaplain, Richard Smith, and three other men were seated around a low card table on the other side of the small fire.

Erasmus and four other young men, whom I recognised as yeoman waiters and grooms of the chambers, were ranged on benches on either side of the long table. Half-empty flasks of sack and brandy and small green-tinged glasses were scattered about the table. All the men except Cobbe had a set of cards in front of them and a pile of coins. Most were already holding them, but as I crossed the room Erasmus started violently and snatched up his cards from the table. If that was the hand he'd been dealt, I hoped for the sake of his purse he did not intend to wager on it. There was no sign of the stacks of paper, inks or quills that I'd seen the day before, but as I glanced at the shelves, I noticed that one of the books was upside down, as if it had been stuffed back with more haste than care. To anyone entering that room, though, it would appear that the men were merely amusing themselves as any gentlemen might after supper, spending a convivial evening gaming and drinking.

I lowered my gaze. I'd sensed from the moment I'd entered that Smith had been watching me closely. I laid the tray down on a chest, pulled the linen napkin from the dish of broth and stepped back, waiting. An aroma of chicken and rosewater drifted across the room.

The younger men relaxed as they saw who had entered, but the expressions on the faces of Smith and those seated at his card table were far from friendly. The three men with the chaplain must be the occupants of the chamber I was obliged to wait upon, and I found myself matching the piss to the man. One who looked to be a similar age to Smith, probably in his forties, had protruding ears that stuck out through fluffy wisps of tawny hair, and with his pursed mouth, snub nose and dull brown eyes monstrously magnified behind the thick glass of a pair of spectacles, he reminded me of a bat. I'd wager he'd produced the cloudy orange specimen. The second man was probably in his late thirties, olive-skinned with a coal-black beard trimmed to a dagger point. Even seated, he was a good head taller than Smith. There was ice in his blood and blood in his water. The last was the youngest of the four priests, judging by his smooth, pale face, but his hair was white long before his years – his should be the almost colourless piss. But I had never counted uromancy as one of my talents.

Smith was still staring coldly at me. 'This is the newest member of Lady Magdalen's household, gentlemen,' Smith said. 'Yeoman Pursglove, who brought Master Cobbe to the Abbey.'

Cobbe's eyes flicked open and he struggled to push himself upright in the chair, wincing in pain as he dragged his leg across the stool. He gave me a wan smile, as if he were about to speak, but Smith cut in.

'Surely you have been told that you are not permitted in this part of the guest hall at this hour, Pursglove?'

'I was instructed to bring up the tray for Master Cobbe before it grew cold. There was none else to come and whoever ordered it had not returned to collect it . . . sir.'

Smith lifted his chin and glared at Erasmus, who was staring at his cards like a desperate gambler who knew he held complete ruin in his fingers. Two bright spots of colour blazed on his cheeks. He scrambled to his feet, dropping the cards, and one fluttered to the floor. He hesitated, half stooping to retrieve it, but changed his mind and stumbled across to fetch the bowl of broth.

'Well, what are you waiting for, Pursglove? Return to your duties. Erasmus will assist Master Cobbe.'

I gave a curt nod and with a flourish I handed the linen napkin to Erasmus. As I strode from the library, I picked up the fallen card and replaced it on the long table – the ace of spades, the card of ill-omen; some even called it the card of death.

Closing the door quietly, but firmly enough to assure them it was closed, I took a few heavy paces along the passageway and paused in front of the next door, laying my head close enough to listen. There was no sound on the other side. I tried the latch. The door was locked. I pulled a thin metal spike from the pocket sewn inside my shirt and inserted into the keyhole. It proved as easy to charm as I had suspected. If Little John, the master architect of the hidden chambers, had worked on this house, he had clearly not expected any of its searchers to be a magician, or even a skilled gilt.

The chamber into which I slid was small – barely wide enough for two men to stand shoulder to shoulder, with a single narrow casement no broader than a man's hand. From the faint light filtering in through the open door from the passageway, I could dimly make out the outlines of a chair and what might be a prayer desk. Was this some kind of chapel, a confessional? Whatever its function, as I'd hoped, it appeared to be separated from the library only by a wooden panel.

I fixed the position of the chair and prayer desk in my mind before I closed the door, plunging the chamber into complete darkness. I groped along the wooden panel until I found a spot towards the far end from where I could hear the voices on the other side, then slipped from my pocket the small green glass which I had palmed while making a show of proffering the napkin to Erasmus. I held it against the wood and pressed my ear to it.

'But to deliberately lie, Father Smith . . . is that not a sin?'

'Have you ever heard me instruct any soul to lie, Erasmus?' There was a murmur of voices which I could not distinguish, but if Smith was asking the question, I couldn't imagine any were dissenting.

'But, Father, if they ask me . . . should I deny my faith?'

A silence fell upon the room and I did not need to see the outrage on Smith's face to imagine his expression, for I had seen it many times on the face of the Fairfaxes's chaplain, Waldegrave, when I was a boy. When Erasmus spoke again, his voice sounded even more tremulous.

'I only meant . . . Of course, I would never do it, Father. I long for a martyr's death. I pray for it daily.'

'They must prove that a Mass has taken place, just as they must prove that you are preparing for ordination. You need neither confirm nor deny anything, but only say honestly that you are a Catholic, which is the truth.'

'But if they should question me about you, Father, or about Father Cobbe . . .'

'Then the answer you must give is that you refuse to involve others. They may put you to the torture, but before they do, they will ask you again, and you must repeat the same answer and keep repeating it even when you hang in manacles. They will desist when they find they cannot break you. And as you suffer and pray, you must ask yourself, what is the worst they can do? Why nothing except kill you, and that will be no hardship, but the greatest gift you could desire, for it will take you straight into the arms of Christ.'

Had Richard Smith ever hung in chains, ever seen a man eviscerated on the quartering block, ever watched a woman's flesh bubble and melt from her bones in the fires? Could you smell that stench and hear those screams and still call it a gift? If you hear a man talk of glories of the battlefield, you know he has never waded through running blood and mangled flesh, never stumbled over hacked-off limbs or felt the heat of another man's open wound on his own cheek.

'Father?' A new voice, one I couldn't identify. 'Will we pray for the soul that was buried in the graveyard at the Mass tomorrow? There is gossip among the servants . . . that another pursuivant . . .'

I stiffened, shifting the glass, for the speaker's words had become indistinct, as if he had turned his face to look at someone else in the room. Was that who they had buried in the town's graveyard, a second pursuivant, like Benet? If someone else had been hunted down and killed, they had evidently not risked trying to convince the authorities it was another suicide, and they had not reported the death.

I tried to move the glass again, and in the darkness my knee hit the wooden desk. The thump was dull, but there was instant silence on the other side of the partition. I held my breath, hoping that no sliding panel or door led directly into this room. I could sense the men on the other side of the wall – tense, listening. But there was no scraping of chairs or footsteps and after a moment or two I heard again the low, even tones of Smith. It did not sound as if he was moving towards the door, but I could not risk staying longer. I knew that Benet was already dead, buried in a roadside grave, and probably killed by someone at the Abbey. Now it seemed there could be another spy lying in that churchyard. I didn't relish becoming a third casualty in their war.

I slipped out into the passageway, making for the small back staircase. A lantern hung over the top of the stairs. The single flame that shone through the horn was just bright enough to illuminate the first three steps and something else, something glistening wet on the boards. I crouched down and touched it. Blood? It was all that talk of torture and death that made the thought leap into my mind. I sniffed my fingers, then touched my tongue to them. Not blood – sauce – pike sauce – and it was still warm. Someone had just passed along here with one of the dishes that had earlier been served in the Great Hall. But this was not the route to the kitchen. And this dish had not been brought for Father Cobbe. A hungry servant who had stolen remains of the banquet to devour in secret? Or was someone else being fed and sheltered up here, someone who had not been in the library?

Chapter Nine

LADY MAGDALEN and her visitors had been woken two hours before dawn, so we servants had barely time to close our eyes before once more we were hastening to the bedchambers with ewers of hot water, so that the guests could refresh themselves, and hefting saddlebags out to the courtyard, where grooms were waiting to whisk them off to the horses, ready for swift departure. As soon as they were dressed, the guests made their way across the inner courtyard to one of the outbuildings and vanished through a rough wood door. The lamps had been dimmed and candles carried low, so that we saw nothing of the faces of those who moved through the dark and silent courtyard.

We were the last to join the ragged procession, and I followed Arthur down a set of stone steps worn into hollows by centuries of monks' footsteps to what, at first glance, appeared to be a storage cellar smelling of damp, mould and tar. It was in darkness save for a few lanterns set on the floor that marked a Stygian path through a twisting maze of farm tools, barrels and tubs, which judging by the stench were used to store salted and smoked fish, herring, pickled oysters, strong vinegars and tallows. The door beyond was opened to us, and the dazzling light in the chapel almost blinded us as we stepped in from the darkened cellar. A wave of incense and beeswax drifted out and now I understood the need for the masking stench of fish and tar behind us. There were so many fat candles burning in the chapel that the heat was almost stifling after the cold outside. We took our places, standing behind the ranks of chairs on which the household and guests were seated.

I knew that Lady Magdalen had endowed her own chapel at Battle, but that had not prepared me for the size or magnificence of the place. The light from the candle flames danced over gold, gilt and silver, glittering on the vessels, crosses and the halos of the saints, some painted upon the walls, others standing as gilded statues. In front of the congregation was an elevated altar the like of which I was sure had not survived anywhere else in England, surmounted by a magnificent silver cross emblazoned with five blood-red stones. On the east side of the chapel was a quire with its own separate altar. It was occupied by the three priests and three of the young acolytes I had seen in the library the night before, including Erasmus.

I nudged Arthur, who was standing beside me. 'The priests in the quire, what do they call themselves? Always good to put a name to the pisspots.'

Arthur chuckled. 'The one with snow on the roof calls himself Henry Holt. Old jug-ears there, he goes by the name of George Bray, and the tall skinny one who looks like he has a rotten herring under his nose, he's Julian Santi. But I warn you, you won't get a smile or a thank-you out of him, even if you were to clean his pisspot with frankincense.'

The other two young men from the library had taken on the role of servers and were standing before the main altar on either side of Richard Smith. The young men had all removed their servants' livery and were clad in plain black robes which any clerk might have worn. But Smith and the three ordained priests were clad in fine silk robes of the kind Father Waldegrave used to don for Mass in the Fairfaxes's house. Their garments were thin and light, and could be folded exceedingly small, to be slipped in the false bottom of a chest, stuffed behind a shelf of books or concealed in the lining of a saddlebag when a priest was moving between safe houses.

Arthur elbowed me in the ribs, grinning broadly. 'Pretty, ain't she?'

'The chapel or the girl?' I asked, following his gaze.

At the front of the congregation, almost a head taller than any of the other women who surrounded her, sat the imposing figure of Lady Magdalen. She was as still as the statue of a saint, her head lifted, gazing at the cross, her back straight as a pike-shaft, in contrast to the young woman next to her. The girl was gazing around, her hands never still, one minute adjusting the folds of the wide ruff about her neck, the next fiddling with her long sapphire earrings and her necklace, smoothing her blue silk skirts, or twisting the curls of her hair that in the candlelight gleamed like polished oak. Clad in blue with a demure white veil covering her hair, she should have resembled the Virgin Mary, but for some reason it was a pagan goddess of summer that sprang to my mind.

'Who is she?' I whispered.

'That's Katheryne, that is. Lady Magdalen is her guardian, though gaoler would be nearer the mark, 'cause the whole Abbey knows the girl doesn't want to be here. She's a born rebel, that one. And as far above you as the lark is to the toad. So, you be on your guard if she makes eyes at you. The old dowager will bury you head down in salts for the crabs to feast on if you so much as glance the girl's way. Guards her virtue like a falcon guarding her chick, though rumour has it she's guarding an empty nest, for that little bird has already been plucked.'

'Does her ladyship have a habit of burying bodies in the marsh, then?' I asked, chuckling to make the question seem like a jest.

His gaze slid to the men seated in the quire. 'She has a habit of burying many things,' he said, and for once he wasn't grinning.

Smith and the two servers bowed the knee, and the lines I knew so well filled the chapel.

'Judica me Deus, et discerne causum meam de gente non sancta: ab homine iniquo et doloso erue me.'

Judge me, O God, and distinguish my cause from the nation that is not holy: deliver me from the unjust and deceitful man.

A gaping pit had opened in my chest. I did not want to hear

this, but the words of the Mass echoed inside my head, coming not from Smith's mouth, but from the dark and twisted labyrinth deep inside me. I deliberately wrenched my gaze from Smith and stared instead at the quire. The priests and two of the acolytes were joining in the responses with the two servers up at the altar –

'. . . *quare tristis incedo, dum affligit me inimicus?*'

. . . why do I go sorrowfully whilst the enemy afflicts me?

But Erasmus's hands were clenched so tightly together that his knuckles gleamed in the candle flames. His eyes were squeezed shut and his lips moved rapidly. He seemed to be muttering the same words fervently over and over again.

Arthur nudged me in the ribs, his tone once again light and cheerful. 'So, impressed, are we?' He waved airily towards the silver chalice and the vessels on the high altar.

'She's fortunate her late husband acquired an Abbey and all its treasures.'

'None of this lot came from the Abbey; leastways, so they tell everyone. There's some who take that with a grain of salt, but Amor – you remember him from Sybil's alehouse? – he says when Cromwell's agent came to make record of all that was in Battle Abbey, he told his masters it was a beggarly house and that not even a dung-raker would give them a thank-you for what was left in it.'

I stared at him in surprise. 'But I thought this was a place of great pilgrimage once.'

I'd been told as a boy that Battle Abbey had once been wealthy enough to possess over a hundred holy relics: not just fragments of the true cross, but the beards of St Peter and St Paul, and even the Virgin Mary's veil, all housed in a magnificent gold-and-jewel-encrusted reliquary. 'I suppose all the relics were carried off by Cromwell's men and destroyed.'

'I dare say they would have been if they'd found any, but Amor reckons the old abbot wasn't the country bumpkin Cromwell thought he was. By the time the agent came back, everything that was worth anything was gone, sold, so the abbot said, to pay their debts.'

In spite of the Mass continuing at the front of the chapel, most of the servants at the back, who probably had little schooling in Latin, were holding their own murmured conversations, flirting or leaning against the walls, unable to keep their eyes open. But Arthur still glanced around with great exaggeration and sidled closer to me as if he were about to impart some vital secret.

'But there's some that say the old abbot hid the Abbey's relics and treasures to save them from Cromwell's bonfires, thinking the wind would change when King Henry died and that England would return to Rome. Then the abbeys and monasteries would be restored to their rightful owners and they could retrieve what was theirs. Amor reckons the cunning old devil hid them in the Abbey somewhere.'

From what I'd seen of the ruins, the church and chapter house had been taken apart stone by stone when the late Viscount's father had remodelled the Abbey for his residence, so the abbot had either found a very cunning hiding place, or more likely had spirited the valuables away to ensure his own comfort in the bleak years that followed. But then maybe it was Cromwell's agent who had decided to store up few treasures on earth instead of heaven.

The ringing of the bell up at the altar severed all whispered conversations and those who had been asleep struggled to open their eyes and kneel as Smith elevated the host. The chapel door opened and the steward came hurrying in. Most of the congregation turned their heads, anxiously following his progress as he advanced towards Lady Magdalen. She did not look at him, but held up her hand, commanding him to stop, her gaze all the while fastened to the wafer held aloft in Father's Smith's hand like a moon rising over a miniature world. Only when she lowered her hand did Brathwayt approach and bow the knee in the general direction of both her and the altar, bending close to murmur something to her. She nodded gravely, then dismissed him with a curt gesture. He backed down the narrow aisle, bobbing as he went, as if he were retreating from the King's presence. Up at the altar, Smith remained frozen, though he did not turn.

'Continue, Father.' Magdalen's voice was calm but commanding.

The Mass continued, the wine was consecrated, the chalice held aloft, but the tension in the chapel was palpable. Though his tone remained low, the pace of Father Smith's delivery had noticeably quickened, as had the responses. Faces kept half turning towards the closed door, as if people couldn't help themselves. Every ear in the room seemed to be straining to listen for any sound beyond the priest's voice, and when someone fumbled with their psalter and dropped it, the hollow bang on the stone floor made one woman shriek with alarm, while a dozen others jerked violently at the noise.

'. . . *sanctum sacrificium, immaculatam hostiam* . . .'

. . . thy high priest offered to thee a holy sacrifice, a victim without blemish . . .

There was a mew, like a small animal in pain. I glanced towards the quire. Erasmus seemed to be staring up at a crucifix. I followed his gaze. In the candlelight and the blue-grey incense smoke rising from the thurible, the painted figure of the bloodied Christ seemed to be moving, as if he were writhing in his torture. Erasmus pushed passed those hemming him in and made for the door, gagging as he ran, his hand cupped to his mouth. He wrenched it open and was gone.

'. . . *Benedicat vos omnipotens* . . .'

As he turned towards us to give the final blessing, Smith's gaze for the first time strayed to the door that led back through the stinking cellar into the cold darkness of the world beyond. As soon as the congregation had joined in the final amen, the priests, including Smith, began pulling off their light silk robes and stuffing them beneath their doublets. Smith and three priests from the library were huddled together with Lady Magdalen.

The chalice and paten and the other vessels were swiftly being borne away by the servers and acolytes. Candles were rapidly extinguished, leaving barely enough light to find our way out by, as Goodenouth, the senior gentleman of the chambers, began to usher the servants towards the door ahead of the guests, whose faces, as they turned, were now veiled in shadow.

After the fug and heat of chapel, the wind in the courtyard, which still lay in darkness, was chilling, and as the kingfisher weathervane had predicted, it had turned to the west, bringing with it a squally rain. Maybe that would dispel the smell of incense which clung to our hair and clothes. We'd have a hard time convincing the leopards that no Mass had taken place if they caught the ghost of that particular smoke.

I drew back into the doorway of one of the small workrooms around the courtyard, watching the guests emerge in twos and threes, though I could see little of them. The acolytes hurried out, ready to resume their duties as servants. Then finally Lady Magdalen stepped out from the cellar. Even in the dark, her impressive height and upright gait were unmistakable. Her chaplain and the bat-like priest walked either side of her, while her ward, Katheryne, trailed behind. There was no sign of the tall priest or the young, white-haired one. Perhaps they had remained to close the chapel, or to pray.

'. . . wherever they reside, they must leave the Abbey and ride inland, then skirt around,' Smith was saying. 'It is vital they do not draw any of the sheriff's men to the coast road until the man has been searched for papers. I doubt they'll find the money. If he had any large sum with him, the boatmen will have taken it.'

'But letters also have a value . . .' Lady Magdalen broke off, glancing at the girl who was standing close behind her. 'Katheryne, return at once to the house and tell my maid I will break my fast with sweet buttered eggs instead of the herring.' She pressed her hand to her gullet. 'The fish I ate for supper still lies heavy on me. Go, make haste, girl, before she brings the wrong dish.'

Katheryne attempted to step quickly around the dowager and the two priests, but slipped on the wet stones. I sprang forward and caught her by the arm, steadying her before she fell to the ground. She cried out, probably as alarmed by my sudden appearance from the darkened doorway as by the fright of the near-fall.

Lady Magdalen gave a little start and peered at me. 'Oh, it is you, Pursglove. Pray tell me, are you a guardian angel in disguise that you appear for the second time to save one of us from injury?'

'It is not just angels who come in disguise,' Smith said coldly. 'Why are you lurking here rather than tending to your duties in the house? You have a habit of being where you ought not to be.'

I bowed curtly. 'One of her ladyship's guests dropped a glove. I came to find it.'

'And you thought to seek it in the dairy, did you?'

'I was making my way back to the chapel to search, but naturally, when I saw you emerge, I stepped aside to make way for you. I hope I know my duty, sir.'

'The chapel is closed,' Smith said, and was about to add more but the dowager cut in.

'Be good enough to escort my ward back to the house, Pursglove. And since she does not seem capable even of walking without causing a fuss, perhaps you will relieve her of the task of informing my maid to fetch me buttered eggs for breakfast. You may tell her I shall dine alone in my bedchamber.'

She gave a sharp gasp, closing her eyes tightly for moment, as if gripped by a sudden spasm of pain, then took several slow deep breaths. I'd wager she was suffering from something more serious than indigestion, though she was determined not to show it. The old lioness was sick and the jackals were creeping in.

I bowed and offered an arm to Katheryne, who brushed it aside and stalked ahead of me across the slippery stones. I caught up with her and, when we were out of sound and sight of her guardian, once again offered my arm. 'The rain has made the courtyard slippery, my lady.'

She seemed about to refuse, but with her next step she almost slipped again. Her soft leather shoes had not been fashioned for walking outside. This time she accepted my arm, but only to steady her as far as the door, and dropped it with distain the moment we passed inside. In the light from the sconces on the wall, I saw her clearly for the first time. She was short and thin, her collarbones standing out starkly below the delicate lace ruff that encircled her neck. She kept her chin lowered and looked up at me from beneath long lashes, making her dark brown eyes appear even larger. The effect might have been one of demure innocence and charm, had her lips not been pressed tightly in a furious pout.

'She treats me as if I am a hound that must be brought to heel. I'd have more freedom if I were a prisoner in the Tower.'

We had reached the stairs and Katheryne climbed ahead of me, holding her skirts up so that just enough of her ankle and calf was revealed to be both modest and provocative. Behind her, I bit back a smile. The girl had clearly practised that for hours.

'Fear sharpens tongues, my lady. Your guardian will doubtless have been greatly alarmed if the steward brought news that searchers are riding this way.' That wasn't what Smith and the old dowager had been discussing, but if either of them questioned Katheryne it must appear that I had heard nothing.

On reaching the landing, she flounced round to face me. 'You're wrong. That wasn't the news he brought. They've found a corpse at the mouth of the river, with his throat cut. Father Smith thinks he was murdered by the boatmen who rowed him ashore from a ship, or someone waiting on shore.'

'Do they know who the victim was?'

'Father Smith was expecting . . .' The petulant expression suddenly vanished and she gnawed her lip, as if she realised that she had said more than she should. She glanced anxiously up and down the passage.

'He was expecting the arrival of another priest, like Father Cobbe, by ship from France,' I prompted.

She lifted her head and gave me a brief smile. 'You know all about that, of course. You rescued him . . . But I don't think the dead man is a priest.'

Smith's sepulchre tones drifted up the staircase as somewhere below us a door opened.

Katheryne clapped her hand to her mouth. 'The old hag's breakfast! I'll tell her maid, Esther, but you'd better hurry to the kitchen and warn the cooks. She'll not be best pleased if she has to eat herring again.' She giggled. 'She was belching like a puddle of frogs half the night, serves her right.'

The studied pose of the coquette had vanished and she looked for a moment like a mischievous child. She turned and once more I noticed how small and slight she was. Her head seemed to be balanced precariously on the ruff, as if on a platter, for her neck looked too slender to support the weight. Anne Boleyn had taken comfort in her little neck, which she hoped the swordsman would have no trouble severing. How old was Katheryne? – fifteen, sixteen, the same age as Lady Jane Grey had been when she had gone to the block. But King James's predecessors had granted a swift beheading to traitors. He was not nearly so merciful, and Katherine would have to swiftly learn to guard her tongue, otherwise she would discover exactly how much freedom was afforded to a prisoner in the Tower.

I hurried down the stairs and along the passageway towards the kitchens. Through the casement, I could now see the bare branches of the distant trees, black against a faint grey light. Daylight would creep in slowly under this heavy pall of clouds, but the guests were already departing with a clatter of iron horseshoes. The riders were enveloped in heavy cloaks, hoods pulled low, faces half concealed by mufflers which none could dispute were needed to protect against the chill wind, rain and the mud splashed up by the horses. It is indeed an ill wind that blows good to no man.

As I passed beneath it, I glanced up at the dead kingfisher dangling from the beam. All of the candles in the sconces had been lit and to my surprise I saw there was not one but three dried birds hanging there. In the darkness of the passageway the night before, I'd noticed only one. Two seemed to agree that wind was coming from the west and set to continue blowing from that quarter. The third appeared to take the contrary view to his brothers and was indicating east. Now what would a soothsayer make of that?

Chapter Ten

PALACE OF PLACENTIA, GREENWICH

'Aim your lance straight between his eyes,' Richard Fairfax instructed his young cousin. 'You've a seasoned horse beneath you. He'll keep running in a straight line as long as you don't drag on the reins. Hold them loose and keep your sights fixed on the Turk's face as you gallop towards him. Strike hard and true. Run him through, whelp! You won't get a second chance.'

Oliver glanced down at his cousin and the knot in his stomach tightened. Those unnaturally pale green eyes were always cold, but just now, in weak afternoon sunshine, they were glacial. Richard released the bridle of the large strawberry gelding and stepped back as it circled round before lining up alongside the long wooden tilt barrier. The Turk was far down the list, too far to make out his face, much less his eyes, but Oliver could see the sun glinting from the upraised simitar and flashing from the red stone in the centre of his turban. His cousin was right: he must not allow those winking lights to distract him.

All around, courtiers and servants alike had paused and turned towards the long stretch of sand. He could hear the murmur of their chatter and occasional peal of laughter. He knew wagers were being laid. He glanced towards the twin viewing towers. Was the King also watching from one of those windows? He had glimpsed James there earlier, surveying the experienced men. Oliver felt every man's gaze upon him. He momentarily closed his eyes, silently begging all the powers in heaven and hell not to let him make a fool of himself.

Those watching began to yell taunts, urging him to get on with it or, if he was too craven, to yield the ground to men with more mettle. Oliver circled the gelding once more and then, with a shout, kicked it into a gallop. The horse did not need telling twice: it thundered down the line of the tilt barrier, as Oliver tried to press himself down in the saddle and keep the point of the weighty lance from sinking. The list was long enough for a horse and rider to settle into a stride, but the Turk was looming all too swiftly. The winter sun hung low and dazzlingly bright. Oliver could see nothing except the flash of that simitar and where his gaze fastened, his aim followed. He hit the Turk on the shoulder and the weighted quintain spun round. Oliver had braced himself for a solid impact, but instead his lance glanced off the wooden figure and shot forward into empty air. He rocked backwards, trying to stop himself from following the momentum of the heavy pole and being dragged over the horse's head. The flat of the metal simitar in the spinning Turk's grip slammed hard against his ribs. The horse felt the impact, reared and bolted forward as Oliver crashed to the ground with a thump that knocked the breath from his lungs.

It was not the first time in his sixteen years of life that Oliver had been thrown, but it was certainly the most humiliating. As he lay gasping like a landed fish on the sand, gales of laughter and ribald comments assaulted his ears. The Scots were jeering the loudest. Several servants had rushed out into the list: two to catch his horse, another two to check that he had not broken any limbs. Oliver struggled to his feet just as they reached him, and angrily pushed away their hands as he saw the grins that they were not even attempting to suppress.

He looked around for Richard and was both hurt and relieved that he had turned his back on the yard; he appeared to be deep in conversation with one of the grooms, as if he hadn't noticed the fall.

Oliver limped towards the archway, trying not to meet the glares of those Englishmen who'd been foolish enough to wager on him at least staying in the saddle, and ignoring the jeers of the Scots who were offering to lend him a donkey or a rabbit to ride, or some birdlime to glue his arse to the saddle. What little dignity he might have retained was betrayed by his knee, which kept giving way, causing him to stagger like an infant and prompting renewed bellows of laughter from those standing around. Fortunately, the appearance of another young rider soon diverted the spectators' attention to the sport of unnerving the next contender, in the hope that his downfall might provide even greater amusement. But Oliver's relief was short-lived, for he had only just hobbled out of the tiltyard when a hand roughly grasped his shoulder and spun him around.

'Are you auditioning for the role of court jester?' Richard growled. 'There are milkmaids in this palace who could hold a lance better than you. You looked as if you were dancing the volta with that Turk. When it spins, use your legs to move the horse swiftly away and stay in the saddle. The King's Accession Day tilt is less than four months away and if you are not to make a complete fool of yourself—'

'I doubt it will work a second time, Lord Fairfax, not until the King tires of his new jennet, at least.'

Oliver inwardly groaned as he felt an arm slip round his shoulders, gripping him tightly. Sir Christopher Veldon always made a point of putting his arm about whoever he was talking to, but Oliver could never decide if he was being friendly or making it almost impossible for anyone to walk away from him. Veldon looked to be in his early thirties, about the same age as Richard, with the distinctive shade of red-gold hair that fuelled the court gossip that one of his ancestors had been begotten in a royal Tudor bed. He certainly already had the corpulent Tudor belly, but that did not stop him from being acknowledged as one of the most skilful riders at the tilt. Oliver wanted to crawl under the nearest barrel and never come out again. 'Fairfax, didn't your cousin tell you that you have at least to break a leg in the Accession tilt to catch the King, or is that what you are rehearsing?' Veldon made a great show of examining Oliver from every angle and his amused study of the back of his breeches made Oliver suddenly aware that he must be covered in sand and probably worse. 'I grant you your young protégé is a comely lad, Richard, straight-limbed, face of a little cherub. But I think the King prefers his paramours to have at least sprouted a beard.'

Oliver could hardly fail to realise who Veldon was referring to; the whole Court was talking about it. He'd witnessed the great spectacle of his first Accession Day tilt back in March. It had been a glorious day, with knights and their attendants arriving on lavish floats, dressed in extravagantly outlandish costumes and all trying to outdo each other in front of the King. Another new arrival at Court, a handsome, flaxen-haired Scot, Robert Carr, had been employed by a former favourite, Sir James Hay, to present Hay's shield and device to the King. Carr had exhibited both his skills and his well-turned pair of legs in a showy display of horsemanship, which had had all the women in the Court gasping, swooning and clapping. But he'd gone too far and had managed to get himself thrown by his horse, breaking one of those fine, muscular legs. If court gossip was to be believed, James had arranged for his own surgeon to attend Carr, installed him in private lodgings at the King's own expense and, or so it was rumoured, had visited him daily while he mended, spending hours at his bedside.

Oliver saw the amused expression Veldon flashed at Richard, and he was furious with himself as he felt his cheeks flaming. 'I've no desire to take Robert Carr's place.'

'Ah, but maybe your cousin has greater ambitions for you. Is that why you are schooling this pretty young man in falling off his horse, Richard?'

Richard snorted. 'He needs no schooling from me to make an ass of himself. He worked that out all by himself.'

'His wits must be sharper than the roan jennet's, then. I hear it was Thomas Overbury who told Carr to throw himself off his horse at the King's feet. Overbury's hardly got the beauty to win the eye of the King, but there's more than one way to gain the King's ear. I hear the Queen has taken to calling Overbury Carr's governor.'

'And if the rumours are true and Carr is knighted and made a Gentleman of the Bedchamber . . .' Richard said.

'Oh, I think we can assume he is already the man *in* the bedchamber, even if he's not yet a gentleman. But yes, if Carr is ennobled then Overbury has a channel to the King day and night. And we will all be swearing that Carr's sweet lips are pomegranates and his eyes are sparkling jewels each time we seek audience with James. Let us hope that Carr falls out of favour before the Christmas honours, or that someone ensures he does. Then we'll be persuading young Oliver here to fling himself off his horse at the next Accession tilt so that the King can kiss him better.' He squeezed Oliver uncomfortably against his padded jerkin, as if he was a child. 'You'd do that to help your dear cousin, wouldn't you, lad? Of course, you don't need James to give you Latin lessons as he did Carr, but maybe he could teach you sorcery instead, and then you'd be able to charm him. But your cousin will be able to tell you all about that art.'

Oliver opened his mouth to retort, but he was aware that Veldon had turned his gaze on Richard when he made this last utterance. Richard had stiffened. Veldon bowed and walked swiftly away, his lips twitching in the ghost of a smile.

Oliver glanced around, assuming that someone was approaching who Veldon did not wish to be overheard by. He had not begun to fathom half of the dark undercurrents that twisted through the Court, but he knew enough to realise that to speak against the King's favourite in the hearing of anyone who might report it was unwise, to say the least. But the small garden where they stood was deserted, and judging by the shouts coming from inside the tiltyard, everyone was in there, watching the sport.

Richard was still glaring after the retreating back.

'What did he mean about sorcery?' Oliver asked.

'He meant Daniel. The man you saw on trial when you first

came to Court. That village bastard foisted on my father. The man who murdered him.'

'But I thought . . . my father said Lord Fairfax died in a riding accident.'

'It was no accident! It was revenge. My father should have hanged the whoreson years before when he found out what Daniel had done, but instead he sent him away, banished him, and was the little bastard grateful his life had been spared? No, he came back. He always comes back. A cockroach, a rat and a stinking malignance will always return, until you cut them into pieces and destroy them.'

Chapter Eleven

DANIEL PURSGLOVE

'You SHOULD HAVE HEARD the howling, Master Yaxley. Scratching and slathering at the walls, and the door rattling in its frame as the beast hurled itself at it. If I'd not put a stout oak beam across it, that creature would have smashed it down as easy as breaking a dried fish-skin. You can see the claw marks on the wood, great gouges they are, deeper and wider than even a wild cat would make.'

'Get away with you, Esau,' the bailiff said. 'Next you'll be telling me that old knucker slithered out from his pool and came hunting.'

The dregs of the afternoon light filtered through the grey clouds, but the rain that had been hammering down since dawn had finally eased to fine mist. An oxcart had backed up into the open door of one of the wooden outbuildings framing the court-yard, and the carter was hefting sacks from the store and loading them up, bellowing his complaints as he worked.

'If there are marks on your door,' the bailiff continued, as Esau emerged again, 'then you more than likely made them yourself when you came reeling home, drunk as a sow, from the alehouse.'

Esau darted a sour look at the bailiff, then returned with his final load before wiping his muddy hands on the seat of his breeches. 'That din started up just afore daybreak. I'd been in my bed for hours. My mother will swear to that. Near frighted her into the next world, it did, when that door shook. And there's more.' He stalked to the front of the cart and, reaching in, lifted a bundle wrapped in old hemp which he thrust hard against the bailiff's belly, forcing him to take it.

I edged closer. The bailiff flicked back the wrapping. A dead cat lay limply on the cloth, its mouth and eyes wide open as if it had died in terror. Water dripped from the matted fur.

'Found her dangling over a beam in my wood store this morning. You going to tell me she drowned herself?'

'Been raining,' Master Yaxley said stubbornly, looking around as if unsure what to do with the sodden corpse he was clutching.

'Aye, it has. But not in my shed. She was drowned, then she was tossed up over that beam as if the beast was playing with her, like she was a mouse and it was the cat.'

'The cat got itself a wetting, that's all, took shelter in the wood store and died,' Yaxley said impatiently. He turned the cat belly up, peering at the throat, then running practised fingers down the limbs before thrusting it back at Esau. 'See for yourself, there's no teeth marks and it's not been caught in a poacher's snare 'cause there's no bones broken and not a drop of blood on her. Now, if you'd brought me that grimalkin of yours with its belly or throat torn out like that doe Matthew Crowhurst found, then I might take these notions of a wild beast seriously.'

Esau dropped the dead cat on to the back of cart and seized the ox's halter. 'You can mock, Master Yaxley, but I'm not the only one's been tormented by this night-creeper and folks are growing afeared and angry.' He tugged the ox until the cart was clear of the door, then clambered up as the wheels rolled, turning back in his seat to have the last word. 'Mark my words, they'll take matters into their own hands if the beast isn't caught soon, and you know what mischief a crowd can do when their blood's up.' He flicked the long whip and the ox patiently plodded out of the yard.

The bailiff spat in the direction of the retreating cart on the ground, and turned to me, jerking his head.

'Mewling scut,' he said disgustedly. 'If he took better care of that cottage of his, the door wouldn't hang so loose that the wind could shake it like a bag of bones. That's all it was, a drat wind.'

'I heard others in the town complain of being disturbed on several nights by the same kind of noise,' I said, 'and the alewife, Sybil, said she'd had chickens taken.'

'Foxes or vagrants,' he said tersely.

'All the same, when people feel threatened in their own homes . . .'

'Aye, well, we're none of us safe in our own homes these days, are we?' He stared up the Abbey. 'There's some of us like to lose more than a few scrawny chickens. And if her ladyship is taken, there's not a man, woman or child on this manor who'll be able to sleep safe in their beds.'

His expression was grim and he seemed far from the man who had cracked jokes about the leopards in front of the servants at supper. But faster than I could have waved a cloth to make a toad vanish, the scowl on his pitted face was replaced by a leery grin.

I turned to see a woman daintily picking her way towards us, her skirts held high to keep them from the dung and mud. She was perhaps in her forties, her black hair plucked back from a high forehead which accentuated her high cheekbones. There was a severity in her dark grey gown, white collar and cap, which reminded me of both a nun and a Puritan. Yet her thin lips were stained a garish vermillion, making her mouth look like a raw sword slash across her face.

'Now there are some creatures a man would be glad to have scratching at his door at night, what do you say, Pursglove?' Yaxley murmured, with a wink at me. Then he called out cheerfully, 'Good day, Esther.'

So, this was Magdalen's maid.

'I bring a message from Lady Magdalen.' She hesitated, as if wondering whether she need venture further across the mud, but plainly decided it was not something she could shout across the yard and continued. I thought the bailiff would spare her the trouble and walk to meet her until I realised he was enjoying the sight of her legs as she raised her skirts still higher out of the puddles.

'Some of the ladies are staying on and Lady Magdalen wishes . . .'

She stopped and looked pointedly at me. I bowed, somewhat deeper than courtesy demanded from a Yeoman of the Chamber to the mistress's tiring maid, but servants in her position usually had the ear of their mistress, not to mention the key to their chambers, and I might need this woman on my side in the coming days.

'Daniel Pursglove, newly appointed to her ladyship's service.'

'Lady Magdalen speaks well of you.' She bestowed a smile with the air of one who was the lady herself rather than her maid. 'Father Smith has spoken of you also.'

'But not well?' I asked, adopting an innocent expression.

A little bubble of laughter escaped her, but she pressed her hand quickly to her mouth to suppress it and regarded me curiously for a moment before turning her attention back to the bailiff.

'Lady Magdalen will be holding vespers at Gray's well this evening and then she'll lead the ladies on a pilgrimage to the holy source of the spring. She wishes you to ensure the paths are clear of fallen branches and bracken, and that wood is laid over the worst of the mud especially around the spring where they will stand.'

Yaxley scowled. 'You don't need to be telling me what needs doing, Esther. I gave the orders yesterday. Been seeing to it for years in all weathers and her ladyship has never had cause to complain, not once.' His gaze slid sideways to the house once more, as if the dowager's spirit might be hovering within earshot. He lowered his voice, taking a pace towards the maid. 'But you want to tell Lady Magdalen that now is not the time to go traipsing through the woods on any pilgrimage, especially after dark. They'll have watchers posted all around the grounds and there are places where the women can be seen this season of year when there's no leaf to give them cover. Their lanterns and candles will light them up like fireships at sea.' He gestured in the direction of the Abbey church ruins. 'Can you not tell her to content herself with saying her prayers at Gray's well? 'Tis out of sight and, as you say yourself, it is the same water that feeds it.'

'I'll tell her no such thing. That pursuivant found out about those pilgrimages to the holy well, and Father Smith says his own hand was turned against him like Judas Iscariot. He was buried like a rabid dog at the roadside, as he deserved. The angels and all the saints protected Lady Magdalen before and they'll do it again.' Her chin jerked up as if challenging the heavenly army to do their duty. 'See that the path is clear.' She stalked away in the direction of the house.

Yaxley glowered after her, rubbing the base of his back. 'I don't know who is more stomachy, her or the mistress. Lady Magdalen's grown as stubborn as the east wind since Smith became her chaplain, barges straight through whatever's in her path, instead of bending round it. Years gone by she used to go to the parish church as the law demands whenever there were services, which wasn't often, for the Dean spends most of his time in Oxford. But Smith's persuaded her that even doing that much to avoid calling down trouble is a sin. I reckon he's convinced her she wants to be martyred and if that's what she's hankering for, she's going the right way about it, without giving a thought to who she'll be dragging to the scaffold with her.'

He growled deep in his throat like a baleful dog, and seeing one of the men beyond the gate, lumbered after him, bellowing orders about clearing the path through the wood.

I turned back towards the house, deep in thought. The pursuivant whom Esther had referred to could only have been Benet. Clearly, the whole household knew who he was. But Yaxley was right: with a murdered man lying out on the marshes, and the sheriff's men convinced that every passing ship was smuggling in priests and spies, Lady Magdalen was taking a huge risk venturing out on another pilgrimage, today of all days. She either possessed the faith of a saint that God would shield her or someone on the Privy Council was protecting her.

But FitzAlan said these pilgrimages had already been reported to the King by others and, no doubt, to the Privy Council too. So, Benet must have discovered something far more significant to get himself killed. And whatever her hold over them, Privy Councillors were hardly likely to have come to Battle and pushed Benet into a pit for her. Whoever had done that lived here. In any raid on the Abbey that might have followed Benet's report, if he'd lived to deliver it, Smith would have been considered a great prize for the leopards and the mistakes that had led to Father Gerard's escape from the Tower would surely not have been repeated. I found myself wondering just how far a man like Smith would go to protect what must be a most agreeable position and, more importantly, his own skin.

I was about to cross the inner courtyard when from the tail of my eye I caught the glimmer of a flame beneath the door of the cellar through which we had entered the chapel a few hours earlier. Instinctively I drew back and ducked into the outer room of the dairy, which was empty, for the maids' work in there was finished until the next milking. I peered through the small casement, but the light had vanished. Moments later the cellar door eased open. Two figures emerged and sidled into the courtyard. Their backs were to me, but there was no mistaking the startlingly white hair of Henry Holt and with him the tall, thin figure of Julian Santi. They seemed to have spent an eventful morning, for their hose and breeches were splattered with mud and green slime and their shoes were caked in it. Each had a leather satchel slung over their shoulders. As I glimpsed the white marks on Holt's sleeve, I felt a sudden chill. Saltpetre blooms on cellar walls. Gunpowder! It couldn't be. No one would attempt that again, would they?

I remained hidden until I was certain that they'd gone into the house, and I had just crossed the courtyard when the door was flung wide and Lady Magdalen descended, magnificent as a galleon in full sail. She was followed by a flotilla of half a dozen ladies wrapped in cloaks and mufflers, though the dowager's face was defiantly uncovered. Each woman carried a psalter and a fat wax candle, shielded from the wind inside a glass vessel, the flames guttering bravely. Though the faces of all the other women were masked by their hoods and scarfs, I did recognise the diminutive form of Katheryne trailing behind the others, as it seemed was her customary place, her small hand holding the glass lantern with such casual indifference, I doubted the candle would remain alight long enough to reach their place of devotion. George Bray came hurrying down the steps behind them, coughing to attract attention; the low pale sun glanced off his thick spectacles, making his eyes look white and dead. For a moment, I saw again the white eyes of the corpses caught among the muddy reeds of an Irish lake. The water turned red, transfigured into blood.

Lady Magdalen glanced round impatiently. 'As you see, Father Bray, I have heeded the words of my steward and Father Smith. I would prefer to make our vespers prayers at the well after sunset, as we have done since I came to reside here, but I will on this occasion keep the nones devotion there instead. But do not ask me again to forego that. These ladies are most anxious to make the pilgrimage and some have come a long way to pray for healing.'

Bray stepped forward, determined to take his place at the head of the procession, but Lady Magdalen flapped him aside impatiently. 'I have been leading the ladies in their devotions for these many years. Nones or vespers, I am equal to the task. There is no cause to risk your life and liberty; indeed the presence of one man among a group of women would only draw attention to our purpose, while ladies alone appear simply to be taking exercise.'

How many did so clutching lighted candles?

'I shall pray for you, Lady Magdalen, for as the sun begins its descent into darkness at the hour of nones, so the spirits of men and women sink too at that hour. They are more open to temptation, and this is the time the demons choose to test them.' Bray inclined his head, in a gesture that was intended to be humble but looked so obsequious I found myself grinding my teeth.

The elderly dowager made a noise that sounded suspiciously like a snort. 'I assume you are referring to those who might be tempted to betray us, for I am sure we will find little to test us in the woods except the mud. Come, ladies. Katheryne, stop fidgeting and keep up. We are not walking out to gather rosebuds.'

Katheryne, awkwardly grasping her votive light with one hand, had been trying to loosen the drawstrings of the tiny embroidered bag dangling from her belt and extract something from inside. As the women processed towards the holy well near the wall of the ruined church, Katheryne followed behind and, as she passed me, she flashed a wide-eyed glance up at me from beneath her long lashes. Her gaze held mine quite deliberately before she walked on. With the muffler drawn across her face it was impossible to see if she had smiled, but I was sure her eyes had not. She had only taken two or three more paces before I saw something drop on to the flags with a tiny metallic clink and roll against the wall.

It was a gilded thimble. It must have dropped from her little bag as she was trying to find whatever she was searching for. I bent to retrieve it and called to her. She turned as I held it out to her.

Instead of exclaiming her loss, or taking it from me, she dragged her muffler down from her face.

'A pretty thing, is it not? Take it to my chamber, Pursglove, and lay it carefully with my stitchwork, will you? It is very special to me.'

Pulling the covering back over her mouth again, she turned and hurried after the women as they vanished around the corner.

I stared down at the object in my palm, certain from her words that she had deliberately dropped it to ensure I went to her chamber. She could then easily accuse me of stealing something from it, or make certain I was caught there, trespassing in the bedchamber of the Viscountess's own ward. Either would see me hurled out from the Abbey and probably a great deal worse. Arthur had warned only that morning that 'the old dowager will bury you head down in salts for the crabs to feast on if you so much as glance the girl's way'. It probably wasn't so far from the truth. But I could think of no reason why Katheryne should want me dead or even dismissed, unless she was annoyed and petulant that I hadn't fallen for her charms earlier that day. Of course, Smith might have convinced her to try to trap me. But from our brief encounter that morning, I'd seen a spark of defiance in Katheryne which I suspected even the Pope might find hard to extinguish.

Either way, I had no intention of walking into that snare. I looked down at the object in my palm. She was right: it was pretty and unusual, with a broad band of decoration around the base and top. Had she meant it when she said it was 'very special' to her?' Thimbles usually came to women as gifts or were bequeathed to them by their mothers.

Out of curiosity I turned the thimble round, searching for initials or a name, but there was nothing except the bands of . . . what were they? Stylised pomegranates and perhaps springs of myrtle, symbols of the Virgin Mary. It was, at first glance, an entirely suitable gift for a young Catholic girl, and yet these were not depicted like those in most churches or even like those in the hidden chapel here. I had seen them carved in this style before, though. And if I was right, then how on earth had this come into the possession of girl like Katheryne?

I hooked my finger into the thimble as I pushed it into the purse hanging on my belt, then stopped and drew it out again. There was something inside it. I took a few paces back into the courtyard and flicked out a slip of paper, folded into a band.

The writing was small and neat, but had those unnecessary flourishes that women are taught by their tutors. 'Daniel, I can help you, if you will help me.'

I laughed. The last time I had trusted a woman to help me was when FitzAlan had sent me to Bristol and that was an episode I had no intention of repeating. Even though we'd only exchanged a few words, I'd have wagered my own cods that the only help I could expect from Katheryne would be in putting my head in the hangman's noose. I dropped the slip of paper into the nearest puddle, grinding it with my heel until the ink washed away and the paper was pulp. Then I went in search of Esther. She could replace the precious thimble and, if she was so minded, report to her mistress that I had not taken the bait.

Chapter Twelve

'PURSGLOVE!' Goodenouth, the senior gentleman of the chambers, came waddling towards me down the long passageway, his face florid. 'Master Santi and Master Holt need the mud cleaning from their shoes.' He thrust a sack into my hands with evident distaste. 'I have already sent their clothes to the laundry, since Erasmus was not in attendance. Return the shoes to their chamber when you're done. As soon as Erasmus condescends to show his face, I will send him up with cold meats and beer for the livery cupboard. A plague of rats could not have cleared it more thoroughly.'

So, Holt and Santi had not only mired their clothes, but had also missed their breakfast and dinner. What had preoccupied them so much in that undercroft?

I carried the sack to the outhouse where the brushes and leather oils were stored, shook out the sack and examined the shoes. Even beneath the mud, it was clear that one pair was almost new, with little wear. The priest seemed to have rarely left the house. The other pair was worn, the leather starting to peel and crack. And from the style and type of leather, I'd wager those shoes had not been acquired in England. These had known more sun than had ever shone from the sky above this land.

The dirt puzzled me. The cellar floor had been wet, certainly, but this was dark: evidently, they had sunk deep into a thick layer of mud. Unless further back in the undercroft conditions were much wetter, this hadn't come from the cellar. As I scraped it off, dried fragments of some reed-like plant, brown and rotting, fell with it. Could this have come from the holy spring? The bailiff had said it was miry there. But the smell . . . I touched my finger to the mud and then to my tongue. Salt! Sea-salt – you don't find that in the woods. The body from the ship out on the estuary – that's what they'd spent the morning doing, searching for the corpse and maybe even disposing of it.

I washed the mud from the shoes and oiled them with far more haste than care. Rowe's steward would have fined any servant who did such a clumsy job, but FitzAlan had provided me with ample money and, in any case, I suspected that here they were more accustomed to servants who did not know how to serve. I hurried up the stairs and, as I had hoped, the bedchamber was deserted.

Whatever letters or documents Holt and Santi had found on the murdered man, I knew they would have taken straight to Smith. The priests were probably all up in the library examining them now. But if they had removed clothes or anything else that might identify the corpse, they would not have risked leaving those nearby. If the satchels they had been carrying were still in the room . . .

I found the satchels quickly enough; they'd been thrust under the beds, without any real attempt to hide them. The first contained only a few crushed and bedraggled herbs, too late in the season to be of use even to the most skilled apothecary, but mostly likely snatched up to provide a reason for being out on the marsh if they were stopped and questioned. The other bag was empty, though it had very recently contained something, for the inside was damp and when I pulled out my hand, I found my fingers streaked with mud and something else – blood.

I wiped my hands and felt under the mattresses. Nothing. Then I turned my attention to the first of the chests that stood beside each bed. It was locked, though the mechanism was so simple it could not have been intended to contain anything of great value and I had it charmed open in no time. The top layers of clothes were, as I had expected, those that any layman might own. If there was anything to be found it would be concealed beneath. But it occurred to me that perhaps the lock had been too simple: it was likely that there was a hidden panel at the bottom, or in the lid. I froze as I heard the creak of wooden floorboards outside and, moments later, the door opened.

Bray ambled in. I was crouching on the other side of the bed, but he seemed to have only one thing on his mind and made straight for the livery cupboard, standing with his back to me, his ears poking out through his disordered hair. He lifted the wine flagon and shook it, muttering to himself as he realised it was empty. I eased the lid of the chest shut, and clicked it locked, seizing one of the pairs of shoes as I rose and coughed. He jerked around. The pewter flagon he was holding crashed to the floor.

'What are you doing creeping around in here?' he demanded, staggering slightly. 'Could have startled me into my grave.' He was clutching his chest and looked as if he might indeed have dropped dead from fright, or maybe it was guilt.

'I was instructed to bring the shoes of Masters Holt and Santi up to the chamber.' I nodded towards the cupboard on the wall. 'Erasmus will be coming presently to refill the livery with meats and beer.' Since that seemed to be foremost in his mind, I hoped it would distract him from noticing that the chest still protruded slightly from under the bed.

'Erasmus will not be on duty for the rest of today.' He was swaying as he stood and his speech had that slow, studied quality of one who is trying not to slur his words. I suspected that he had consumed the better part of that flagon before his companions had returned.

'Is he sick?' I asked, nudging the chest back with my foot. 'He looked unwell when he hurried from the chapel.'

Bray grunted. 'A malady of spirit, not body. But Master Smith has the cure. He has laid upon him an exercise in faith that will strengthen his resolve.' He frowned, staring at the shoes in my hand. 'Those are Julian's.' He pointed to one of the beds.

'Master Santi will have to invest in a new pair of boots if he is to make regular excursions to the estuary,' I said, arranging the shoes at the foot of the bed. 'Mud and saltwater soaks deep into old leather once it starts to peel.'

Bray peered at me through his thick lenses. 'He told you where he was going?'

'I trust they succeeded in their task,' I replied carefully.

'Reached the body before it was discovered and made certain it would not be found by the sheriff's men, at least not for some days.' He crossed himself. 'God have mercy on his soul and God damn the wretch who killed him.'

'It was thieves, then?'

'Robbed of his purse. I expect it was a large one.'

I was tempted to push my luck and try to coax the identity of the murdered man from Bray, for he certainly wasn't as guarded as Smith, nor, I concluded, anyway near as astute, even when he hadn't been drinking. However, even he might become suspicious if I pressed him directly. As they say, there are more ways to kill a dog than hanging.

Bray was gazing disconsolately at the barren livery cupboard.

'If Erasmus is not returning to his duties today, I'll fetch the meats and beer.'

He beamed and nodded gratefully. 'Wine, Pursglove, there's a good soul. I have a delicacy of the stomach. The physicians say I must take the utmost care. Clement, the Yeoman of the Cellar, knows which suits me. But not a word to the steward, mind. The man must have the digestion of a hog, for he has no appreciation of the havoc beer and rough wine can cause.'

'I will speak to Clement alone, Master Bray.'

'I never used to suffer with it so, but days in hiding with nothing but cold broth through a tube once a day . . .' he shuddered. 'And worse food in prison. Is it any wonder . . .?' He was still muttering to himself as I softly closed the door and I found myself suddenly feeling sorry for him. I had tasted that prison fare. If he had suffered that diet and had every reason to fear he might again, I could hardly grudge him a good wine while he had the chance.

THE LAUNDRY ROOM on the far side of the courtyard was deserted. I had wagered on the women from the village not coming in to wash on a Sunday. It was cold and damp. Wind funnelled through the open slits high in the roof, and the narrow casements above my head had only iron bars set in them, no glass or shutters. The fires in the stone pits, used to boil the water, were banked down under smouldering peats, ready to be stirred into life on Monday morning, and no heat escaped them. Buck tubs and cauldrons were lined up around the room and wooden racks on which sheets and garments could be hung swung from pullies suspended from the stout beams, ready to be hauled up and down. Barrels of lye and pots of evil-smelling slimy soap stood in the opposite corner, along with ash balls, brushes, scrubbing boards and the stout wooden staves used to pound the bed linens and coarser clothes. The place stank of lye, damp wool and wet wood. It reminded me unpleasantly of a gaol and no doubt could be used as one if the need arose.

But as I'd hoped, several coarse linen sacks stuffed with soiled clothes had been heaped on boards in one corner, ready to be washed. With another glance outside I quietly closed the stout door and peered into the first sack.

Whatever had been in that satchel had left mud, saltwater and traces of blood on the inside. The priests had returned wearing splattered clothes, so what they had thrust into that bag must have come from the murdered man. If you wanted to ensure that a body was not found or, if it was, could not be identified, the first thing you'd do would be to strip it and let the crabs, gulls and fishes do their magician's work and make the flesh vanish. You couldn't risk leaving the clothes to be found, so you'd bring them back and let the chattering washerwomen soak them in their steaming tubs with the mountains of other washing in the thick, grey, soapy soup.

I had no illusions that I'd find letters or papers in the dead man's garments – even sewn into linings or hems, Santi and Holt would have searched thoroughly for those – but the sight of Santi's shoes had reminded me that there was more than one way to tell where a man was from and that any clue would be a start. The bag I was looking for would likely be near the top of the pile, and as soon as I unfastened the cord and put the bag to my nose, I knew I had found it. The stink of wet marsh silt and slime was unmistakable. I found three shirts all stained with blood, but the stains were mired over with silt and faded by the saltwater, so that the washerwomen would be unlikely to notice anything in the dimly lit and steamy room except filth and stench, neither of which were in short supply in this weather.

But on examining them closely, I thought I could tell which had been worn by the murdered man, for the blood stains on the two priests' shirts were on the sleeves and low down on the chest where they had lifted the body. On the third, the edges of the stain, though faint, were mostly at the top of the shirt where blood must have run down from a wound in the throat. I examined the garment closely, likewise the hose, doublet and woollen breeches rolled with it, but they were the kind of clothes any traveller might wear for a cold sea journey, if he could afford wool, for they were warm and serviceable. And to my disappointment I could see nothing which might mark any of them as Spanish, Flemish or French, indeed they seemed more English in fashion and cut than foreign.

I heard footsteps outside and the creaking and whine of a handcart. I hastily stuffed the garments back into the sack, cursing under my breath as one of the bone buttons on the dead man's doublet snagged on a loose thread at the mouth of the bag. I tugged and the button tore off in my hand. I pushed the doublet down into the bag and slung it back on the pile. The cart trundled past the laundry and, as the sound faded, I eased the door open, and slipped out.

I had almost reached the house again when I realised that I was still clutching something small and hard – the button. The light was fading fast, and lanterns had been lit in the courtyard and candles set in some of the casements. Standing beneath one, I could see clearly what I had not noticed in the dimness of the laundry room. The bone button was inscribed with fine lines. They were too shallow for the pattern to be distinguished by touch, but the lines had been darkened with a black dye and now I could see what it was – a ship and a castle. I stared at it with a sudden prickling of familiarity. I had seen the image many times since FitzAlan first plucked me out of the Hole in Newgate gaol and sent me to find the gunpowder conspirator, Spero Pettingar. It was the emblem of Bristol. The man lying stripped and naked in the ooze of that estuary may not have been Bristol-born, or even English, but I was willing to wager he had at least passed through that city, and recently too. Had the message Smith had been so anxious to recover also originated in that city, the city that FitzAlan had called the nest of Jesuits?

Chapter Thirteen

I HAD OFFERED TO TAKE Erasmus's watch in the passageway outside the priests' chamber that night, and Goodenouth looked relieved. He was not a young man and the responsibilities of supervising the servants looking after so many guests had strained him to the point of exhaustion.

I watched him limping away in the direction of his own chamber, his hand pressed to his back and a small bottle grasped in his fist.

'He'll not be making his rounds tonight,' Arthur said, staring after him. 'That cordial the apothecary makes up for him has him lying in his cot as like to a corpse as a herring is to a fish. They could light twenty barrels of gunpowder beneath his bed and he'd not hear a single bang, nor be able to move a muscle if he did.' He nudged me and winked. 'So, if you want to slip out to Sybil's alehouse, he'll not know you've left your post.'

I faked a yawn. 'After the hour we were roused this morning, I'd fall asleep face down in the beer.'

He caught the yawn himself. 'Aye, mayhap you're right. Doubt if I could walk there myself, much less stagger home after a jug or two, and it's not often I'll admit to that.'

All the same I was pleased that Goodenouth would not be prowling the passageways; it would make what I had planned even easier than I'd hoped.

I had ensured that the livery cupboard was more than amply stocked with manchets, meat, pastries, beer and of course a large quantity of wine for George Bray. I'd had to perform some deft sleights of hand to extract more than the usual allocation of food and drink from the kitchen for the gentlemen's chamber. I didn't want any of them to have cause to call for me and find me absent. They wouldn't hesitate to report that, if they did.

I laid my bed roll in the passageway outside their door, watching the other yeoman take up their places at intervals along the passageway as most of the candles were extinguished, leaving only a couple of lanterns alight at either end. The creaks of the beds in the chamber beyond were gradually replaced by snores both from the priests within and from my fellow servants. The early start and the extra work for the visitors had taken its toll on all, and I found myself struggling to stay awake.

But the thought of Bristol was buzzing around in my head, like a trapped blowfly. FitzAlan had been sure that the many ships that sailed in and out of that port and any of the tiny harbours hidden along the river were being used to smuggle spies and Jesuits into England, and to carry traitors and those hunted by the Crown to safety on the Continent. I'd had my suspicions about who might be forging the necessary travel documents there, though I'd been unable – FitzAlan might have claimed *unwilling* – to obtain proof.

But even within England, it was safer and often quicker to move a man trying to escape detection round the coast by ship, rather than across country. Any man travelling by road could expect to be stopped and questioned a dozen times a day and every innkeeper and loyal citizen had been ordered to watch and report any man passing through their village or taking lodgings in their street that they did not recognise. I was beginning to think that this Abbey and Bristol were more closely linked than I had realised. As Yaxley said, the same water fed both the holy well and the spring in these woods, but was Battle the source or the mouth of that dark, underground stream that ran unseen all the way to Bristol?

I crept along the passageway, stepping carefully around the slumbering servants, blankets pulled over their heads against the draughts, and climbed the stairs, taking care to tread close to the wall where the steps were less likely to creak. There were no sleeping servants on the upper floor and yet I could hear something: not snores or groaning bed ropes, but a faint mewling sound, like the whimper of a hound in pain. I froze and strained to make out where it was coming from. But almost as soon as I caught it, the cry died away. An animal or bird outside on the roof, perhaps.

I lit a chamber candlestick from the lantern burning at the head of the stairs and edged forward, pausing at every door to listen until I reached the library. Once more I pressed my head close to the door but could hear no movement inside. I was relieved to find the door locked. That at least suggested it had been secured for the night and that the room was empty. It only took me moments to gain access.

The library was in darkness. I set the chamberstick down where its light would not be seen through any chinks in the shutters. Then I began to search. If a house was raided, the bedchambers of anyone suspected of being a priest would be torn apart for evidence. Smith was shrewder and more careful than most. He would not have kept anything in his own room which might incriminate him, much less papers taken from a murdered man. So, there was a good chance that he had hidden them in here.

A letter or message could be slipped into or behind any one of the scores of books, and there were dozens of other places in a room of this size where a paper might be hidden: below floorboards, beneath tables or shelves, behind panelling . . . it was going to be a long night, probably a week of long nights. But the first thing to do was to check if there were any documents left to be found. I moved the candlestick to the fireplace and, taking a poker, began to gently rake through the cinders, searching for any trace of paper ash, or dark stains from burnt wax that might have been a seal. As I bent over the task, examining the grey wood ash, I heard again the soft cry I had caught at the top of the stairs. It was clearer here, and there was another sound too, like something tapping against wood. A bird, probably, huddled on top of the chimney for warmth as they often did on cold nights. But any heat must be rising from a different flue, for it suddenly dawned on me that these ashes were cold.

I rose and crossed back to the table. Inks and quills stood ready and the ground ink was wet. Someone had used it today. The fire had been blazing in here on Saturday night, probably until the priests went to Mass the next morning, yet these ashes were not merely cool, but cold. I scraped more back and found beneath them a log which had not burned completely away. It was wet. The fire had been deliberately extinguished and cold dry ash added on top to make it appear that it had been allowed to die away. It was something they might well have done if they were expecting a raid, but if they wanted it to seem that the room had not recently been used, they should have removed the wet ink. Smith would never have made such a basic mistake.

The noise I had made scrabbling into the heart of the ash had evidently driven the bird away, if it was a bird, for there was now silence. I stood motionless and then the faint knocking came again, but there was a new sound, hoarse and barely above a whisper.

'Christ and all the saints save me . . . save me . . . save me.'

I leaned into the flue, careful not to look up in case any soot was dislodged. The sound was louder inside, though it was not coming from above me on the chimney, but to the right of me. I ducked back out, moved to the side of the hearth and ran my hands over the walls. They seemed to be solid stone. I knelt and tried again. Only on the third pass did I find it: a small, thin gap between the stones at thigh height, just wide enough to insert a knife blade.

I drew my blade along the crack until I found what I was looking for and heard the faint click. I pushed on one side, but another click told me I had fastened it again. I inserted the knife and depressed the catch, this time pushing on the other side, and a small section of the wall swung open. The stone wasn't a deep block like the rest of the wall, but a slab fastened on to a wooden door behind, though the stone was thick enough that when tapped on the outside no one would hear it ring hollow. It was the hallmark of the hunchback whom Catholics called 'Little John', and this was undoubtedly his handiwork. I crouched down and pushed the chamberstick inside.

Had it not been for the cry I'd heard, I would have been convinced the hiding place was empty, for the space was bare and as narrow and low as a dog kennel. Then the stench rolled out: piss, shit and the acrid smell of sweat, the kind produced by fear, not by labour. Still I could see nothing. Dropping to all fours and pushing the candle carefully in front of me, I crawled forward until my head and shoulders were inside the tunnel.

Erasmus was huddled on a narrow ledge above the tunnel, in a gap behind the fireplace. His back was pressed hard against one side and, to keep his balance, he'd been forced to sit with his knees drawn up to his chin and his feet pressed against the opposite wall. A taller man would have had to sink his head on to his chest to wedge himself into the space. Though my candle flame was by no means bright, he was squinting and wincing in the sudden light after what must have been utter darkness. His fist was pressed to his mouth as he struggled in vain to suppress his moans and whimpers.

'Erasmus, it's me, Daniel. You can come out now.'

He shook his head vehemently, like a terrified child being urged to jump into a river.

'There are no searchers, no leopards. You don't need to hide. It's safe to come out.'

Again, he shook his head. He'd been in there some hours, judging by the stench of him, probably ever since he'd run from the chapel before dawn.

'The leopards didn't come to the Abbey. The guests have all gone now and Father Smith and the other priests have long been sleeping easy in their beds. They wouldn't have retired if they feared a raid.'

He lifted his head slowly. Sweat had run down his face, leaving black streaks of dirt and dust. But it wasn't hot in this hiding place; an icy draught gusted through it from some unseen vent. At least a man wouldn't suffocate in here, provided no one lit a fire.

'Father Smith . . . Father Santi . . . asleep.'

'Heard them snoring myself as I came here.' It wasn't strictly true that I'd heard Smith, but he didn't need to know that. 'Whole household is asleep, exhausted after that swarm of visitors. Look, I'll back out and you follow. I think I saw some wine left on the table.'

'Don't take the light,' he pleaded.

'I'll leave it just outside the entrance to guide you out.'

I shuffled backwards, pulling the chamberstick with me. I was amazed he'd managed to shut the door and find his way up to that ledge in such darkness, especially if he was as panicked as he'd appeared to be when he'd fled the chapel. Perhaps he'd had a candle which had since burned out.

It took a few minutes before his head finally emerged and, once outside, he remained on his hands and knees, seemingly unable to rise, gasping as if he was struggling to breathe. He clutched me, staggering, as I helped him to his feet. The cramped position he been sitting in had deadened his legs. I dragged him to a chair and sat him down. He stank.

A flagon and empty glasses still stood on the table. I blessed whichever servant had neglected to void them. I flipped up the flagon lid and caught the heady aroma of wine, cinnamon and ginger – hippocras! Now that was a rare drink to be served, even in a place such as Battle Abbey, except on the occasions of great feasts. Smith and the others must have been celebrating something that they'd learned from the murdered man's papers. But I'd lost any hope of searching for those tonight.

I poured out the remains and gave the glass to Erasmus, but his hand was shaking and he could barely bring it to his lips without spilling it. He was staring fixedly at the hole from which he had emerged, as if he feared some creature of darkness would come slithering out and drag him back inside.

I didn't know who in the household knew of its existence, but we could take no chances. I pushed the panel shut and heard the click. Then I took some of the soft wood ash from the fire and blew it gently over the crack. As a boy I'd watched Father Waldegrave cover a hidden door like that, when he thought he was unobserved. The leopards looked for signs of dust being disturbed.

Erasmus finally wrenched his gaze from the panel. 'F . . . Father Smith . . . you're sure he is asleep?'

'He's retired for the night,' I said. 'But we had no raid, nor, I think, does he expect one now.'

'I know . . . he said the steward was bringing news of a body, not . . .'

'Then why did you need to conceal yourself in there?'

Erasmus shrank deeper into the chair. 'Father Smith said I should spend the night in there . . . strengthen my faith. Unworthy . . . weak!' He struck his chest with his fist in a gesture of *mea culpa* as he rasped out the self-accusation.

'You are indeed, Erasmus.' The words were quietly spoken, low and measured.

The young man's eyes flashed wide in alarm and I spun round. Smith was standing in the open doorway. He closed the door soundlessly behind him. 'You say you want to be ordained and return here to save souls and strengthen the faithful. How you do you expect to strengthen others if your own faith is so feeble that it will not bear you up through such a small test? Fear itself is not a sin. Even our Lord shrank from the agony that lay ahead for him. The sin lies in surrendering to it. You must draw your strength from prayer, for prayer overcomes all fear.'

Erasmus had dragged himself to his feet and was standing, his head bowed. Smith's nose wrinkled as the stench of shit assaulted him.

'You have soiled yourself! Can you not even control your own bowels for a few hours? Father Oldcorne did not void himself for a week when he was hiding, out of respect for the fellow priest who was with him. Christ and his saints gave him strength to bare his discomfort.'

'It was the flux, Father Smith . . .' Erasmus mumbled to the floor, his face flushed. 'If I'd not had the flux—'

'The ale we drank at supper last night was sour,' I said quickly. 'I too have suffered for it today.'

It was pure fear that had made Erasmus's bowels turn to water. I'd seen it many times the night before a battle when I served in Ireland.

Smith turned his scowl on me. 'Was it you who tempted Erasmus from his vigil?'

He stared pointedly at the glass which the young man was still clutching, as if I'd coaxed him out with wine as a master might lure a dog from hiding with a scrap of meat.

'I found him unwell – the flux. I thought the wine might settle his stomach.'

'Do you have a calling to be a physician, or an apothecary, perhaps? First you come to the aid of a man in a trap, then Lady Magdalen's ward, and now you seek to cure gripes of the belly? Perhaps it is you who should be seeking ordination, or are you planning simply to be canonised, Saint Daniel?' His eyes narrowed. 'And how did you get in here? Was that another of your miracles? I know that door was locked. I made sure of it myself.' He pulled the key from his pocket and weighed it in his hand, as if to assure himself that it was still in his possession.

'It was not locked, sir. Perhaps someone came later to check that the fire and lights had been made safe for the night. That's why I came up here. I saw a candle flame from the yard and came to check it hadn't been left burning, since the hour was so late. But I must have mistaken the room.'

Smith locked eyes with me, but I'd learned to stare down tougher men than him. I'd been raised by a priest, one harder even than this one.

Finally, Smith turned away. 'Get yourself cleaned up, Erasmus. We shall speak more of this alone.'

The young man scuttled to the door, walking sideways so that the chaplain shouldn't see the shaming stains on his breeches. I bowed and followed, turning slightly in the act of closing the door.

'You will learn nothing from Erasmus, Pursglove,' he said softly, 'because he is entrusted with nothing. *Alii nulla curiositate videant quae sunt in sanctuario priusquam involvantur alioquin morientur*. Divine instruction from the book of Numbers that you would do well to take to heart, Pursglove, particularly the last phrase. *Alioquin morientur.*

I shook my head. 'I never learned that tongue, Master Smith.'

'Oh, I think you did, Pursglove, I think you understand it only too well. But let me jolt your memory. "Let not others by any curiosity see the things that are in the sanctuary before they be wrapped up, otherwise, they shall die." *Morientur*, Pursglove. Remember that word –*They shall die.*'

Chapter Fourteen

THEOBALDS HOUSE, CHESHUNT, HERTFORDSHIRE

'TEN THOUSAND, DE YE KEN!' The King's voice was raised in such fervour that Cecil could hear every word echoing down the length of the Green Gallery while he was still heaving himself up the stairs.

'Every noble in the land must play his part. I will demand it. I'll tolerate no gainsayers.'

Cecil winced. Surely, even James had learned by now that neither the Parliament nor the House of Lords would grant him yet another vast sum, simply because he demanded it, without more concessions? And those he would stubbornly refuse to make.

Lord Salisbury paused out of sight at the top of the stairs, taking a deep breath to steel himself. He still could not reconcile himself to the knowledge that Theobalds was no longer his house. True, James had granted him the Hatfield estate in exchange, but both men knew Cecil had got the worst of the bargain. It would be years before the house he was obliged to virtually rebuild there would equal this. He bitterly regretted entertaining the King here on his journey from Scotland to claim the throne, and those lavish masques he'd subsequently organised for him since. If he had not made Theobalds appear so attractive . . . But whenever a Sovereign bestows the multitude of titles and lands that he had heaped upon Cecil, he always expects a generous return for his largesse. Favours granted by kings are swiftly forged into fetters for lesser men.

Cecil mounted the last steps and entered the Green Gallery. There was nothing to equal it in all England. Its size impressed every visitor – it was over one hundred feet long – but its painted walls astounded them. They reflected his father's twin obsessions – cartography and heraldry. Fifty-two trees were painted on the walls, representing the counties of England, and from each of the leafy green branches, shields depicting the arms of the land-owning nobles of that district hung down like multicoloured fruit, together with symbols representing the produce for which each area was famous. Painted around and between the trees were exquisitely detailed maps of the cities, towns and villages to be found within the domain of all the notable landowners, from esquires to highest-ranking nobles. Little wonder James had coveted the house, for these walls alone showed any English monarch at a glance what Master Shakespeare had been pleased to call *this royal throne of kings, this sceptred isle.*

But James wasn't admiring his *other Eden*; he was twisting about in an ornate chair, an open book clutched in his hand, jabbing his finger at a page, apparently lecturing the only other occupant of the gallery. The solitary member of his audience did not appear to be listening and was gazing out of one of the balcony windows, transfixed by the sight of several cages being removed from a covered wagon. Cecil had passed them on his way up and had been informed by a disgruntled porter that they contained a small crocodile, a beaver, several flying squirrels and a highly aggressive sable that seemed to be the source of both the savage rasping snarls and an abominable stink. Despite its diminutive size, none of the servants seemed keen to unload the little beast, it having already savaged the hand of the last man who'd touched the cage, as the trail of bloody drops across the floor testified.

The figure by the window looked round and Cecil recognised the blond hair and flamboyantly coloured jerkin of the King's new favourite, Robert Carr.

James, on seeing the young man give a curt nod, turned in his chair and beckoned Cecil into the gallery. 'Here's my best beagle.'

Carr laughed and Cecil ignored him, making a deep bow to the King. But James continued to wait, his heavy-lidded gaze flicking pointedly towards Carr, like a father insisting that his two children should kiss and make up. Cecil made a small bow in Carr's general direction without taking a step towards him. 'I trust your leg gives you no further trouble, Master Carr?'

Every man and woman at Court knew it was prudent to express concern at least, even if they could not bring themselves to feign admiration for the young man. It was not, Cecil supposed, a greater pill to swallow than being obliged to inquire after the health of the King's favourite tiger or, in this case, his pet ape.

'Robert gives trouble to no one,' James cut in, glancing down at his own twisted leg. There was a razor-sharp edge to his tone, and it occurred to Cecil that the King's constant attendance at Carr's sickbed stemmed in part from James's loathing of his own lameness and his fear of seeing such an athletic young man condemned to the humiliation of the same lifelong affliction.

But as rapidly as the sun emerges after a summer storm, James's eyes were flashing with excitement again. He brandished the book aloft, like a preacher raising the Bible as testimony to the truth and divine authority of his words.

'*The Perfect Use of Silkworms*. Nicholas Gesse has made an excellent translation. I'll warrant you'll not yet have read it, but you will. All England will. Italy and France have set themselves up as masters of silk and we have been forced to bend the knee to them and pay through the nose for their silks. No more. The mulberry tree upon which the silkworms feed grows well in England. There are several in these very grounds; why should there not be a score, even a hundred trees or more on the lands of each of my Lord Lieutenants? The silk women of London make a fine living producing their silk laces and ribbons, but how many more might they employ if the raw silk upon which they depend was produced in England, and on such a grand scale and of such fine quality it could be made not just into cords, but cloth too? And think of the beggarly men and women who might be gainfully occupied in the making of it. The parishes will no more need to devise fruitless employment to provide for their destitute.'

Having lost interest in the scene outside, Carr had wandered over to the King and James had pulled him down on to a low stool close by his own chair. All the while he was talking, his fingers were restlessly smoothing the wrinkles on the back of Carr's jerkin and adjusting the hang of his collar, as if Carr was a small child and he was the boy's father making his son look fit for company. Many ministers and nobles at Court would have been affronted that they had been left standing in the King's presence while this upstart was practically sitting in his lap, but Cecil ignored the slight. James's interest in a toy seldom lasted long. He had dismissed eighteen courtiers only a few weeks ago for no greater offence than that they bored him and he didn't like their clothes. He'd soon tire of this one.

James was still babbling about his new obsession. 'The author is of the opinion that silkworms fed on white mulberries instead of black produce a thread which is finer and does not break as easily, but he cautions the white mulberry is a tree that requires abundant sun and warmth, and a mild winter, which are not be found in England.' As if to prove the point, a gust of east wind rattled the casements and the smoke from the two fires blazing in the hearths swirled in the chilly draught. 'Therefore, we shall plant black mulberries. British silkworms will eat British leaves just as my beaver now devours the wholesome bread of England with a hearty appetite in place of the foreign herbs it was doubtless accustomed to nibbling in its native land. Ten thousand sapling must be ordered at once, so they are ready for planting in a year.'

So, it was trees he intended to demand from the people this time, not pounds. That was a little more palatable, but not much. Cecil cleared his throat. 'Sire, Parliament will never agree to pay the cost—'

'The landowners will pay. They will see it as their patriotic duty to support such an industry and they shall certainly make a profit from it, if they pay only three farthings for a sapling. The more they buy, the less it shall cost them: say, a hundred plants for six shillings. Now that's a bargain they'll not refuse.'

'But it will be many years before the trees are grown mature enough to turn any kind of profit on that.'

James flapped his hand dismissively. 'If they really plead poverty then they may buy the seeds and raise their own, though that will take even longer. I will write to them all, starting with the largest estates. They'll not turn down the chance to invest in such a great enterprise.' He gestured towards the painted trees on the walls, hung with the produce for which each shire was famed. 'We will soon have to paint new fruit on every tree in here. A mulberry with its wee worm, or maybe a silken jerkin such as Carr favours.'

Cecil's jaw clenched.

James squeezed the young man's shoulder. 'Go, put on that new one I ordered for you.' He nodded to Cecil. 'Lord Salisbury is agog to see how it becomes you, are you not? I had the tailor cut it so that the cloth swings free and light catches it as it moves. The shades are continuously changing, light and dark, like water running in a Scottish burn. It is the finest art of the silk weaver.'

Carr shrugged and ambled from the gallery. Cecil breathed a sigh of relief as the heavy door closed behind him. It amused James to have Carr change his clothes several times a day. It was bad enough that the King bought himself a new suit of clothes every ten days, as Cecil knew all too well from the outrageous bills presented by his tailors. It was to be hoped he didn't intend to buy as many for Carr. But for once Cecil was grateful for the distraction; with luck, the young man would take a long time preening himself. What he had to say was for the King's ears only.

Cecil bowed. 'Sire, there is some intelligence I must share with you, for the safety of your own person, so I trust you will pardon me if I come swiftly to the meat of it. Rumours have reached me that someone is shortly to be smuggled back into England, someone who we believed had been spirited away from our shores, like the gunpowder conspirator John Gerard, in the entourage of the Spanish Ambassador.'

James's gaze had strayed back to the book, but he suddenly laid it down and leaned forward in his chair, his full attention now fixed on Cecil. He gestured impatiently for him to sit. Lord Salisbury ignored the stool vacated by Carr and moved a chair closer.

'And you picked up this *rumour* in the Paris Garden in Southwark? An evening at the bear-baiting, was it?' James said. 'I'm told that's where the Spanish Ambassador's servants meet their agents, for you canna tell a maid from her master at nightfall there. I don't doubt you have your own men lurking among those dark trees, scavenging for any juicy wee morsal.' He leaned back in the chair, pressing his fingertips together, studying Cecil carefully. 'Or did you learn this somewhere a touch more intimate, maybe?'

If James was hoping to see a flicker of disquiet, the smallest twitch of alarm cross Cecil's countenance, he was to be sorely disappointed. His minister's expression was as impassive as those of the bronze statues that graced the mantel in the entrance hall below.

'The intelligence came from outside London, Sire, from the city of Bristol.' This last word was uttered as softly as the hissing of a viper, but Cecil knew James had heard it. He saw the whitening of the knuckles as they gripped the arms of the chair, the almost imperceptible jerk of the spine, and the tiny bulge of the muscle as the jaw tightened beneath the sparse beard.

'A message from a Spanish agent in the city was intercepted,' Cecil continued. 'A close watch is kept on the city, Sire. With ships coming and going between Bristol and every port in England, and indeed every country in the world, the Spaniards would be fools not to have installed an intelligencer there, far from London. Anyone gathering information there need not exert himself more than a fisherman who hangs a net across a river. He simply sits back and waits for the fish to swim in.'

'This message – the man who is returning. If he was smuggled out by the Spanish diplomats, then you think him another of the conspirators?'

Cecil crafted his reply even more carefully than usual. 'It would appear that he set sail within days of your Majesty uncovering the Gunpowder Treason plot. The exact date of his departure is not yet discovered; perhaps it was even before the day of Fawkes's arrest. A king may sign a death warrant without witnessing the felon's subsequent execution, just as a traitor may light the fuse of a plan without staying to watch the explosion.'

'Pett . . . gar,' James whispered, but his overlarge tongue mangled the word, for every muscle in his face was rigid with tension. He crouched forward, so low in the chair he resembled one of his own lions preparing to spring, snarling, at the bars of his cage.

'You spoke, Sire?'

James pushed himself up from the chair, and stood clutching the back of it, staring wildly about the room. 'You think this man, this Jesuit, intends to try again to assassinate me.' His hand had slid to the hilt of his sword, but Cecil suspected he did not even realise he was grasping it.

'It is not known if he is a Jesuit, but it is unlikely he would risk returning unless he has another plan to set in motion, one that requires his presence in England. We must assume he intends to act or persuade others to do so.'

'This agent whose message you intercepted. He must know more.' James rounded on Cecil. 'Why is he not already under arrest and in the Tower being interrogated? You've plainly known about him for months, and yet you've let a foreign agent roam around the King's port at will, without let or hindrance. Maybe it is you who should be in chains.'

Cecil's tone remained calm and even. He was accustomed to the threats of monarchs and of men. They slid off his crooked back like autumn leaves. 'If the agent was arrested, he would simply be replaced by another, and while we were trying to uncover the identity of their new man, he would be free to work unobserved. A snake in plain sight poses much less danger than the viper coiled beneath the bed. And we have our own agent in Bristol, a double agent, a man who has his trust.'

'Another of your turncoat priests?' James snapped.

Cecil ignored the question. 'If we arrest the Spaniards' man, we will endanger our own agent and his services will be more vital than ever if another plot is being hatched. In this case, Sire, we should take heed of the wisdom of the parable and let the wheat and tare ripen together. Root out the tare and you will destroy the wheat.'

'Aye, but when the enemy are hiding in the wheatfield you must burn the whole crop to smoke him out. I don't care how many bushels of wheat you have to destroy, Lord Salisbury. Find that traitor before he destroys me and throws the whole kingdom into bloody civil war. Remember this, my little beagle, when they murder a king, they hang his hounds from the same tree.'

Chapter Fifteen

5TH DAY OF DECEMBER 1607

DANIEL PURSGLOVE

'IF I WAS YOU, I'd fetch the water from the holy well next to the ruins, only mind you don't let her ladyship catch you,' Arthur said. 'She'll think it sacrilege. It'll be dinner time before they get the courtyard water running again, if they ever do, and they'll have to thaw it all over again before supper.' He crossed to the small window in the passageway and scratched a witch mark in the form of a daisy wheel in the frost which had formed on both sides of glass.

'Drive off the ice wolf,' he said, with a somewhat embarrassed grin. 'My grandma always did that at the first real cold snap of the year, said it kept hunger from our door.'

We had woken to a glittering frost, with puddles and horse troughs turned to solid ice. Winter had descended almost overnight, and servants were scurrying from room to room, stoking up fires and trying to heat enough frozen water for the household to wash without chilling themselves.

'Kindly move aside!' The command came from Magdalen's maid, Esther, sounding as imperious as her mistress. She lifted the lid of the chest next to where I was standing. 'Hold your arms out.'

I set down my pails, and obligingly stood while she piled heavy cloaks on top of me while Arthur made lewd gestures behind her back.

'You'll be wanting something warm to slip under your skirts to keep the cold out, Esther.' He winked at me.

'The only thing any decent woman in this house will be wanting under her skirts is a rat trap to keep you out,' she retorted, lifting her chin as if she was affronted.

Arthur chuckled.

There was a flash of blue in the winter sunshine as three dried kingfishers tumbled out from where they had been tucked in among the clothes to keep the moths from them. Esther scooped them up and dropped them back in the chest, before relieving me of the cloaks she had selected. Then she swept off towards the stairs.

I took Arthur's advice and headed towards the ruins of the church. White mist hung frozen in the air, sparkling in the glacial sunshine, the sharp grains of ice stinging like sand against the eyes. Trees and walls, flags and grass were glazed in silvery-white, so that even with straw rope bound over boots it was hard to keep upright.

The well stood on the ancient cloister garth, close to what remained of the old church wall. It was an impressive structure, at least from the outside. I couldn't see the water as I approached, for it was surrounded on all sides by a massive wall, a good foot or so higher than my head. There were stone steps on either side to reach the well itself, but I had never yet climbed them. Remembering Arthur's warning, I glanced back at the house. The frosted windows would, I hoped, blur any view of the grounds, and none of the windows would be opened in such bitter weather, but I thought I caught a glimpse of a shadow in one of the upper casements that darted away as I turned. *The King has eyes and ears everywhere.* I knew it wasn't only Smith who was watching me. The question was, were those other eyes inside or outside the Abbey?

The steps were as slippery as glass, but I was not the first to climb them, judging by the impressions of boot marks in the frost. Clearly the other servants sent to fetch water had had the same idea. Black streaks on the stone marked where countless votive candles had been lit by those who'd climbed these steps to pray, and brown, withered bunches were all that remained of what had once been summer posies. As I reached the top, I found myself staring down into a deep pit, seven foot or so below me, and as wide and long as an open grave. But that was not what made me catch my breath, for the pale winter sun had risen far enough to illuminate one corner of it, and I imagined, for a moment, that I was staring down into a well of scarlet blood.

I'd heard the legends, of course, that the gore of those thousands slain at the Battle of Hastings had soaked into the earth here and that the earth, in sorrow, forever wept blood. They say the same fiery star that had ghosted across our skies all through the months of autumn had hung in the darkness above England before that great battle, foretelling Harold's defeat and death. But then William no doubt blessed it as a good omen. Good or bad, it was not only kings who were slain in battle.

Suddenly I was not looking down into that well, but into a lake in Ireland, red with the blood of men and their families slaughtered by the soldiers of an army to which I had once sworn allegiance. Their blood was on my hands, though I hadn't lifted a sword or fired a musket. But flaming stars are not sent to proclaim the slaughter of thousands. Those deaths count for nothing when weighed against the thrones of kings.

'My thimble was empty when it was returned to me, but you didn't reply.'

I was so startled by the sound of a girl's voice that I almost slipped on the ice and came near to plunging down into the blood-red pool. I heard a little bubble of laughter.

Katheryne was standing below me in the shadow of the steps, muffled in a fur-lined cloak and hood.

'Fetch your water first, then come down. There's a rope and bucket in the corner.'

I filled the pails and clambered down. She was shivering now and pulled her cloak tighter.

'I would not advise you to climb those steps today, my lady. If you wish to pray, it would be safer to do so down here.'

'It's you I came to see. I told Arthur to send you here.'

If Arthur had encouraged me to come here at her bidding, what else had she persuaded him to do?

'I need help.'

'Then you should ask your guardian or Master Smith to advise you,' I said curtly.

'They are why I need your help. They both say Bethia ran off, but she wouldn't do that. She wouldn't leave me. She was the only one I could confide in, you see. That's why they sent her away.'

'Bethia?'

'My tiring maid . . . she vanished over a month ago.'

'If her ladyship told you that your maid left, why should you question it? And Father Smith is a priest.' I couldn't quite bring myself to say that he wouldn't lie, but I couldn't see why he'd trouble to lie about anything as unimportant to him as a runaway maid.

'Bethia was in a strange mood the last few days, troubled about something, but that last night when she left my chamber, she noticed my flask of rose oil was almost empty and she said she'd fetch more when she brought the washing water in the morning. She wouldn't have said that if she meant to run away, would she?'

'Lady Magdalen or Steward Brathwayt might have dismissed her on the spot, if she was discovered stealing. But I can see no reason why they would not have told you afterwards.'

'Bethia was no thief,' Katheryne said furiously. Two bright red patches flared on her cheeks and not simply from the cold.

'Then she must have run away,' I said. 'You said she was in a strange humour. Perhaps she only made her mind up to leave after she helped you retire. A harsh word from one of the other servants . . .' *or that bastard, Smith. Given what he had done to Erasmus a few nights ago, I could easily imagine him reducing*

a servant girl to tears for no greater crime than flirting with a
stable boy.

Katheryne shook her head with annoyance, as if I was being deliberately obtuse. 'Father Smith has persuaded Lady Magdalen I should be sent to Brussels to enter a convent and take the veil. She's old. She'll die soon,' she added, with the cold callousness of youth. 'So, she wants me to spend the rest of my life praying for her soul and for her dead husband too.'

I could imagine the dowager delighting in the prospect. What better example of piety and faith than to inspire your young ward to become a nun. It would also ensure that a headstrong young girl would be placed out of all temptation, with no risk of her bringing disgrace to the family. Half the guardians in England, even the Protestant ones, might have been sorely tempted to do the same if they had a ward like Katheryne to contend with.

'But I have refused to go!' she announced, with a defiant lift of her chin. 'And Father Smith said Bethia was encouraging me in disobedience, because she's . . . not a Catholic.'

She had looked away as she added these last words and I was left with the distinct impression that they had not been what she'd started to say.

'They sent her away to punish me and they think without her, they'll be able to break me. But they won't.'

I half expected her to stamp her little foot and spit the words out like a child. But they were said with a quiet determination and, for the first time, I glimpsed not a spoiled, flirtatious girl, but a woman with eyes full of a pain beyond her years.

When I spoke, it was in a gentler tone. 'Lady Katheryne, you asked for my help, but you must realise that as a servant I cannot begin to persuade Lady Magdalen against this course of action. I doubt anyone could, except her grandson. If you wrote to Viscount Montague . . . Is what why you sought me out? You want me to get a letter to him?'

'Bethia used to carry my letters . . .'

'To Viscount Montague?'

Again, her gaze darted away from me. 'Not to him.'

'Then to the man who gave you that thimble?'

Her eyes flashed wide, then she slowly nodded. I was beginning to understand. Pomegranates and myrtle – if they meant what I thought they did, Smith would be appalled. Katheryne was playing an extremely dangerous game. She had not been exaggerating when she'd claimed Bethia to be her only friend. Every man and woman in the country would condemn her.

'And, I take it, Lady Magdalen doesn't know of this man?'

She shook her head, her eyes wide. The thought of her guardian discovering this secret seemed to terrify her, and if I had understood aright, she had every reason to be frightened for his life and for hers.

She glanced around to ensure we were still alone. 'In the town there is a tanner who regularly takes a cart to London to sell his leather. He would carry a message sometimes for money. Bethia was to have taken a token there the night she was sent away, warning of my guardian's plans, but I don't know if she delivered it for there's been no word from London since. Bethia may have gone to London herself. The man is kind: he would take her in, help her to find a new position.'

'Has it not occurred to you that Lady Magdalen or Master Smith might have intercepted the message and that is why your maid was sent packing?'

'They would not have understood the meaning of the token I sent; not even Bethia knew, and Father Smith would have had me locked up, if he'd even suspected . . .'

That I did not doubt.

'I need to know if the token was delivered . . . if he is coming to help me. Please!' She had placed her hand on my arm, her head lowered, gazing up at me from under those long lashes. It was the worst thing she could have done. My memories of Bristol were still too raw.

I withdrew my arm. 'You should try your charms on one of the stable lads, my lady. I'm sure they'd be only too eager to carry your tokens for a coin or even a smile. Your maid has already been dismissed for her friendship with you. I've no wish to find myself cast out upon the road.' I stooped to pick up the buckets.

'If they did, you'd have to go back to sorcery, wouldn't you?'

I straightened up slowly, keeping my expression neutral. She was leaning in the angle between the wall of the holy well and the steps. All trace of the coaxing, helpless girl had gone. She had lifted her chin and was watching me. Even though her face was stiff with cold, the trace of a triumphant smile played around her mouth.

'A sorcerer? Aren't you afraid I might turn you into a frog and throw you down the well, or maybe you think I can send you flying off to London on a distaff?'

'I think you can turn eggs into pigeons.'

'A broody hen can work the same magic.'

'And I think you can make coins vanish and appear inside a whole apple. You can make a bird burst into flames and come out of the fire and fly away. I saw you in London. You conjured a rose and gave it to a girl in the crowd. I wished then you'd given it to me. And the next market, I insisted to Bethia I had to buy new gloves so that I could walk that way again, but you weren't there. They said you'd been arrested and they told me why.'

I forced myself to laugh. 'I haven't even been able to get a rose to bloom on a bush, much less in my hand, and if I could make coins appear in apples, I would not need to be carrying water to earn my bread.'

'I saw your firemark when you were entertaining the crowd. I thought it was a live snake twisted about your neck. For a moment, I even saw it writhing towards me. No other man has a mark like that. I could not mistake it. I recognised it at once when I saw you coming from the chapel.' Her eyes narrowed. 'Father Smith hasn't trusted you from the hour you arrived and if I told him what I know . . .'

We both knew she did not need to complete her threat.

'But I won't. Not yet. I could help you. You came here to learn something. I hear them all talking when there are no servants in the chamber. I could find out things you'd never discover.'

'I came here because I needed to get out of London. And since I am not a wealthy man, I needed to earn enough to fill my stomach with good food and find a roof to sleep beneath that I did not have to share with lice-ridden goats or hounds. It was mere chance and my good fortune that Lady Magdalen offered me a post.'

'And how long do you think your *good fortune* will last when they discover they have a sorcerer or maybe worse in the Abbey?' She gave a cold smile.

Any sympathy I might have had for her and her lover was frozen by that smile. But I couldn't deny that the little vixen had a point. I did not trust her an inch, but she had every reason to hate Smith and the dowager. She would certainly not be loyal to them, and would relish the idea of passing on anything she might overhear, simply out of revenge.

'I may be able to discover if Bethia delivered anything to this tanner, if you tell me who he is and what she was to have brought to him.'

'A comb, a wooden comb, nothing that anyone would trouble to steal.'

'And what message was the recipient supposed to learn from that?'

'I painted the shaft of the comb with roses, so that he might know my love for him remained true, but the thorns of the roses enclosed a little cat, so that he will know I am held prisoner.'

The tip of her little pink tongue slipped over her lower lip and she gazed up with wide eyes, as if she wanted to make me see the soft and innocent kitten she was. But I had learned long ago that the sweetest kittens bare the sharpest claws.

'And you will take a message to the town for me, Daniel?'

'In time, I might be persuaded. It would depend on what you could tell me.'

'About that man they found with his throat cut. You were interested in him?'

I laughed. 'If a man dies in his own bed no cares who he is, but if he dies with a knife in his back suddenly the whole world becomes curious.'

She smiled, this time with genuine amusement. Virgin, nymph and witch – Katheryne could transform from one to another faster than a halcyon spinning in the wind. Which one had this unknown man fallen in love with, or was there a fourth buried deep inside that only he could see? I pitied the Mother Superior of any convent which had the misfortune to admit her as novice.

Chapter Sixteen

IT WAS NOW THREE DAYS since the freeze began and the cold bit deeper than ever. As soon as the servants' supper ended, I hurried to the gentlemen's chamber to check that Bray had not emptied the livery of food and wine before supper. The priests were still at table in the Great Hall and from there would go to the library until they retired for the night. With luck, I would not be wanted again until morning. I had expected to find the chamber empty, but Erasmus was already there. It had been nearly a week since I had rescued him from the hiding place and we had barely spoken in the past few days, for he usually spent his evenings in the library with the priests and seemed to go out of his way to avoid me at all other times, retreating quickly whenever he caught sight of me.

He bent to poke at the fire, though it was burning cheerfully. 'There is a great chill in here,' he announced, as though this chamber alone had been cocooned in ice. 'The gentlemen will need their beds heating tonight, Pursglove. See that you are ready with the warming pan as soon as they retire.'

I cursed under my breath. 'Wouldn't they prefer you to wait on them at that hour?'

'Father Smith . . . has a task for me . . . I shall be delayed.'

He was circling the room, trimming wicks and returning to do it again as if he was not aware of having already done it.

'He is not going to force you into that hiding place again, is he?'

Erasmus shook his head like a dog with canker. 'He did not force me!' he snapped. 'I choose to endure it . . . to strengthen my soul . . . It was God's will . . . But no, I have work to do elsewhere tonight, important work.'

'Is another ship expected?'

He looked at me for the first time, with cold contempt. 'What do you know of any ship?'

'Like the one that brought Father Cobbe,' I suggested. Smith might have tried to persuade me that Erasmus knew nothing of any importance, but that had only convinced me that Smith feared he did, even if his young acolyte was not aware of its significance.

Erasmus's gaze darted to the door. 'I don't listen, I don't know anything.' His long skinny hands briefly rose towards his head, as if he was about to press them over his ears.

'None of us actually listens, Erasmus, all the same, we can't help but hear,' I said, and laughed. 'The Montague estates are so large, and their business affairs so vast, I should think ships and messengers must be coming almost weekly from London and Bristol with documents to be signed and bills to be paid.'

His head jerked up at as I said Bristol, and he studied me, frowning. But that look wasn't the startled reaction that I'd anticipated. There was something else in his expression. He crossed to the door and opened it, half stepping out, and I thought he was leaving. But he took a step back in, closing the door, and remained there, still facing it, with his hand on the latch.

'Father Smith speaks of Bristol. He has made inquiries there. He knows . . .'

'Knows what?' I asked, trying to keep the urgency from my voice.

But Erasmus was staring fixedly at his hand on the door latch as if it was some strange animal. He swiftly lifted the latch and hurried out, closing the door firmly behind him, leaving me kicking the nearest bed in frustration.

I had thought, after I'd rescued the little rat from that hole, that Erasmus might be willing to talk, but he was probably going straight to Smith to report what I'd just said as a means of redeeming himself. He'd nearly let something slip himself, though, so maybe, at least on this occasion, he wouldn't dare.

But just what had Smith discovered? Was it possible he knew Waldegrave, the old priest who that arch-thief Skinner and his castle rats in Bristol had dubbed the Yena? That quotation in Latin – had Smith learned that I'd been taught by Waldegrave as a boy or was it simply a test to discover if I was the lowly and uneducated servant I pretended to be? But if Waldegrave had told him who I was and what I'd been doing in Bristol, I'd already be lying in that lonely grave alongside Benet. A leopard doesn't change its spots, but they say a yena can change its form at will, so maybe the miraculous had happened and that old bastard, Waldegrave, had actually vouched for me instead of betraying me. But a transformation like that would take more than miracle.

I WAS MAKING FOR the main gate when I saw the young lad Giles scurrying in, straw stuffed into the tops of his shoes and down the front of his jerkin, and his vermin sack slung over his shoulder.

'Been emptying your traps, lad? But it's late to be bringing the heads here. Master Yaxley will have finished for the night. Best wait till morning.'

'I want paying tonight.'

I nodded. He probably had a family who were waiting on what he could bring home if they were not to go to bed hungry, or a father demanding ale-money. It happened.

But I couldn't linger to ask more. The priests would return to their bedchamber straight after their prayers around ten of the clock. But that should be time enough at least to discover when the tanner had last seen Bethia.

The night had brought no relief from cold, rather the reverse. The sky was cloudless, the stars like shards of ice in the blue-black expanse. Puddles glittered in the moonlight and the frozen ground was treacherous, so that even in my boots I found myself forced to slow my pace to stop myself from slipping.

A familiar voice rang out behind me. 'Hold hard there, Dannet!'

I groaned. Arthur! I did not want company tonight. I thought about pretending I hadn't heard, but his footsteps sounded too close. I waited and he came rolling up, clapping a friendly arm about my shoulder.

'You're in a hurry to get to Sybil's – desperate for a flagon of Knucker's Milk, or is Sybil who takes your fancy? I warn you, Dannet, there's many a man tried to breech her ramparts, but she's not raised the white flag yet, not to any of them. Still, you're better carved than most of the gargoyles round here, you might win her over with that silver tongue of yours.'

'Already got my eye on someone. That's where I'm off to now, but I might join you for a flagon later.'

He grinned, nudging me with his elbow. 'You'll have a fair thirst on you by then.'

He waved cheerfully enough as we parted company on the corner. There were few people about in the town on such a cold evening and those who were scurried as swiftly as they dared towards the warmth of their hearths or the welcoming lights of a tavern.

The row of tanners' houses was not hard to find. Even on such a bitter night, the stench of fermenting urine was pungent. Master Tiploft's house was easy to pick out too, for as I'd been told, it was far better appointed than the others in the row. Evidently the fine leather he produced fetched good sums in London.

The woman who answered my knock at the door glared at me. 'He's not hiring, especially not strangers. There's men from Battle lining up to work for him.'

'I do wish to speak to him, Goodwife Tiploft, but I am not seeking work.'

She reached around the door frame and lifted the lantern that hung outside, tilting it so that she could appraise the quality of my boots and clothes. 'Can see from your hands you've never worked in this trade. But if you've come on tannery business it'll have to wait till tomorrow,' she added crossly. 'You're letting the cold in.'

'Is Master Tiploft at home?' I persisted. 'I only want to ask your husband a question, then you can shut the door.'

'He's my brother, not my husband, thank the good Lord. And I'll shut my own door whenever I please, without your leave.'

She made as if to do so, but curiosity got the better of her.

'What do you want to go questioning him about anyway? Are you one of the sheriff's men?' She held her lantern up again, combing the light across my cloak in search of a badge of office.

'I wanted to ask about a package he may have carried to London.'

'Robert's no smuggler,' she said indignantly. 'You ask anyone in the town, and they'll all tell you the same.'

I wager they would. They'd all swear there's not a single smuggler in the shire. 'I am sure he's not. And rest assured I'm not one of the sheriff's men. I work at the Abbey.'

If I thought that would placate her, I'd badly miscalculated. Her expression became wooden.

'He swears he saw nothing that night and it's no good anyone saying he did. He'll not budge. You tell them. He saw nothing.'

'Which night, Mistress Tiploft?'

She stared at me, bewildered. 'I don't . . . You best speak to my brother.' She jerked her head towards the end of the road. 'You'll find him with Myrna most nights when he's home. Cottage behind the well. She's another baggage, like that girl from the Abbey. Husband's at sea, or so she says.' The woman suddenly shot out her hand and touched my arm, her tone almost pleading. 'Tell that girl from the Abbey to leave him in peace. We don't want more trouble. If he was taken, what would happen to his children and to me?'

Before I could ask more, she snatched her hand away and closed the door so hurriedly my cloak almost became jammed in it.

Myrna's cottage was much smaller than Robert Tiploft's, but the gate was new and well oiled, the shutters on the window recently repaired, and the door had been neatly patched, as if Tiploft or some other man had found endless tasks that needed to be done as an excuse for spending time there.

I had expected my knock to be answered by Myrna, but after I had rapped several times, the door was flung open by a man, dressed only in a shirt and breeches which seemed to have been adjusted in some haste. He wore no hose, but despite the cold, his face was flushed. He had evidently snatched up a heavy iron skillet as the nearest weapon and now brandished it in my face.

'She told you to go drown yourself! If I catch you . . .' He stopped and peered at me in the dim light emitted by the fire behind him and a single candle far back in the little room. 'Who are you?'

I ignored the question. 'Master Tiploft, your sister told me I might find you here.'

'Did she indeed? And what business is it of . . . ?' His tone suddenly changed. 'Has there been an accident? My little lads, they're not hurt?'

'All is well at your house and I regret having to disturb you, but I work at the Abbey and they only let us loose at this hour.'

At the mention of the Abbey, he stiffened just as his sister had done, and with an anxious glance back over his shoulder, he stepped swiftly out, pulling the door closed behind him. He shivered as the icy air enveloped him.

'What does the Abbey want with me?'

'The Abbey doesn't,' I assured him. 'But I understand that on occasions one of the maids would ask you to take something to London with your leather.'

'And who told you that?'

'Lady Katheryne. She said her maid, Bethia, would bring you these things and you'd fetch things back for her. A thimble, perhaps.'

'Bethia had a young man in the city. She couldn't write, so she'd send him little messages that way. No harm in that, is there?'

Is that what he really believed, or was that the story he had been schooled to produce if his part in this was discovered?

'No harm at all. Though I don't expect the old dowager would approve. I dare say that's why Bethia was so anxious to keep it from her.' I laughed. 'These pious old crones forget what it's like to be young and in love.'

'Not just the old women,' he said sourly. 'My sister's as bad. Expects a man to live like a monk just 'cause his wife up and left.' He shivered again, wrapping his arms about him and shuffling from foot to foot. 'So, what brings you here?' He was suddenly suspicious again.

'Only that Bethia has received no answer to the last token she sent, the painted comb.'

He frowned. 'I took no comb to London.'

'It would have been over a month ago when she gave it to you.'

He shook his head. 'I've not clapped eyes on her since before Saint Crispin's Day. Thought she finished with all that. Pair of them had fallen out, maybe, or he'd found another wench. London's a big city, full of pretty maids and obliging ones too.'

'Did he seem that kind of man to you?'

Tiploft shrugged. 'Never saw him. I left whatever she gave me at the Wrestler, the coaching inn, hard by Bishops Gate, and I used to call in there on my way back to see if there was anything to be fetched back here . . .' Something seemed to strike him and he took a threatening step towards me. 'Hold hard! Why would Bethia tell you she'd sent something when she hadn't? And while we're about it, why are you here asking questions about it instead of her?'

He tried to pushed me back against the wall, his arm across my throat, but the ground was slippery and as I sidestepped him, he fell. The heavy iron skillet clanged against the ground. I heard a cry of alarm from inside and hurried away before he could get back on his feet.

I couldn't decide if Tiploft really believed he was carrying tokens from an unlettered tiring maid to her sweetheart, or if he knew the truth. And what exactly was the truth? Were they really messages sent between lovers or between those who had a quite different purpose? What had Tiploft seen? Whatever it was, someone from the Abbey was threatening him into silence.

I had been walking with my head down, avoiding the puddles of ice that were gleaming silver in the starlight. One false step and I'd come crashing heavily on to the frozen ruts and stones, like Tiploft. I was relieved to see lights shining out from the Abbey gatehouse. The cold was biting, even through my cloak, and I was beginning to wish I had demanded a thicker one from FitzAlan, not that I could imagine that Scotsman paying for a fur-lined one for me, not even if the fur in question was rat.

I was about to turn in towards the gate when something caught my eye further ahead on the road. There was a dark shape on top of the wall which surrounded St Mary's churchyard: it looked like a giant bird or a monstrous bat silhouetted against the stars. The eyes can often play tricks and I thought I must be staring at part of a yew tree that was overhanging the stones. But as I took a pace closer, the creature sprang off the wall and vanished inside the churchyard. Whatever it was, it was no tree. If a wind had been blowing, I might have thought it was a piece of sailcloth bowled along in a gale. But the breeze only had strength enough to carry a few dry leaves. I hurried up the road past the Abbey gatehouse, towards where I had seen the creature disappear.

St Mary's church was in darkness. I had yet to see it otherwise, for I'd been told that the Dean of Battle spent most of his time at Oxford University and had not returned to conduct services for almost two years. But the moon and stars were bright enough to reveal the black outlines of wooden crosses, stones and humps of earth marking the graves. Twisted yew trees circled the burial ground like demons, determined not to let a single soul escape them. All that was as it should be, and I could see nothing moving.

I followed the path to the church itself, then edged round it on the frosted grass, until I reached the northside. The grass and weeds had grown long over the summer and now lay beaten down and tangled. My cloak caught on a clump of old brambles. It was plain that few people ever came here, afraid to set foot on this side of the church even in daylight, for it was here they buried the unbaptised, the thieves, the paupers and the strangers whom no friend or family had claimed. Most of these graves lay unmarked, though a couple bore crude wooden crosses made from lashed branches, fashioned out of pity for a beggar, while heavy rocks had been dumped on others to keep the malevolent corpse from rising. If what I had seen was a ghost or demon, or even a beast hunting its supper, this place would be its abode.

I'd drawn my dagger, but there was no sign of the figure I'd glimpsed moving before, though in the darkness any man or beast crouching low to the ground would have been impossible to distinguish from the hillocks of earth. I ducked back against the church wall and slid down on to my haunches. Keeping my knife firmly grasped in my hand, I waited to see if any creature would emerge.

As my eyes adjusted to the shapes around me, I realised that I was staring at something I had thought at first was a branch hanging down from one of the yew trees, but though the ever-green fronds were stirring in the small breath of wind, this was shaking. I stood up and walked towards it, but before I was half-way across, a creature leaped from the tree on to the wall. With a wild shriek like a great bird of prey, it vanished. But whatever manner of beast it was, I was sure now it was made of flesh and blood, for I'd distinctly heard the rattle of gravel on the track as it sped away.

A clock chimed, the bell reverberating through the icy air. It was later than I thought. Avoiding the snaking brambles concealed in the tangle of old grass, I started towards the gate and road that led back to the Abbey, walking the opposite way around the church from the path I'd followed, thinking it to be a shorter route. But as I reached the corner of the church, I saw something that made me stop. A grave had been dug in a place that could not be seen from the path I'd taken earlier or even by anyone entering the church. It was not new, but it must have been dug in the last few weeks, for even in the dark I could see the earth had not yet settled. A wooden cross marked the place. But something lay on top of the earth mound, shining in the moonlight.

I knelt down. Smooth white pebbles, glittering with veins of quartz, had been carefully placed on the blood-dark earth. It must have taken considerable effort to collect the stones, for I'd seen none like them lying in the earth in these parts. They had been painstakingly arranged in a pattern, over where I assumed the chest of the corpse must lie beneath the mound. I stood up and stared down. There was no mistaking the design: six petals inside a circle, a daisy wheel. Either someone was anxious to protect the corpse from the Devil, or they meant to pin the dead down in the grave and prevent them from rising to work their evil.

Chapter Seventeen

SHADOWS

I HAVE NEVER SEEN HIS FACE. Only the shadow of him as he vanishes out of the door. The heels of a pair of soft leather shoes, which make no sound except for the creaking of one of the floor-boards. When he returns to guide me back inside my cell and locks me in, his face is hidden by a tattered hood and black mask, a bird's beak, a raven's. He is the shadow of a raven. I know he wears the mask for our mutual protection; I know it because they have told me. The beak is stuffed with herbs that will prevent contagion. Is there fever out there? Has the plague returned again? Or I am the one who is infected with the pestilence?

I reek worse than a plague corpse. When I return to my cell, I can smell my own stench, thick as a Thames fog in the tiny space, ordure and urine, stale sweat and sour breath and something else. I know it well, I smelled it often enough in my former life – grave mould. It grows stronger by the day, as if I am already buried beneath the earth, buried alive, but not alive. I will not live again until my task is completed.

I uncoil from the tiny cell, emerging into the windowless room beyond, like a giant insect wriggling from a chrysalid, blinded by the flame of a solitary candle after the utter darkness of my cell. I have no candle in there. The smallest pinprick of light might be seen in a chink, through a crack, and the space is so small that I might easily set fire to myself or even suffocate in the fumes. I have no candle for our mutual protection – I know it, because they have told me. I only see his shadow when he moves, for I am squinting so hard against the violence of the light, that he is without substance in the gloom.

... terra autem erat inaniset vacuus ...

... and the earth was without form and void, and darkness was upon the deep ...

Is that what God saw, this formless shadow that He would mould into a creature of substance, into a man? But this man, if he is indeed a man, is gone before I can make him flesh and bone and blood, before I can give him a name. Is the shadow keeping me alive or is it keeping me dead?

A fire burns in the hearth in this room, and I cling to its heat, trying to rub the warmth and life back into the blocks of ice which are my limbs. I know I will pay the price, pain and madding itching as blood flows back, but it must be. My belly rumbles. Bread and wine are laid ready on the table, and herrings. Loaves and fishes. Is it a fast day, or do they fear to give me meat that seals the bowels and festers in the belly when you cannot move? They dare not give me physic to make me void it. There is no room for a bucket or pan in my cell. I must wait until nightfall, ignore the cramp in my guts when it comes, supress the burning in my bladder. I must wait ... wait.

Books have been placed ready for me, paper stacked neatly, quills cut, the ink in the dish freshly wetted. All this I know without looking; it is always done.

Pones coram me mensum.

Thou hast prepared a table before me in the presence of my enemies.

But who is my enemy here? For the Devil comes in many guises, even an angel of light. And those very walls that protect a man from the wolves that circle outside, trap him with the serpent that lies coiled within.

Chapter Eighteen

DANIEL PURSGLOVE

THE ROOFS GLITTERED with thick white frost, and every stone and twig was sheathed in ice as if it had been dipped in glass. Straw and dried bracken had been scattered across the courtyard and old sacks laid down to give some purchase, but it had made little difference for they had frozen overnight and were now as slippery as the stones beneath. Lavender-grey smoke from chimneys and from the fire the stable boys had built in the yard rose vertically into the powder-blue sky, ghost ladders ascending to heaven. The lads crouched around their blaze, the white fog of their breath masking their faces, and stretched out hands purple with cold as they waited for the pails of frozen water to melt.

It was hard to breathe. The freezing air seared your lungs and made your eyes stream, and in spite of the brightness of the morning, no one from the house was eager to venture outside. Even a brief task meant piling on coats, dragging on boots, and binding coils of straw rope around feet to keep from slipping. Maids and manservants peered out of doors and casements, calling for the lads to fetch water or wood, but they were either ignored or met with jeers of 'fetch it yourself' from the bolder ones, none of them willing to tear themselves from the warmth of the fire.

A woman edged in through the archway and stared about her, as if unsure who to approach. Her head was swathed in a shawl drawn up over her mouth and nose. Her arms were crossed over her chest, holding a coat made of sheepskin closed; the stained and patched leather gloves she wore seemed too large and stiff for her to grasp anything. The boys ignored her and she seemed fearful of approaching the door of the house, but finally her gaze alighted on me and she gingerly edged towards me.

She mumbled something I couldn't understand, through the folds of the woollen shawl covering her mouth. Her pale blue eyes stared up at me anxiously and her face was so pinched and pale, I thought she must be begging for food.

She pulled the cloth from her face. 'I know you. You're the man Sam brought to the cottage.'

'Alys!' I recognised her now. 'Are you looking for Master Yaxley? Does your husband need help . . . is it poachers again?' She had told me that they never came to the Abbey. Something serious must have happened to bring her here.

She crossed her arms more tightly. 'I don't rightly know if I should bother Master Yaxley . . . he might think . . . If Matthew comes back, he'll be fighting mad if he knows I told the bailiff. And I wouldn't, not in the usual way, but it's that cold, you see. If he's fallen . . . broke a leg . . .' She kept glancing behind her at the archway, as if she was on the verge of fleeing back home.

'Alys, you said *if Matthew comes back*. Is he missing?'

She nodded miserably. 'He's not been home since yesterday afternoon and he told Sam he'd be back for his supper afore dark. If he's had a fall on the ice and been lying out all night . . . Sam's been out looking and he can't see sign of him. Matthew's not a man to go drinking, not like some. Can't abide going near the town. Too many folks, too much noise, he says. But he'll be in such a fury if he learns I came here. Maybe I best go home. He might already be there, wanting his breakfast.'

'I hope that is so, Alys, but in this weather we can't afford to wait. If he is lying hurt out there then he must be found quickly.'

I didn't add that if he had been caught in another of those man traps, like Cobbe, and lain out all night in this cold, it might already be too late; the despair in her eyes told me she already feared that.

*

165

WITHIN HALF AN HOUR a small group of men and lads who could be spared from their duties had assembled in the courtyard on Yaxley's orders. Most seemed to have clad themselves in every winter garment they owned, rope knotted round their waists since their coats had been pulled over so many layers they would barely fasten. Straw and raw sheep wool peeped over the top of stuffed boots.

Yaxley clambered up on to the mounting block.

'I dare say this a waste of time. Most of you won't have dealings with Crowhurst, but any that have will tell you he's a churlish bastard with a sour temper, so he's more than likely taken umbrage at something that poor wife of his has done and gone off to a whore's bed for the night or got himself drunk and is sleeping it off in a haybarn. Though Alys reckons her husband's a saint who's never looked at another woman or been the worse for ale, if you can believe that . . .' The men laughed and gave each other knowing winks and digs.

'Then why are we tramping around in the woods when we could be toasting our backsides by a warm fire?' one of the men sang out. 'It's cold enough out here to freeze the cods off a demon in hell.'

'Aye, that it is,' Yaxley said. 'And if one of you clotpoles was lying out in it with a broken leg, I dare say you'd be glad to think someone was looking for you. So, we'd best make a search just in case, for no man could last a second night out in this. Can't use the scent-hounds, they'd not pick up a trail when it's as bleat as this, so it'll have to be men.'

'We'll make a good search for him,' another said. 'But if I come back from tramping round in those woods and find he's been sitting by some alehouse fire all this time, I'll break his miserable neck, never mind his leg.'

'You'll have to stand in line,' someone else called out and there were a few more nods and grunts.

The bailiff held up his hand for silence. 'You'd best get going; there's not much daylight this time of year. Pair up and stick together: that way if you find him and he's hurt, one of you can come back and fetch a bier and the other stay with him. Keep to his patch. If he fell or got himself caught in a trap, it'll be when he was making his rounds. If we find him or the search is called off, I'll blow three blasts on the horn. When you hear that horn, come back fast as you can and there'll be a hot mulled ale waiting for you.'

After some debate about how to pair up and the direction to head for, the men set off. Yaxley had already sent Alys home, but said he'd follow her and question Sam to see if he could learn any more from the lad about where his father might have gone.

But the sun was already dropping behind the skeletal black branches of the trees before we finally heard the three blasts of the horn sound out across the woods. A clamour of rooks flapped up into the rose-pink sky and wheeled in circles, cawing mournfully. Servants gathered at the door and casements as, slowly, in twos or fours, the men and lads came plodding into the courtyard, stamping numbed feet, their faces stiff with cold, noses red and cheeks flushed. As soon as the horn had sounded, a cauldron of spiced ale had been set to heat over the fire in the kitchen, and two maids with ladles stood by, ready to thrust a warm beaker into each icy hand as soon as gloves were stripped off.

A shout went up from an upper casement. Two men had been glimpsed carrying what looked like a man between them. Those below rushed back out to help, but the burden they carried, slung between two poles, proved to be an eviscerated deer. They had found the frozen carcass, they said, but the ground around it had been too hard for even a shod horse to leave fresh tracks. It seemed Crowhurst had disturbed poachers in their work, and had given chase, or they had attacked and silenced him.

SUPPER IN THE servants' hall was a subdued affair. The woods had been ringing with the cries of searchers calling Crowhurst's name. If he was out there and had not been able to cry out then he was surely in a bad way. A couple of the men were all for resuming the search with lanterns and torches after they had a 'good belly full of hot food' inside them, but others had shaken their heads. Darkness and this cold were a lethal combination. Any man could fall and break a leg or find himself caught in a trap and if there were poachers about, men who were ruthless and desperate, they could pick them off one by one. Better to resume at dawn, it was agreed, and if it was warmer by morning, they might be able to use dogs.

But as we drained our ale and finished mopping up the last of the stewed chicken and prunes with bread sops, Master Yaxley strode in, peeling off his gloves and rubbing his fingers over the large blaze in the heath. His face was so stiff with cold it was hard to tell if he was smiling or grimacing. He could scarcely move his jaw enough to speak. Someone thrust a hot poker into a beaker of ale and handed it to him. He drank it with evident relief, both hands wrapped around the warmed cup, before wiping his mouth and setting it down. All eyes in the hall were riveted on him.

'It's good news I have for you. Just come from Crowhurst's cottage. Went to get something of Matthew's for the scent-hounds to sniff at in the morning, in case we could use them. But he's already back home and safe. Seems he spotted a blood trail and took it for a wounded beast or man, followed it as far as the marshes, but he slipped and hurt his back. Found himself a bit of shelter last night, but his back got worse sleeping on the ground and it's taken him the best part of the day to drag himself back home.'

A babble of voices and grins broke out, some cursing Crowhurst for a fool, though without any real malice, others giving thanks that he was safe and even more thankful that they wouldn't have to spend another day in the freezing weather searching the woods. Beakers and tankards were swiftly refilled. This was a cause for celebration, though a very swift one, before we were all chivvied back to our duties. Even if Crowhurst had been a saint risen from the dead, the candles in the bedchambers would still need trimming and the piss-flasks set out ready for the priests.

As we rose, a man leaned across the table, frowning. 'So where exactly was this blood trail, do you reckon? Must have been a good way off manor land, else why did none of us run across him as he was limping home? 'Cause, if you think about it, whichever direction Matthew came from he'd have to have passed through the woods we were searching to reach his cottage. And he must have heard us yelling for him, especially if he was limping at a snail's pace.'

'Surly beggar refused to answer, I expect,' another man said. 'Heard one of the stable lads say Crowhurst wouldn't even return a greeting if you offered it. If you ask me, it's as well he's stuck out there in the woods by himself all day, miserable old devil. But it's that wife of his and the lad I feel sorry for.'

'Aye, well, maybe one day she'll get lucky and a poacher will finish him.'

Chapter Nineteen

BEAR GARDENS, SOUTHWARK

THE APE SCREAMED, clinging to the saddle of the horse as the dog leaped up at it. The horse was galloping wildly around the edge of the pit. Three of the hounds ran towards it, barking and snapping at its legs and belly. It was swerving so violently that the ape would have been thrown off into the snarling pack had it not been tied on. As it was, the terrified creature slipped from the saddle, dangling sideways from the bucking horse until another of the dogs jumped up and almost caught its arm between his jaws. Finally, it managed to haul itself upright, its teeth barred, as it shrieked in fear and fury. Laughter and shouts rang out from the servants, labourers and apprentices who were standing in the stalls, and some tossed pieces of mutton pies or fruit at the ape as the horse careered round the inside of the wooden wall.

But their masters, who could afford to pay twice as much to be seated on the tiers of benches above stalls, barely glanced at the spectacle unless their attention was caught by a particularly loud scream or howl, which signalled a beast was wounded. They were occupied in earnest business discussions, legal or otherwise, frequently glancing about them to ensure that no eavesdroppers had edged too close. Others shouted for food, drink or pipes of tobacco from the vendors who hollered their wares as they roamed among the crowd.

One dog sprang at the horse from behind, trying in vain to reach its diminutive rider, and slid off, its claws raking down the horse's rump. The horse kicked out with his hindlegs: one hoof crashed against the wooden wall; the other caught the dog in the ribs, sending it rolling over and over, howling and whimpering. It dragged itself away and crumpled, cringing against the wooden boards. A man leaned over, caught the dog by its spiked collar and hauled it out of the pit. They always set the young and inexperienced dogs on the horses and monkeys. Once they'd learned how to dodge the trampling hooves, they'd be ready for the bulls and bears, if they survived that long.

Oliver feigned rapt attention to all the activity in the pit. His cousin, Richard, had invited one of the many bare-breasted whores to keep him company in the gallery. The women, most of whom looked old enough to be Oliver's mother or even his grandmother, huddled around the braziers at the entrances and flashed open their cloaks to briefly display their wares. They edged away from the warmth of the fires only to entwine themselves around men who looked as if they were wealthy enough to pay for company and a drink or two. Oliver had tried to ignore the mocking and teasing catcalls of the women, but he felt his beardless cheeks flame. It wasn't that he didn't want to sample all the pleasures he'd heard such women had to offer, but thus far in his life, he'd rarely even kissed a girl of his own age and could not face being humiliated by these succubi in public. He needed to be alone with one of them, preferably in the dark, until he was sure he had mastered the art.

The whore sat astride Richard, rocking back and forth as he fondled her breast. Christopher Veldon, sitting on the other side of Richard, was watching them with some amusement, evidently finding her gyrations more entertaining than the baiting of the ape. Judging by Richard's swift breaths and grunts, Oliver guessed her work was almost done. She squealed as Richard crushed her nipple in his fist and pushed her off his lap. Her knee hit the wooden boards hard and she cursed him roundly, raising her hand to slap him, but he caught her wrist.

'Claws away, malkin, or I'll tie you to a saddle and see what the dogs will do.' He nudged Oliver, who was staring fixedly at the horse and ape being led out of the pit. 'Here coz, a gift for you.' He placed the woman's arm he still had in his grasp on to Oliver's lap. The woman's expression changed in instant from a sulky pout to a coaxing smile, and her fingers began to creep like a burrowing mole towards his codpiece. Oliver, who had not been expecting this, shot bolt upright, batting her hand away as if a rat had leaped on him. He felt his face burning again as gales of laughter rang out all round him.

None laughed harder than the woman 'My! He's a tender little lambkin, isn't he? He'd make a lovely Juliet, if he'd a mind to go on stage.' She leaned forward so her two pendulous breasts brushed his face, and pinched his cheek. 'Maybe you should find a handsome Romeo for him.'

All those within hearing cackled with laughter, but Veldon, glancing across the pit, suddenly frowned. 'Speaking of Romeos.' He gestured towards a figure pushing his way along the row one up from their own on the opposite side.

The gallery and stalls were still only half occupied, but they were filling up fast with those anxious not to miss the main attraction of the bear-baiting, on which heavy wagers would be made. Regulars had their favourite hounds and champion bears too, celebrated for the number of dogs they had killed. Oliver peered across the pit. It was hard to see any face clearly, for the late-afternoon light funnelling through the open roof above only illuminated the arena, while the gallery was in the deep shadow of the wall and its overhang, which provided those who had paid for the privilege some protection from the icy breeze from the river. But even in the semi-darkness, the blond hair, broad shoulders and multicoloured jerkin, doublet and hose of Robert Carr made him stand out like parrot in a flock of crows.

Peering around the whore to where Veldon had gestured, Richard absently dropped a few coins into her palm and pushed her towards the aisle. The woman shrugged and ambled away.

'Who's that with Carr?' Veldon asked. 'I can't see from here.'

The man seated beside the King's favourite was older, his hair and dagger-point beard darker, and his attire, though elegant with a large ruff and silver buttons, was of such a dark russet hue that it merged into the smoke-stained walls, making it appear that his disembodied head was being served up on a white platter.

'None else but Thomas Overbury, Carr's governor,' Richard announced.

Thomas Overbury had turned towards Carr and appeared to be delivering an earnest discourse on something, but his young friend did not appear to be listening. He was watching a large mangy brown bear being led and prodded into the pit. It was tethered by a chain to a post fixed in the middle of the ring while a couple of men distracted it with small lumps of raw meat that they tossed towards it.

'The brains are endeavouring to counsel the brawn, without much success it seems,' Veldon said.

Richard snorted. 'Overbury should know you don't reason with a highland bull; you take a goad and prod him. He should ask the pigmy there to school him in the art of mastering dumb beasts.' He gestured down at the ring.

The great mastiffs had not yet been released and while they were being fetched, a dwarf, clad in yellow and scarlet, had cavorted across the bloody sand and darted towards the bear. He poked it with a sharp stick, dodging away as it lashed out. He pranced and turned somersaults, coming so close to the beast that it seemed as if those claws must rake his face off as they lashed at him. But the dwarf seemed to know the reach of them to within an inch, for the bear continually struck empty air. The crowd shouted their approval and the little man turned to make extravagant bows, deftly catching the coins they tossed.

It would be a while before the event between the dogs and the bear commenced, and Oliver saw Carr mutter something to Overbury before making his way towards one of the entrances, while Overbury remained seated. Perhaps he was going to relieve himself in the jakes outside, or buy himself a hot pie or even a whore – for he flirted shamelessly with any pretty woman, servant or lady, at the Court and, apart from the Queen, who didn't hide her dislike of him, most women seemed to welcome his attentions.

Beside him, Oliver heard Richard give an amused grunt. He was no longer watching Carr's progress towards the steps, but instead his attention was caught by three men in the stalls who had turned away from the prancing dwarf and were evidently keeping track of Carr as he moved along the row above them. Now they followed, making for the same exit, though Carr seemed completely unaware that he was being observed.

Richard nudged Veldon. 'I think there is some sport to be had outside.'

Both men rose swiftly and made their way along the bench, and Oliver, after a moment's hesitation, followed. At the entrance, the aroma of hot spiced meat and saffron cakes mingled with the stench of dung, piss, mouldy straw and rotting offal from the dozens of dog kennels and bear cages that were clustered close by. They had to push against a tide of people who were battling to get inside out of the bitter cold and secure a good view.

Oliver quickly lost sight of Veldon and his cousin. But as he extracted himself from the throng, he saw them further ahead, hurrying towards the dense grove of trees in the corner of the garden furthest away from the river. It was a spot which even he knew had something of a reputation, especially at night, favoured by those who did not want their activities to be observed. It was a haunt of the night creatures – doxies and Ganymedes, thieves and fences, procurers of poison and stranglers for hire. Hidden away from the prying gaze of the river traffic, they were free to pursue their business under the cloak of darkness, for the watch rarely ventured inside unless they were well supported by armed soldiers – it wasn't worth getting your head stoved in or your eyes stabbed out to arrest a couple of lads with their breeches down. And even though it was mid-afternoon, the grove did not look welcoming beneath the heavy grey clouds.

Oliver glimpsed flashes of scarlet and emerald green among the dark trunks and in the same instant heard Richard's voice. It sounded as if he was issuing some kind of challenge. Suddenly ashamed that he had hesitated, Oliver dragged his sword from its scabbard and hurtled straight towards where he thought he'd seen movement. Much to his chagrin, his bold dash was hampered by strands of dead bindweed and other tendrils that twisted around his legs, but he ploughed on, trying not to lose his footing on the icy ground.

One of the three men Oliver had seen leaving the bear pit was standing directly behind Carr, who was kneeling on the frozen leaf mould. Carr's ruff had evidently been ripped from his neck and lay trampled close by. And in its place around his throat was a loop of hempen rope. His captor was holding the ends in his two great fists. The rope was pulled tight but was not yet choking Carr, who was trying to get his fingers beneath it, though every time it seemed he might succeed, his assailant jerked his fists, half strangling his victim, making him gasp and cough.

Richard and Veldon had both drawn their swords and were squaring up to the two other men, who had taken up positions a few feet in front of them. One was a gangly, hunched-shouldered youth who was tossing a knife expertly from hand to hand and grinning, as if to ask which of them wanted to taste his blade first, while his companion, an older man with a pock-marked face and drooping, thickened eyelids, was bouncing the end of a stout cudgel against his palm. In open ground, a short cudgel and a dagger would be no match for swords, but the men had chosen their spot well, for the trees grew close together here; their weapons would be far more useful when wielded among branches and trunks.

Their gaze darted towards Oliver as he lumbered up, evidently wondering if he was part of the swordsmen's company or had his own reasons for being among the trees. That glance was their undoing. Richard lunged at the youth with his sword. Both the young man's hands were stretched out in front of him as he juggled his knife, and Richard's blade sliced straight down the length of his right forearm, cutting through cloth and opening the flesh beneath to the bone. The lad shrieked, dropping the dagger and clamping his arm tightly with his left hand. Blood welled out from between his fingers, but Oliver didn't wait to see that. He was nearer to Carr than Veldon, and had sense enough to realise that he could do little else between tangled trees than to use his sword like a lance.

Oliver ran at the man who was clutching the rope, his blade held out straight in front of him. But the man saw it coming and leaped back, dragging on the noose around Carr's neck and toppling him sideways. The Scot's not inconsiderable weight was now suspended from the rope the man was gripping. Carr was scarlet in the face, gagging and choking as he tried to drag the noose away from his throat. He managed to get one leg planted on the ground and levered himself upright, smashing backwards with his fist. Oliver heard the crunch of bone as the powerful knuckles connected with his assailant's nose. The man dropped the rope and reeled away.

Oliver turned back to see Richard wiping his blade on a clump of grass, while Veldon was already sheathing his. Of their opponents there was no sign, except for the trail of blood from the youth's arm, shining wet on the frosted ground.

Richard dug the point of his sword into the trampled ruff and hooked it up, offering it to Carr, who regarded it with disgust. He plainly had no intention of having that cleaned and mended. Richard shook it from the blade and let it fall.

Carr briefly massaged his throat. There was a dark red rope-burn around his neck, but he seemed more concerned with brushing the dirt and leaf mould from his clothes and straightening his attire. 'Swaggerers! They ken I'm a Scot and they followed me.'

'Into the woods?' Veldon raised his eyebrows. 'What business brings you in here, Master Carr? You should be more circumspect. Men seen coming from this place are always assumed to have something to hide.'

Carr glowered at him. 'I was in the jakes. They hemmed me in. One of them pulled a dagger and forced me in here. When the King learns of this, he'll have them all hunted down and their miserable carcasses hung in chains.'

'You came close to being hung yourself,' Richard said, 'or garrotted at least. It's fortunate we saw the men following you.'

'Then you should have called the guards and had them stopped sooner. They'd be locked up by now and I wouldn't have been put to the trouble of fighting them off.'

'We fought them off!' Oliver burst out indignantly.

'I don't need a laddie with arse fluff for a beard to do my fighting. But it was a lucky strike you made with that sword of yours, Lord Fairfax. It'll make it easier to prove the man's guilt when the King's men hunt him down.'

Richard inclined his head as though he was accepting Carr's thanks, which Oliver realised had still not been offered. And nor would they be it seemed, for Carr walked away without another word, though Oliver noticed with some satisfaction that he was limping. This afternoon's events must have aggravated the newly mended leg.

'We should have let those Swaggerers finish him,' Oliver said furiously, griping his sword hilt. 'Why did you follow him out here, Richard? I thought you couldn't stand him. If you'd just let those men do their worst . . .'

A broad grin spread across Veldon face's, as if he suddenly understood. He wrapped an arm around Oliver's shoulder and nodded towards Richard. 'Your coz is as cunning as a fox and twice as devious. Watch, listen and learn from him. *Dad* will be all concern when he learns his favourite laddie was almost killed. Carr will no doubt spin him a tale in which he comes out as the hero, but he'll have to mention the three of us at some point, especially Richard. When those men are caught, we'll be needed as witnesses, if Carr's to have the satisfaction of seeing them hanged. Since they did him no real injury, he'll have no proof they intended to, unless we testify. How else is an Englishman at Court to win the favour of a Scottish King and get him to pay off his debts, except by defending his favourite Scot?'

'Debts?' Oliver frowned and glanced at his cousin. He had inherited the whole Fairfax estate. Surely, he couldn't . . . ?

'Didn't you know, lad? Your dear cousin's tastes are even more extravagant than Carr's, and he has expenses besides, a great many, I would wager. The men he employs don't take promissory notes or cast-off clothing in payment. Timely accidents have been known to pull men out of such mires, but a man's father can only die once. Isn't that right, Lord Fairfax?'

Chapter Twenty

DANIEL PURSGLOVE

THE THUMP OF STEEL striking wood carried through the trees and across the frozen meadow on the cold still air. That was no task for a man with an injured back. But as I approached the cottage, I saw it was young Sam wielding the axe, splitting logs on the stump of a tree. His broad frame was more than equal to the task of swinging the blade, but he was doing so without any skill, clumsily chipping at the stump more often than the log. When he did hit the target, he smashed it rather than split it, sending splinters of wood flying in all directions, threatening to impale anyone within range. Presumably this task was not often entrusted to him, which was probably the only reason he was still in possession all of his limbs.

I called out a warning and he turned. A slow smile spread across his face as he recognised me and lowered his axe. His cheeks were scarlet and his nose was running in the cold.

'That task will warm you even before those logs are burning.'

'My job, this'll be now. Father says I'll soon be as good as him if I keep at it.'

It was strange to hear that Crowhurst was giving him encouragement instead of shouting at him for being a clumsy ape. But maybe his back injury had reminded him that he needed the boy.

'Lady Magdalen has sent physic for your father and some food for you all. Is your father inside?' At the mention of food, Sam's eyes had gleamed, but now he suddenly looked as wary as he had when I'd first come across him in the forest. He glanced anxiously towards the closed door of the cottage, as well he might. Crowhurst had seemed to me exactly as the bailiff had described him – a surly bastard – and I couldn't imagine that pain had sweetened his temper.

'He'll be glad of what I've brought, I'm sure. But you don't need to come in.'

I was aware of the boy silently watching me as I made for the door and knocked. The door opened a crack, just enough for me to glimpse the worn, faded face of Alys. But no one opened their door wide in that bitter weather. The cold, once it barged in, would not readily depart. I repeated what I'd said to Sam and indicated the sack I carried. She hesitated, glancing behind her into the room. Then she reached out to take the bag, but I held on to it.

'Lady Magdalen wants me to see how your husband fares, Alys, and ask what else he might be in need of . . . also, about the blood trail he was following. I won't trouble him for long.'

'Let him in, Alys,' a man's voice called out.

I pushed the door wider and slipped in, closing it swiftly behind me.

The room was dim, almost dark, after the fierce blue of the clear sky and dazzling frost outside. The shutters had been closed to help keep out the cold, and the only light came from the flames of the fire dancing in the hearth. I didn't know how Alys could see to do her spinning, but then she had probably been spinning and weaving, plucking birds and baking bread every day of her life since she could toddle and, like most goodwives, could have done it all blindfolded.

The door to the room that served as storeroom and bedchamber was open, no doubt to allow the heat from the fire to warm both rooms. Beneath a heap of blankets and sheepskins, I could just make out the shape of a man lying in bed.

'Good morrow, Goodman Crowhurst. You were kind enough to let me share your supper and hearth the day I came to Battle. I am sent to return the favour,' I called out. I turned back to the scrubbed table and began to lay out the food and preserves I'd brought. I handed Alys a freshly killed goose. 'I was instructed to tell you that your husband should have a broth made of the brains, liver and guts to help him mend. But I think a good helping of roast goose meat would get him on his feet quicker. It would me. What do you say, Goodman Crowhurst?' I called out.

'Aye, a grown man needs a good bit of flesh to keep his strength up, not pap for sucklings, isn't that right, Alys?' He sounded almost cheerful, much more so than the night I'd met him.

I pulled out a small vial. 'Syrup of poppy . . . if your husband is in great pain or cannot sleep. And this . . .' I held up a sealed earthenware jar, 'an unguent to be rubbed on his back where the injury is. I'm told the sooner this is applied, the swifter he will recover. Shall I do that for him, while you pluck that goose?'

Alys dropped the goose and snatched the jar from me, clutching it against her chest. 'I'll rub it on. He can't abide having anyone else tend him.'

'At least let me help you turn him, then. He's a heavy man and if he can't move—'

'We'll manage,' she cut in firmly. 'He hates anyone to see him weakened like this, specially another man.'

I should have expected that. It would be galling to a man like Crowhurst who prided himself on his strength and independence to be rendered helpless.

'Then I'll leave you in peace, just as soon as I've had a word with him.'

She stepped in front of the door as if she would bar my way, but this time I would not be dissuaded and moved her firmly aside. I squeezed into the small room, ducking beneath the ropes and snares dangling from the beams and trying not to impale myself on the billhooks and scythes which hung on the walls.

'How do you fare, Goodman Crowhurst? Lady Magdalen wishes me to tell you that she is praying for your swift recovery. But she also anxious to know . . .'

I trailed off, staring down at the face and shoulders of the man lying prone beneath me. His face was thinner than I remembered, though pain and exhaustion can make the fittest of men look drawn and gaunt overnight. His features, beard and dark hair were very similar to Crowhurst's, but there was one thing I was certain that was different – his nose was straight. It had never been broken. Whoever this was, he was not Alys's husband.

'He's tired and his back is paining him a great deal. You should leave him be.' Alys was standing in the doorway, watching me anxiously.

I glanced back down at the man lying in her bed. He had closed his eyes. I had seen men in pain more times than I could count – those who bore agony without complaint and those who made certain the whole world knew – and I was certain this man was neither in pain nor asleep. I was almost tempted to boot him out of bed to prove it. But I caught sight of Alys's fearful expression. Had I caught Alys with her lover? But she didn't seem the kind of woman who would dare do such a thing, however much she might crave affection.

I walked back into the main room. Outside I could hear Sam was once more absorbed in the attempt to split the logs. He was a good-hearted lad, but an innocent, and Alys would never trust him not to let something slip to Crowhurst about any visitors she'd entertained.

'Alys,' I said quietly. 'On my honour I will say nothing about that man in there, but if Master Yaxley learns that your husband did not injure his back, he will be furious, as will the rest of the men who wasted a day searching for him, not to mention Lady Magdalen.' I gestured towards the fat goose and the other provisions on the table.

'But Master Yaxley knows he hurt himself. He came here last evening and talked to him. And you've seen for yourself, my husband can't move out of his bed, he's that stiff. Maybe that salve will get him right.'

'But that man in your bed is not Matthew,' I protested.

182

"Course it is. Who else would it be?'

'But that's not the man I met the night Sam brought me here after his stone-boat turned over. You said the man who came home that evening was your husband and you called *him* Matthew.'

'Aye, that's him.' She jerked her head towards the man lying in the bed.

She turned away and pulled a sack half filled with an assortment of feathers from the wall. She sat down on the low stool by the fire and began to pluck the goose, adding the feathers to those in the sack. Her head was bent as if she was concentrating on the task, but I sensed it was simply to avoid looking at me. I would get no more from her.

I wrapped my cloak more firmly about me and braced myself to step outside into the blast of icy air.

As I put my hand to the latch, Alys said, 'Please thank Lady Magdalen kindly for the vittles and physic. She's a good soul. None more Christian than her.'

As I closed the door behind me, Sam paused with his axe in mid-air and smiled uncertainly. I didn't want to cause any trouble for the lad. I nodded towards the pile of smashed wood. His aim wasn't improving, but at least they'd have kindling aplenty.

'You've worked hard, lad. Your father will be pleased when he comes home and sees how much wood you've cut.'

His gaze slid towards the cottage door. 'Father can't get out of bed, that's why Ma says I must do it.'

'Have you spoken to your father today?'

Sam nodded.

'And does he seem changed to you?'

He stared at me, his brow creased.

'Did he look different when he came back after being lost?'

'He hurt his back.'

'Was there anything else that was different about him?'

Sam beamed. 'He didn't shout.'

He carefully balanced another log on the tree stump, arranging it several times with deep concentration, and I knew I was forgotten.

EVEN BEFORE I reached the door of the withdrawing room, I could hear the raised voices – Smith's angry growl, Katheryne's tone shrill and indignant.

'I will not forget her! And you cannot banish me as you did her.'

'Your guardian may most certainly banish you, if she sees fit. You are fortunate that Lady Magdalen has allowed you to live in this great house thus far, but she could easily send you to spend your remaining time in England in a far less agreeable place.'

'As I have told you repeatedly . . .' Magdalen's tone had not lost its authority, but she sounded exhausted, as if she longed to be left in peace by everyone, 'your maid was not dismissed by me. She ran away of her own volition, no doubt seduced away some rogue. She was a wanton.'

'She wouldn't—'

Tempted though I was to walk away, I knocked in the hope of preventing Katheryne from blurting out something in her fury that we'd both regret.

The dowager was seated on one side of the hearth, her fingers spinning her rosary ring, though whether she was praying for patience or simply soothing her nerves was hard to say. Smith was standing on the other, warming his backside at the roaring blaze, his jaw set hard, and Katheryne stood a little way off, her whole frame quivering with pent-up rage.

I avoided catching her eye and bowed to Magdalen. I knew without looking that Smith was glowering at me, but the dowager offered me a relieved smile, as if she welcomed the interruption.

'Well now, Pursglove, did you deliver the food and physic to my woodward?

'I did, my lady, and his wife asked me to thank you for your great kindness.'

'And how fares her husband? Is he recovering?'

'He was in his bed resting his back, but I think he will recover well, though he seems changed.'

'Changed?'

'Not the man he was, that is, not as I remember him. Do you know Matthew Crowhurst, my lady?'

'What a strange question. As far as I can recall I have never had cause to speak to him or any of the woodwards. I rely on Master Yaxley as bailiff to give them their orders. But are you suggesting that the man is dissolute, or' – her gaze briefly shifted to Smith – 'that he might be a danger to my guests?'

'No, not at all,' I said hastily. 'He and his wife speak of you with great loyalty, my lady. He is proud that his father and grandfather held the post before him.'

She smiled graciously, as if she expected no less. But still she looked puzzled. 'Master Yaxley tells me he was following a trail of blood when he fell. My bailiff was certain it came from the deer they found slaughtered. Is the woodward of the same opinion? He doesn't believe it might have been . . . a wounded man?'

I glanced at Smith. He was watching me carefully.

'With the great freeze, the ground in the forest is as unyielding as granite, my lady. It would be impossible for any man, even a skilled woodward, to tell, unless the blood came from a foot or paw and left print of its shape. You would either need to find where the creature was first wounded or where the trail finishes to be sure. Do you wish me to try?'

'No,' Smith said quickly. 'That will not be necessary. The bailiff knows this estate and the lands round about. If there is another wounded beast to be tracked down and dispatched, he will do it.'

'If that is the only reason for hunting it,' I said carefully, 'he will not need to trouble himself. A night out in this cold would send any wounded creature into a sleep from which it will never wake, beast or man.'

The old woman held up her hand to silence whatever retort Smith had been about to make. 'Pursglove has carried out my orders faithfully,' she said firmly. 'As *I* knew he would. We should allow him to return to his duties.' A slight shudder convulsed her frame, as if from a sudden stab of pain. But a moment later she had regained control of herself and sat as still and upright as before.

I bowed. 'My lady.'

I closed the door and stood for a moment, listening, but they had lowered their voices.

I walked away and moments later heard the door open and close again. Katheryne hurried towards me. Lightly gripping my sleeve and with a finger to her lips, she pulled me forward, opened the door of a small chamber and beckoned me inside.

'If someone should come in . . .' I warned. I was only too aware how it might appear – a male servant behind a closed door with Lady Magdalen's young ward and future nun. I'd be flogged from one end of the shire to the next. I had come dangerously close before in my life and I had no desire to risk it again, especially not for Katheryne.

She gestured towards the fire. 'Then tend to that.'

I knelt and picked up the poker. She was good at this; too good.

'So, what news?' Her eyes glittered in the firelight. 'Did you speak to the tanner?'

'I did.'

'Well?' she demanded impatiently. 'What did he tell you? Did Bethia go to London with him? Did he deliver the comb? Did he bring something back for me?' The questions tumbled over each other.

'A bargain is a bargain. Tell me first what you have discovered about the murdered man on the marsh.'

'Oh, him. Why are you so interested? He's dead.'

I rose and took a pace, as if I intended to walk out.

'All I learned was that he was bringing letters and money from two priests newly arrived from France and smuggled into a port on the other side of England. I don't know who the money was for – whoever killed him stole that. I don't think the letters were for Father Smith, though, but for someone else. But he wanted to read them.'

'Do you know where the letters are now?'

'They've been delivered, that's what I heard Father Smith say. He said something about orders to move him.'

'Do you know who they were talking about?'

'I didn't hear any more. You're lucky I heard that much. They don't talk in front of me. Some things they don't even say in front of my guardian. She won't hear talk of treason or plots even in jest.'

'Treason?'

Katheryne suddenly looked frightened. It made me wonder again about those tokens she had sent to London. Had they really been intended for a lover, or for someone else? Even if she were naively and innocently acting as a messenger for someone conspiring against the King, her youth would not save her from the scaffold. It was rumoured King James had even had a cat hanged for treason in Scotland.

'There are no plots,' Katheryne declared, 'except against me. I told you, they want to send me to a convent in Brussels. That is the plot.'

But she had said they had orders to move *him* – could this man possibly be Spero Pettingar? Yet if Katheryne was to be believed, the orders had not been intended for Smith, so if it was Pettingar, then Smith was not the one shielding him. The messenger who'd been murdered had passed through Bristol. The two priests had been landed in a port on the west of England and were probably still being hidden there. Waldegrave could even now be forging the documents they needed to travel, or the papers that would be needed to move this unknown man.

'The blood trail that woodward Crowhurst was following . . .' I said. 'Why does Lady Magdalen think it might be a wounded man?'

She shrugged impatiently. 'Father Cobbe got caught in a trap, didn't he? Maybe she thinks someone else did.'

'Are they expecting someone else to arrive here, then?'

Her chin jerked up. 'I won't tell you anything more, unless you tell me what you learned from the tanner. A bargain is a bargain,' she mimicked.

'And I will keep my side of it,' I said. 'Bethia never delivered that last token to the tanner. He is sure of that, and nothing was left at the Wrestler for him to bring back.' I wanted Katheryne to be certain I had spoken to Tiploft. If this was more than an innocent exchange of lovers' messages, she had to realise that I had knowledge I could use if I chose. I needed her to trust me, if I was to learn more. Though I did not begin to trust her.

Her eyes had widened in alarm. 'Then, he never received the message . . . he doesn't know . . . he isn't coming for me.' An expression of childlike hope suddenly blossomed on her face. 'But if Tiploft took Bethia to London, she will have kept the comb to deliver herself. So, he may have already set out. He could even be here in Battle.'

'Your maid did not ride with the tanner to London, nor anywhere else. He hasn't seen her. It seems your guardian spoke the truth when she said Bethia ran off; perhaps she too was in love.' *Or more likely, she became alarmed by whatever she thought she was becoming mixed up in.*

'But she didn't! Look at this.' Katheryne fumbled in the little bag at her waist and pulled out a brooch in the form of a ship in full sail. She held it out in her palm. Even without handling it, I could see it was fashioned from cheap, base metal, not the kind of ornament any woman of Katheryne's rank would have worn.

'This is Bethia's.'

'How can you be sure? It looks like a fairing. I imagine half the lads in Battle have bought their womenfolk something like it.'

'Bethia always wore this when we went out. I'd know it anywhere. I saw one of the maids wearing it and asked her where she got it. At first, she said it was hers, but I knew it to be Bethia's, because I remember when she caught the edge of it and the top of the mast broke off, just there, you see . . . ? The girl finally admitted she'd found it pinned to Bethia's best cloak after she left. Bethia would have taken this with her if she'd planned to run off and she would never have left her good cloak behind. Father Smith must have sent her packing without even giving her time to collect up all her things.' She tucked the little brooch back in her bag.

'When someone is cast out of a great house in such haste,' I said, 'there is always a scene which at least one of the servants would have witnessed, and you can be sure every person in this manor and probably everyone in the town would know about it before nightfall.'

I could certainly testify to that. When George Fairfax had banished me from his hall when I was a youth, I swear there wasn't a man, woman or child in the place who hadn't watched from a doorway or casement as I was hurled out on to the road and the great gate was slammed against me.

'I think the mostly likely explanation is that Bethia gave this maid her cloak, a bribe to buy her silence, because the maid caught her packing. Maybe she even helped Bethia to steal away.'

Katheryne started to protest, but seemed suddenly deflated. 'Will you take—'

I knew what she was going to ask and held up my hand to cut her off, gesturing towards the door as if I could hear someone outside.

I motioned her to stand back where she could not be seen when I opened it, then I slipped out and hurried away. I had no intention of carrying any of her tokens even as far as the tanner's house, much less London.

Chapter Twenty-one

'FANCY SHARING A FLAGON OF Knucker's Milk with me?'
Arthur said.

'Or something warmer?' I replied. For once I didn't make
excuses. I suddenly longed to get out of the Abbey.

'That you, Pursglove?' a muffled voice sounded behind me.
'Hold hard, I want a word.'

I groaned. If that was a message to say I was to wait on the
gentlemen's chamber again in place of Erasmus, I'd find myself
sorely tempted to lock him in a hiding hole myself. I would have
pretended I hadn't heard, except that Arthur had already turned
round.

Yaxley came lumbering towards us. 'Lady Magdalen tells me
she gave orders for you to be sent to Matthew's cottage with
vittles. I'd have taken them.'

'I imagine she thought as bailiff you had more important
things to attend to than running menial errands.'

Arthur grinned. 'Aye, if there's any shit to be shovelled, it's
us they send for. We pag whatever they want, to wherever they
want it pagging; same as pack mules, us.'

'You *will* be shovelling shit if you don't watch your tongue,
my lad.' Yaxley turned back to me. 'How's Matthew doing? Did
Alys say he was on the mend?'

'He was in bed when I saw him and he seemed cheerful
enough.' I didn't want to cause trouble for Alys, but my curiosity was growing. 'Did Crowhurst seem himself, to you? I mean
the same man as he was before?'

Yaxley grimaced, seeming to consider it. 'Took a fair bit
out of him, spending a night and best part of two days out in

that cold. It'll probably be a while before he's back to his usual churlish self.'

That might well be so, but broken noses don't suddenly straighten themselves after one night in the cold. Not unless he'd been bathing in that holy well.

'What was that about?' Arthur asked, as we walked away.

'Do you know Matthew Crowhurst?'

'Can't say that I do. Don't have much to do with any of the woodwards. They've rarely any cause to come to the Abbey and I don't go wandering about the forest.' He gave a mock shiver. 'Can't see the attraction myself, always something lying in wait to sting, scratch or bite you. Now if the good Lord had created a tree that sprouted mutton pies instead of leaves or a bush that blossomed with gold coins, I'd willingly go for a woodland stroll. He should have had me to advise Him when He was creating them. I'd have told Him what was needed.'

'Do you remember Lady Katheryne's maid, Bethia?'

'Aye, that I do.' He gave a leery grin. 'Buxom wench, she was. Bubbies as big as plum puddings and twice as sweet. Not that I got to taste her wares. They say there's plenty that did, though. But she wouldn't give away her favours for nought, and she'd not look twice at a short-arsed clown like me.' He tweaked his own bulbous and pitted nose.

'So, what happened to her?'

'Rumour is the old lady and that chaplain of hers didn't approve of her flirting and had her sent away.' He leaned in closer. 'But I don't reckon it was her having an eye for the lads that got her thrown out, more that she wasn't of the faith, if you get my meaning. So, I suppose they thought they couldn't trust her, what with the comings and goings in the house. They say the chaplain persuaded Lady Magdalen to pay her off with a good sum, more than good, enough to keep her mouth shut and go quietly. Esther says they found an old widower to marry her, which Bethia wouldn't have minded if he was wealthy enough and not likely to trouble her long in this life. It's what she'd always hankered after. And he'd die a happy man, that's for sure.'

'They must have thought she knew something if they paid her off like that, knew more than the rest of us. Do you reckon she saw something, or someone?'

'Aye, well, most servants have other reasons to keep their mouths shut, as well you know, Dannet.' He gave me a sideways look and I wondered for the first time what had brought Arthur to the Abbey. He must have had some cause to need a place to hide, but though he'd clearly been raised a Catholic, I'd wager it wasn't a summons for recusancy that had brought him here. No one could accuse Arthur of being pious.

As we slipped into Sybil's alehouse, all heads swivelled towards us. I swiftly shut the door against the blast of cold air that entered with us. The parlour was full of men crammed on to the benches on either side of the long table, tankards of steaming mulled ale in front of them, but a swift glance nonetheless told me that these men had not retreated here for an evening of convivial drinking and gossip. They had loosened coats and capes, but they hadn't removed them, even though the great heap of logs burning on the hearth and the press of bodies had well warmed the little room. And stacked against the walls were not just a few sticks which the more aged or infirm men might need to walk on slippery paths, but all manner of staves, cudgels, pitchforks and threshing flails. It seemed every man in the room had come armed. While the expressions and tones of those who greeted us were not hostile, the tension was palpable.

Arthur nodded towards the stack of makeshift weapons. 'What's afoot, lads? Have those Spanish buggers invaded, or are you after some sport hunting Scotsmen tonight?'

A few men chuckled. Jacob, the stonemason, waggled the stem of a pipe at Arthur. 'Night-creeper, that's our quarry.' He took a long suck on the pipe and handed it to his neighbour, slowly blowing out a stream of black smoke before he continued.

'Been at it again. Getting worse it is. This morning, my wife's two sows were found dead in the knucker-hole.'

'Likely they'd gone to drink, slipped on the ice and fell in,' Arthur said.

'They were bedded down in their hog pound on account of the freeze and she'd melted water for them to drink their fill before she shut them in there. Someone or something had opened the door to that pen and driven them into that spring. Takes a sharp stick and a pail of swill to get those lazy sows moving, even on a fine morning; take a demon from hell to get them to shift from a warm pile of straw on a bleat night like the last.'

'It was the knucker that took them,' old Amor wheezed from his place next to the fire. 'That's what he do – slithers out from his hole in the dead of night and snatches hogs and sheep for his supper.'

Jacob gave the old man a withering look which was entirely wasted on him, since he was, as always, staring fixedly into the bright flames.

'There wasn't a bite or claw mark on my pigs. Died of drowning they did. So, unless that water-dragon of yours can open doors . . .'

Walter's mouth twisted into his lopsided smile of grim satisfaction. 'Just like I told you, it was a demon I saw, plain as day. Ten foot tall it was.'

'Grown, has he?' Arthur said, with a wink at me. 'I swear last time you said he was only eight foot tall.'

'Ten foot or twenty foot, makes no difference,' Jacob said firmly, waving an empty flagon at Sybil. 'Whatever the creature is, if he tries anything tonight, we'll be ready for him.'

The men continued to argue about the nature of the night-creeper and how best to catch it, while Sybil refilled the flagons with strong ale and the communal pipes with plugs of tobacco. They say ill blows the wind that profits no one. And though Sybil might have lost some of her hens to the night-creeper, she was certainly profiting by him that night.

A little before ten of the clock, when the Abbey gate would be locked, Arthur and I began fastening our cloaks and steeling ourselves for the shock of the cold after the warm fug of the smoky ale room, but we hadn't even got as far as the door when we heard a sound that made every man around that table freeze in mid-act. The demonic howl and wild shriek cut through the babble of voices like an axe blade through flesh. There was a great banging, as if iron pots were being clattered together. For a moment, I thought it was another skimmington, like that awful one I had witnessed in Bristol, when the mob had surrounded the house of the Catholic cordwainer and his family, pounding on the walls, door and shutters with staves, billhooks and iron bars, howling for their blood.

Everyone, except old Amor in the corner, sprang up, scrambling for the makeshift weapons they'd stacked against the walls. Several had imbibed too much of the strong mulled ale. All tried to crowd out through the small doorway at once, jamming themselves into the narrow gap, so that it was a few moments before one person could wriggle free and burst out. The rest followed, exploding into the street beyond. I hurried out after Arthur. Outside, the men were staring up and down the length of the road. For several minutes we could hear nothing except a babble of questions.

'In the Devil's name, what was that?'

The frightened faces of women and children peered anxiously from the casements in the cottages along the streets. A few of the men had stopped to light torches at Sybil's hearth and now came hurrying out with them, the flames casting a flickering red and orange glow over the knot of men, their faces tense with cold and fear.

Some of the men were arguing about where the sound had come from, while others tried to hush them to listen, then just as we were all beginning to think we must have mistaken the sound, there came another piercing shriek, like a giant bird of prey, that seemed to set the cold stars trembling in the darkness above us.

'That way. It came from down there!'

The men turned as one and hurried down the street. Arthur and I followed, though I kept to the back of the group, not for fear of what lay ahead, but seeking to preserve my own limbs. Many of the men, already unsteady on their feet, were flailing their arms as they struggled to keep their balance on the ice-covered road, and their scythes and burning torches were swinging so wildly that they were in danger of slicing off each other's ears or setting fire to anyone who was within range.

'There! See it!'

The men in front stopped so suddenly that those behind smashed into them, cursing and shouting. But soon all had fallen silent and were staring ahead. A figure was standing on the sloping roof of a low wooden outbuilding, a workshop of sorts, which had been errected against the stone wall of the yard. The creature was dark against the stars, like a hole cut out of the sable sky, a giant bird with two ragged wings and a long, curved beak. It stood swaying, turning its head to stare at us. Neither the men from the alehouse nor the beast on the roof moved. The only sound came from the rasping breaths of the men, panting white clouds of mist into the frosted night air.

'Get him, before he flies off,' Jacob growled.

He lumbered towards the workshop, his cudgel raised. After a moment or two of hesitation, the others suddenly surged forward. The creature shrieked, though this time the cry seemed to be one of alarm. It moved awkwardly across the frozen roof towards the higher, more steeply raked, roof of the cottage, which stood a few yards away across the yard. The men yelled out, thinking it was about to flap its wings and fly across the gap, but whatever it was, it made no attempt to launch itself.

'Come on!' someone yelled. 'We've got it trapped.'

The men rushed forward, several slipping and crashing down heavily on the ice. That seemed to sober them, for as they drew closer, they began to move more cautiously, clearly unsure how to tackle the creature. The workshop roof was low, but it was still several inches above the heads of the tallest man in the group and the beast had edged back to the centre of it. It seemed unlikely that any of the heavy weapons would be able to reach it, and even if they were thrown, at that angle they would simply clatter away without touching it.

The great bird was crouching as if preparing to spring down, talons and beak ready to rip at throats, faces, eyes. Those at the front of the group hastily drew back.

'Give us that,' Jacob demanded, snatching a torch from the nearest bearer. He hurled it towards the beast, the flames arcing scarlet and yellow through the dark sky, but the creature saw it coming and leaped aside. The torch clattered on to the roof. The flames shot upwards before the creature kicked it off and it plunged down, scattering men. For the first time, the beast's motion looked all too human, and suddenly everyone seemed to recognise that whatever was up there, demon or revenant, was more man than bird.

Jacob darted forward and snatched up the torch again, waving it above his head like a solider lifting the colours to rally his comrades. 'Set fire to the hut! Burn it.' He ran forward and held the torch against the tarred wooded wall until a streak of bright orange flame darted up the wood. The fire had caught. The men cheered and those who carried torches rushed to lay theirs against the wooden walls on the three sides they could reach.

Flames licked up the walls of the workshop and a thick curtain of acrid black smoke from the burning tarred timbers rose into the night sky. I could see little of the roof now, except glimpses of the figure lit by the hell-red glow of the flames, looking more like a ghost or a demon than ever. It seemed to dissolve and reform in a thousand different shapes before our eyes as the smoke twisted over it.

A scream came from behind us. We all whirled around. The door to the cottage had burst open and a woman stood in the doorway, shrieking in alarm as she watched the hut burn. Her husband pushed past her and came rushing out in a nightshirt, clutching an iron poker as if he meant to stoke the blaze.

'My workshop! My tools!' he bellowed. 'All my stock. What have you done?' He stared at the blaze in horror, then turned on the nearest person, who happened to be Walter. 'You beef-witted scuts. You boiled-brained maggots!' He swung the poker at him.

Walter only avoided having his skull cracked open by ducking smartly. But the poker caught him a savage blow across his shoulder, and he fell to his knees with a howl of pain. The man raised the weapon again and probably would have pounded Walter's head to a pulp had not several of the group leaped on him and wrested the poker from his hand. The woman had stopped screaming and had run barefoot across the frozen yard to fill a pail in the nearby trough. But the water was frozen solid. She tried in vain to smash it, but she may as well have tried to get milk from a stone. She hurled the pail down in frustration and turned to face the men. In the light of the leaping flames, tears glittered in her eyes and shone wet on her cheeks.

'Why?' she asked helplessly. 'Why would you do such a thing? What have we ever done to harm you?'

'The night-creeper, Goodwife Kemp,' Jacob said. 'That's who's the cause of this mischief. Tormented the whole town, it has, but we got it now, see!' He swung his arm round in triumph, pointing to the roof of the workshop as the flames and smoke billowed up around. He gaped. The roof was empty. The night-creeper had vanished.

Chapter Twenty-two

SHADOWS

I HEAR VOICES. The stones carry the sound, like the claws of mice scrambling behind the panels, and the rasp of rats' teeth on the beams; louder and louder, closer and closer they come. The rats shriek and scream as they fight, kill each other, desperate for food. They multiply. Will they break through into my cell? Will they swarm all over me, gnaw at my hair, my face, biting through sinew, stripping flesh from bones? When the shadow of the raven comes to lead me out, will he find nothing but a heap of dry bones?

Et dixit ad me fili hominis putasne vivent ossa ista?

And he said to me: son of man, dost thou think these bones shall live?

I hear voices, but not words, like the tapping of the death-watch beetle as it burrows through the timbers, ticking away the minutes through the darkness, through days and nights that are always darkness. The deathwatch clock that never reaches the hour, never chimes the dawn, never tells the day of my release. Am I already dead? Lying in a grave hearing the living walking above me, walking over the earth mound, not knowing I am beneath them, listening.

The walls are whispering, muttering, plotting. I hear voices. Are they friend or foe? Are they the voices of those who bring me food, who hide me, or the voices of those who are searching for me? A thump, a bang, a shout, a grating of stone, a clang of metal, a clatter of footsteps echoing through the walls, and I fear they have come. They search, measure, tap, probe, rip, tear, expose until they find the catch, until the door slides open, until I am revealed.

It falls silent. But I am not fooled. The leopards are prowling around, waiting, watching until I can bear no more, until I emerge, and then they will pounce. That's what they do. They pretend they have gone. But they wait. Whisper and wait, until there is a sneeze, a cough that can no longer be suppressed, a leg that jerks in a violent spasm of cramp and thumps against the wall. They will wait until my eyes will not stay open for a single minute more, until my head lolls back, knocking against wood.

The deathwatch doesn't tell the hour; it only counts the heartbeats, tick, tick, tick, as I wait, as they wait, counting down to death.

Chapter Twenty-three

DANIEL PURSGLOVE

'But what exactly is alleged against this woman?'

A commotion instantly erupted in the courtroom, like a clamour of rooks startled from their nests, each voice rising to a shout as it tried to make itself heard over all of the others. The magistrate thumped on his desk and, in the resentful silence that followed, his gaze darted over the gaggle of men and women who circled the lone figure.

On the evening I had called upon the tanner at his lover's cottage, I had not glimpsed the woman herself, but from his sister's description of 'the baggage', I had assumed that Myrna would possess the kind of voluptuous charms that had seduced not only the mariner who was her husband, but many other men in Battle too. But the woman who stood trembling in the centre of that crowd was, at least at this moment, far from what I'd imagined.

Beneath the torn and charred shift, she looked slim, almost boyish in her proportions. Her head hung low and her long greying hair, which in months past had been dyed a startling brimstone yellow, hung loose and draggled. There was a livid scarlet sear across her forearm and her bare shoulder was red and badly blistered above the charred shift. She was shaking violently and rocking, probably more from the pain of her wounds than from the cold of the small magistrate's court. The magistrate and his recording clerk were seated by the fire, blocking any heat, and the rest of chamber, which had clearly not been used for some time, was as chilled as a crypt.

The magistrate leaned forward, searching for someone among those lining the walls, before finally pointing at Jacob. 'You, Goodman Dericote. You came knocking, demanding a hearing. You tell me of what crime you accuse Goodwife Nash.'

Jacob took a step forward. He looked as if he hadn't slept much and though he'd clearly put on his best clothes, the sticky tarry smoke was still etched into the creases of his face. Arthur too bore the traces of it still along his hairline. It took strong soap and lengthy scrubbing to rid yourself of it, as I had discovered.

'Myrna is the night-creeper that's been plaguing the town. Keeping us all awake at night, stealing chickens and scaring my pigs into drowning theirselves.'

A babble of voices rose again, some in support of Jacob, others indignantly proclaiming the woman's innocence. 'It was never her,' Arthur whispered beside me. 'Some of the other old cats in the town, maybe. Myrna wouldn't have the time; she's got her hands full most nights.' He sniggered, then tried to straighten his face as the magistrate rapped hard on the table.

'You will all be called to make your statements, but in the meantime, I will have silence. Otherwise, I will have you all wait outside and call you in one at a time to give testimony, and looking at the number of people here, most of you will be cooling your heels out there in the freezing cold for some hours.'

That had the effect he wanted: while the crowd looked sullen, they kept silent.

'If you make an accusation against your neighbour, you must have proof to offer, Goodman Dericote, otherwise she'd be within her rights to bring charges against you for slander.'

Those who had been protesting Myrna's innocence nodded smugly at each other.

That seemed to unnerve Jacob a little. He glanced warily at the clerk, who had dipped his quill in readiness and, in spite of his youth, was regarding Jacob in the manner of a schoolmaster waiting for the correct answer from a backward pupil.

'Proof – there's proof for all to see, sir. Those burns! We cornered the night-creeper on the roof of Goodman Kemp's workshop and tried to smoke it down. But the building caught alight and the creature was trapped on the roof among the flames.'

'Creature? Master Dericote. I thought you were claiming Goodwife Nash is the night-creeper.'

'That she is, sir. She can turn herself into a huge black bird with a savage beak and great talons and in that guise performs her mischief. Then, come dawn, she turns herself back into human form again. There was an old woman over in Wartling used to turned herself into a cat each night and suck her neighbours' cows dry of milk. Farmer laid a trap in his field, and caught the cat by its foot, but when he went to release it and kill it, she scratched him and got away. Next day, everyone in the whole village saw the old woman limping badly. She'd tried to hide it, but her foot was all bloody, just like the cat. So, they knew her for a witch.'

'And what does this have to do with the events of last night?' the magistrate said coldly.

'The night-creeper was up on the roof among all the flames, and then it vanished before our very eyes, flapped away, it did, on great black wings, but see, it had to fly through the flames, so it must have scorched its wings. Look there!' He pointed at Myrna, with the exaggerated drama of a bad actor. 'She's burned on her arm; that proves she was up on that roof.'

The magistrate leaned forward and rapped the clerk sitting in front of him smartly on the shoulder, making the young man splatter the ink across the desk. 'This is important testimony. Have you diligently recorded his every word?'

The clerk was hastily sprinkling sand on the ink blots. 'I did, sir. Yes, sir. Shall I read it to you, sir?'

But the magistrate had already turned his attention back to Jacob.

'Now let us be very clear, Goodman Dericote. Am I to understand that you are accusing Goodwife Nash of being . . . a witch?'

There was a sharp intake of collective breath. Myrna moaned and sank to the floor. Clutching her head in her uninjured arm, she rocked back and forth.

An icy fist gripped my bowels. Barely a year had passed since I had found myself where this woman was now, accused of sorcery for no other reason than that I earned my living performing sleight-of-hand tricks to amuse the crowd. If I had been clumsier, my tricks less skilful, they would have seen them at once for what they were, but a cross that turns by itself, a bird that burns then flies away, that they could not explain, so it must be witchcraft. I knew only too well what this poor wretch was facing. Even Jacob seemed suddenly to understand the enormity of what he had begun, for his eyes widened and he stared wildly at the crowd like a deer brought to bay by hounds.

'Well, Dericote,' the magistrate snapped. 'Is that the charge you are bringing against Myrna Nash?'

'I . . . I didn't mean . . . not a witch . . . not that.'

'Then what precisely did you mean? It seems to me that if a woman can transform herself into a bird and fly about the town causing mischief and harm, she could only do this by means of the dark arts of magic and that would condemn her as a witch.'

Myrna's hand clenched as if she were fighting desperately to lift herself out of the mire of pain and shock. 'No, no!' She struggled to rise, then sank back to the floor. 'My cottage . . . someone threw a burning brand through the casement when I was abed . . . There was a blaze . . . curtains round my bed caught . . . but I pulled them down . . . put it out.' She lifted her right hand, which was red and swollen, so much so that she could not open her fingers. 'Burned myself on the drapes. Threw them in the yard. You can see . . . see they're black and charred.'

'She burned them herself to cover for her wounds,' Tiploft's sister jeered.

'I am perfectly able to examine the accused myself, my good woman, without any prompting,' the magistrate said sternly, peering over his spectacles at her. 'And I warn you again, I will have you all wait outside if you interrupt once more.' He surveyed the courtroom. 'Did any among you see the brand being thrown or witness Goodwife Nash's attempt to extinguish this blaze?'

In the silence that followed you could hear the crackle of wood burning on the hearth.

'Goodwife Nash, did you see who threw the brand?'

'I was asleep, sir.'

'Then do you know who might have done such a wicked thing to you?' When Myrna did not reply, the magistrate raised his head and looked at the crowd. '*If* this woman speaks the truth, does anyone know why someone might have cause to try to set fire to her cottage?'

'Only half the wives in Battle,' someone muttered and there was a ripple of laughter.

If he heard it, the magistrate chose to ignore it.

'Since no one can corroborate her account of how she came by her injuries, I must ask if anyone in this courtroom, besides Dericote, actually saw this creature you call the night-creeper on the roof of the workshop, or indeed at any time earlier in the evening when the disturbance began?'

All the men who had been in Sybil's ale-room raised their hands, including me, but before the magistrate could call anyone forward, Myrna staggered to her feet and stumbled towards the clerk's table, gripping the edge with her good hand for support as she cradled her burned arm beneath her breasts.

'Maybe there's no one who saw the brand thrown, sir . . . but there's one who knows for certain I'm not the night-creeper. He was with me when the howling began, and we heard the clatter of men running past and saw the torches. That's when he left, sir . . . case there was trouble.'

'And the name of this man who you claim was with you?'

Myrna looked across at the crowd of men, as if she expected one of them to step forward. The women in the group also looked towards the menfolk, searching their husbands' faces for signs of guilt. The men had all adopted nonchalant expressions of innocence, though it was plain that one of them must be feigning.

I glanced at Tiploft. He was engrossed in studying a slip of paper, frowning as if it was of great importance. His sister was studiously not looking at him. Either she knew something or she suspected, but did not want it proclaimed in front of the whole courtroom.

'So, Goodwife Nash, it seems that no one is willing to confirm this tale of yours. You leave me no choice but to send you to be questioned—'

'Forgive my interruption, sir.' I stepped forward, making a formal bow.

I should not get involved. This is not my fight . . . not my fight.

The magistrate glanced up, irritation written large on his face, but my courtly bow seemed to arrest his curiosity. 'And who might you be?'

'Daniel Pursglove, sir, in service at the Abbey.'

'And are you the man the accused claims to have kept company with last evening?'

Several of the men nudged each other, grinning, while the women muttered behind their hands. Behind me, I heard Arthur's laugh.

'No, sir, but I believe I can save you the trouble of having this woman examined further. I was among those who ran after the night-creeper and saw it on top of the workshop. The night-creeper had the appearance of a bird, but I am convinced it was neither a bird nor a human transformed into an animal form. And whoever it was, it was not this woman.'

There were several jeers and shouts of protest. The magistrate held up his hand to silence them, but kept his attention fixed on me. 'And how can you be certain of that, Goodman Pursglove, unless you know who it was? Do you? The truth now, for I shall have you swear a statement under oath.'

'I do not know who or what it was . . .' I saw the satisfied looks and nods exchanged among Myrna's accusers. 'But I will swear on oath to this – when the workshop was set alight, it could only be done on three sides, because the fourth backs on to a stone wall. The night-creeper had only to jump, not fly from the roof, on the fourth side, and that it did, under cover of the thick smoke. So, its wings or arms would not have been burned. If it was burned at all, it would have been on the feet and legs, for when it was on top of the roof, the flames were burning up the wooden walls and rose no higher than its knees. That burn' – I pointed to Myrna's shoulder, 'was made by something hot falling down from above, as she says, most likely the burning bed hanging or the brand that was thrown in.'

'None of us saw the moment she vanished; flames could have licked her if she fell,' Jacob said stubbornly.

'What say you to that?' The magistrate looked genuinely curious.

'Indeed, they could have, but not the flames from that burning workshop. Sir, look at Jacob's face and at the faces of the other men who were there last night.'

The magistrate beckoned to Jacob. 'Come closer. The light is poor.'

Jacob reluctantly shuffled towards his table and stood awkwardly as he was inspected, as if he feared he might have sprouted horns or fur without knowing it.

'What am I supposed to see, Goodman Pursglove?'

'The wooden walls of the workshop had been coated with tar and Jacob's face still bears traces of the tarry smoke, as does every man who was there.' I indicated Arthur. 'He scrubbed his face with good soap, as did I, but his hair-line is black with it. It sticks like glue.'

Arthur rubbed vigorously at his scalp, glaring furiously at me.

'And your point is?'

'My point, sir, is that if this woman had been on that roof, the tar in that smoke would have stuck to her too. More so to her than to us, since she would have been in the thick of it.'

The magistrate plucked at his lip, considering the matter. 'She could have washed it off as you did.'

'But not from her burns. The tar would have been driven deep into them. She would have been in agony had she tried to scrub those burns as vigorously as it would take to remove tar from them, and the blisters on her skin are for the most part unbroken.'

He beckoned to Myrna. She looked terrified and her legs buckled beneath her as she tried to walk the few paces from the clerk's table towards his. I caught her by the waist and steadied her, supporting her as she crossed. 'Courage,' I whispered.

The magistrate seized her injured arm and dragged it towards him till it was outstretched. She gasped in pain. Holding her limb close to the candle on his desk, he peered at the wounds for what seemed like an age. Then he released her so suddenly she crumpled again to the floor.

'Are you a lawyer, Pursglove?'

'A servant, sir.

He grunted. 'You reason like a lawyer, and you know what they say: "a good lawyer makes a bad neighbour". And in my experience, a dangerous servant too. I shall warn Lady Magdalen about you.' He glowered at me, then addressed the gathering.

'There's not enough evidence to bring a charge against this woman or send her for trial at the assizes. She is at liberty to return to her home. And I give orders that no one is to trouble or vex her there. See to it, Petty Constable.'

He gestured to the clerk, who added a final word and, with a flourish, began to gather up his papers. As if a sluice gate had been opened, a torrent of furious and indignant chatter burst out.

Goodman Kemp pushed his way through the men and strode up to the magistrate's table, ignoring the constable's attempts to help Myrna to her feet. 'And who's going to pay for my workshop and the tools and leather?' he demanded furiously. He jabbed his finger towards Jacob and the men gathered around him. 'They burned it to the ground.'

His wife stepped out beside him. 'How's he supposed to earn a living now? We'll starve and be put out of our cottage. End up living on the parish. They should pay.' She jerked her head towards Jacob.

'The night-creeper was on their roof making mischief,' Jacob protested, looking thoroughly insulted. 'The beast would likely have destroyed his workshop, if we hadn't stopped it.'

'You *didn't* stop it!' Kemp yelled. 'And my workshop *was* destroyed . . . by you!'

The magistrate sighed loudly. This was going to be a long sitting for him and his long-suffering clerk. I slipped out and made my way back up the path towards the house. Arthur hurried up beside me.

'You know what you've done, don't you? Set half the town against you, that's what. Dericote and his cronies are not going to forget this in a hurry. You made them look proper fools. They'll be out for revenge. What's Myrna to you anyway? You've not been sampling her wares, have you?'

'I don't like injustice,' I snapped. 'And they *are* fools if they really believe she's the night-creeper.'

'If you're so sure she's innocent, then it's likely the night-creeper will go on the prowl again, and if it had when she was safely chained up in gaol, it would have proved that she'd not done it, so they'd have had to let her go. Now if that great bird or whatever it is swoops down tonight, they'll be blaming her again. Not a good move of yours, was it?'

'Even if she was chained to the wall in a witch's bridle, Tiploft's sister and those other harpies would have claimed the night-creeper was a demon she'd summoned and sent against them.'

Waldegrave's words echoed in my head: when a witch is arrested, her interrogators are so convinced that her imp will come to her that a shadow darting across the wall of her cell is enough to convince them that they have seen what was never there and does not exist. Waldegrave and I both knew how the minds of the King's interrogators reasoned. Whether you were accused of treason or sorcery, even the proofs of your innocence could be twisted by those determined to prove you guilty into a hangman's noose.

'Myrna's got reason enough to hold a grudge against half the town, the way they gossip about her,' Arthur said. 'So, suppose she did summon that demon bird to do her bidding, like you say. Then your proof about her not being burned on the roof is worth no more than a flea's turd, have you thought of that, Dannet?'

'I think the men she entertained might have noticed her summoning a demon while they were in her bed, or are you going to claim she enchanted them as well?' Seeing from the expression on Arthur's face that he was considering this as a serious possibility, I continued hastily. 'Besides, innocent or not, Myrna wouldn't survive a week in a freezing cell in this weather, especially with those wounds, so it would be a death sentence before she was ever brought to trial.'

'Better hers than yours. 'Cause I'll tell you another thing, Dannet: whether or not the magistrate tells Lady Magdalen what you did in there, word will get back to her, it always does, and to Smith too. He doesn't like having any bastard around who's cleverer than him. Makes him nervous, and what he says goes in this household now. You best keep low and out of sight, else you'll be finding yourself freezing your cods in a ditch or lying dead in some pit.'

'Like that pursuivant, Benet?' I asked.

He stopped in mid-stride and stared at me. 'He jumped in there. Guilt, most likely, that he was about to condemn a kind old lady. Couldn't bring himself to do it.'

'Then why not simply walk away and keep quiet?'

Arthur's expression had grown savage. 'That bastard Cecil probably had some hold on him, threatening him or his family. You must know the jade's tricks that man uses. He promises to spare your life or your kin if you deliver him someone else in return. A life for a life, except Cecil demands three lives for your one, a dozen even, and then the lying toad doesn't keep his part of the bargain.'

I was startled by the anger and bitterness in his tone. He'd never seemed to take anything seriously before, except his flagon of Knucker's Milk.

'Cecil arrested someone you cared for?'

He stared off at the frosted black bones of the distant trees, glittering in the pale winter sun. 'A woman I loved, and her brother and parents too. It was the brother Cecil really wanted. There was talk he'd been a friend of Guy Fawkes, maybe mixed up in the plot somehow. My Helen knew nothing of that, or of her brother's friends, but they took her just the same. It was an old priest who delivered their names. I don't know what Cecil gave him in return, maybe just the chance to save his own miserable hide, maybe a good deal more. They say that little ferret has a clutch of tame priests he's turned. There's ordinary Catholics risking their lives to protect the clergy and pleading with the priests to hear their confessions, and all the time those holy men are feeding back every word to that black-hearted knave. I'd herd the lot into gibbet cages and hang them as high as I could in yonder trees to starve to death. Let the night-creeper feast on them. Now if Myrna could conjure the demon to do that, I'd be defending her myself, louder than any man in this town.'

Chapter Twenty-four

THE SHARP RETORT woke me instantly and I found myself on my feet and crouching low before I was fully awake. For a moment I thought I was back on the battlefield in Ireland, until my senses kicked in and I realised I was in the darkened hallway of the house. There was a second bang, louder even than the first, and the door to the gentlemen's chamber was flung open. Holt staggered out, stumbling as if he'd been shot, but he was only dizzy from waking so suddenly.

'What's happening? Are we being raided?'

'No, Master Holt, all is well,' I said soothingly, steering him back through the door. 'It is only more trees exploding in the frost.'

Most nights since the freeze began, we'd heard the sharp cracks and booms in the silence as distant trees burst and great branches sheared off, but it was tearing the nerves of the priests to shreds. Holt, suddenly aware that he was standing barefoot in a freezing passageway clad only in a nightshirt, shivered violently as I ushered him back to his bed. Santi too had struggled out of bed and was standing by the window, peering out anxiously. Bray had slept through both the noise and the alarm of his brothers, and was still snoring peacefully: I suspected that the quantity of wine he had drunk the evening before had sent him so solidly asleep that not even cannon fire would have roused him. But I didn't blame him for that; without it, the horrors of prison come creeping back like tormenting bedbugs in the darkness.

I lay down again in the corridor and burrowed back beneath my cold blanket to snatch a few more hours of sleep. But I couldn't get warm. I turned over, wrapping the blanket tighter. A pale flash in the darkness caught my eye. Someone was creeping softly down the staircase at the far end of the passageway. I could see nothing of them, only the tiny distant candle flame as the figure descended, and then I caught a muffled clang and a dull thump of wood knocked against wood.

I rose as quietly as I could and, with the blanket still swathed around me, I edged along the passageway, carefully avoiding the places where I knew the boards squeaked. But by the time I reached the staircase, whoever had been descending them had passed out of sight around the bend, leaving only the momentary ghost-glow of the light they carried, until that too was swallowed up by the darkness. But something else still lingered, the unmistakable stench of a shit pail. I'd emptied enough of those this past month to recognise that particular fragrance anywhere. No one would empty a piss pail in the middle of the night, especially in this freeze, unless . . . unless it came from the chamber of someone whose presence in the house was being kept a secret even from loyal servants.

EACH NEW DAWN seemed to bring a greater intensity of cold. We woke stiff and aching from a restless night, in spite of heaping all the blankets and cloaks we could beg, borrow or steal on our pallets. Although a fire burned in every hearth, by daybreak the inside of the casements was covered in a layer of thick frost, delicately patterned as if silver fern leaves had been pressed against the glass panes. Pails of ice had to be thawed each evening and set around the fires all night, to keep them from freezing again, otherwise it was mid-morning before anyone could melt ice enough to wash themselves, much less water the horses, dogs and livestock. For even the water in the holy well, which never froze, had frozen.

Erasmus had set me the task of raking out the ashes from the priests' chamber and taking them outside to cool and store, ready for the laundry women to make their washing lye. It was dirty, dusty work, but at least the embers were warm, which is more than I could say for Erasmus's manner towards me. It had grown, if anything, even more frigid and imperious. Although I had rescued him from the hiding place where Smith had imprisoned him, he was plainly mortified that I had been witness to his fear and wretched state when he emerged, and I seemed to be a constant reminder of his humiliation. He was trying to punish me for it by giving me all the worst tasks he could think of. It certainly wasn't the first time in my life that men had tried that, but I'd always found a way of getting my own back. In this case though, I knew I could not retaliate, at least not yet. Arthur was right: Smith was watching for the smallest excuse to get rid of me.

I stepped out into the courtyard and could not resist glancing up at the casements on the upper floor. I'd spent what remained of the night thinking about that nocturnal shit pail and wondering if this hidden man was the secret that Benet had discovered, the information that might finally persuade the Privy Council to issue a warrant to have the Abbey raided. But they already knew priests were being hidden here. Whatever Benet had discovered had to be something more than that.

I was certain whoever they were hiding was not concealed in the library. There might well be half a dozen priest holes in there, some real, some decoys, but that baked gammon I'd smelled the first night I'd ventured on to the forbidden floor had been carried past the library door. Curiosity was, as always, tormenting me, like a madding itch I couldn't scratch, but I knew it would be futile to search that whole top floor for him. If he was lying low in a hiding place, I could search all day and all night for a week and not find it. A dozen leopards might hunt for days to uncover a well-concealed hole, and they could rip off panelling, prise up floorboards and smash through plaster and stone. I could barely risk a gentle tapping. And even if I did uncover his hiding place, of one thing I was quite certain: once I'd seen his face, I'd never be allowed to leave Battle alive. But they couldn't keep anyone hidden for ever; sooner or later, a rat must emerge from its hole.

Still preoccupied, I pulled my muffler up over my nose, and was trudging across the yard with the pail of ash when a rattle of furious yelps jerked me out of my thoughts. A scrawny dog was darting in and out of the archway, barking furiously, which had in turn set off all the other dogs in the Abbey, first those in the stables, then, like a gathering wave, the hunting hounds in the kennels beyond, whose yaps and howls carried on the frozen air as far as the outlying cottages, rousing their dogs to join the canine chorus. I thought at first the dog in the courtyard was a stray, desperate for food or warmth, but I saw that it was running back and forth between the archway and a group of four men, gingerly picking their way between the granite-hard cart ruts. Two of the men were carrying a willow hurdle with a long bundle covered in sacking lashed to it. The other two walked either side, steadying the hurdle each time the bearers slipped and stumbled, so that whatever lay on it wouldn't crash to the ground.

The steward came bustling out, alerted by the barking, and directed the men towards the empty laundry room in the court-yard. Two trestles had already been set up inside to receive the hurdle. The men laid their burden down upon them and stood back, glancing at each other and at the steward, until he pressed a coin into the hand of each man. Then, whistling to their dog, they trudged wordlessly out beneath the archway and back down the track.

'Have you no work to occupy yourselves?' Brathwayt snapped at the curious stable lads. 'If not, I can find you enough to keep you hard at it till midnight,' he warned, and the boys vanished like rabbits diving down burrows.

The steward gave a grimly satisfied nod, then beckoned to me. 'You! Pursglove! I warrant you've a strong enough stomach. Stop whatever you're doing and give me a hand.' As I stepped into the laundry, he nodded grimly. 'Close the door. If one of the young maids chances by and glances in, she'll start caterwauling and that'll set them all off.'

I pushed the door closed. Brathwayt lit a lamp from one of the fires in the stone pits that had been left banked down in preparation for boiling the laundry water. A yellow glow lapped around the room.

Brathwayt nodded grimly. 'Better take a look at what they found.'

But I already knew what was under the sacks. I recognised the shape only too well; I'd seen more corpses in my life than any sexton.

The cords strapping the body to the willow hurdle had frozen, and the smouldering laundry fires held their heat tight to themselves like misers. So, it took several minutes before we could loosen the knots. The steward motioned me to move aside, while he pulled the sack from the head and shoulders of the body.

There was no doubt the man was dead, yet he lay on his side curled up as if he were asleep. Crystals of ice glittered on his hair and in the thick black beard. I was standing at the bottom of the hurdle and in the feeble lamplight could see little of his face except a cheek and forehead. They were so pale beneath his weather-beaten tan it seemed as if a brown pigment had been painted on to a white marble statue. His shirt, what little I could see of it, was frozen to his body. No sane man would wander about clad only in a shirt in this bitter weather, even in his own house. It was little wonder he'd perished. But as Brathwayt moved the lamp across him, I saw something that made me start. I only glimpsed it for a moment; I couldn't be certain. It was probably just a trick of the flickering light.

'We should remove the rest of the sacking,' I said. 'He may have wounds.' I stepped closer, reaching out to seize the covering, but the steward gestured irritably for me to stand back.

'What's the point? Even if he was injured, bandages and physic are hardly going to bring him back to life now.'

Footsteps crunched across the yard outside and the door was jerked open, almost flattening me behind it. Richard Smith and Henry Holt bustled in, closing the door behind them. Their gloved hands snaked out from beneath heavy cloaks, as each made the sign of the cross before swiftly darting back beneath the folds.

Smith took a few paces towards the head of the corpse and stood looking down. 'Who found him?'

'Lad from the town out collecting firewood. Found the body when he went into one of the old charcoal burners' huts in the woods. They've not been used in years. He said he went in to get warm, though more likely he meant to wrench out some poles and take them home to burn. Save him the trouble of searching for fallen branches.' Brathwayt gestured towards the corpse. 'No knowing how long he's lain in there. Could be hours or days. This cold would keep a man's body fresh as a new-laid egg for weeks.'

The door crashed open again and the bailiff lumbered in, breathing hard, his breath billowing out in white puffs.

'Heard they found a corpse in the shaw,' he wheezed.

'They did,' Brathwayt said. 'Master Smith thought it best to bring him straight in here, until—' At a sharp cough from Smith, the steward stumbled in silence.

Smith bent and peered more closely at the face. 'Do you recognise him, Master Brathwayt?'

The steward shook his head. Smith gestured to Yaxley, who shuffled forward and peered at him as Brathwayt held the lantern closer. The bailiff straightened up. 'Don't reckon he's from these parts. Look at his shirt. Poor stuff it is and filthy. Been sleeping rough. Mostly likely he's a vagabond who came abegging this way and took shelter against the cold.'

'He might as well have slept in a ditch for all the protection those old burners' huts would give now,' Brathwayt said. 'They should have been cleared away long ago,' he added, glaring pointedly at Yaxley, who he clearly considered had failed in his duties.

'There were left on the Viscount's orders, to give shelter when the men are hunting.'

'Then they should have been kept in good order,' the steward retorted. 'They could collapse in a puff of wind. And suppose Lady Magdalen or one of her guests were out walking and went inside to take shelter from the rain—'

Holt swiftly intervened, his gloved hands fluttering out from the warmth of his cloak in a gesture of conciliation. 'I'm sure Master Yaxley will give his orders as soon as the weather is clement enough to commence such work. But it is this unfortunate man's soul that should concern us now, isn't that so, Father Smith?'

Smith looked down at the corpse with an expression of mild disgust, as if it was a headless sparrow brought in by the cat. 'Without knowing who he was, we cannot know if he was a Catholic or indeed what manner of man he was.'

'But if he was sheltering so far off the highway on manor land, Father Smith, rather than in the town, it would appear he was making his way to the Abbey to seek alms or even . . . *sanctuary*.' Holt's voice dropped to a reverent whisper on the word. 'Lady Magdalen's reputation for piety and compassion makes it likely that he came here because he was of the true faith.'

'Or he was being paid to keep watch on the Abbey,' Smith snapped, staring down again at the man's shirt. 'He could easily be another pursuivant, or at least working for such a man. Have you considered that, Father Holt?'

'In that case, he is in even greater need of our prayers if he has gone to his judgement with such a sin upon his soul,' Holt countered stubbornly.

Smith's head jerked up and he glared at Holt. 'Then he deserves damnation. You know full well, Father, that the prayers of the whole Catholic Church will not spare a man so much as an hour of suffering, unless he truly repents. And I can assure you, pursuivants are so blinded by heresy and greed that even when they stand before the gates of hell, they will still be claiming they did God's work.'

Holt bowed his head, his eyes lowered towards the corpse. 'As you rightly say, Father, if he is a heretic, our prayers will not help him,' he murmured, 'but nevertheless we are commanded to pray for our enemies. And if there is even a chance this man was a Catholic—'

'My time is too valuable to waste debating this further.' Smith's tone could have frozen the hottest fire in hell. 'Very well, then, if it will content you. But let us make haste.' He impatiently bunched up his cloak, preparing to use the folds to cushion his knees from the icy flags.

But I'd listened to enough prayers for the dead in my lifetime, prayers for men I knew as brothers, men who should not have died. 'Shall I seek out the petty constable in the town, Master Brathwayt, and have him send word to the coroner?'

All the men whipped round to stare at me. Smith's startled expression made me wonder if he'd even noticed me standing in the dark shadows behind the door. 'No,' he said sharply, recovering himself. 'It will not be necessary to trouble the coroner or the constable. I would not subject the coroner to such a hazardous and unnecessary journey in this weather. One that could very well prove fatal. There has been no foul play here. It is plain that this man simply died of hunger and cold as, I fear, many of the poor will before the thaw sets in. His was a natural death, no different from that of anyone who dies of old age or a fever. The coroner and jury cannot be called from their work to examine a corpse every time some passing vagrant happens to reach the end of their days.'

He knelt, motioning all of us down on to the cold flags, before reciting a rapid prayer for the man's soul. Then he clambered to his feet. 'It will be impossible for the gravediggers to do their work with the ground frozen so hard. We don't know how many days or indeed weeks it might be before he can be laid to rest, and if he is placed in the chapel there is a danger of putrefaction setting in, not to mention the distress it may cause to Lady Magdalen and her ward each time they enter to pray. I think it would best to store the body in one of the outbuildings well away from the house, where the cold will preserve him until he can be buried.'

'Just what I was going to propose myself, Master Smith,' Brathwayt said, dragging the sack back over the head and shoulders of the corpse.

The bailiff glowered at him, plainly still smarting from the jibe that he had neglected his duties. He addressed himself pointedly to Smith. 'There's a hut backs on to the church ruins, mostly used for storing scythes and such like for haymaking. It's cold as a crypt in there and no one has cause to go there this time of year.'

'Are you sure the roof and walls of this hut are sound?' Brathwayt asked. 'We don't want stray dogs or foxes feeding on him.'

'Solid as these walls, Master Brathwayt, and while I'm there I'd best fetch you back some rat traps. I hear the little devils have been making merry in your stores. It's a wonder you didn't see to it before, knowing they'd be driven indoors by this bleat weather.'

Brathwayt opened his mouth to retaliate, but Smith cut across him.

'Very well, Master Yaxley. I dare say you and Pursglove can manage to carry the body to this hut between you. And, Pursglove –' his gaze locked with mine – 'you will keep silent about this matter. I see no reason to distress Lady Magdalen or any of the other servants with this sad affair.' There was menace in his eyes, colder and harder even than the ground outside.

The two priests made the sign of the cross once more over the body, as if they were commanding it to remain dead, and hurried from the laundry, closely followed by the steward.

Yaxley eyed the corpse balefully. 'If Master Smith wants this kept quiet, we'd best shift it on a handcart along with a few tools or cords of wood. Else some idle scullion is bound to spot us carrying the body, and the news will be halfway round Battle faster than fleas jump. I'll fetch a cart. You best stay in here and stop anyone from coming in.'

The moment he had closed the door behind him, I moved swiftly to the head of the corpse and pulled the sack up, just far enough to expose the man's face. I lifted the lamp and crouched down. This time I was certain that what I was staring at was no illusion. The man's nose was bent, as if at some time in the past it had been broken and mended crookedly. I knew that face. I had seen it before, the night I'd come to Battle. This was the man whom Alys had first claimed was her husband and Sam's father. The man I'd known as Matthew Crowhurst.

The rumble of wheels outside jerked me into action and I had just enough time to pull the sack down and replace the lantern before the latch clicked down and the door swung open. I hurried forward to help drag the small handcart inside. Yaxley had already stacked a few tools on top with a piece of old sailcloth. Between us we hefted the frozen body on to the cart. Curled up as it was, it was awkward to load, but once there, its outline, covered with the sailcloth, was easily disguised by the tools and no one giving it a cursory glance would have guessed that the corpse of a man lay beneath.

Before the freeze, the courtyard would have been swarming with servants and stable lads finding some excuse to linger in the fresh air, but today not even the most hardy were venturing out. We were so heavily muffled up that if anyone from the house caught a glimpse of us trundling the cart across the yard, they would not recognise us from behind. That was just as well, for the sight of the bailiff and a Yeoman of the Chamber engaged on such a task together would have engendered more than simply curious stares.

The wooden shed on the other side of the roofless church had been built using a section of the church's ruined wall as its back and the ancient monastery flagstones for its base. The interior was dim and unlit, but the shaft of bright frosted light from the open door revealed walls and floor stacked with sickles, scythes, pitchforks, blades and many kinds of spades, their wooden shafts gleaming with oil and their blades thick with a coating of grease to keep them from rusting. The steward might have accused the bailiff of neglecting his duties, but he seemed diligent enough in overseeing this work at least.

With its flagstone floor and stone back wall, the hut felt colder inside than out. The body would probably stay frozen in here even longer than the earth in which it would eventually be buried.

There was no table or bench on which to lay the corpse, but Yaxley indicated the far corner where it was darkest. 'We should set it straight down on the flags, I reckon. They'll keep it chilled, and he'll not care what he's resting on.' He dragged aside a small fruit press, and as he came back to the cart, I positioned myself at the head of the corpse. As we lifted the body to carry it over to the corner, I used my arm to drag the sack up from his face as if by accident.

We laid it down and I crouched, as though I was intending to straighten the sack I'd dislodged. 'Master Yaxley, look! Isn't this Matthew Crowhurst?'

He came closer and peered down, though the light was so poor in that corner, it would have been hard to tell a rat from a rabbit.

'Nay, that's not Crowhurst.'

'Look again,' I urged. 'Step to this side so you're not blocking the light from the door.'

He did, but shook his head impatiently. 'I grant you there's a resemblance. Same thick black beard. Matthew looks like he's wearing a bear's pelt on his chin and on the rest of him too. And he's a bear's temper to match his hide.'

'Master Yaxley, I stayed the night in Crowhurst's cottage when I first came to Battle. I know it's him. I couldn't mistake that broken nose.'

'Matthew's nose is not broken, never has been. He's been my woodward for years. You think I wouldn't recognise his ugly face as well as I would my own? I'd wager it was well after dark when he came home the night you met him. Never comes home till the working day's been drained to its dregs, I'll give him that. And there'll have been naught but a single tallow burning in that cottage of theirs. If Alys had dared to light a second, even to do her weaving, he'd have flown into one of his rages about her wasting his hard-earned pennies. Been there myself of an evening, many a time, and know for a fact you wouldn't be able to recognise your own mother's face in that light.'

I wouldn't even be able to recognise my own mother's face in broad daylight.

Yaxley prodded the corpse with his boot. 'Hurry up now, cover it over. It's as cold as a witch's dugs in here. And mind you keep your mouth sealed. Master Smith meant it and he can be a hard man if you cross him.'

Chapter Twenty-five

I EASED OPEN THE DOOR to the courtyard, closing it behind me as silently but as swiftly as I could, for the blast of icy air that rushed into the passageway would alert anyone passing more forcefully than a clanging bell or barking dog. Though the casements were all shuttered for the night, and the ones in the servants' hall had even been stuffed with rags in an attempt to keep out every last sliver of draught, the occasional gale of laughter or angry shout still escaped, which made the silence in the courtyard all the deeper.

Torches burned on the walls, the yellow flames climbing almost straight up into the inky sky, as if they were altar candles, for there was scarcely a breath of wind. Under their light, the frost which gilded every stone or fallen leaf glittered gold. The straw and old sacks that had been scattered had frozen to the ground and were almost as treacherous as the ice they had been laid to cover. I crunched across. The hounds heard me, but gave only low yaps and huddled together deeper into the straw. They plainly had no intention of rising from what little warmth they had created beneath them.

I held the lantern I'd brought beneath my cloak, knowing that a moving light, however small, could easily be seen, but even after I'd left the courtyard, I needed no flame to light my way. Starlight and moonlight bathed the track beyond with sharp white light, throwing into relief the prints Yaxley and I had made earlier in the day and the snake lines of the handcart wheels. But there was another set of footprints, running in parallel. There was no snow on the ground and the impressions of the tracks in the frost were faint, but just to be sure, I planted my steps where the frost was already marked, so that I didn't leave another trail.

The door on the hut had frozen to the frame and it took a deal of pulling before it sprang open with a crack that echoed from the stones of the abandoned church. I drew the lantern from beneath the cover of my cloak, made my way across to the corner where we had laid the body, and removed the sailcloth. I ignored the man's head and dragged off the sacking that covered his body and bent legs. It was stuck both to the corpse and to the stones beneath. Yaxley had been right about the flagstones keeping him fresh. I wondered if the stones had felt as cold this when the old monks once padded across them in their sandals or knelt on them through the long night vigils over their dead.

The corpse was clad only in a shirt and breeches, both encased in ice. The feet beneath the sacking were bare, the sprinkling of black hair on the toes standing stark against the blue-whiteness of the skin and nails, the toes black at the tips. And there was something else: three deep blue-black lines around his ankles. I recognised those marks, for I bore ones like them. The skin on my ankles had healed and the livid red marks faded to brown, but they were still there: the marks of the irons which had been loaded on me in Newgate prison, before FitzAlan had offered me a means of escape. This man's legs hadn't been fettered in irons, but he had been tied up. I moved the lantern upwards. His arms were behind him, pressed together, the fists clenched. I tried to peel back the shirt, but it was welded to his body with ice. Warming my own numb fingers several times over what little heat I could draw from the lantern flame, I managed to drag up part of one sleeve, tearing the brittle cloth. Again, I found the same lines bitten deep into the flesh of his wrists, but no sign of the cord or rope used to bind them.

I ran the lantern light over the body, examining him as carefully as I could, and though I couldn't move his frozen limbs or straighten him to examine his belly, I could see no blood or wounds upon his back or chest. Once more I dragged the sacking off the head. I was even more certain this time that this was the man I'd seen in Crowhurst's cottage that first night in Battle. I held the lantern lower, to examine the bent head more closely. His mouth was partly open, and the candlelight bounced off something pale and smooth between his lips. I lifted the shoulder, tilting the head to get a better look.

The side of the face on which the corpse had evidently been lying was almost black, but the frozen lower lip on the uppermost side was torn, like the cloth I had ripped on his sleeve, though there was no sign it had bled. He must have been in a struggle and what I could see was probably a broken tooth. I hooked it out. Not a tooth, a bean – a dried white bean. I glanced round and spotted a small blunt hook hanging on the wall. I slipped it between the jaws. Two . . . three . . . four . . . five more beans slid out and dropped into my hand.

Maybe Smith had been right and he had been desperate enough for food to try to chew on a handful of hard, dried beans, or at any rate swallow them to fill his empty belly. But though he may have been hungry, he certainly hadn't been starving, at least not for any longer than a few hours or days at most, for he was well muscled and looked better nourished than most crofters I'd seen. I moved the lantern back to his bare feet. The soles were horny, as might be expected for any man who toiled outdoors, but the skin wasn't torn or filthy. He certainly hadn't walked through the woods barefoot in the hours before his death.

I replaced the sacks so that it appeared nothing had been disturbed, and then, covering the lantern again, retreated from the hut. I stood outside in the freezing air, watching my breath billow up white against the jagged ruins of the Abbey church, the stones gilded silver in the starlight. Nothing stirred. Not even an owl called out. But as I turned away, a single long howl split the darkness, like a wolf baying at the moon.

The sensible thing to have done on such a night would have been to have to surrender to what my numb fingers, face and feet were begging me to do and return as fast as I could to the warmth of the Abbey's hearth and a hot mulled ale. And if I had done that . . . But curiosity has always coaxed me into following her, like the bawd she is, and so, turning my back on the safety of the Abbey, I edged into the woods.

The distant howl reverberated through the air once more, and before it died away, all the hounds and curs in Battle town started to bark and yowl. Every wolf in England was dead, and yet I was as sure as I could be that the cry I'd heard had not been made by any farmer's dog.

I found the rough track through the woods that I hoped would lead me to the old charcoal burners' huts, but even though most of the trees were leafless, in places the branches were so densely intertwined that scarcely any moonlight penetrated. I calculated that I was far enough from the house to risk uncovering the lantern again and held it low. The dead undergrowth was trampled on either side of the path, the old stems not bent, but shattered like broken glass, presumably by the boots of the men who had walked on each side of the makeshift bier. If so, I was on the right path.

The huts, when I eventually found them, stood so deep in the woods that had it not been for the lad searching for firewood, the body might easily have lain there for weeks or even months before it was discovered. If the thaw had set in, the ravages of decay and vermin would have made the face of the corpse unrecognisable.

The remains of three conical huts stood in a clearing, casting dark shadows in the shafts of moonlight writhing through the wood. One hut had collapsed as Brathwayt had predicted, the few poles of the frame that still remained slumped sideways, caught by the branches of a tree. The old turfs which had once covered them mouldered in the shallow ditch that encircled the hovel. The lad who had been foraging for wood here had probably hastened its demise as he plundered it for kindling. The other two huts still stood upright, though some of the overlapping turfs had fallen away, leaving dark holes in the skins, as if giant insects had burrowed out of a rotten pear. I covered the lantern again and circled them in the darkness, watching and listening for any sign of movement. It was so silent I could hear my own breath crackling as it froze in the air.

I began with the hut closest to me. There was no door, but a small portico of poles and turf which would once have protected the entrance from wind and rain, though now it sagged at a drunken angle. Crouching down, I swept the lantern light inside. Old leaves were scattered among blackened and rotting vegetation on the earth floor. A dead robin lay on the ground, its claws clenched as if it had tried in vain to cling to life. But there were no footprints inside on the frosted soil. The corpse had not been found in this one.

As soon as I shone the lantern inside the second hut, I saw that the ground had been recently trampled. The iced-coated weeds, like those along the path, were smashed. I ducked inside, hoping the hut would not collapse on top of me as Brathwayt had warned. But this one seemed more solid than the others; it was evidently the one favoured by hunters. A plank of wood had been balanced on two sections of tree trunk to form a makeshift seat and a circle of scorched stones marked where fires had been kindled, though no fire had been lit for some time, for weeds had grown up through the ashes. Several pairs of feet had walked over this ground and the rough outline of the curled-up body was still marked in frost. It seemed to have been frozen to the ground beneath; it must have taken some effort to prise it up.

But there was nothing to show that the dead man had been living here and no sign of his clothes or boots. The meanest beggar always found a few rags or some gleaned wool to bind round his feet, even those accustomed to sleeping under the stars, for no man would be able to walk far on stony roads or through brambles without some protection. The lad who found him might have stripped the corpse, reasoning that the dead have no need of boots or coat, so why shouldn't the living make use of them? Yet the body had been frozen solid; the arms and legs couldn't be straightened. No one could have removed his boots, much less his coat. He had been stripped while he was still warm, probably while he still lived.

I lifted the plank from the logs to see if anything had been stuffed beneath. There was nothing except an old, dried mutton bone gnawed by sharp little teeth, and that had clearly lain there for some time . . . but then I noticed something else. It was only a little paler than the earth and dried leaves on which it lay, which is why I nearly missed it. I held it up in the lantern light.

It was a length of cord. It had been knotted in two places, but whoever had removed it had done so hastily or had been unable to loosen the knots, for it had been cut through. I wound it tightly around my wrist, once, twice, three times, then examined the faint indentations on my skin. I was in little doubt that this had made those marks on the arms of the corpse. The cord had been cut off after death, when the body was frozen in its bound position. It had probably been dropped on the plank and had slipped underneath. Surely, if the men who'd brought the body to the Abbey had found it trussed up, they would have said as much. Besides, why would they cut the bonds of a frozen corpse?

The man or woman who had tied him and left him to die of the cold had wanted to make the death appear natural, so far as they could. But it was murder, no less than if his throat had been cut – though someone who recoils from carrying the sin of murder on their immortal soul might well reason that if a man perishes of cold, then it is God who has taken that life, not them, just as they might argue a Divine hand, not a human one, slays the man who dies when he *falls* into a hole.

The ice wolf was gnawing into my bones as I crunched back towards the Abbey; even my teeth ached with cold. My fingers were so numb inside my gloves that had it not been for their stiffness, the lantern would have fallen from my hand. My feet were clumsy, stumbling over the tree roots, slippery as the puddles of ice, and I didn't relish crashing down on to the rock-hard ground, forced to lie out all night with a broken leg, so in spite of the siren lure of warm fires and hot ale, I couldn't hurry. But something in the woods was moving fast.

Twigs and branches cracked and snapped as it charged towards me. A hunted stag? A herd of rampaging pigs? Either could kill a man if he found himself in their path. With clumsy fingers, I dragged my dagger from its sheath and swung round to face the animal, hoping that the lantern light would be enough to make it veer aside. But it kept coming. As it burst from the trees, I glimpsed a creature like a giant black bird with a monstrous curved beak. It charged into me, hurling me down on to the frozen earth.

The lantern was dashed from my hand and spun away. The candle flame was extinguished, plunging the path into darkness. The beast was on top of me, its full weight pressing down on my dagger arm, its beak inches from my face. I thrust my left arm upwards into its throat and pushed as hard as I could. It was wheezing, gargling, trying to roll away from me as its head was forced backwards, but it couldn't seem to free itself. I pulled my arm back from its throat and punched the side of its head. It shrieked, jerking back, and I pushed again. Something tore and the creature rolled off me. It was only then that I realised what I had felt against my face was not fur, or feathers, or even a cold beak. It was cloth.

Though I could see no more than the black shape crawling away in the moonlight, I scrambled up and sprang at him, knocking him flat to the ground. I locked my arm around his neck and jabbed my knife against his back, digging the point through his clothes and into his skin hard enough to make him jerk and then go rigid, afraid to move.

'On your knees.' I dragged him upwards by his neck. His fingers dug frantically into my arm as he choked, but I kept the dagger pressed into his back. In the shaft of moonlight, I could see the monstrous bird beak, just as I had seen it on the wall of the graveyard. But now I realised what I was looking at: a black cloth mask that hung down over his neck, with a stuffed cloth beak over his nose.

'So, it seems I have caught the night-creeper.'

'I am not him. Let me go! The night-creeper is a foul demon, a spirit.'

'Oh, I think I could easily prove to you that the night-creeper is flesh and *blood*.' I pushed the dagger a little harder until he squealed. 'Would you like me to do that, or would you prefer to show me your face?'

He didn't move.

'I can push the blade in up to the hilt, nice and slowly, so that you have plenty of time to change your mind, though it might prove too late when I pull it out.'

He moaned and suddenly wriggled in my grip, trying to break free, but that only jerked the sharp blade in the cut, making him cry out. He lifted his arm and pulled off the hood.

On such a cold night, the face that peered up at me was damp with sweat. His eyes glittered in the moonlight, a strange mixture of fear and exhilaration.

'Erasmus!'

Beneath his wisp of a beard, his Adam's apple rapidly slid up and down. I lowered the knife and he clambered unsteadily to his feet.

'You? The night-creeper. The one who's been terrorising the town.'

'No, no, you're mistaken. I only wore the mask to keep out the cold—'

He broke off as he felt the point of my dagger beneath his jaw.

'There's an innocent woman sick with fear that she'll be charged with witchcraft and hanged, or worse. You tell me the truth, or I swear I will march you back into that town and let the people you have tormented beat it out of you.'

'No, please . . . I can't help it . . . Not my fault . . .' He mumbled, trying to speak without moving his jaw. 'Have to do it . . . Can't stop.'

I lowered the knife and as if the blade had been holding him upright, his legs gave way and he slumped against a tree, sliding down the trunk until he was crouching on the frozen leaf litter, his head cradled in his arms. For a few moments he said nothing, but his chest heaved as he tried to supress a sob.

Then he raised his head. 'I know . . . I know it is wicked, but I can't stop myself. I am possessed by an evil spirit who takes hold of me and forces me to do such things. Day and night, I can think of nothing except the leopards coming and how I shall be forced to endure the priest hole, for hours, days, shut up there in the dark, listening to them tearing the house apart, listening to them coming closer and closer. Lighting fires to suffocate and roast us alive if we are hiding near chimneys. Even Father Oldcorne could only endure eight days in the hole before he surrendered . . . then he was dragged to the Tower. Do you know what they do to them in there? They hung Little John by his wrists in irons again and again until his belly burst wide open!'

His eyes were screwed shut, as if he was trying to shut out a horror that was unfolding right before him. 'Day and night the evil spirit that possesses me whispers these things, tells me over and over again that I am weak, a coward; that I will not be able to endure the agony. Like Judas, I will betray Father Smith, betray the Holy Church, betray our Blessed Lord Himself and be eternally damned. And when I try to sleep it's worse – all night the demon goads me with these visions and nightmares.'

He bit his fist.

'The demon will only give me peace when I am running through Battle, making them afraid. When I hear them cry out in terror and scream, then I have all the courage in the world. I am as powerful as any leopard. I am the one bringing terror. The evil spirit is stilled then and its tormenting voice is silenced. And when it is over, I can return and sleep without nightmares.

I am calm then, but as the sun begins to set, I can feel the demon stirring and I know it will awaken. I cannot sleep or think . . . its voice pounds and pounds in my head. It will not let me rest . . . I have to run. I have to . . .'

I wanted to shake the snivelling little rat till he howled. but the utter misery of this tormented wretch cowering on the ground was plain to see, even in the dark.

'It makes you feel powerful, does it? How powerful would you have felt if that mob had succeeded in burning you alive when they trapped you on the roof? If you fall into their hands again, they will kill you, just as surely as you have killed their chickens. And I reckon you deserve it!'

'No! No, I did not kill any chickens! I swear on the Blessed Virgin. I bang on their shutters and shriek just to frighten them, that is all I do, I swear.'

Seeing him quivering on the ground, his eyes glittering with fear in the starlight, I found myself believing him. For a moment I had wondered if Crowhurst had discovered his secret and Erasmus had tied him up to silence him, but though the young man might have lashed out and struck him blindly in a panic, he would not have had the nerve to strip him, much less return to a corpse and remove the cords. He was not Crowhurst's murderer.

But I'd have gladly murdered Smith if I'd found him alone in these woods. He had frightened and humiliated an earnest young man, and reduced him to this wretched state. A century ago, when it was not a crime to be a priest, Erasmus might have passed his life peacefully in a little village, baptising babies, burying the dead, and he would have served both God and his parishioners well. But he was not equal to this deadly game of subterfuge and terror. He'd never make a soldier for his Sovereign or his God.

His hand grasped my ankle. He was staring up at me, his eyes shining wet. 'You won't tell them. You won't give me away,' he pleaded.

For a fleeting moment, it occurred to me that I could use him, demand information as the price for my silence. But he'd never hold his nerve long enough to steal so much as a bent pin from Smith without giving himself away. Smith had broken him, as Waldegrave had once tried to break me.

'No, I won't, but only because I don't want your death on my conscience. The townspeople would storm the Abbey if they ever learned the night-creeper was in there, and if they didn't string you up from the Abbey walls, they'd bury you up to your neck in the marsh at low tide and wait for the sea to roll in. I hear that's what they do in these parts to those who upset them.' I crouched down. 'But you must confide your fears to one of the priests. Maybe Father Holt could help you, if you were to ask him.'

I wouldn't have chosen to confide in any priest myself, but he was the only one here I'd seen display a shred of compassion, and it had to be someone in the Abbey.

'Don't tell Holt anything about the night-creeping, Erasmus! If you value your life, don't mention that to another living soul. But tell him of your fears of being trapped in one of those hiding holes. Some men can tolerate being shut up in such small spaces, but others can be driven mad by it. See if Holt can't find another place for you far from Battle Abbey, another way of serving the Church without becoming ordained.'

'But I must train for the priesthood. Father Smith says that every man is needed. I am called,' he said desperately.

'All the more reason that you must find someone to help you.'

'Do you really think Father Holt can rid me of the demon?'

'Talk to him,' I said firmly. I was sure the only demon possessing Erasmus was the fear that Smith and others had instilled in him, but if Holt could exorcise that, or at least get him away from Smith's control . . .

Erasmus was shivering violently now, and I wasn't much better. I couldn't feel my feet. I dragged him upright.

'Now you take yourself back to the Abbey, while I get rid of this.' I gathered up the ragged cloth mask. He reached out as if he was going to snatch it back from me, like a drunkard who cannot turn his back on wine.

'Go!' I ordered.

Erasmus needed help, and swiftly. I only hoped that Holt was equal to the task. I waited until I heard his footsteps crunching away into the distance, then walked into the trees until I found a patch of brambles. I'd have liked to bury the mask, but there was no chance of making even a shallow grave for it. So, I ripped it up as best I could, hardly able to hold the hilt of my knife now, and pushed the pieces beneath the leafless brambles, hoping that they'd simply be taken as rags by anyone who chanced upon them. As I did so, another thought struck me. Where had Crowhurst's murderer disposed of his clothes?

Chapter Twenty-six

SALISBURY HOUSE, THE STRAND, LONDON

CECIL LIFTED THE GREAT SCROLL of paper on to his desk and unrolled one end of it, securing the edges of the plan with an assortment of small books and a sander pot made from a twisted goat's horn with two brass feet to keep it upright. He had other sanders, far more valuable, but this one had amused him ever since he'd received it as a boy. When his own daughter, Frances, was only four years old, she had announced firmly that it was the tail of a baby dragon. He found himself smiling at the memory. She had always been an engaging child and now, at fourteen, she was blossoming into an enchanting young woman, despite having lost her mother, Elizabeth, when she was only three.

Elizabeth had been a good match at the time, and he had not regretted their marriage since, though she had possessed neither the beauty nor intellect of a woman like Catherine Howard; but then very few did, and perhaps it was just as well, for they were not the qualities that made for a faithful wife. But he had grieved for Elizabeth, in his own way.

William and Frances had sorely missed their mother too in those first few months after her death, but some might say it was a blessing Elizabeth died when she did, for at least she hadn't lived to see her brother George arrested on the orders of her husband and executed for High Treason. It was four years since Cecil had uncovered the plot to kidnap James, but his questioning of those conspirators had fortuitously exposed a far more deadly plan, to kill 'the old fox and his cubs', and to put

James's cousin Arabella Stuart on the English throne. Cecil had realised from the start that if his wife's brother George Brooke was involved, then George's elder brother, Lord Cobham, and his friend Walter Raleigh would be mired to their necks in the same treachery. They had all confessed after a sojourn in the Tower and all had been sentenced to death. But George had had the gall to write to Cecil demanding that, as his brother-in-law, he should obtain a pardon for him, daring to suggest that Cecil owed him such a service. Cecil had naturally done no such thing, but the demand still rankled, even after George's severed head had been tossed into the basket.

George's brother Lord Cobham had indeed been reprieved by the King, just moments before the axe was about to descend on his neck; he still languished in the Tower, where he would remain until he rotted to death unless he could convince Cecil that he might be of some use to him, as Sir Griffin Markham, another of the conspirators, had done. Markham was even now furnishing Cecil with extremely useful information from his exile in the Low Countries, where his part in the conspiracy had made him something of a hero in the growing community of English Catholics who'd fled there. But even Cobham's great friend Raleigh could find nothing more flattering to say about Cobham than that he was a 'silly and base fool'. And an agent who couldn't open his mouth without contradicting himself was no more use to Cecil than a watchdog who couldn't bark.

At the time, Cecil had wondered whether his wife would have begged for George's life had she still been alive. And though he would never have admitted as much to anyone, sometimes in the long dark nights a malicious demon whispered in his head that Elizabeth might have gone further than simply pleading for her brothers; she might actually have joined them in the conspiracy, betraying not only her Sovereign but her husband as well. Would he have had his own wife arrested as he had her brothers? Would he have stood in the shadows listening to her interrogation in the Tower? Would he have let her go to the scaffold without begging for her to be pardoned? He grimaced. *Proditoribus necesse est mori. Traitors must die.*

Having set the stage with the carefully arranged scroll of paper, Cecil walked to the door and sent the servant waiting outside for his steward. As the steward entered, he saw, as he was intended to, his master examining the plans for the new wing at Hatfield House, though Cecil could have drawn them himself in every detail from memory. But he knew well that if what a man *sees* matches what he *hears* then he will not even think to question it.

The steward bowed and waited in respectful silence. He was a short, compact man and though not a crookback like his master, nevertheless his height, or lack of it, had given him an advantage over other men who had coveted such a post in Lord Salisbury's opulent household. At Court, men seemed to deliberately stand straighter and closer to Cecil than they did to others to emphasis his small stature, and he had no wish to be reminded of it at home.

'I have been expecting a box to be delivered containing samples of marbles which might be used to floor the new hall at Hatfield.' Cecil spoke without looking up from the plans. 'I gave you instructions that it was to be brought straight to me upon my return. Has it been put aside by one of the servants and forgotten?' He darted a glance at his steward as he said the last word, to catch the slightest flicker of anxiety or guilt.

But unlike most men Cecil had cause to question, on this matter, at least, the steward had nothing to hide.

'My lord, no box has been delivered. They say this frost has the whole country in its jaws.' Seeing his master's eyebrows twitch, the steward bowed hastily to acknowledge his foolish mistake. 'As, of course, you will already have been informed, my lord.' *He probably knew that before God did.*

'I understand the box was to be delivered from the port at Winchelsea, my lord. But the rivers are impassable because of the ice and I think few souls will venture to bring a laden cart or wagon so many miles on roads so treacherous. I heard of a dozen accidents just yesterday, with horses breaking their backs and carts crushing people against walls or rolling back down slopes when the wheels started sliding. I will remind all the servants that the box is to be brought to you at once when it does arrive, but while this frost lasts . . .' He spread his hands helplessly.

Cecil nodded and dismissed his steward. He was not an unreasonable man. Other masters might take their frustration out on blameless servants, but that only built a smouldering resentment and he wanted to ensure loyalty.

The marble samples were not needed. He had already chosen the fine black and white slabs that would checker the floor of the huge hall, but the samples were intended to conceal what he hoped would be a file of papers, too many and too lengthy to be disguised in the usual form of a cryptic letter or concealed in the hollow of a book. He was expecting to receive names, addresses, codes and routes, details of ships and whether or not their captains were aware of the true identities of their passengers. He wanted to be told, at least in part, how men were being moved from the ports to the towns, who was financing them, and even the names of illiterate farmers who might have been persuaded to leave a loaf of bread and a little cheese in a barn for the faceless strangers who arrived after dark and left long before dawn.

When frost touches a spider's web, every invisible thread is exposed, every turn and twist revealed, the whole exquisite shape of it laid bare. Cecil had seen tantalising glimpses of the web – the thread that ran through Bristol, for one. He had received names from that city. He had a list of ships. The priest there had done well. He had delivered one end of the network, but Cecil needed the other. When you have both ends of the rope in your hands you can tie it into a noose.

But most priests were not so easily persuaded to change their coats. When men are truly convinced that heaven awaits them on the far shore, when they are certain they will receive a martyr's crown, they embrace pain and reach out for death. But from one genuine coin, you can counterfeit a hundred forgeries. So, one turned priest can be used to train a dozen fake ones.

Cecil had taken great pains to assemble his little cell: men who could pass themselves off as priests and lay brothers to infiltrate the network; who could travel with genuine priests being smuggled in and out of England; who were willing to be arrested when houses were raided and spend time incarcerated in the miserable chambers of the Tower to convince the others that they were genuine. These men could become the very enemy they despised in thought, word and deed, and yet still retain their loathing of the foe.

Cecil removed the sander and the books from the end of the plan and watched it curl itself up like a beaten prisoner. His steward was right: he could not expect any news from Battle, not until this freeze was ended. But if boxes could not be moved, then neither could people. For the moment, the ice was holding them prisoner almost as securely as the grim walls of the Tower would do. He could wait. He had schemed and waited for months to put James on the English throne. The skill of a master chess player lies in anticipating the moves his enemies will make before they have even planned them, then setting up the traps for them to play into. *Espice, adspice, prospice. Look behind, look here, but always – look ahead!*

Chapter Twenty-seven

DANIEL PURSGLOVE

THE CONICAL CHARCOAL BURNERS' HUTS were scarcely more inviting in the winter sunshine than they had been in moonlight. I had to admit Brathwayt had had a point when he accused the bailiff of neglecting this part of the estate, and the woodward, Matthew Crowhurst, had also been remiss, if this section fell under his responsibility. Young trees had sprung up in what must have once been a wide clearing, but though leafless, they were being choked by snakes of dark green ivy, so that little of the pale winter sunlight filtered through the dismal grove to the cold ground. Tangles of old brambles and frost-blackened nettles scrambled over piles of rotten wood and a warped and broken sledge. The charcoal burners had evidently abandoned their dwellings hastily, or perhaps had intended to return the following year but had never come back. Maybe they'd fallen victim to one of the waves of plague.

But pigs had created paths through the undergrowth, and other animals too, for there was a quantity of old bones scattered about – rabbits, squirrels and sheep. And not just bones, for as I poked about with my staff, I found half-dismembered carcasses too, chickens and crows reduced to hollow skins of feather shafts, beaks and skulls by maggots and vermin. The place resembled the lair of some dragon or monstrous beast. Old Amor, Sybil's father, would probably say it was certain proof that the knucker had risen from his bottomless pool to feast on his prey.

But I was only interested in one corpse. I crossed to the hut in which the man I knew as Matthew Crowhurst had died. Although I'd found the cord inside, I was certain the interior of the hut would reveal no more, for I had searched it as thoroughly as I could by lantern-light. But outside, there might still be something to be uncovered – signs of a meeting or a struggle, perhaps. I began to circle the hut, moving outwards in ever-increasing spirals to search the ground and bushes around it.

As I'd noticed the night before, the men who had collected the body, and probably also the lad who'd dragged his bundle of wood, had trampled the dead undergrowth and broken twigs. There was no way to be certain now how many people might have been here the night Crowhurst died. But however he'd got here, it had not been by cart. There were no wheel marks. Yet there was something. It had been partly obliterated by footprints in the deep frost, but there were two parallel tracks just visible here and there, broader than cart tracks, and lighter too.

I followed them away from the huts, bending slightly so that the low sun caught the faint grooves at the angle where they could best be seen. I had walked only a dozen yards when I saw a patch of leaf mould, slightly darker than the surrounding forest floor, half overhung by a clump of rotting deadly nightshade. Someone had been digging there. I scraped the disturbed ground with my boot heel. The first few inches of leaves and earth came away in slabs, but the ground beneath was frozen solid. Whoever had tried to dig had discovered, like me, that they could not get down more than a hand's breadth.

Using one of the old hut poles, I prodded and poked beneath the sagging mass of dead weeds and bracken around me, until finally I snagged the edge of the bundle and hooked it out. A coat had been wrapped around something heavier. It was stiff and it crackled with ice as I pulled the folds apart to reveal a pair of worn, leather boots. Whoever had stripped and bound Crowhurst and left him to die had evidently tried to bury those boots and failed. Hose and other garments could be cut up and scattered as I had done with the mask, even burned, but disposing of thick leather boots was not so easy.

I had been so intent on retrieving the bundle that the sound had crept up on me before I was conscious of it: footsteps crunching the ice, twigs snapping. I crammed the boots back into the frozen hollow of the coat and tossed them beyond the rotting weeds, then turned. A man was moving towards the huts between the trees. I shifted my grasp on the pole, prepared to use it as a weapon if needed, and edged closer.

The man, his back to me, was moving clumsily towards the hut where Crowhurst had been found, carrying a sack over one shoulder. He was talking, though I could see no one else near him, and it was only as I took a few paces closer that I recognised the voice. It wasn't a man, but a boy.

'Sam!'

Startled, he turned too quickly on the treacherous ground, and came crashing down. The sack flew from his hand. 'Clotpole, clumsy clotpole!' he shouted, but I knew he wasn't addressing me.

I hurried forward, careful not to slip on the same patch of ice, and hauled him up. He rubbed his hip and peered at me.

'You shouldn't be here. No one comes here,' he said stolidly.

'Then what are you doing here, Sam?'

'Looking, that's all.' But his gaze darted towards the huts and the expression of guilt was unmistakable.

Did he know Crowhurst had been lying dead in there? Did he think he still was?

'What are you looking for? Perhaps I can help you.'

'Father says I'm to tell him if I see anything amiss. I'm his eyes and ears, see. Eyes and ears, Sam. Eyes and ears,' he repeated in a singsong tone.

'And how is your father?'

He shrugged. 'Cold.' Again, his gaze darted towards the huts, before returning to a patch of ground in front of his boots.

I retrieved the sack. It wasn't heavy, but as I handed it to him, I felt something stir inside it. 'What have you got there, Sam?'

He snatched it from me. 'Nowt . . . navens, that's what. Navens for my ma's pot.'

If that was a bunch of roots then they must be mandrakes, not navens. Whatever was in there was alive and wriggling. He'd probably been snaring woodcock or rabbit, but it was hardly something to lie about. As a woodward's son, he was entitled to take any small game he could catch or find on manor land so long as it was for the family's table.

He shuffled uneasily from foot to foot. 'You shouldn't be here,' he repeated. 'Are you going now?'

'I'm leaving . . . Sam, sometimes things happen that we didn't mean . . .'

I trailed off. There was nothing to be gained by getting the boy to confide in me. I couldn't help him, even if he told me the truth. What I had learned in Bristol had reminded me all too firmly that a just cause is not the same as innocence in the eyes of the King's judges, and truth can be twisted into a noose as easily as lies.

As I walked away I glanced back, hoping to catch the lad making for the hut. But he was standing where I had left him. Slow he might be, but not stupid enough to move until he was quite certain he could do so unobserved.

If Sam had tied his father up in there, perhaps to escape a beating, not understanding that it would kill him on such a bitter night, he might have returned to release him or even bring him his supper in the form of a rabbit for the pot, not realising he was dead. But even as I considered this, I knew that it couldn't be the whole story. He and Alys were certain Crowhurst wouldn't return. So, Sam must either have intended to keep his father prisoner in the hut, or he knew Crowhurst was dead. Then again, it might not have been Sam who'd killed Crowhurst, but Alys. Crowhurst was a powerfully built man, but she could easily have fed him a herb to make him sleep and dragged him here on Sam's stone sledge. I couldn't decide if Sam was trying to protect his mother from the gallows or she was trying to protect him.

Chapter Twenty-eight

THE BOY GILES WAS CROUCHING near the small fire in the bailiff's stone hut, his bony hands stretched out over the glowing logs, his legs spread wide. His sack lay empty on Yaxley's table, the vermin he had trapped and killed laid out in a neat row – the severed head of kite, two or three small birds, a weasel that looked as if its skull had been smashed with a hammer, and four large rats. I caught again the stench of rotten meat. The rats looked fresh enough, but the filthy, bloodstained sack had probably not been used for months, if not years.

'No wonder you're cold, lad, you must have been out for hours to have caught yourself so many.'

He half turned his head. 'Master Yaxley said to wait here till he gets back. He'll pay me then.'

He had just finished speaking when the bailiff himself lumbered up to the door. The leather-bound ledger in which I'd seen him previously record the list of Giles's vermin haul was pressed beneath his arm. His other hand was pressed to the small of his back, as if it was aching again. His head jerked up when he caught sight of me.

Giles sprang to his feet and I moved further into the workshop to let the bailiff pass, glancing again at the haul laid out on his table. 'Young Giles should get a good bounty for those. He did well to find any creature abroad in this weather. I would have thought they'd all have gone to ground.'

Yaxley grunted. 'They get hungrier than ever when it's cold, and bolder. Rats are raiding kitchens and barns in broad daylight in the town; not even the sight of man or dog scares them off. Easy as picking mushrooms after rain to catch them at this season, isn't that right, lad?'

Giles obediently nodded, but looked far from convinced.

Yaxley patted the ledger under his arm. 'Record every beast killed in here. Proof the manor's keeping to the law and trapping vermin. We don't want to give those bastards any excuse to raid us. Her ladyship's got enough trouble to contend with, without us bringing more to her door.'

He laid the ledger reverently on the table as if it were Holy Writ and opened the page, running his stubby finger down the list and checking the tally. The book was old, bound in worn leather with a fish-shaped oil stain on the front. It was the same one I'd seen Steward Brathwayt hand to Yaxley in the servants' hall the night he'd come to caution us about the leopards. The bailiff heaved a box on to the table, drew out a small bag of coins, and began to count them out. Giles took a pace closer, his pinched face suddenly showing interest as he watched the small stack of coins grow, licking his lips as if every one was a bite of food.

Yaxley glanced up. 'Summat you wanted, Pursglove?'

'Just a warm,' I said.

'Hard work warms a man better than any fire. You want me to find you some?'

I slipped out swiftly before he could, shutting the door behind me. But something was nagging at me. If that ledger merely contained a record of the vermin caught and the bounty paid for it, then why would Steward Brathwayt have had it the night before the Mass? And why had Yaxley taken it into the house again this afternoon? Brathwayt might simply have been checking up that Yaxley was doing his duty and actively hunting down vermin as the law demanded, as anxious as the bailiff not to give the sheriff's men any excuse to enter and search. But from what I'd seen of Yaxley and Brathwayt together, I couldn't imagine the bailiff tolerating the steward overseeing his work; they were, after all, of equal rank in their own spheres.

But messages could easily be brought into the Abbey hidden inside the animal carcasses, removed by Yaxley and slipped between the pages of the ledger to be carried into the house, the book handed to the steward in plain view and returned the same way. No one watching the manor would look twice at an urchin like Giles, knowing that he regularly came with his gory haul. Even if he was stopped on the road or in the town, few of the sheriff's men would relish poking around inside severed heads or sticking their fingers into the bellies of decomposing rats. I felt almost elated. I was finally getting somewhere.

THE FIRES HAD BEEN banked down for the night and my 'gentlemen' had retired to the beds I had warmed for them. It was so cold in their chamber, I was certain they wouldn't venture out of bed to relieve themselves in the night and would simply reach for the pisspots I'd purposely set within reach of each man. I wouldn't be missed, for an hour or so at least.

I had almost reached the door to the courtyard when it creaked open. A figure crept into the dimly lit passageway, swathed so heavily in mufflers and cloak that it was impossible to tell if it was a man or woman. I pressed back in a dark doorway, shadowed between the pools of light cast by the few candles still burning in the sconces on the walls. The figure paused, unwinding the scarves and throwing back the hood. I grinned. It was only Arthur, creeping back after a night's drinking in the alehouse.

'Is this how you disport yourself in a godly household, sirrah!' I growled in what I thought was a fair imitation of Smith's voice. Arthur evidently thought so too, for he gave a strangled squawk and at once began blabbering excuses, until he realised who was standing there, and then he hurled his boot at my head. I ducked and it thudded to the flags.

'Dog heart! Rat turd! Suppose you think that was funny?'

'Hilarious,' I said blithely. 'I wager you've been at Sybil's, though I'm amazed even the lure of her beer would tempt you from the hearth on a night as bitter as this. You could freeze your cods off.'

'Wouldn't be any great loss if I did, since Bethia left,' he said gloomily. 'She was the only woman I had eyes for.' He affected a comic lovesick pose and laughed. 'Anyhow, it's worth it just to get away from the Abbey. I reckon the old monks had more sport here than we ever do. Not that there was much to be had at Sybil's tonight, either. There's trouble brewing.'

'What kind of trouble?'

'Night-creeper's been heard again, and there's some poultry taken from a barn. But it seems you convinced a good many that Myrna couldn't have done it. Anyhow, that burn of hers turned bad and she's racked with fever. So now, thanks to you, they're starting to say the Abbey is the cause of it all.'

I felt an icy hand grip my guts. Had they somehow discovered the night-creeper was Erasmus?

Arthur sat on one of the chests, rubbing his feet vigorously through his hose to warm them. 'They're back blaming it on that body her ladyship had buried in the churchyard.'

'You told them it was a vagabond.' *Just like Smith had claimed the frozen man in the old hut to have been. Battle was proving to be a remarkably unlucky place for beggars.*

Arthur shrugged. 'I was only guessing. No one died at the Abbey, so it must have been a beggar, seeing as how they buried him so close to the north side of the church.' He lowered his voice, glancing up and down the passageway. 'Couldn't have been any one they were hiding here, could it? Else they would have buried them quietly in the ruins of the Abbey and said a proper Mass for them.'

He was right: whoever was in that grave could not be a priest or any fugitive from the Abbey. I'd wager everything I owned on it being another pursuivant, silenced, like Benet, before he could make his report. Though they could hardly claim it was suicide again, neither would they be able to stomach the thought of a heretic resting in the hallowed grounds of the Abbey – which meant they only had one option, to bury him quietly at night in the graveyard of the Protestant church before his paymaster realised he was missing.

'Another Benet who met with . . . an unfortunate accident?' I suggested.

Arthur glanced uneasily behind him. 'You don't want to be asking those sorts of questions,' he whispered fiercely. '*Knowing* can put a noose round your neck as easily as *doing*.'

But, as always with Arthur, his mood switched in an instant and he turned his attention back to his frozen feet. 'Like I was telling you, Dannet, the Abbey buried the body in the Devil's arse where they put the thieves and murderers, and gave him no Christian service. So, the townsfolk have taken it into their heads that whoever is down in that grave must have been wicked when he was alive and worse after he died. He won't lie quiet. They reckon the only way to put a stop to his mischief is to open the grave and cut off his head with a gravedigger's spade. Then burn the corpse to ashes.'

'But that's just alehouse babble, isn't it?'

Arthur grunted with amusement. 'Walter was as bold as a lion on ale, certainly. He was all for digging up the corpse tonight, till Sybil pointed out that if it was the night-creeper down there he'd have clambered out of his grave with the rising moon and already be prowling the town. So, he'd likely tear Walter's head off with his bare hands if he came at him with a spade. She said they'd have to wait until the sun was up and the corpse was back lying beneath the sod again. But I reckon they'll do it come morning, once the sun rises and the wraiths have melted away. I warned you Jacob Dericote wouldn't take kindly to being made to look a fool in front of all his friends by someone from the Abbey, and he's determined to prove himself this time. Walter may think better of it when he sobers up, but I'll wager a pound to a penny Jacob'll do it.' He yawned and shivered. 'If I don't get some sleep, they'll be taking me for a wraith. I swear that bastard rouses us earlier every day.'

I turned as if I was making for the stairs, but as soon as Arthur had vanished towards the servants' hall, I returned to the courtyard door and slipped out. The shock of the icy air almost stopped my breath, but at least that would keep everyone else inside. I drew back into a narrow space between two of the small outbuildings, where the light from the torches on the walls couldn't reach me. There wasn't a breath of wind. Even the flames of the torches seemed frozen, their hearts blue and cold beneath the scarlet fire. Drops of water from the melted frost ran down the walls behind them, freezing again before they even reached the ground.

I examined each of the windows that overlooked the courtyard for any blades of light cutting into the darkness from cracks beneath the shutters or chinks in them. I watched to see if any of the lights flicked or vanished, showing that someone was peering through, but all were steady, which was as well, for it might take me several minutes to charm the lock to the bailiff's workroom. Usually, I'd be able to do it in a heartbeat, but I knew my fingers would be clumsy as an old codger's in this cold and the mechanism was bound to be frozen.

But as soon as I tried the door, I discovered it wasn't locked. Yaxley had either grown careless or didn't fear thieves. Though it might be an old recusant trick: the leopards would instantly be drawn to any room that they found locked and tear it apart in the belief that something valuable, illegal or nefarious must lie within; an unlocked room, like an unlocked cupboard, attracts far less attention.

A small fire, banked down under glowing peats, smouldered in the stone hearth, bathing the workroom in a dull ruby light. I used it to light the candle I had brought with me. If the bailiff noticed a burned candle on one of his sconces or in a lantern, he'd know at once someone had been in here.

There was a stack of old ledgers on the shelves, but I ignored those and opened the small chest on the floor beneath. Like the door, it was unlocked. On the top, I found the cash box from which I'd seen Yaxley take coins to pay Giles. As I lifted it out, I could feel something sliding around inside, but it wasn't the bags of coins. They'd all been removed. The box was empty, except for a small iron disc, probably a holy medal, about as wide as a man's thumb ring. One side was embossed with what I assumed would be the image of a saint, but as I held it up to the candle-light, I saw it was a wyvern, a two-legged dragon with a serpent's tail. Perhaps it was meant to be the old knucker who haunted the pools in those parts. It might even be an amulet to ward it off, though Yaxley hadn't given me the impression he felt in need of protection from the knucker or any other monster. I slipped it back in the box and turned my attention to the three ledgers stacked in the chest. The one with the fish-shaped oil stain was lying on the top of the pile. That was what I'd come looking for. I lifted it on to the table and moved the candle closer.

The entries, written in a rough though legible hand, carefully recorded the number and kind of each bird and animal brought by Giles and others over the years, and the bounty paid for each creature, as law required, so that the manor could prove it had been diligent in killing vermin, and could not be fined for neglecting the law. I turned to today's tally – one weasel, one red kite, three swallows, four rats.

I flicked right through the ledger, even shaking it over the table. No notes. No loose pages. I checked the cover and binding for places where notes or letters might be concealed but they were glued tight, no hollowed-out spaces inside the covers. I took the ledger to the banked-down fire, holding the pages over the heat. As a field messenger in Ireland, I had once witnessed the capture of an Irish messenger. The papers he carried told us nothing, merely advice from a father to his baby son, in case he should die on the battlefield. But when the letter was held close to the heat of a candle the real message appeared between the lines. A clever trick, and one I had later used to entertain my audiences. *Abracadabra* and words appeared as if by magic, written by a spirit hand. The ink was the juice of a lemon, visible only when heated and which vanished again as it cooled, as if the words had been blown off the page by a ghostly breath. I tried heating several pages, but no message magically appeared. It had been a long shot, for neither the steward nor the bailiff struck me as men well schooled in the tricks of the intelligencers, though I'd have wagered Smith was.

It was beginning to look as if their system was as simple as I'd imagined, just a note smuggled in with the dead vermin, then slipped between the pages of the ledger to be removed by the steward or even Smith himself. If that was the case, then I would find nothing incriminating in Yaxley's workshop. I turned the ledger so that the stain was uppermost, as it had been when I'd removed it from the chest, but as I replaced it, I noticed a streak of white powder on the cover. It must have come from Yaxley's table, for there was a thin white trail across it which had transferred itself on to one of my sleeves. From the smell and texture, it was probably cornmeal, though I didn't taste it, remembering Yaxley's jibe to Brathwayt – he might well have been using it to make rat poison. I carefully dusted off the book and my clothes. Then, with a final glance round to ensure nothing was out of place, I slid out and hurried back to the house. If old Goodenough took it into his head to make one of his nocturnal inspections, I didn't want him to find my bed empty.

THE SUN HAD RISEN over the graveyard of St Mary's, but only the pearly glow behind the dense fog betrayed that. The mist had frozen in the air. Tiny grains of ice clung to my cloak and coated my lashes so I could hardly open my eyes, though that might have been as much to do with lack of sleep as the cold. The priests had gone to the chapel before dawn, the old dowager along with them, and that meant that I had scarcely lain down before we were all summoned again to help them dress and to tidy their rooms. I swear I used to get more sleep in the army, and that was precious little. But, in truth, I wasn't too sorry, for it meant I could slip out early and with luck no one would miss me.

Gravestones and wooden crosses loomed in and out of the dense mist, as if they were prowling around behind the white curtain. Humps of earth reared up and seemed to sink again behind me. Ravens and crows cackled at each other like marketplace crones from the dark yews or the church tower, as if they could see their unsuspecting prey approaching. I stopped and listened. Except for the birds, there was a heavy, muffled silence. But there was a strong smell of woodsmoke in the air, as if a bonfire had been lit close by, though I could see no sign of it, nor of anyone working in the graveyard. Maybe Arthur was wrong, and Dericote and his drinking companions had thought better of desecrating a grave when they sobered up, or were still sleeping off the ale.

The path to the church door seemed much longer in the mist that it had done even in the dark when I'd pursued the night-creeper. But eventually I found the church door and slid into the shelter of the porch. I had barely settled myself before I heard voices. One among them was trying, but failing, to make the others whisper, but the rest seemed to be determined to talk even louder than normal, as if to drive off any ghosts who had not heard the cock crow and might still be lurking in the mist. As the voices moved towards me, one yelped, then cursed vigorously. He'd obviously slipped on the ice or barked his shin on a gravestone. This time several of the men bade him hold his tongue, fearful that he was cursing on hallowed ground.

About half a dozen figures lurched out of the mist, only to be swallowed up again almost at once, but I recognised Dericote's voice. Keeping well back, I followed the sound around the corner and almost collided with them. They had stopped in front of the grave on which I'd seen the daisy wheel symbol the night I'd followed the creeper there, though there was no sign of the mark now, or even of the pebbles from which it had been fashioned. The sign must have been laid there by one of the townsfolk in a vain attempt to prevent the demon from clambering out, but as far as they were concerned it had failed to work. Now, in place of the pebbles, the mound was covered with the remains of a fire. The charred wood still smouldered, thickening the dense white mist with grey smoke.

Those men standing nearest me carried pickaxes and mattocks strapped across their backs and a couple of spades, one of which must belong to a gravedigger, if Arthur was right and they intended to decapitate the corpse.

'Earth should be thawed enough to dig now,' Dericote said. 'Been burning since dawn.'

There were murmurs of admiration at his foresight. 'Threw some salt on the flames while I was at it,' Dericote said, clearly relishing their approval. 'It'll hold him down there in his grave till we've finished our work.'

Everyone fell silent as the implication of what Dericote had said began to dawn on them. The night-creeper was down there, in that grave, waiting. The men didn't move. It seemed no one wanted to be the first to disturb the earth, fearful of what might rise shrieking out of it. I, on the other hand, was eager to see what this dead man looked like. There was only a slim chance I'd recognise him, but FitzAlan might know him if I could provide a good description, always assuming they'd left the corpse with a face.

Finally, one of the men muttered, 'Maybe we'd best say a prayer afore we begin.' He turned his head to look at his fellows and I glimpsed his face. The tanner, Robert Tiploft. I hadn't expected to find him among Dericote's gang. Plainly, he'd do anything to prove Myrna Nash's innocence.

'Pray for the man's soul?' someone asked.

'For *us* . . . protect us against the night-creeper's vengeance. Too late to pray for *his* soul.'

There was a collective mumbling of 'Christ defend us' and 'Deliver us from evil', and what sounded more like curses against the Devil than prayers. Dericote seemed to realise it was up to him as unofficial leader to strike the first blow against the demon. He dragged the remains of the charred wood off the raw mound of earth with his mattock, then raised the blade high and brought it crashing down, embedding it in the thawed earth. He heaved and a slab of earth and ash slid from the grave and burst into dust on the ground. The men watched the second strike, and seeing that it didn't elicit any howls or shrieks from the grave below, they picked up their tools and began to dig. They swiftly worked through the first foot or so of earth, saying nothing except for the occasional exclamation when soil dug up by one man was carelessly flung on to another's boots or breeches. But their progress slowed as they encountered the frozen soil. Pickaxes replaced spades.

There was a sharp cry, causing several of the men to stumble backwards in alarm, slipping on the ice or falling over the charred wood. Dericote and a couple of the others stood their ground, but held their tools in front of them in both hands, as if they feared they would have to defend themselves.

'Was that you squealing, Walter? What did you want to do that for?' Dericote demanded.

'It's the corpse. I can see the shroud. Nearly put my pick through it.'

'Can't be. We're nowhere near six foot down.'

'He was trying to climb out,' Walter said. 'That proves he's the night-creeper. Told you, didn't I? Said it was a demon I'd seen.'

'More likely, the body wasn't buried deep enough,' someone else muttered, inching forward to peer down. 'Remember it wasn't the sexton that dug the grave, but men from the Abbey and at night too. They were likely in a hurry or didn't know how to make a proper job of it. Skilled work, it is, digging a decent grave without it collapsing halfway through.'

They had all inched back to the hole and were peering down. The mist was beginning to thin and melt away, and an ash-pale light filtered through it. I crept a little further back, anxious not to be seen.

'Someone'll have to get in there and use the spade to dig him up,' Dericote said.

No one moved.

'It was your idea, Jacob. I reckon you ought to be the one to do it.'

Dericote looked round, as if still hopeful that someone else would volunteer, but finally he nodded. He sat on the edge of the hole and, with two men steadying him, he lowered himself in until he was standing thigh-deep, pressed hard against the edge of the hole and plainly afraid that if he trod on the corpse it would cry out, or that a hand would shoot up and seize his ankle. He tried to dig the frozen earth, but the angle at which he was standing made that impossible, so he scraped at it with the mattock.

'The shroud's tied over his head and bound round the neck with a stout length of rope. Soon as I get it off, you hand me the sexton's spade.'

Walter dangled the spade over the open grave as Dericote bent to cut the shroud rope. He grunted, sawing with evident effort. Then he thrust the blade between his teeth to free his hand and wrenched apart the stiff folds of frozen cloth. It surrendered with a loud crack. He stood up so swiftly that the top of his head clanged against the flat of the spade Water was holding out, and he was sent sprawling, face down, on top of the corpse.

Arms reached in to haul him out and he stood at the side of the hole, swaying and rubbing his pate. He flapped his arm over the grave, his face turned away from it, as if he couldn't bring himself to look.

'It's a girl down there and . . . and her throat . . .'

Chapter Twenty-nine

IT TOOK SOME TIME to haul the body out, for the woollen cloth of her shroud was frozen to the earth. But eventually they heaved her up and carried her further behind the north wall, out of sight of the path and road beyond. I followed, no longer seeing any reason to hide. I was as stunned as if I'd been hit on the head like Dericote. I'd convinced myself that another Benet was buried down there, but whoever the woman was, she could not be a pursuivant.

They had laid her on the grassed-over mound of another grave and one of the men was endeavouring to rip away the shroud covering her body. They glanced up at me, and Dericote scowled, but he was too preoccupied by his startling discovery to do more than growl. The others barely gave me a second glance, their gaze immediately drawn back to the corpse.

Signs of decay had set in, but the cold had evidently arrested them. The woman was probably around twenty years old, her tawny hair lying in tangled curls about her shoulders. The mounds of her breasts, though badly discoloured, still protruded above a gown cut low enough to reveal that she had in life been well endowed. Her lips had shrunk into a ghastly rictus grin and her skin was peeling. Her head lay at an unnatural angle and the cause was only too plain to see. In her throat was a gaping black hole, stretching from ear to ear. It was so deep that it had almost severed her neck down to the spine behind, exposing a sliver of bone shining white in the growing light. The strands of her hair were matted with dried blood, which had run down her breasts into her gown.

Dericote glanced around. 'Anyone know her?'

'Aye,' Robert Tiploft said heavily. He stood up, wiping his hand over his eyes. 'Though she's the last person I ever thought to find buried here. Bethia, they call her. She's a tiring maid up at the Abbey. Leastways, she was.'

So, Katheryne had been right all along: her maid hadn't run off, or if she had, she certainly hadn't got far. Had the old dowager known all this time that Bethia was lying in a grave just beyond the Abbey walls?

Dericote clambered to his feet. 'Well, it's as plain as a pikestaff why our town is troubled. She's been torn out of this world so violently that her spirit can't rest. She's seeking vengeance on her murderer. Trying to show us the wrong that's been done to her. Her blood is crying out from the earth, like Abel's against Cain. We should carry her straight back to the Abbey. They buried her here, so they must have seen her corpse and known what was done to her. Likely they know who did it an' all. It must've been one of them. She wants us to take her back and demand justice for her, poor wench.'

'Now hold hard,' Tiploft said. 'You can't go accusing Lady Magdalen of murder. She's got powerful friends. We'll all find ourselves hauled up in front of the justices for slander.'

'I didn't say it was the old woman herself,' Dericote said. 'Stands to reason she couldn't have done this, not at her age. But there's plenty up there who could. Men coming and going in secret, foreigners too. Stick a knife in your ribs quick as look at you, they would.'

Walter caught his arm. 'Robert's talking a keg of sense. The magistrate is the late Viscount's cousin. He's dined at the Abbey many a time. You go bringing trouble to their door and they'll bring it fourfold to ours.'

'The whole town is already troubled by that,' another said, jabbing a finger towards the corpse, but studiously avoiding looking it. 'Until her murderer is brought to justice, there's none of us will get any peace.'

Dericote nodded vigorously. 'That's the meat of it!' He glowered at Tiploft. 'Anyway, I thought you wanted to prove your whore innocent. Not so sure of her now, is that it?'

Tiploft's hands clenched around his pickaxe and he took a menacing step towards Dericote. 'You're just making trouble for Myrna because she wouldn't have you. It wouldn't surprise me if it was you who threw that firebrand into her cottage.'

Dericote lunged at him and two of the men moved swiftly to separate them, wresting the pickaxe from Tiploft's grasp.

Dericote, unable to reach Tiploft, rounded on me. 'Did the old lady send you here to spy on us? Did she tell you to report back what we mean to do about the girl, or was it someone else up at the Abbey who sent you?'

Several of the men slowly advanced towards me, but I kept my arms at my side, offering no resistance, though my fingers were close to my dagger hilt beneath my cloak.

'No one sent me. Half of Battle knows what you had planned this morning. You hardly made a secret of it in Sybil's alehouse last night. I came because I was as curious as you were to see who was down there. But if you want to confront the Abbey, I'm certainly not going to talk you out of it. The girl's murderer should be brought to justice. No woman deserves that fate.'

I was itching to point out that this corpse did not, in either height or form, resemble the night-creeper we'd seen on the burning roof, but if they had convinced themselves her spirit or a demon could transform into that diabolical creature, then it might be all to the good. Erasmus would not stalk the streets again – at least, I devoutly hoped he wouldn't – so, if the night-creeper fell silent and the townspeople believed it was because they had unearthed a murder victim, they would not go looking for anyone else. I confess I didn't much like the young novice, but I blamed Smith for making him into the creature he had become, just as I blamed Waldegrave for taking the boy I was and turning me into his aberrant creation. These priests thought they were God. And they were the ones who should be brought crashing down to earth, not those they tormented.

Dericote scowled. He had been looking for a fight and was furious that I wouldn't rise to the bait. '*I* say we take her straight to the Abbey,' he repeated, as if I'd argued against him. 'We'll carry her to the church door, while you two fetch the parish bier from inside. You take her feet. You lift her shoulders opposite me.' He pointed at the various conscripts as he assigned them to their tasks.

Dericote crouched on one side of Bethia and wriggled his hands beneath her shoulders, lifting the body as he stood up. But the man on the opposite side lost his grip. The frozen corpse rolled out of Dericote's grasp, tipping over on to its side, and thumped back down on to the icy mound. Something was jolted out of the gaping wound in her throat and rolled on to the grass. There was a gleam of white in the pale sunshine, and I realised as I stared at it that it wasn't bone I'd glimpsed in that terrible wound: it was three dried beans, their smooth, creamy skins smeared with blackened blood.

Chapter Thirty

ALTHOUGH IT WAS ONLY a short walk between St Mary's church and the Abbey, I had managed to lose the grim procession before they reached the gatehouse. I would certainly not be allowed to remain at the Abbey if Smith or the steward saw me in their company. Fetching the parish bier had taken a little time, and even when the corpse was safely borne aloft, the bearers were obliged to walk with slow, clipped steps. If any of them slipped on the ice, they'd all come tumbling down like a tower of cards.

I knew their progress would be further halted by the black-robed porter at the gatehouse, who, if he treated them as he had me when I'd first arrived, would fetch someone out rather than let them in. So, I got inside well ahead of them, but instead of making my way up the drive to the house, I doubled back and hung around on the other side of the great archway until they thundered on the gate. Then, while the porter had his back to me answering their knock, I slipped into the tiny circular room in one of the little gate towers. The squint in the little chamber proved a good vantage point to see and hear all that went on beneath the archway. Generations of porters and others must have made good use of these holes to spy on the Abbey's visitors, ever since the ancient monks had built the gatehouse. The old abbots might have trusted God, but they did not trust their fellow man.

The porter permitted Dericote and his companions to set the bier down in the passageway between the two gates, but no amount of stamping of feet, blowing on numbed hands or even, in desperation, a proffered coin would induce him to permit any of them into *his* lodge to warm themselves at *his* fire. Since the tower where I found myself was as cold as a crypt, I took a grim satisfaction in this.

Dericote had grandly demanded to speak to Lady Magdalen, but when the porter did eventually return, he was not accompanied by the old dowager but by Smith, who swept into view, muffled against the cold in a heavy fur-lined cloak.

At the sight of him, several of the men in the group shuffled towards the back, heads down. I couldn't see Robert Tiploft anywhere and guessed he had quietly slipped away before the party reached the gate.

'Who speaks for you?' Smith demanded, sweeping his gaze around the small crowd of men, like a schoolmaster seeking the ringleader of the mischief among his errant pupils.

A couple of them took another step back and several darted glances at Dericote, who lifted his chin defiantly.

'It's Lady Magdalen we want to speak to.'

'You expect a frail, elderly woman to risk her health and limbs walking to the gatehouse on this ice?'

'No need for her to come here. We'll go to the house, which is what we'd a mind to do anyway, if this fellow hadn't kept us cooling our heels here.'

He beckoned to the others and took a pace forward. The porter raised his staff across his chest as if he meant to knock Dericote down if he tried to pass, but Smith didn't move.

'State your business and if it is a matter that concerns Lady Magdalen directly then she shall be informed.'

'It concerns her ladyship alright. There was a corpse brought from the Abbey and buried in the parish graveyard by her men at dead of night. All Hallows' Eve, it was. I reckon they chose that night, knowing there's none would venture near a graveyard after dark on that day.'

'And yet you claim men from the Abbey did? It is good to know you think they have more courage than any townsman.'

'The Devil looks after his own,' someone muttered from the back of the men.

Both Smith and Dericote turned sharply, but with mouths covered by mufflers and hats pulled low, it was impossible to see who had spoken.

'These past weeks, the town's been plagued by a night-creeper, tormenting folks in their cottages, scaring women and children half to death, and stealing and killing fowls, and pigs too. And it all began when that corpse was buried in the churchyard, so this morning we determined to put a stop to it. We opened the grave to see what was down there and deal with it, once and for all.'

'*Deal* with it?' Smith said, his tone more glacial than the ice outside.

Dericote shifted uneasily. 'Aye, there are ways . . . If the corpse won't lie still in the grave, then you have to destroy the corpse, so the demon has got no human body it can use to make mischief.'

'Are demons so weak, then, that they cannot do the Devil's work except through the frailty of human flesh, not even to say *dead* flesh?'

Dericote opened his mouth, but seemed unable to find an answer. 'You best take a look at what we found.' He turned towards the bier and gestured to Walter. 'Show him.'

Walter bent with difficulty and unpeeled the shroud as far down as the woman's shoulders. The porter took a step closer, the better to see, then jerked back, his eyes bulging. 'Christ have mercy!'

Had he recognised the girl, or was it the wound on the corpse which had startled him?

Smith had not moved and his face betrayed no shock or even disquiet, and I was certain then he already knew exactly what lay beneath that shroud.

The porter's evident shock seemed to have restored Dericote's swagger.

'See, is it any wonder her poor tormented spirit is haunting the town? Master Tiploft recognised her at once, says she's one of the Abbey's tiring wenches. Goes by the name of Bethia. Isn't that right, Robert?' He turned towards the other men, and only then seemed to realise the tanner was not among them. 'Anyhow . . . that's what he said. We all heard him.'

'Can't be,' the porter said. 'Young Bethia left the mistress's employ long since. Must have been two or three days after Saint Crispin's Day.'

'Well, is it her or isn't it?' Dericote snapped. 'Lady Magdalen ought to be able to tell us, if you won't.'

'The light is poor here,' Smith said.

The porter, his jaw clenched, stepped into his lodging and emerged carrying a lantern, which he held over the face of the corpse and, taking a deep breath, glanced down.

'That's her alright . . . isn't it, Master Smith?'

'The unfortunate girl does resemble the maid,' Smith said, though he did not appear to have even glanced at the corpse again.

'She's seeking revenge on the man who did this to her.' Dericote sounded almost gleeful. 'She won't rest until she's got justice. That's why I must speak with her ladyship. She'll want to know her maid was foully murdered. The constable will have to be sent for.'

'Of course,' Smith said. 'And Lady Magdalen will be most gratified that you and your fellows are willing to deliver yourselves into the hands of the law and confess your crime in order to bring about justice for her poor servant. I trust they will not be too severe with you.'

Dericote gaped at him. 'This isn't my doing! I didn't murder the wench. It was me who persuaded the others to dig up the corpse. I'd not have done that if I'd killed her. Stands to reason, I'd have tried to stop them opening the grave if I'd done it, isn't that right?' He appealed to the small knot of men, who nodded their support.

'He was the one talked us into digging her up,' Walter said. 'It was his idea.'

Smith raised his eyebrows. 'Was it indeed? Then, this man is likely to receive the harshest sentence, if you are all willing to testify that it was him who convinced you to violate a grave on consecrated ground and steal a body from its resting place.'

Dericote jerked as if he'd been struck in the back, and it was a moment or two before he found his voice again. 'Now see here, we only opened that grave to rid the town of the night-creeper.'

'And if you are fortunate and the constable and magistrate believe you, then desecrating a graveyard might be the only crime you are charged with, but from what I know of them, a few noises in the night or a goodwife's chickens going missing will hardly be taken as proof that a revenant is stalking the darkened streets of the town. So, they might well believe that you had other motives for grave robbing. They might begin to wonder if you intended to sell the corpse to an unscrupulous apothecary to use in the making of his physic and theriacs, or even to sorcerers who would use the parts for their spells, and you lost your nerve when you realised that even villains would start asking questions when they saw what you'd brought them. They would demand that you paid them for disposing of a murder victim, and I imagine the silence of such men is not cheaply bought.'

Dericote and his companions were staring from one to another in growing alarm, their eyes glittering with fear in the lantern light.

'You could even find yourselves accused of necromancy.' Smith had been speaking calmly and dropped his voice to a near-whisper on the last word, as if it was too fearful to be uttered aloud. Dericote's face was freezing into a mask of terror as the realisation slowly sunk in.

'But . . . But I didn't . . . I never . . .'

Smith regarded him in silence, letting the threat do its work. The men had backed away from the corpse and were edging towards the great door, only now seeming to realising they were cornered, trapped inside the Abbey gatehouse.

'Speaking for myself, I know you all to be godly men, honest and true. I think that you all acted in the belief, all be it misguided and foolish, that you were saving your fellow townsmen, and some of them might even call you heroes for being willing to fight what you thought might lie in that grave. But you must see how your actions could be interpreted by those who do not live in the town and do not know you. It would be a cruel injustice to see you hanged and your grieving wives and children cast into penury.'

He paused. Every face was turned to him and they seemed to be holding their breath. 'Leave this unfortunate girl here. Tonight, I will see that she is reinterred with all proper rites and prayers for her soul, so that her spirit will find peace and not trouble you again. It is likely that her murderer will never be discovered. Since the killer has not struck again, he was doubtless someone passing through the town, a pedlar or a drunken mariner who will not dare to return.'

They nodded vigorously, willing to settle for any explanation that would allow them to escape.

'Return to your homes now and I caution you for your own safety to speak of this to no one, not even your wives. The King has listening ears everywhere and if even a whisper of your actions should reach the justices . . .' He did not need to finish the warning.

The men crowded behind the porter as he unlocked the gate. They sped out, only turning to make swift bows and mumble their thanks to Smith when they were safely outside.

As soon as the gate had been relocked behind them, Smith bent to cover the girl's head again and, motioning to the porter to lift the other end, they carried her through his small room and into the old chamber beyond. I seized the opportunity to slip out and hurried swiftly back towards the manor deep in thought, running through my mind exactly what Smith had said, or rather what he had cleverly not said.

He had convinced Dericote and the townsmen that the murderer was someone from outside both the Abbey and the town, and they had been only too eager to believe that. They were so relieved to catch the rope he had thrown to drag them from the mire in which they'd found themselves that not one of them had thought to question who had buried the girl and why. Maybe that would occur to Dericote or one of the others in time, but I doubted now whether they'd dare to raise it, given what Smith had threatened.

The explanation could be as innocent as Smith or Steward Brathwayt merely wanting to spare an old lady and her young ward the pain and sorrow of learning their tiring maid had been violently murdered by a ruffian or drunken seamen. The shock and fear that there was a killer stalking the town could easily finish off some elderly women, but somehow, I thought it would take a lot more than that to frighten Magdalen into her grave.

Bethia had probably died the same night that she was supposed to have delivered that token to Tiploft. He could have been lying about not receiving it. Tiploft could easily have killed her, or someone else could have murdered her to stop the message being taken to London, just as they killed Benet to prevent him delivering his report. *The killer has not struck again*, Smith assured the townsmen, but he had. And his victim lay frozen in the hut behind the ruined Abbey – the white beans in his mouth were proof of that.

Chapter Thirty-one

THEOBALDS HOUSE, CHESHUNT, HERTFORDSHIRE

'THE KING RISES!'

There was a scraping of chairs, and a snowstorm of linen napkins was cast upon the remains of the banquet as the whole company struggled to their feet. With the marshal leading the way, James limped from the dining room, his hand pressing down on the shoulder of the young page, who from his pained expression was trying hard to remain upright under the weight and walk in a straight line. But had it not been for his weak and twisted legs, James would have been perfectly capable of walking without weaving across the hall, unlike most of his inebriated guests and courtiers.

Oliver had been discreetly watching him and marvelled at the quantities of strong wine his Sovereign had managed to imbibe without apparently any effect. Maybe the chrism with which kings were anointed really did give them godlike powers. But it was evident many of the guests and most of the courtiers had not been rendered divinely immune. Some were swaying, grabbing for the table or each other to steady themselves as they waited, giggling as they watched a man overbalance into the remains of a cream trifle. Chairs and other obstacles were hastily dragged aside by the servitors as the company began to form up, preparing to follow their leader in order of precedence, which meant that Richard and Sir Christopher Veldon were well to the back.

The Spanish Ambassador and his entourage had been the honoured guests, and the King's favourite, Robert Carr, had found himself ousted from his place at the King's table and so was obliged to walk far behind James in the ragged procession that trailed after him. But Carr had latched on to his friend Sir James Hay, whose shield he had presented in the tilt the day he'd broken his leg. In company with several of the other Scots, they had managed to position themselves ahead of Richard, Veldon and a number of the other English nobles, who were darting murderous glances, sharp as rapiers, at Carr's broad back, muttering that he should be mucking out the King's stables, not aping his betters in the King's dining hall.

'Someone needs to show that young upstart his place,' one growled, quickening his pace as if he meant to do it there and then. But Richard and Veldon hastily caught up with him, linking their arms through those of the disgruntled man and hauling him back.

'Patience,' Richard cautioned, his green eyes glittering like ice in the candlelight. 'Let Carr ride high for now. You know the old proverb: the more you stir up a piece of shit, the worse it stinks. We'll scrape him off our shoes yet.'

Veldon laughed. 'And they also say, the harder you stamp on a turd, the broader it grows. I wouldn't soil my boots on him.'

As the bottleneck in the doorway eased and the procession moved forward, Oliver found himself trailing behind his cousin and his companions, managing to drop even further back than protocol demanded.

Oliver wanted to ensure Lord Salisbury had taken his seat before he arrived, so that he could find a place to stand where he'd be hidden from Cecil's view. 'Out of sight, out of mind' was a maxim he had always tried to follow as a small boy to escape trouble, and he certainly didn't want to find himself on Lord Salisbury's mind. Being summoned to the Tower in the middle of the night and questioned by Cecil about Richard and his recusant father was a memory that still, nearly nine months later, gave him nightmares from which he woke trembling and sweating. Even now he could barely bring himself to look up at the grim water gate, the Traitors Gate, as they had dubbed it, when he passed it on a wherry, dreading another midnight summons. But Lord Salisbury had not questioned him again, and Oliver was more than anxious to ensure that he didn't.

The hall was full by the time Oliver entered. The King and the Ambassador sat on a raised dais reached by a short flight of steps, which were flanked on either side by two narrow cascades of water that bubbled from urns at the top and emptied into tiny dark pools at the bottom. The twisting ribbons of water gleamed gold in the light from the many candles that illuminated the room.

A huge tree with long branches spreading across the wall stood to one side. The artificial trunk was covered in pieces of real bark and from the branches hung silk leaves cut to resemble those of the mulberry. Pearly-white worms, as big as snakes, swung down on fine silken cords, slowly revolving round and round, turned by some unseen mechanism, which presumably also made the stuffed peacock perched on top of the tree open and close its iridescent wings as if it was about to take flight.

Half a dozen musicians were playing on sackbut, harpsichord, lute, violin and bandora to accompany the singers and dancers clad in jerkins and gowns layered with feathered swathes of red and orange, and hung with baubles resembling peaches, apples and nuts. In one corner, a corpulent elderly man, playing the part of Bacchus, reclined on a bank of grass beneath a bower festooned with bunches of grapes. He was half naked but for the deerskins draped over his great belly and a voluptuously curled wig perched on his head, held in place with a wreath of vine leaves. A group of young girls, scantily dressed as wood nymphs, sprawled around him, pouring wine from flagons for anyone who proffered their goblet. But since most of those holding out the cups were too owl-eyed to hold their goblets steady, and the girls too drunk to pour with any care, wine was spilling over guests and floor. But it only added to the howls of laughter and merriment when guests or servants slipped on spilled wine or squashed fruit and came crashing down, sending whatever they were carrying flying upwards to shower themselves or others.

In another corner, beneath a mock oak tree, a muscular centaur posed on a carpet of fallen leaves and acorns. Oliver guessed the beast had been formed by two men, with the one at the back bent over and covered with a horse's hide, while the more fortunate man in front stood upright holding a bow with a quiver of arrows slung over his shoulder. Thick rusty-red strips of what appeared to be fox fur had been stuck to his chest, back and arms, and heaped around him were piles of dead game, including birds of every size from wrens to herons, a boar with long yellow tusks and a hart with black dried blood trailing from its nose.

Skinny lads, probably only two or three years younger than Oliver, had been dressed up as Pan-like creatures, with shaggy breeches made from fleeces and goats' horns protruding from their wild hair. Each held a hunting dog on a leash and they were trying to distract the hounds and lymers from the bloody carcasses by slipping them pieces of pastries and pies when they thought no one was looking. Oliver winced; he hoped for these young actors' sakes those dogs were not the King's favourites. They'd all be vomiting by morning and the Master of the Hounds would have the lads whipped till they howled if he caught them.

Oliver spotted Carr again. He had noticed him earlier, surrounded by young women, and judging by their coquettish gestures and tinkling peals of laughter, he seemed to be charming them as much as he did the King. But one by one their mothers, husbands and fathers had reclaimed them and ushered them back with stiff smiles which froze to ice the moment they turned away. Now he was leaning against one of the pillars, gazing up at the dais, his shoulders hunched, scowling like a sulky child.

To Oliver's surprise, after Richard's warning about ignoring the King's protégé, he saw Richard, Veldon and the man whom they'd restrained earlier strolling towards Carr, greeting him warmly as if he was a boon companion. They stood close to him, smiling and talking. Whatever was passing between them, it certainly did not look like an exchange of insults. Veldon placed what appeared to be a brotherly arm around the Scot's shoulder and guided him towards the door on the far side, with Richard and the other man threading their way closely behind.

Resentment bubbled up in Oliver. Richard had made no attempt to include him in his circle of friends that evening. He'd almost ignored him. But now, here he was, treating this upstart stable hand as if he was his dearest friend in spite of everything he said behind his back. At the bear-baiting, he'd allowed Carr to insult and humiliate him, even joining in the laughter. *I don't need a laddie with arse fluff for a beard to do my fighting.* Oliver felt the blood rush hot to his head. Each time he had thought about it, he had grown more angry with himself for not running Carr through with his sword, instead of driving off his captor. Even if he hadn't actually gone as far as killing Carr, he could at least have let his blade slice across that handsome face, cut off that arrogant nose. Carr wouldn't have looked so pretty then. And Oliver could have claimed it was just an accident; he was, after all, only a beardless boy, Carr had said as much, so, a *boy* could hardly be blamed if that sword had slipped—

A hand gripped the back of his arm, and he spun round, his fists clenched, a hairs breadth from striking out, and found himself staring into the face of Lord Salisbury. Oliver gave a puppy-like yelp and jerked backwards, his taut muscles instantly melted to water by Cecil's sudden appearance and the chilling realisation of how close he'd come to striking the most powerful man in England after the King, and some whispered even more so.

'You seem a little tense, Master Oliver? Not enjoying the spectacle?'

Oliver made a bow that was far deeper and longer than the occasion demanded as he struggled to think of some reply that would not land him in trouble. He was dimly aware that Cecil had organised the entertainments for James on previous occasions;

if he was responsible for this, then he might very well take anyone not enjoying themselves as a personal insult.

'I am in awe of the vision, sir,' Oliver stammered. 'The trees . . . they look as if they're really growing . . . from the ground.'

In his dealings thus far with Lord Salisbury, the great man's expression had been as inscrutable as a death mask to Oliver, but now he could have sworn that just for an instant a look of pain flitted across his face.

'If you had been here in my father's day, you would have seen six trees in the great chamber that even the birds thought real, and a crystal cave with a fountain from which water cascaded as if from the heart of Eden. The ceiling above that chamber was divided into the signs of the zodiac and, at night, lights shone through holes to reveal the constellations of stars in each sign, as well the sun and moon.' He gazed upwards as if he could still see it. 'All revolved by means of hidden wheels so that the full glory of the heavens could be seen inside this great house, even if it was as dark as the Devil's breeches outside.' He glanced at Oliver and gave a small laugh. 'And youth, of course, doesn't believe a word of what age remembers.'

Oliver felt himself sweating. Had he looked as if he doubted what Lord Salisbury had been telling him? The truth was he was so preoccupied with worrying about why Cecil was talking to him at all that he'd barely taken in anything the man was saying. It was far too warm in the hall – roaring fires, too many people, and enough candles burning to make a midday sun look wan. Sweat trickled down his nose.

'I heard this was once the finest house in England . . . though it's magnificent now,' Oliver added hastily, remembering the King now owned it. He was desperately willing Lord Salisbury to move on to someone else. Even the most innocuous topic of conversation was laced with hidden traps and caltrops, any one of which could prove fatal.

'Your cousin and Robert Carr have struck up an amiable acquittance,' Cecil said, as if he was merely remarking on the weather. He was looking towards the door through which the four men had vanished, yet Oliver had the unnerving feeling that if he allowed his own gaze to follow, Cecil's soulful eyes would dart back to fasten on him. 'That will please His Majesty. Relations between the Scottish and English courtiers are not always so cordial, as you may yourself have had occasion to observe, Master Oliver.'

The sweat on Oliver's face and chest was now ice-cold. Lord Salisbury must have heard how the Scots had baited him into drawing a sword in the King's presence when he first arrived at Court. Couldn't a man even piss in his own chamber pot without Cecil hearing it?

'But if an Englishman gallantly comes to the aid of a Scot and saves him from being robbed or worse, that would certainly create a bond. It would seem Lord Fairfax is becoming quite the hero . . . Do you recall our little discussion in the Tower—'

If Cecil said more, Oliver didn't hear it. For the door opened, and a procession of men and women trailed in, each carrying a cornucopia spilling rainbows of cloth and silks, while others carried horns or baskets crammed with fruits, nuts, cheese and spices. Some bore trays of confections and cakes, roasted birds and small beasts re-dressed in their own feathers and fur, or artfully stitched together by the cooks to create piglets with cocks' wings and heads, or salmon with rabbit legs and scut tails. Each bearer staggered up the small flight of steps to the King's dais where one by one, kneeling, they offered their gifts, while declaiming verses about all the bounty of his kingdom and of the seas and lands beyond being laid at the feet of their gracious Sovereign.

At least, Oliver guessed from the few who managed it, that was the intention. But the bearers and actors had been drinking for several hours. Most muddled their lines, slurred them or forgot them entirely. Several teetered on the stairs, tottering backwards down a step or two before making another attempt. Oranges tumbled from wicker horns, bouncing down the steps;

golden saffron showered the head of one elderly courtier standing too close; and three green parrots with yellow heads, the only birds to have escaped roasting, broke from their keeper and flew round the hall, bestowing copious quantities of liquid dung on those below.

Although Oliver had not dared to drink as much as he would have liked, for fear of making a fool of himself, in the stifling heat he was also beginning to feel decidedly bowsy. His brains had been replaced with wool and he found himself staggering sideways as he craned to watch the parrots. He glanced round furtively, hoping that Cecil hadn't noticed, but to his relief the hunchback had moved away and he could no longer see him.

Two girls carrying baskets of fish tried to mount the steps side by side, each determined to wriggle ahead of the other. Their wicker baskets locked together and, unable to move forward or disentangle themselves, one tried to push the other back by forcing a trout into the mouth of her companion, while the other retaliated by beating her with a large eel, sending her tumbling into one of the streams beside the steps. The fish spilled from her basket and slithered down the cascade, leaping and shimmering as if the water had miraculously brought them to life again.

Far from showing displeasure, the King appeared to find the drunken fumblings of the actors hilarious, calling out ribald comments and jokes, and when one man made four unsuccessful attempts to remember his speech, each time getting no further than the first three words, James jabbed him with a stick and sent him somersaulting backwards down the steps, as the company rocked with laughter.

It was only as the dazed man was hauled to his feet and dragged out that Oliver noticed that Richard had returned to the hall and was now standing close to the dais. He couldn't see Carr or Veldon, but so many had crowded together to watch the procession that it was hard to distinguish one man from another in the haze of candle smoke and the press of bodies. A few, encouraged by the King's jokes, were hurling nuts and apples at those actors who were still attempting to present their bounty to James, as if they were playing a game of cockshy, trying to knock the players off their feet or make them spill their baskets.

The procession seemed to be drawing to a close and the last figure entered, a man clad in a short but flowing white robe girdled with a silver belt, his flaxen hair crowned with a chaplet of laurel leaves. He was carrying a boned pullet on a silver platter. The butter-roasted carcass was frosted with sugar and cinnamon. Glittering red garnets had been inserted into the empty eye sockets and its head had been split in two and pressed down, so that one half faced right, the other left, giving the appearance of a two-headed bird, each adorned with a savage hooked beak moulded in gilded marchpane. The pullet had been stretched out, its wings spread wide to resemble the emblem of the double-headed eagle, symbol of the imperial might of a great empire. The pork- and barberry-stuffed dish was, as all the Court knew, a particular favourite of the King, but the way the bird had been dressed was surely intended to remind the Spanish Ambassador that Britain was more than the equal of Spain.

Close behind the mock eagle came two male servants carrying white napkins. It was plain that James and his guest would be tasting this offering at least.

It was only when they had almost reached the steps that Oliver saw the platter-bearer clearly and realised that it was Robert Carr. He seemed to be concentrating too hard: like a drunk man dared by his friends to walk the top of a high, narrow wall, he was placing each sandaled foot with exaggerated care. The crowd was still laughing and yelling jibes and jests. They were too far gone in their cups to restrain themselves from that. Besides, the King himself was joining in, but those who had held fruit ready to throw glanced uneasily towards James and let their missiles drop to the floor.

Carr approached the bottom of the steps and paused, to bend his head, but also, it appeared, to try to decide which foot to lift first. Oliver could not be certain of what happened next, even when he tried to recall the events in the sober light of dawn. He thought he saw Richard move forward, though candlelight often gives the illusion of movement where there is none. He thought he saw the tip of Richard's sheathed sword jerk up between Carr's knees, or maybe, as others swore afterwards, the Scot simply stumbled on a nut or slipped in a puddle of wine. But there was no disputing the result. Carr's leg shot from under him; he teetered for a moment, trying in vain to regain his balance, and pitched forward. The greasy bird shot from the platter and up on to the step above, before slithering down on to the marble floor. The crowd roared with laughter and James seemed to find it funnier than any of them. Carr staggered to his feet, his face flushed and furious, which only stoked their merriment.

Two of the hounds, excited by the noise and the smell of the butter-roasted chicken, ripped their leashes from the hands of the young lads who held them and raced towards the bird, sliding and slithering to halt at the same moment and seizing the pullet between them. They twisted and snarled at each other as they tried to wrench it from their rival's jaws. Those standing too close were showered in drops of grease as the dogs shook the bird. As one tore off a leg, the other hound fell backwards, the remains of the carcass clamped in its jaws. The two dogs dropped to the floor, gnawing the chicken. The young lads tried to haul the hounds away, but they would not relinquish their feast. Men and women were clutching each other, howling with mirth.

Then those at the front of the crowd suddenly sobered up as if a pail of cold water had been hurled over them. It took some time for those further back to comprehend what was happening, but they too fell silent. The dogs had dropped the meat and were lying on their sides, trembling and convulsing. Foam bubbled from their mouths as they shrieked in agony. They twisted and arched, thrashing around, whimpering piteously. Then the only sound to be heard in the hall was the cascades of water. Even the parrots had fallen silent, peering down in seeming awe for, far beneath them on the cold marble floor, the hounds lay dead.

Chapter Thirty-two

DANIEL PURSGLOVE

I KNEW EVEN BEFORE I reached it that someone was inside the library. They had left the door slightly ajar, but as they moved silently across in front of the pale light emanating from the room, they threw a dark shadow out across the passageway, too distorted for me to make out who it was, except that it was a woman. I had hoped I would find Smith's lair empty. All of the guests and the household were at dinner. I had glanced in and seen Smith attacking a chicken pie with a hearty appetite, as if he'd spent a morning galloping in a hunt. The sight of the corpse with her throat slashed had certainly not turned his stomach. So, who was up here? One of the maids? Even as I pictured the household eating, I realised who was missing from that table.

The door opened wider, and before I could retreat, Katheryne stepped swiftly into the passageway. It was too dark to read her expression, but I thought I detected a slight jerk of surprise. She'd probably heard footsteps and known someone was approaching, but I wagered she had not been expecting me.

'I was waiting for you,' she declared, a little too firmly for it to ring true.

'Were you indeed, m'lady? And how did you know I'd be coming up here?'

'I thought you would come to make the library ready, for when the Fathers retire from supper. And you have.' She gestured to the flagon of wine I was carrying.

My own excuse, turned round on me. I was annoyed. I had hoped for a few minutes alone to search for any message that might have been delivered in that ledger, but there was no chance of that now.

'Why did you wish to see me, m'lady? Whatever it is you want, you'd better make haste. Erasmus may be coming up soon and you shouldn't be seen here.'

She glanced uneasily over my shoulder, biting her lip between sharp white teeth. For a moment I thought she must have heard about Bethia, in spite of Smith warning the men to keep silent.

She took a step closer, lowering her voice so that I had to lean in to hear her. 'They are expecting a ship . . . two nights from now. I know they mean to put me aboard and take me to the convent in Brussels. Since they banished Bethia, I've had no word from London. He will not know I am to be moved. Please, you must help me to get away. You need only find me a place close by where I can hide and wait for him. The tanner will carry a message.'

If Tiploft was innocent of Bethia's murder, then I would wager the sight of her body would be enough to warn him off carrying more messages, and if he was guilty . . .

'How do you know about this ship?'

'Father Smith received a message yesterday.'

'Yesterday? How? How are these messages delivered?'

'A boy, I think, someone from outside the Abbey. I heard Father Bray mention it once to Father Holt. He told him he'd seen the boy arrive so there must be news.'

So it *was* Giles who carried the messages in his sack of vermin.

Katheryne gave an impatient shake of her head. 'But that doesn't matter. Don't you understand? They mean to force me on to that ship. I heard them talking about delivering the precious cargo safely.'

'Cargo? And did they say you were the cargo?'

For the briefest of moments her gaze slid to the door next to the library. So she too had discovered that much could be overheard from that tiny room. '"A valuable tapestry", they said, one that must not be damaged, but I know they meant me. What else would they be sending to Brussels? For weeks, Father

Smith has been talking about the Monastery of Our Lady of the Assumption. It was established for nuns from England and they are asking for more postulants. He's convinced Lady Magdalen I should be sent there, because I will be with women of my own rank and tongue. Mary Percy has taken the veil there. Lady Magdalen knew her father, Sir Thomas Percy, though she does not speak of it, except to Father Smith.'

And little wonder, I thought, since Percy had been executed for High Treason. Though it was his wife, Anne, who had planned and instigated the rising against Elizabeth, and persuaded her husband into it, even riding with his troops when heavy with child for fear his mettle would fail him. Anne would have forfeited her own head on the block had she not fled to Flanders with the child, and if rumours were to be believed she was still plotting against Elizabeth with her last breath.

I had assumed that if Smith and the old dowager intended to send Katheryne to a nunnery it was to keep her away from this lover of hers, or from other unsuitable suitors. But if the Viscountess really was planning to send her ward to a convent where Mary Percy and her friends were living, then FitzAlan's suspicions of the wily old woman were not unfounded. If Mary Percy was half the woman her mother had been, then this English convent in Brussels was not only a refuge for those escaping Cecil's nets, but a magnet for those plotting against the King, and Magdalen's ward would be placed at the beating heart of it. If that was their plan, though, Smith and the old lady were taking a huge gamble, unless they were convinced that once under the influence of Mary Percy and her sisters, the recalcitrant girl would be persuaded to their cause. But then this whole tale of being spirited off to the Low Countries and forced into a nunnery could simply be the romantic fantasy of a bored young woman.

'My lady, if you heard them speaking of tapestries, is it not more likely that is exactly what they meant? The finest tapestries in Europe are woven in Brussels. Half the great houses in England have imported them. Lady Magdalen has probably commissioned one from a weaver there, for the chapel or the library. If the scene is one that the authorities might consider overtly Catholic, a depiction of a saint or the Virgin Mary, then she will not want to land it in any of the ports where it risks being seized or destroyed by the King's men. So, it must be smuggled in.'

For the first time, I saw tears spring up in Katheryne's eyes, though they did not spill over and she dashed them angrily away. She was frightened. And maybe she had good reason to be, though she didn't know it, for even as we spoke, her maid and confidante was lying within the Abbey gate with her throat slashed wide open.

We both looked around as we heard the sound of voices below us. She stared up at me in mute appeal before walking away. Momentarily possessed by some rash impulse, I touched her arm and she glanced back. 'I will keep watch over you, my lady. And if I believe there is any danger, I will act. You have my word.'

But even as I said it, I was already regretting that word.

I ANTICIPATED that Smith would have Bethia's corpse removed from the Abbey as soon as the servants and household had settled for the night. Before it grew dark, I had managed to slip back into the inner room of the gatehouse and had swiftly patted over the corpse. But there was nothing more to be seen on her body – no signs that her wrists and legs had been tied like Crowhurst's – and there was no doubt as to the cause of her death. No one could claim this to be self-murder or even an accident. I had hoped to find the comb she had been carrying for Katheryne, but her pocket was empty, though that told me little, for it could easily have fallen out unnoticed when she was attacked, wherever that had been. Then again, Tiploft could have been lying when he said she had not come to him that night. But it was plain that all her corpse owned now were those beans. And whoever had stuffed them into the open wound of her throat had also pushed some into Crowhurst's mouth. Was it a message, a warning of the fate that awaited anyone who talked? But warning to whom? Who was that message intended to silence?

I was intrigued to know who Smith would trust to rebury her, for he could not do it alone, if indeed he was even prepared to soil his hands to help lift the corpse. I was sure that it was Smith who had given the order for her to be buried in St Mary's graveyard, and whoever he now instructed to reinter her would be the same men who had dug her grave. He would not risk drawing others in.

I couldn't follow them to the churchyard; even at night I would be too easily visible on that stretch of open road. So, I slipped out of the gatehouse on the pretext of going for a mug or two of mulled ale and a game of cards, at which the porter sighed and wagged his finger in grave reproof, reminding me that gambling was forbidden until Christmas and Steward Brathwayt would fine me heavily if I was caught by the watch; but he let me pass.

A cold hard moon shone down over the graveyard, glittering on the frosted ground. The wooden crosses and the yew trees rose silver-white, ghosts of themselves, as if they would sink back into the earth at cockcrow. Taking care to circle the churchyard close to the wall, so as not to leave a trail of footprints in the frost, I made my way to the northside of the church and hid behind one of the yews. I was some distance from the open grave, but the moon was so bright, I thought I would be able to recognise the men at least by their shape or voices.

I waited, breathing through my muffler and shuffling my feet to keep the blood from freezing. Even my eyeballs felt skinned by the bitter chill. But there was no sign of them. No rumble of cartwheels or crunch of feet on ice. They must come soon.

The heap of earth lay piled by the grave, casting a shadow over the dark pit. I shivered, and not from the biting cold. I had seen many die over the years, in battle, on the executioner's blocks, in prison and in the streets. Somehow seeing another man's death seems to ward off your own, as if your place in the death cart has been taken by some other victim and you have been spared. But that dark pit reminded me there was no escape in the end. And if I didn't find out what Benet had discovered, a grave might be opening its jaws for me within weeks. FitzAlan had forgiven my failure once; I couldn't count on him doing so again.

If I could intercept just one of those messages. Katheryne had confirmed my suspicions that Giles was bringing them in, and if she was right about the ship, Giles would surely deliver another soon. I needed to get hold of that boy's sack before he handed the contents to Yaxley.

I'd been a fool to promise to watch out for the girl. But I was convinced she was mistaken in what she thought she had heard. I didn't for one moment believe that Lady Magdalen was ordering tapestries, I'd said that merely to calm Katheryne, but still it nagged at me. As I had told her, the finest tapestries in the world came from Brussels. It would be foolish to speak of sending a tapestry *to* Brussels. Such a clumsy code would arouse the suspicions of even the most beef-witted servant or beetle-headed official. This ship was not taking someone out, but smuggling someone in. Tapestries were valuable, delicate and worth a king's ransom. Whoever they were bringing in was important to them, far more important than any ordinary priest.

My feet were so cold now that if I didn't move soon, I'd find them welded to the ground. The burning curiosity I'd had to find out who had known of Bethia's death was cooling as rapidly as my hands and face. I plodded my way back to the gatehouse, stamping the feeling back into my legs as I went. I ignored the scowls and grumbles of the porter dragged from the warmth of his hearth. He'd be even more sour when Smith's minions roused him from his bed when they came to remove Bethia's corpse.

As I trudged towards the house, a scrawny cat crossed my path, pausing to stare at me. Her eyes glowed green in the light from the lanterns on either side of the gatehouse. I watched her pad away, wondering how she could bear to walk on such frozen ground when my own feet felt like blocks of ice, even through thick boots. I was so intent on getting back into the house and a warm hearth that, had it not been for the cat, I probably wouldn't even have glanced down at the path, but now I noticed there were two sets of parallel lines in the frost. One pair ran between the courtyard and the gatehouse, while the other set, which were deeper, led from the gatehouse out towards the woods. There were three sets of footprints beside the lines. But Smith couldn't be intending to bury the body here in the Abbey grounds. Until the thaw, they could no more dig a new grave for Bethia than they could for Crowhurst. They must be taking Bethia to the tool shed to lie beside him. There would soon be enough corpses in there to make a charnel house of it. My curiosity was stirring once more and, in spite of my longing for a fire and some hot broth, I followed.

Even in the darkness, it was an easy trail to trace. The tracks of the handcart were plainly visible in the frost, for the weight had shattered the brittle grass blades, just as wagons crushed the stems of the clay pipes that littered the streets of every town. But it was impossible to say how far ahead of me they were; the night was full of noises. The stars, dazzlingly bright and sharp in the black sky, had turned the forest beneath into glass. Dried leaves cracked and shattered under the lightest tread. Twigs on bushes snapped like icicles when you brushed against them, and small explosions echoed through the forest as branches burst in the cold. By now the men should already have reached the shed and deposited the body. I braced myself to retreat quickly if they returned the way they'd come; I'd have a hard time convincing them I was merely out for an evening stroll. But just where I expected the tracks to turn towards the hut, I saw that they had veered away and were now leading deep into the woodlands. They were heading for the charcoal burners' huts.

Ahead of me, through the black skeletons of the trees, I glimpsed a light. Not a lantern, but the bright orange flames of a torch, and almost at the same moment, I caught the murmur of voices and sounds of breaking wood. I edged closer, crouching down behind a holly bush, but the three figures were not even glancing around them. A blazing torch illuminated the whole clearing. The small handcart was drawn up beside the hut in which Crowhurst had been found. One held the torch, while two of the men carried the rigid bundle that I assumed to be Bethia inside, and they must only have had time to lay her down before swiftly backing out again. They vanished around the other side and from the splintering and cracking it sounded as if they were ripping the wood and dried turfs from one of the half-collapsed hovels, which they then took into the hut where Bethia's corpse now lay. They worked in silence. They were so heavily wrapped in cloaks, hats and hoods that it was hard to make out who they were at first. But I had seen Smith often enough by then to be convinced that he was not among them.

One of them lifted a small keg from the cart and vanished inside again. After a few moments he emerged, still holding the keg, placing it with care back on to the cart, while his companion pulled handfuls of straw from two sacks and pushed through the entrance to the hut. The two men who had been carrying the wood and turfs retreated a little way into the trees. The third returned to the hut and thrust the flaming torch through the doorway, holding it there a moment or two until the dry straw caught alight, before hurrying back to join his companions. All three crouched down, their attention fixed on the hut.

The flames caught the dry straw and there was a sound like a sudden gust of wind as the fire blazed up and licked around the poles of the hut, catching dried grass roots in the turfs that were sliding and tumbling to the ground. The bones of the hut were laid bare and the fire licked up the wooden frame, sending golden sparks shooting up into the darkness.

For a moment, in the blaze of light, I saw the body of the girl lying inside, trapped in a burning cage. Behind the dancing flames, she seemed to suddenly uncoil, as if she had come to life and was trying desperately to crawl to freedom. Then the hut exploded: fragments of the wooden poles and pieces of burning cloth and hair were hurled into the black sky and tumbled over and over, gold and scarlet, as they drifted back to earth, and with them came the stench of burning flesh and bone.

There was nothing left now, except a fire. What remained of the other two huts was also ablaze and with minutes they too had collapsed into a heap of fiery wood and smouldering turfs. I knew what had been in that keg; whoever had laid the gunpowder, it had been skilfully done. No one would find any trace of a corpse in those embers, and anyone in the Abbey or the town hearing the distant bang, muffled by their closed shutters, would probably convince themselves it was just another tree exploding in the frost.

The three figures rose from where they had taken shelter and edged towards the burning hut, throwing back their hoods and pulling the scarves down from their faces as they warmed themselves in the blaze. One stumbled over something at his feet and stared down before bending to retrieve it. The firelight flickered over the object, black and scorched, but I could see clearly what it was – a human hand, Bethia's hand. He stared at it for a moment then tossed it into the flames, as if it was nothing but a gnawed chicken bone which a man discards after a meal. Then, as the three of them turned towards the cart, preparing to leave, their faces were lit up like actors on the stage. The sallow face of Steward Brathwayt, the dagger-point beard of Julian Santi and the unnaturally white hair of Henry Holt.

Smith had told Dericote and the others that he'd ensure Bethia's spirit would not trouble them again. She'd be 'reinterred with all proper rites and prayers for her soul'. If he had lied about that, he had certainly kept his promise about one thing: she would not trouble them again. There was no danger of Bethia's corpse rising now, not in this world . . . nor in the next.

I didn't want to risk them seeing me ahead of them, for the bright moonlight and glow of the fires would catch any movement. So, I crouched in the bushes and waited until they vanished from view, then followed, slowly.

All was as still as the grave as I slipped into the manor. The fires in the woods were already dying down and only the ghost of a dark red glow lurked among the trees, nothing that any casual glance would notice.

As I tiptoed along the passage, the light from the night candle burning on one of the sconces caught the bright copper breast feathers and the iridescent blue wings of the kingfisher wind vane. There were two of them hanging there, one pointing south, the other west, like an old married couple who had quarrelled about where the wind was coming from. They were both wrong, for bitter cold could only be from the north or east. But since there was no wind . . .

Two kingfishers, but yesterday there had been three. Maybe one had simply fallen down, rotted away, but they were not supposed ever to decay, which is exactly why the maids kept them in linen cupboards and wool chests, for dried kingfishers were known to preserve the cloth and give it a sweet perfume. Was young Giles paid to catch these beautiful creatures too? It was to be hoped he didn't bring them to the manor in his bloody sack with the stinking crows and putrid rats.

I whirled round and retraced my steps, staring up at the birds. That was it! How could I have not seen it at once? Ever since Giles had brought his hoard the day before, a little worm had been boring away so deep inside my mind that I hadn't been able to pluck it out, but now it suddenly wriggled forward and I saw what had been gnawing at me. The vermin that were listed in that ledger – a kite, rats, weasel and three swallows. This was the middle of winter, and not just any winter but one that was colder than most people could ever remember. And there were no swallows in England at this season.

Some people said swallows slept all winter in flocks beneath the waters of the lakes or seas; others claimed that they flew to warmer climes or even to the moon. But wherever they went, they did not remain here in the cold and bitter months. So, how had the boy caught them in December? He hadn't. They had been caught back in the summer and dried like the kingfishers, so that they still looked fresh. That would explain the cornmeal on Yaxley's table where the bailiff had laid out the vermin while he recorded them. If they had preserved the swallows in the same way that the maids dried kingfishers, then they'd have gutted them and used the cornmeal to sop up any fluids while the flesh beneath the feathers desiccated.

The messages were not hidden *in* the vermin; the birds and beasts *were* the message. The type of animal and the number of each one must have a coded meaning. Yaxley recorded them in the ledger and carried it into the house for someone there to decipher. If anyone had inspected the boy's sack, they would find the contents tallied exactly with the record the bailiff was required by law to keep. The book was legal evidence that the estate was paying a bounty to ensure vermin were hunted and killed. I couldn't help grinning at the elegance of the jest. Giles and the bailiff probably had no idea what each animal or number stood for, so they couldn't betray the code's meaning, whatever ruthless methods might be employed to interrogate them.

But someone in the house did know: Steward Brathwayte – maybe, Smith – almost certainly. The code could potentially be a complex one. There were perhaps as many as fifty different birds and beasts, then varying numbers of each type, with perhaps even a separate meaning assigned to different combinations. No one could keep a code like that in their heads, not even a priest like Smith. He must have the cipher written down somewhere.

I glanced up again at the kingfishers. How did they fit in? Probably a series of simple messages or warnings to others in the household, or to someone who regularly called here. And who hung these birds? An image flashed into my head of the flash of bright blue as three of them had tumbled to the ground. I'd been standing in this passageway as they'd fallen. I tried hard to recall the scene and then it came back to me. Of course! Who else would be trusted?

Chapter Thirty-three

'OH NO, YOU DON'T, young Arthur. You've been keeping me dangling too long,' I said. Clamping my arm firmly around his shoulder, I steered him away from the path that led to the gate-house and guided him towards the woods.

Above his muffler, his eyes opened so wide in alarm that he resembled one of the pop-eyed dogs that wealthy women keep to amuse themselves.

'You promised me that you'd show me a way in and out of this place that didn't involve going through the gatehouse.'

He let out a huge snort of laughter and his eyes crinkled in a mischievous grin. 'Wondered what you wanted for a minute, but if that's all, I suppose I can trust you with such a valuable secret. Not that you haven't got a rare talent for making enemies, but I have to hand it to you, you make enemies of both sides and the middle too, and there's not many can do that.' He grinned again and glanced back towards the Abbey to ensure we were not being watched. 'Come on, then.'

We followed the route that poor Bethia's corpse had been taken the night before, but we had not yet reached the clearing when he stopped. 'What's that smell? Stinks worse than the Devil's crotch.'

As we emerged from behind the trees, Arthur stopped again. Three blackened circles marked where the huts had stood, and scattered across the ground were pieces of charred poles, ash from the turfs and fragments of what I knew must be cloth, bone and flesh. But the pieces were so small and badly burned, they were unrecognisable. I tried to walk on, but Arthur hung back, scuffing his boots through the remains and kicking the charred fragments.

'Thought I saw a red glow over the trees last night, but never took much notice. This bitter weather plays all kinds of tricks on your eyes and ears. It must have been these huts going up. What do you reckon? Night-creeper been up to his mischief again?'

He suddenly crouched down. His fingers were clumsy in his thick gloves and it took several attempts to pick up whatever he'd seen. He blew the ashes from it and held it up in the sharp winter sunlight. It was a jawbone, charred from the fire, but the too-human teeth still clung firm in their sockets. 'This place is littered with old bones. They say ten thousand men were lost at the Battle of Hastings, so I suppose there's bound to be a few breathed their last on this spot. Do you reckon this is one of them? Or maybe it's the bones of one of those old monks.' He tossed the jaw back into the ashes and I found myself wincing, though she could suffer no more hurt or indignity now.

'All I ever find is bones,' Arthur said. 'Why couldn't I dig up a sword from the battlefield with a ruby on the hilt big as a hen's egg, or a purse of gold from a pikeman's pocket?' He raked another heap of ashes hopefully with his boot.

'Trust me, not even a king would be fool enough to go into battle with a jewelled sword, and most pikemen wouldn't have a gold piece to their name, much less a purseful of them. You'd have more luck searching for a monk buried with his treasure. Come on,' I urged him. 'Which way now?'

'You should have been a steward the way you nag . . . getting as bad as old Brathwayt,' Arthur grumbled, but obligingly trudged towards a narrow track that led through the trees on the other side of the clearing. I was about to follow when something pale caught my eye among the dark roots of a tree. I took a few paces towards it. It was a small pile of dried beans. They lay in a nest of what looked like charred twigs. I bent closer, then jerked upright. The beans, white and shiny as pieces of marble, were cupped in the palm of what had once been a human hand, burned so thoroughly that only the clawed, black bones and charred sinews remained. It was a right hand; the hand one of those three men had tossed into the fire.

As soon as Arthur showed me his secret way out, I knew that it was not the one I was looking for. It must have been the one Erasmus had used when he was tormenting the town, which was why he'd run into me that night when I was returning from the charcoal burners' hut. But if Smith was planning to smuggle someone from a ship into the Abbey, it would not be by this route. Behind a dense thicket of trees and bushes that screened it, the wall of the Abbey grounds turned at a sharp angle, and in the corner a heap of broken stones and blocks had been piled up to form a series of rough but serviceable steps that made it possible to scramble up on to the wall. The way up or down on the other side was provided by the roof of a jakes and a barrel positioned next to it. A narrow, overgrown track led from the privy and threaded between the two cottages that shared it to a wider lane beyond.

'You mind the lid is on that barrel before you jump down on it. There was a lad from the Abbey, clambered up on it in the dark one night after a few ales and fell in. Found himself up to his neck in the ancient shit from that jakes that the old woman was using to grow her beans. Took nearly a week of washes to rid him of the stench and old Brathwayt wouldn't allow him back into the house till it had gone, swore the lad stank worse than henbane, which is saying something, because he won't allow any of us to use that. Sensitive little soul is our steward.' Arthur chuckled.

The word *beans* leaped out at me from his chatter, but I was sure it had no significance for him. Every goodwife in England with a patch of garden or scrap of land grew beans along with their herbs and worts. It would be no help in finding out who had murdered Crowhurst or Bethia.

According to Arthur, the privy was no longer in regular use by either of the cottagers and was only visited by a young girl who once a day brought food to her ailing grandmother and who emptied the old widow's piss pail into it. The other cottage was occupied by a man with a harelip who couldn't make himself understood. He kept his shutters closed and his door bolted for fear of the local children who tormented him.

'So long as you use the twitten after dark, there's no one to see, for the old biddy's tucked up in her bed and she's as deaf as an adder, and the man couldn't tell a soul what he saw even if he was put to the rack.'

But though the route would suit Arthur and many of the servants, especially the young lads for whom climbing drunkenly over a wall only added spice to a good night out, I could not imagine it suiting the purposes of Smith, or the other priests. Not that they would disdain the idea of making use of a getaway route via a jakes; I'd often heard Viscount Rowe's guests tell stories of fugitive priests found hiding in stinking sewers or beneath the privies of the recusant houses. But this route out of the Abbey emerged in the centre of Battle town. Ideal for those whose only goal was a tavern or whorehouse, but anyone smuggling men or goods would know that all the roads leading from Battle to the coast were closely watched. They would not risk bringing precious cargo through that way. There had to be another way in and out, but if there was, it was plain Arthur didn't know it, and I suspected that few of the servants did.

I GLANCED UP at the kingfishers in the passageway. I found myself doing that every time I passed beneath them, convinced the number or direction would have changed. But the two still hung facing away from each other. As a boy I'd read an old tale of how the son of the Day Star perished at sea. His wife, Alcyone, daughter of Aeolus, god of the winds, was so grief-stricken that she drowned herself. The gods took pity on them and turned the pair into kingfishers, so that they could be reunited. But it seemed this pair of halcyon lovers had quarrelled.

The rustle of skirts made me turn. Esther, Magdalen's maid, was hurrying along the corridor towards me, her arms, as always, full. I offered a small bow, not so deep that she'd think she was being mocked, but enough to flatter her rank as the mistress's personal maid.

'May I carry that for you, Mistress Esther?'

Her grip on the bundle tightened and she moved it away from me, like a child determined not to allow a treasure to be snatched, but not before I had glimpsed a leather travelling bag, partly covered by a blanket.

'I'm sure you have your own duties, Daniel. The steward was looking for you earlier. He won't be best pleased if he finds you loitering here.'

'I was intrigued by the halcyons. They don't seem to know which way the wind blows.'

'There is no wind, or hadn't you noticed? So the birds hang idle, like you.'

I ignored the jibe, taking a step sidewise as if I were trying to peer back along the gloomy corridor at the birds, but actually to ensure she couldn't easily slip past me.

'I could have sworn there were three the other day. Pity you had to throw one away, Mistress Esther. Such pretty feathers.'

Her body jerked as if she had been pricked.

'It is you that hangs them, isn't it?'

'Sometimes . . . sometimes they are needed elsewhere, to keep out the cloth worms and other vermin from the linens.'

'Pursglove!' The summons came from behind me.

I cursed under my breath. The steward was marching down the passage towards me, his great belly jiggling as if he had a live squirrel under his coat. Esther squeezed passed me and was gone.

White puffs of breath spurted from the steward's mouth as he approached, like a man sucking on a tobacco pipe, and it was a few minutes before he could speak. 'Erasmus will not be waiting on the gentlemen tonight, Pursglove. See that you make ready their room for the night before supper. Make sure the livery cupboard is well stocked. They will be retiring early.'

'Early? But these past nights they've sat up in the library until late to take warmth from the great fire there.' *Not to mention the numerous cups of hot spiced wine.*

'You questioning my orders, Pursglove? Have a care. You'll find it a long cold winter on the road.'

'I was anxious to know when the gentlemen would require their beds warming, Master Brathwayt.'

'Warm them . . .' – he hesitated, his gaze flicking briefly towards those kingfishers – '. . .while they are serving the last course at supper in the great hall. Then you need not disturb them again.'

They weren't going to bed, of that I was sure, at least not until their business was done. Swallows return, yes, but they leave too. Judging by that travel bag, it seemed Katheryne had been right after all; they were going to put someone on board that ship. But I was convinced she was not the one being taken. They would not need to involve the three priests to do that. I'd wager the person being smuggled out was the man they were hiding in that secret chamber. It seemed the rat was about to emerge from its hole.

Chapter Thirty-four

SHADOWS

MY NECK SPASMS in an agony of cold and cramp, as if it is clamped in an iron fetter, crushing the bones. I cannot turn my head. But from the corner of my eye, I see lights, dazzling through the darkness. I've seen them before, lights flashing across my vision like flaming stars, blue and white, red and yellow. I don't know if my eyes are open. Open or shut, I still see them.

I see faces too, faces of the long dead, glowing pale as the moon, and faces of the living. I think they still are living, but they too may be dead now. And they are dead to me, for I can no longer give them their names. I *must* not speak their names. But in truth I no longer know which face owns which name. I no longer recognise friend from foe. How long has it been – hours, days, weeks, months?

He spoke to me through that ragged black mask, through that muffled raven's beak. 'It is almost time.'

Almost time . . . but when he did say that? How long ago – hours, days, weeks? My stomach no longer counts the days for me. It has forgotten how to measure hunger.

I wake to the smell of toast and violets, tobacco and bacon, when I know they must be sweat, ordure and piss, *my* sweat, ordure and piss. I see lights where there are none.

I cannot move my head, and yet now I see an orange glow, a yellow dart of flame. I smell smoke. And I know I cannot open that door until he unlocks it; *if* he unlocks it.

He said, 'It is almost time.'

'Time is, time was, time is past,' said the alchemist's brazen head. And then it was gone. Too late, too late to question.

'Almost time', and then it will be over.

The yellow flame is brighter now. The smoke smells stronger.

Chapter Thirty-five

DANIEL PURSGLOVE

IT WAS THE BLACKEST NIGHT I could remember since the great frost began. The setting sun had bathed the woods in blood-red light, so that it seemed the whole world was burning, but as it vanished, darkness seeped in as a chill tide, and with it the silence, as if the whole Abbey had sunk into a grave-pit and been buried beneath the frozen earth.

The household had assembled for supper at five, but even the flames of the fire and the candles reflected in the silver dishes and glasses looked strangely pale, like corpse lights. The voices, when anyone spoke at all, were subdued and hushed. No one, it seemed, had an appetite for the usual debate and argument over some obscure point of theology or politics. I snatched what glimpses I could of the Great Hall. I could see no sign of Smith, or Katheryne, but the four priests were there, sitting around Magdalen. Erasmus was missing, as I'd been warned, but then none of the other acolytes were present either. I was relieved by that. I had feared, after what Brathwayt had said, that Erasmus might have gone missing, up to his old tricks in the town or shut up in the hiding hole again. The steward was there in his accustomed place at the head of the table over which he ruled, along with several more of the senior servants, but like the priests, they were mainly eating in silence. The tension was palpable and though I suspected few, if any, of the servants understood the cause, nevertheless they plainly felt it.

I hoisted the heavy basket of food and drink needed to replenish the livery cupboard and made my way upstairs to the gentlemen's chamber. I left the basket there and crept along the corridor towards Katheryne's room. Her absence from supper disturbed me. Could I have got this wrong? Was she the person they intended to put on board that ship? I'd promised her I would watch over her. It had been a moment of idiotic weakness, triggered by the genuine fear I'd seen in her eyes. I hadn't come to Battle to rescue some spoiled girl, especially as it might very well get me thrown out, or worse, much worse. But I couldn't very well retract my promise to her, and, I tried to convince myself, she might have learned something more in the last few hours that would be of use to me.

I reached her chamber and was about to knock softly, but before I could, I heard floorboards creaking as if someone was moving stealthily across the room towards the door. I hurried past, gambling that whoever was emerging would turn towards the stairs. I pressed myself into the slight recess of the doorway beyond. Esther came out, closing the door behind her and locking it. As I'd hoped, she hurried towards the stairs without glancing round. I inched back and listened. If Katheryne was in there, she was certainly not pacing about or, as I'd expected, furiously rattling the door. But then, if she wasn't in the room, why would Esther have bothered to lock the door? Unless it was to delay anyone discovering that.

I removed the spike I always carried inside my shirt and let myself in, taking care to relock the door behind me. It would buy me a few moments to hide if Esther returned, or worse still, Smith. The small room was dark, except for a single candle that guttered on a spike beneath a small statue of St Catherine, the wheel at her feet and a palm frond in her hand – Katheryne's heavenly patron. Seeing the saint's long, unbound hair, I was reminded that among her other responsibilities, the saint was also protector of cloistered virgins. I wagered her statue hadn't been placed here at Katheryne's request.

The curtains around the bed had been drawn as if the girl had already retired for the night. And I'd no wish to alarm her by suddenly dragging them open. I called out softly several times, but there was no answer. I moved to the head of the bed and lifted the curtain, prepared to clamp my hand across her mouth if she screamed. The ghost-glow of the votive candle barely reached the bed, but in the cavernous gloom I could just make out a pale form. Katheryne was lying on her back, the covering drawn up to her chin, her hair loose beneath her nightcap and brushed out over the pillow, like a fresh corpse laid out for the relatives to view. For a moment, I thought she was dead. I held my hand close to her mouth and, after what seemed like an eternity, felt a warm breath on my cold fingers.

But she wouldn't wake, not even when I shook her. She had clearly been drugged. I twitched back the coverings, praying to her saint that, at least for the next few moments, the girl would remain asleep. She was dressed in a nightgown. They wouldn't carry her on to a ship in such flimsy garb in summer, much less in this bitter cold. Aside from the fact that she'd freeze to death, I couldn't imagine that Lady Magdalen would countenance her ward being seen clad in night attire by anyone other than her maid. I was as sure then as I could be that Katheryne was not the swallow who would be flying from these shores.

I let the bed hanging fall and crossed back to unlock the door, glancing once more at the impassive face of St Catherine. She was also the protector from sudden death. It was a strange irony that the King, who feared an assassin lurked behind every door, had renounced the protection of such a saint, while those who still prayed to her as they hung in agony in the Tower must be longing for the mercy of a quick end. I found myself nodding to St Catherine as I passed. I hoped neither her namesake nor I would be requiring her services before this night was over.

I had just inserted the spike into the lock again when I heard the boards creak and footsteps coming along the passageway. Too late to escape, I moved to where the door, when it opened, would shield me from the sight of anyone entering. The steps halted. Someone was standing outside, listening. I expected to hear the key rattling in the lock. I held my breath. The footsteps moved on. They did not belong to Esther or any of the other servants, who wore soft leather or cloth shoes inside the house. These shoes had hard soles.

I unlocked the door as swiftly and soundlessly as if I were magically opening a chest to amaze a crowd, and peered along the darkened corridor, to see the sword-straight back of the old dowager making her way towards her own chamber. She was walking more slowly than I had ever seen her do before. Her hand was pressed to the small of her back as if she were in pain, the same gesture that Bailiff Yaxley made in off-guarded moments. She sagged against the panelling, resting for a moment, before quickening her pace, as if yearning to reach her own bed. While she refused to allow her aging body to betray any sign of weakness before others, it was evident that the strain of protecting her Little Rome was taking a cruel toll on her health.

If the Viscountess had withdrawn from the Great Hall, that was the signal for the end of supper. The priests would start for the rendezvous with the ship soon. But there was no sign of them in the chamber they shared or the library. I hurried to the Great Hall.

In contrast to the heavy silence of supper, the room was now ringing with the clatter of dishes and shouted orders. Servants rushed about voiding the tables, bearing away tablecloths, glasses, flagons and bowls, while the young lads snatched up sops of soft wheaten bread or other delicacies, cramming them into their mouths whenever they thought the senior servants weren't looking. But the priests and Smith were nowhere to be seen. While I'd been wasting time with the girl, they had gone.

Although I knew every minute that I remained inside the house meant that my chances of finding them were diminishing even further, I could not step outside without dragging on heavy boots, gloves and cloak. I snatched up a lantern from among those left ready by the door, and stepped out into the freezing night.

The courtyard was strangely dark. A single torch burned on the wall, in place of the usual half-dozen. One of the young scullions slipping and sliding across the ice towards the house was nothing more than a moving shadow until he passed through the small puddle of light cast by the torch flames. This was deliberate. No one inside or outside the Abbey would be able to see who was entering or leaving.

As I walked away from the door, the bubble of lantern light caught something red on the ground. I moved closer. Half a dozen boot prints showed up starkly against the thick layer of white hoar frost, as if someone had walked through a pool of blood. I crouched down and held the lantern closer. Not blood – mud: red mud trodden down into the ice. It was almost frozen over, but not quite. Someone had walked across here not many minutes ago. It could have been the stable lad I'd seen crossing the yard, except where would he or any of the servants have picked up wet mud on their boots on a night as cold as this? Even if he'd tramped across a ploughed field, the earth was frozen solid. You'd have to be . . . of course!

The door leading to the cellar and the hidden chapel was shut, but not locked, nor, I was relieved to discover, was it barred from the other side. Locks I could charm in a flash, but lifting oak beams on the other side of a stout wooden door was beyond even the legerdemainist's art unless the trick could be prepared in advance. I slipped through and descended the ancient stone steps into the cellar.

When we had come to Mass in the chapel, lanterns on the floor had guided us through the labyrinth of farm tools, barrels and tubs of stinking tallow, oil, salt fish, and vinegar, but tonight I had only the lantern I carried and the vault was so wide and high, its light scarcely penetrated a hand's breadth in front of me, as if the flame was cowering inside the lantern, crushed by the weight of darkness around it. I couldn't see any clear path. I suspected the ladders, kegs and saw-horses had been deliberately moved to conceal the way through. I stood still, listening hard. Nothing stirred.

But I was sure this must be the way in and out of the Abbey. When I'd seen Santi and Holt returning from searching and disposing of the corpse of the murdered messenger, they had emerged from this cellar, but the fragments of reeds and mud I'd seen on their shoes had certainly not been acquired in the chapel, nor from the stone floor of the cellar. No wonder the cunning old dowager had built her chapel down here. If there was a raid while Mass was in progress, she could smuggle the priests out by an underground route, before the leopards had even dismounted in the courtyard above.

I threaded through the stores and tools, pausing every yard or so to sweep the lantern light across the walls. I had to move carefully to avoid knocking against the assortment of tools, planks and chains, which would send the noise echoing through the stone vaults. There was now no sign of the chapel door, but instead wooden racks filled with small kegs covered the section of the wall, roughly where I remembered it to be. But I wagered the entrance to the tunnel would not be found in the chapel itself. I moved on.

A cavernous black archway gaped in the pale stone, the entrance partly blocked by an old fruit press. Beyond it, the lantern light revealed another cellar narrower than the one through which I had passed, with tall pillars supporting the vaulted ceiling. Here and there the roots of the trees above had twisted down between the stones, like bone-white snakes, poised to strike. The candlelight caught something hanging high on the stone tracery of the vault. At first, I thought they were large dead leaves, stirring slightly as if ruffled by a breeze, except the air was as still as a tomb. Then I caught the smell, like cat's piss, strong enough to make the eyes water. They were bats, dozens of them. I knew they could creep through a gap barely wider than a man's finger, but those cracks between the stones in the ceiling made by tree roots would be in the ground when seen from above. The bats didn't burrow down into the earth. They had not flown in that way.

I clambered around the old press, skirting the pungent heap of bat dung, and as I did so, realised that it was not frozen solid. Though the air in the cellar would have felt cold on any normal day, it was certainly not as icy as the earth above now. A couple of old barrels stood near the entrance, but unlike the main cellar, this branch of it had little stored in it, at least little that was recognisable. The dark mounds at the base of the pillars and along the walls stank of mould and decay. Several times I was forced to stop and listen, unable to tell if the movement I thought I'd glimpsed was human, or shadows darting between the pale bones of the pillars and gliding over the walls. A drop of water falling or the scrabbling of tiny claws, even my own footfalls, echoed and bounced off the stone, until I couldn't tell if they were coming from above, in front or behind me.

Candlelight flickered across the solid wall in front of me, a dead end. I walked along it, then back towards the main cellar, searching the opposite side. There was a breeze on my face, a draught of icy raw air, and then I saw it. The entrance was not hidden, but even from a few feet away it appeared not to be a doorway, but simply a sealed-up arched casement like the others on either side. The dark hole looked like a shadow cast on to the wall by the stone casing that surrounded it. Only the draught of air betrayed that it was not. It was set into the wall just above my head and would appear to anyone glancing round the cellar to be nothing more than one of the many old monastery windows, long since sealed up as the ruins were buried.

Something metallic clattered to the stone flags in the main cellar, echoing through the vaults. Hard on its heels came a stream of muffled oaths. Taking cover behind one of the pillars, I wrenched off my heavy cloak and dropped it over the lantern. In daylight, the pillar would not have been wide enough to cover me, but if whoever was approaching was armed with only a single lantern, I should be just another of the deep shadows.

A faint glow of yellow light spread across the darkness in the far archway. Two, no, three people were approaching, their shoes grating on the layer of grit and dirt that covered the flags, occasionally muttering and cursing as they stumbled or bumped into the obstacles. The one in front held the lantern. He had the stout girth and height of Father Bray, though it was hard to be sure it was him, for all three wore long cloaks and black cloth masks covering their faces, hair and necks. The lantern light caught only the glittering eyes of the first man, peering out from holes cut through the cloth. The second figure was being pushed around the old fruit press by the person bringing up the rear of the little group. At first, I thought the man at the back was merely guiding him, for he kept stumbling, but as they skirted the pile of malodorous bat dung, I saw the man with the lantern take a firm grip of him. The two men were now propelling him between them. The figure in the centre was slighter than the other two, and shorter. His head lolled forward as if he was drunk . . . or else drugged.

Katheryne! They *were* taking her to the ship tonight. She *was* the precious cargo.

They came to a halt beneath the arched hole in the wall. The man with the lantern held tightly to Katheryne's arm, supporting her, while the other hurried to the far corner and retrieved a short ladder buried under a heap of dirt and straw, which he positioned carefully against the wall beneath the opening. The lantern bearer climbed up, then, kneeling in the old casement, firmly gripped the top of the ladder. Katheryne was pushed and guided up by the man below, who finally scrambled up after them. They pulled the ladder up over the edge of the lip. The lantern light faded and then vanished, leaving only the dark hole.

I had seen another ladder near the entrance to the cellars, but dared not waste time returning for it. One of the old barrels would suffice, if the wood was not too rotten to bear my weight. I rolled it over under the casement, scrambled up on to it and heaved myself up on to a broad ledge. On the other side, a tunnel curved away into the darkness. Its floor was only about two or three feet below the ledge, not nearly as far down as the base of the cellar on the other side. I cast the lantern beam upwards and saw a ceiling vaulted like the ones behind me, but the bottom of the tunnel was formed from jagged rubble, loose soil and broken stones which must once have been part of the Abbey. It resembled the lair of a giant worm which had burrowed through the earth and all that lay buried beneath it.

It was risky to leave the lantern uncovered. Even a single candle in darkness could be seen a long way ahead, but the way underfoot was treacherous. As if to prove it, there came the rattle of stones and a shrill cry, as if one of those ahead of me had slipped. I couldn't see their light, but they could be close, the twists and turns of the tunnel concealing the glow.

A rat darted past me, and as I inched round the curve, the light caught three more, scrabbling at something pale and smooth in the debris. They skurried into the darkness, but as soon as my light had passed the spot, I could hear their claws on the stones as they scampered back. Were they feasting on the skull of an ancient monk, or the bones of the dead of the great battle that had placed a foreign king on the English throne? The bearded star with the tail of fire had heralded that invasion, which was to change England for ever. Had it returned to warn of another? Was there a new war coming, Catholic against Protestant, rebels against their King, another ten thousand men slaughtered on some muddy field, as there had been here? The idea seemed unthinkable, and yet if Pettingar and the plotters struck again, if the foreign troops came across the sea to support them, England might again witness such a slaughter. I left the rats to their bones.

Dressed stone and rubble had now given way to rock and earth, still uneven and rough, but more solid, and I was able to quicken my pace, knowing that the men ahead of me would be doing the same. I stopped abruptly as voices drifted back to me. They were returning already! I wondered how swiftly I could retrace my steps, but the voices faded and as I edged forward again, I felt a blast of icy air, as if I was leaning over a deep well.

Covering my lantern light once more, I emerged into a pearly mist which hung a foot or so above a river, its waves and eddies hardened to cold steel. Slabs of ice jutted up from the surface where they had been pushed and squeezed as the water froze. The bare branches of trees, bending to touch the shaggy reeds, were locked together by the frost. The marshy ground was petrified to rock, but the night air crackled as if the glass stars were falling from the black sky and shattering on the iron earth below.

A rough wooden landing stage poked out into the river and a small boat was moored beneath it, but even from where I stood, I could see from the jagged spars that the ice had crushed it as if it was an eggshell. If the plan had been to carry the drugged girl down river to the estuary and row her out to a ship waiting offshore, they must surely have realised long before this that it would be impossible.

I could hear a low muttering, but could see no one. There was another sound too, snorting, as if the fog were pouring out from the nostrils of a monstrous dragon. I edged further out on to the bank, trusting to mist and darkness to cover me. The ice and frozen air bounced and distorted the voices, so that they seemed at first to be coming from all around me, then through the curtains of white mist, I saw the yellow spheres of lantern lights, rainbow-haloed by the fog. I glimpsed dark cloaks and something else. Horses! That was what I'd heard snorting. But they couldn't have come through the tunnel; they must have been brought here by someone else. One of the men was cursing furiously, and from the way the mist was swirling around them, like water in a witch's cauldron, they were clearly having trouble holding the beasts still enough to mount them, or perhaps Katheryne was resisting. Even drugged, she would not suffer herself to be put on a horse without a spirited fight.

I couldn't be sure how many men I might be dealing with – two certainly, probably three, because someone must have led the horses here, but there could be others. I moved away from them, searching until I found a tree with a long branch overhanging the frozen river, stout enough to bear the weight of the lantern. Using a long strip of cloth slashed from the bottom of my shirt, I suspended the lantern from the tree, taking care to keep the light covered all the while. Then, sacrificing a second strip of my shirt, I tied the handle of the lantern so that it was held up tight against the branch. I stuffed a short length of a hemp-cord match into the knot, and held the candle flame to the end, blowing gently until it caught alight. As swiftly as I could, I circled round to the other side of the group of men and horses, then groped over the hard ground until I found a fist-sized stone which I could prise loose. I waited, dagger in hand.

I'd learned this trick from a man who'd earned a good living swindling the gullible by conjuring Oberon and Titania, King and Queen of the fairies, who he'd claimed could make those they favoured as rich as Croesus, but he'd had ample time to prepare his scene. I could only improvise. I saw the light give a tiny jerk and threw the stone hard on to the frozen river. It landed with a crack, the sound thundering like a musket shot, just as the rag binding the lantern to the branch burned through. The lantern swung down and out like a pendulum on the length of cloth I'd used to suspend it. The momentum of the weighty lantern propelled it in and out again in a steady sweeping movement. The men, who had fallen instantly silent at the retort, spun round to peer through the darkness.

There was cry of alarm as a horse, spooked by the noise, reared and broke free from the hand that held it. I heard its hooves crashing down on the ice as it galloped away. The other beasts must have broken loose and followed, or else the men had let them go as they stared at the light. It loomed in and out of the swirling mist. For a moment, even I thought it was being held by someone moving towards us, though I knew it was only an illusion of the fog and the rocking lantern.

Feet began pounding over the ground, the ice-sheathed grass and reeds snapping beneath them as they scattered. I ran towards them. One still had hold of Katheryne by the wrist, but she was trying to free herself from his grip. I charged between them, using my weight to break the man's grasp, and my elbow to smash him in the belly. With a groan, he crumpled to his knees. Guessing they would retreat to the tunnel, I grabbed Katheryne's arm and dragged her the opposite way, pushed her, face down, into a mass of willow scrub, and pressed her flat to the ground. The splintering crunch of iron-shod hooves and the men's pounding footsteps faded away, and the silent world of darkness and ice seeped back.

In that stillness, the strange realisation which had been fighting to be heard over my more pressing concerns finally won my attention. The thin, bony wrist I had been dragging along was hairy, and the body pressed beneath mine had none of the soft curves I was expecting. I sat up and yanked off my captive's cloth mask.

Chapter Thirty-six

'WHAT THE DEVIL are you doing here?' The words exploded from me even though every sense told me I shouldn't be speaking above a whisper.

The face that peered up at me through the darkness was as white as bone, the features pinched with cold and fear. Any sense of exhilaration he had been gripped by on the night I had unmasked him in the Abbey's grounds had vanished. Erasmus slithered backwards across the frozen grass of the riverbank like a startled lizard, cringing as if he thought I was going to punch him, which I was sorely tempted to do.

I crouched, breathing hard, the cold air burning my lungs.

'Where is Katheryne?' I growled. 'Have they already taken her to the ship?'

I could see little of his expression, but his glittering eyes stared at me as if I were speaking in some foreign tongue.

'Lady Magdalen is forcing Katheryne to go to Brussels. They're taking her to the ship tonight.' Even as I said it, I realised what this little runt was doing here. 'You were the decoy, weren't you? They're taking Katheryne to the ship by another route. Answer me!' I grabbed him by the front of his cloak, jerking his face towards mine. I didn't trust myself to pull my dagger to threaten him. I knew I'd use it.

'Not . . . Lady Katheryne. Me! It is me they are taking to the ship.'

'You! But they were dragging you along. Why would they need to force you to go on board? I thought that was what you and the rest of Smith's little acolytes wanted, to be chosen for training in the seminaries of Europe. You'd have been begging for the honour of being the first.'

He shook his head miserably and, as I released my grip on him, he slumped down among the brittle reeds, like the punctured bladder of a court jester.

'Not to train for ordination. I'm to be sent to the Carthusians. I am to be a monk. Father Smith says I must do penance for the rest of my life, if I am to save my soul.'

No wonder they'd had to drag him down that tunnel. I knew little of the Carthusians except that they were said to be the most austere monastic order in the whole of Christendom, living like hermits in solitary cells in the monastery, not speaking even to each other, eating their meagre meals alone and leaving their tiny cells only for prayers and for solitary labour in the garden. Imprisonment in the Tower must have seemed a more inviting prospect for a young man.

'Why? Erasmus, why would Smith send you there?'

'It's your fault!' he spat. 'I should never have listened to you. You told me to confess. You said he would help me.'

'I said you should confide your fears about being arrested, not make your confession, and I said you should talk to Holt about it, not Smith. He was the one who terrified you in the first place, shutting you in that hole.'

'I told Father Holt, but he went to ask advice from Father Smith.'

'Holt broke the seal of the confessional!'

If what Robert Cecil had claimed was even half true, there were priests who had been prepared to see hundreds of men, women and even children blown to pieces rather than divulge what had been told to them in confession. Jesuits like Garnet had willingly been hanged, drawn and quartered rather than break that sacred seal.

Erasmus hung his head. 'I didn't make confession to Father Holt. If I had, I would have had to tell him about the night-creeping, so I talked to Father Holt about my fears . . . of the hiding place, that's all, just talked, like you told me to. But when Father Holt told Father Smith what I was afraid of, Father Smith sent for me and ordered me to make my confession. I had no choice. I had to tell him everything, else I'd be damned.' His voice cracked as if the ordeal of that scene was still racking him.

'And for this night-creeping, Smith is forcing you to become a monk.'

I'd known from the first the man was a bastard. He reminded me in so many ways of my boyhood tormentor, that malicious devil Waldegrave. Skinner and the castle thieves in Bristol couldn't have chosen a more apt name for him when they dubbed him 'the Yena'. Maybe that's why I'd detested Smith on sight. I'd recognised instantly what kind of man he was, but even I found it hard to believe Smith could so cruelly wreck a man's life, especially one who had looked up to him and blindly trusted him.

'Father Smith says . . . some of the townspeople exhumed a grave. They found the corpse of a girl and brought her to the Abbey. It was the maid, Lady Katheryne's maid, Bethia. The one they all thought had run away, only she hadn't. She'd been murdered. Father Smith thinks I killed her! Half the Abbey knows she used to sneak out after dark. He said if I was out night-creeping and found her alone . . . He said, I must have . . . forced myself on her and she threatened to tell her mistress and Lady Magdalen . . . so . . . so, I killed her to keep her from talking. But I didn't! I swear on the Blessed Virgin. I didn't touch her . . . not at night, not like that.'

'But you had touched her before.'

He turned his face away, though in the darkness neither of us could read each other's expression. 'I liked to talk to her sometimes . . .'

'And did this talk lead to something more, fondling, kissing?' I pressed.

'She was a wanton. She thought it a game to inflame a man, especially those of us she knew were celibate. I saw her deliberately leaning over the holy well once so that her breasts fell out from her dress and hitching her skirts to her bare thighs when Father Santi passed to make him look, then after that I heard her giggling with one of the other maids that if she got the chance she could make even the Pope's prick stand to attention and salute her.'

A *wanton*, that's what Magdalen had called Bethia. Had the old dowager already known the girl had been murdered before her corpse was dug up? Erasmus could well have killed Bethia in a panic for the reasons Smith had suggested, but what cause would he have to kill the woodward, Crowhurst? This little maggot might have been able to overpower a girl, but even in a fit of madness he would have been no match for a strapping woodsman like Crowhurst, and I was convinced that the same person was guilty of both murders.

'Father Holt said no woman in the house was safe while I was living there. Father Smith said I was a rabid dog who should be killed and buried at the roadside before I could harm others.'

The same words Smith had used about the pursuivant Benet and the same fate which had befallen Benet too.

'I begged him to let me go. I swore I would leave Battle, leave Sussex and go to Bristol or London. But Father Smith said he couldn't trust me. I might attack another girl or start night-creeping again, and I knew too much about the manor and those in it. I was weak, a . . . a coward. If I was arrested and questioned, he said, I'd sell anyone to save my own skin, I'd tell them everything. But I wouldn't. I swore on the sacred blood that I wouldn't . . .'

It wasn't often that I found myself agreeing with Smith, but in this, the bastard probably had a point. Erasmus would only have to hear the jangle of prison keys to fall on his knees and vomit up every scrap of information he knew. Though it was Smith who had turned Erasmus into this pathetic wreck.

He was shivering violently, his teeth chattering so that he could hardly stammer out the words.

'I didn't kill her . . . But I can't be a monk, not like the Carthusians. I'd go mad shut up in one of those cells for hours. I can't be closed up, I can't . . . But if I don't go, he'll kill me, I know he will. He'll have to. He's right. I'm a coward, a miserable coward and I . . .'

I threw myself on to him, clamping my hand across his mouth. He tried to fight me off.

'Don't move, listen!' I hissed into his ear.

Horses were coming towards us, their iron-shoes striking the stones and cracking the ice. But I was sure it was not the beasts that had bolted. There were more of them and these horses had riders; I could hear the creak of leather, the jangle of metal and the rhythmic dull thud of sword sheaths against the riders' thighs, musket stocks against saddles. Any man who has ridden to war knows those sounds. It means that the horsemen had their weapons close to their gloved hands, not slung across their packs or shoulders. These were men who were armed and expecting to use those arms on the instant. Thus far, the mist and darkness had hidden us, but if the riders passed too close . . .

I dragged Erasmus to his feet and propelled him towards the bank. 'Cross the river here. The mist lies thicker on the other side and the ice will bear your weight. They'll not risk the horses by crossing over. Once you're across, keep moving quickly away from the bank. You need to get out of musket range. They'll fire if they see movement. Hide for the night and take the London road as soon as it's light. Join a group of travellers if you can, or hitch a ride on a cart, but keep going. Smith won't risk following. It's the sheriff's men you have to avoid.'

I didn't have time to tell him what to say if he was stopped. I could only trust that Smith and the priests had at least taught their acolytes that much. He didn't move, but stared at me, his eyes huge and glittering.

'Go, Erasmus! Now!'

The troop was getting closer; if he didn't go quickly, they'd ride right into us. I hauled him upright and gave him a shove towards the river. He slipped and let out a startled yelp. It wasn't loud, but every sound was magnified.

A command rang out from one of the riders, and the horses were pulled up as they listened. Erasmus suddenly came to life and chose that moment to scramble down on to the frozen water, shattering the ice-sheathed reeds as he blundered through them. It was too late to grab him. Another command was shouted and the horses were urged forward through the clinging mist.

I strode towards them, treading heavily and swinging my arms at the bushes, to create as much noise as I could. Spectral-black figures emerged and vanished through the curtain of white. A shout told me they had spotted me, and moments later I was surrounded by six men-at-arms, ice glinting on their metal helmets. Their mounts, snorting dragon smoke, circled restlessly. One man urged his horse closer and jabbed the point of his sword towards my throat.

'Show your face!'

I cursed silently. I couldn't see his face clearly, but I recognised that voice and the way he hunched in the saddle. These were the same group of sheriff's men I'd run into on my first night in Battle. I only hoped they didn't recognise me. I pulled down the muffler but kept it covering my lengthy beard and the firemark on my neck.

'Be a cold night for hunting, good masters,' I said, adopting a rougher accent from the one I'd used when they'd stopped me on Diligence. 'Game's gone to ground.'

'Not the game we hunt. Ship was spotted at anchor off the estuary. No lawful business being there. Been horses on that shore waiting for her. Found their dung. No cart tracks. So, they weren't smuggling wine. Must have been vermin they were bringing ashore, human vermin. You seen any riders pass this way, sirrah?'

'In this fret? The old knucker himself could have come crawling out of the river and I wouldn't have seen him.'

The man pushed the point of his sword into the layers of cloth around my throat, jerking the blade upwards. 'Don't bandy words with me, hedgepig. I'm tired, hungry and frozen to the marrow, so for two pins I'd slice you open and warm my fists in your steaming guts.'

One of the men who'd been circling round trotted back to the sergeant. 'Don't reckon this one came from the ship, sir. No horse tethered round here and he'll not have turned it loose. Be needing it.'

'Of course he didn't,' the sergeant snapped. 'Look at the fool. The only animal this beef-wit has ever ridden is an ass like himself.' He turned back impatiently to me. 'There's something familiar about you. I've seen you before.'

'Aye, good master, few months back. Cart broke its wheel,' I said vaguely, trusting he and his men had ridden past enough stranded carts for them all to blur into one.

'So, what are you doing lurking out here on such a night?'

'There's more than one way to keep warm on a bitter night and she could set Jack Frost aburning.'

The men within hearing laughed and even the sergeant gave a grunt of amusement, but peered through the fog. 'Don't recall seeing cottages on this stretch of the river.'

'Old fishing hut, good master, well hidden. Her husband's handy with his fists . . .'

The men laughed again, joking about the remarkable merits any woman would have to possess to be worth exposing their cocks in a fishing hut on such a night, before the sergeant sharply ordered them to ride on. He turned the horse to follow, but before he moved off, he leaned down and seized my shoulder. 'I've seen you before and it wasn't with a broken cart. You best thank God I've more important quarry than you to hunt this night, else I'd be running you back tied to my horse's tail, and trust me, I know better ways to make a man's cods burn than slipping them between the thighs of a slut.'

I waited until the crunch of their hooves had faded. There was no sound from the river other than the sharp cracking of the ice. I hoped Erasmus had crossed and would have the wit to seek shelter until daybreak, when he could travel without arousing suspicion.

I couldn't risk returning through the tunnel. They might well have left someone on watch to ensure they were not followed, or at least sealed the other end to stall any attack. My best hope was to find the place Arthur had shown me in Battle town and scramble over the wall, if I could make it without running into the patrol again. But it was going to be a long, cold walk.

If horses and riders had already been waiting at the estuary for the ship before the sheriff's men arrived, then they had expected to receive a message or a cargo. A *human* cargo, if there was no cart, as the sergeant had said. I was pretty sure that Erasmus being sent out on the ship was an afterthought. They must have only recently decided on that plan, and I couldn't imagine Smith describing him as precious cargo. He would have been only too happy if Erasmus had fallen overboard. They could well have taken the unseen person in the room to the ship, or at least intended to, but he wasn't the one the riders on that beach had been waiting for. My first instincts had been right and I cursed myself for not trusting them. The tapestry had been brought from Brussels, not sent to it. They had smuggled someone in tonight, and I had been looking the other way. They'd probably allowed Katheryne to think she would be put aboard to create a diversion. That scarcely mattered now, because if the horses had left the cove before the sheriff's men arrived, then it seemed likely they had already brought their precious cargo safely ashore. So, where was he now, and what was he here to do?

Chapter Thirty-seven

THE TWITTEN, as Arthur had called it, which led to the privy and the Abbey wall was as dark and silent as the grave. The old widow and her neighbour in the cottages on either side of the path had like Battle's other inhabitants long since retired to bed, fires banked down and candles extinguished, as if the town had been encased in ice and would not emerge until spring. Once away from the river and marsh, the mist vanished, but even so I had to feel my way down the narrow lane, using the wall of the cottage to guide me, for even the mirror-bright shards of moonlight couldn't reach down into the blackness between the two cottages. I was about to step out into the yard behind them when a noise burst through the stillness with the force of a cannon blast.

Poultry squawked and a woman shouted. Moments later, heavy footsteps came pounding down the alley. I slipped around the corner of the yard and flattened myself against the wall as someone ran past me and scrambled up on to the barrel. He threw a bulging sack over the wall, then heaved himself on to the roof of the jakes and dropped down on the other side. Though I could not see his face, the flailing, clumsy movement and the lumbering stride were unmistakable. I would have wagered my horse, Diligence, that it was Crowhurst's son, Sam.

Whoever was chasing him had not given up. Boots crunched down the lane towards the far end of the twitten, then paused as their owner peered down it, breathing in great rasps. The cold seared the lungs of any man who attempted to run in this weather. The footsteps moved off further down the lane. There was a yell, as if the pursuer thought he'd spotted something, and answering bellows from some of the houses, demanding to know who was disturbing them. But no lights appeared in either of the cottages that backed on to the privy. Arthur was right: the old woman was deaf and her tormented neighbour was probably shrinking deeper beneath his bedclothes. I crept towards the barrel. Sounds of laboured breathing came from the other side of the wall and muffled whimpers of pain. Sam was still there.

As stealthily as I could, I climbed up on to the roof of the jakes and peered over. I could make out the shape of someone sitting on the ground, his back against the wall. Sam jerked his head, craning his neck to stare up at me. He tried to rise, but fell back with a groan. I clambered down the other side and crouched beside him. He had covered his face with his arms, rolling on to his belly on the freezing ground, as if he feared a beating.

'Easy, lad. It's me, Daniel. You remember me, don't you, Sam? Stayed the night in your cottage. Look at me.' He slowly peeled one arm from his face, peering up warily. 'Whoever was chasing you has run on down the road, but we'd best get you deeper into the trees in case he decides to retrace his steps.' I extended my hand and he grasped it, but gave a yelp of pain, clutching his knee and rocking. As I prised his hands away and felt it, he flinched.

'You've dislocated it, Sam.'

'Will they . . . cut my leg off?' he stammered through clenched teeth. 'I'll not let them cut it off . . . I'll not.'

'Then we'd best pop it back quickly before more damage is done. This will hurt, lad, but it'll be over in a flash. Lie still and bite on this. If you yell out, you'll bring half the town running. And then this knee will be the least of your troubles.'

I pulled off one of my leather gloves and stuffed it in between his jaws before he could argue. I was no bonesetter. But I'd held down men and boys while others pulled. It was easier with two, but Sam's father had already died from cold; I wouldn't risk leaving the son to fetch help, and such an injury could cripple you for life if it was left too long untreated.

It took three attempts. The boy arched in pain and sweat popped out on his forehead, freezing almost at once, but he didn't let a single sound escape him. When it was over, he sighed with relief and leaned forward, massaging the joint, moving it tentatively to assure himself it still worked, as I pulled my glove back on. The leather was thick, but he'd bitten right through it. I allowed him to rest for a few minutes but dared not risk letting him lie there much longer.

'Come on now, Sam, try to stand.' I put an arm around him, hauling him upright. He winced and stumbled as he took a step. 'It'll be a day or so before that feels right again. I'll help you to your cottage.'

He stopped dead. 'Can't go home . . . have to . . .' He was staring anxiously around.

'Is this what you're looking for?' I picked up the sack lying a few yards from the wall. The moment I felt it, I knew what I'd find inside – two chickens, their necks broken.

Sam made a grab for the sack, but I held on to it. He started to protest, but the sound of voices and weighty footsteps told me that his pursuer was coming back down the road, and now he had company. If they saw our prints in the frost and the scuff marks on the barrel . . .

With one arm supporting him, I pulled Sam towards the cover of the woods and did not let him stop until we were deep inside. I set him against a tree trunk and motioned him to stay silent. Distant voices and the clattering of wood drifted towards us through the glacial air. They were searching the yard. Someone clambered on to the roof of the privy, shouting back to the others, but he didn't attempt to climb over the wall. Finally they seemed convinced that no one was hiding behind it and we heard them moving away. Silence flowed back.

'You do realise that if they'd caught you, Sam, they'd have thrown you into the town's gaol, and that's after they'd thrashed you black and blue. What possessed you to go stealing chickens? Is your father still sick?'

The boy slowly shook his head.

'Then you surely have meat in the pot, and I can't believe that Alys would have sent you out to steal. If you'd come to the Abbey, they would have given you food.'

'First, I took birds and rats from the gibbet. I waited till there were lots of one kind, 'cause Father couldn't count past five, so he didn't know if one or two were gone. Sometimes he'd notice there weren't so many as he'd put there. Then he'd shout and curse that someone had thieved them, but Mother told him kites or wild cats took them. But then a man came from the town. Wanted to buy them. Wanted them fresh, he said, soon as they were killed. Paid well for them. So, Father didn't leave them hanging any more.'

'But what did you want them for? Did the manor pay you for what you brought them?'

It was probably not uncommon for enterprising lads to steal vermin from a woodward's gibbet line and claim the bounty from unsuspecting churchwardens or landowners in a neighbouring parish, though it was surprising that Sam had thought of that trick, unless other lads had put him up to it.

'Have to feed them, else they'll die.' He made a half-hearted attempt to grab the sack again, but his arm fell limp.

'Show me.'

He shook his head. 'Won't let you kill them.'

'I know you won't, Sam. You'll fight for them, like you risked your life to steal the chickens for them. I won't harm them, I swear.'

He hesitated for so long, I thought he'd refuse, but finally he nodded.

We picked our way through the tangle of bare trees. Sam was limping but, suddenly determined to reach the place, he forged ahead, sometimes following a rough path for a few yards before turning aside and ducking under branches. I wondered if he was deliberately trying to ensure I couldn't find my way back, but then realised that, in spite of what Alys had told me, he at least knew enough about the woods not to risk wearing a regular track which could be followed by someone else.

He dropped to one knee, dragging his injured leg behind him as he crawled beneath the low branch of tree that in the moonlight reared up like a giant bear, shaggy with a thick pelt of ivy. I followed and found myself scrambling down into a small sunken clearing. It was surrounded by a circular stone wall. Brambles and herbs had crept over it and burrowed between the stones, dislodging sections. A low arch was set into the wall, enclosing an ancient stone trough. It was filled with water; where it had trickled over the edge, it had frozen into glittering stacks of ice, but I could hear the gurgle within the wall. A spring was still bubbling up from far below the earth.

Sam, ignoring the spring, limped the few yards across to the other side of the enclosure to what appeared in the moonlight to be a mound of earth standing hard against the wall. He lifted swathes of dried bracken from the front of it, laying them aside carefully, and removed several branches beneath. A pungent musky stench rolled up, so strong it felt like a punch to the nose, making the eyes water. Sam seemed prepared for this, for he drew back until the strongest wave had passed, then beckoned me closer.

I peered into the darkness; something was moving down there. In the bone-white light from the moon, I caught three pairs of glowing green eyes turned towards me, and heard a high-pitched bark first from one, then all three. Sam crouched awkwardly, his injured leg extended, as he tried to light the stump of a candle with the flint iron from his tinder box. I took it and managed to get the small flame burning, then held it cautiously in the entrance. I found myself peering down into a small beehive stone hut. From the outside, the thick walls appeared only three or four feet high, but the floor of the hut was dug well below ground level, so that a man might easily have stood upright in the centre.

Three foxes were staring up at me. The largest lay on a heap of straw and dried bracken, scattered with fragments of gnawed bones. The other two foxes ran agitatedly around her. They were smaller and leaner; presumably they were spring cubs, now full-grown. They were both tethered on long chains, bound around a heavy stone. But I saw why there was no need to leash their mother. Half her front leg was missing, the stump healed into a naked lump of purple flesh.

'Took her from Father's trap before he found her. Trying to bite off her own paw, she was. Could feel her cubs, moving in her belly. Three, there were, blind as kittens, but one died soon after it were born. Father would have chopped her head off with an axe and drowned her cubs, like he drowned the cat I found, so I had to hide them . . .'

He opened his sack and tossed in one of the chickens. The young foxes leaped on it as if they were pouncing on live prey, seizing it between them and tugging furiously, giving ear-piercing yelps and throaty clicks that sounded as if they were beating rapidly on drums. Sam beamed fondly, his face aglow in the candlelight. 'She likes me. Doesn't mind I'm an addlepate.'

'And when you couldn't take vermin from the gibbet for them, you stole poultry from the townsfolk.'

'I didn't take all of them,' he said sullenly. 'The rest will have chicks, so they'll get new hens.'

'Aren't you scared to come out at night? I thought you were afraid of Wild Tom.'

'Wild Tom only comes to the cottage when Father calls him. He takes the lubbers, like me. Snatches them while they're sleeping and they don't never come back. He ties them up and throws them in the salts to drown them, like their mothers ought to have done when they were born. But he won't come again.'

'How do you know?' *Had Sam discovered Erasmus was the night-creeper?*

'Father won't call him.'

'Your new father, you mean, don't you, Sam?'

He flinched, ferreting in the sack for the second carcass. 'I have to feed her. She'll be hungry.'

'Who killed your old father, Sam? Was it you? Did you help your mother to do it?'

He turned, his eyes wide with alarm. Even the squabbling young foxes seemed to sense his distress and fall silent.

'He's not killed! He went away, but he's not ever coming back. If I don't tell, he won't ever come back.' He pressed his balled fists between his teeth, biting his knuckles hard in his agitation. 'I don't want him to come back. He beats me and then he shuts me out of the cottage . . . hear him beating her and her crying. I can't get back in to stop him. But when he's asleep, she creeps out and lets me in. I have to be very quiet then, so as not to wake him. I told her that when I'm a man I'll beat him till he's dead, so he can't hurt her again. But when I said that, it made her cry again. She said that's what she was afeared of. But my new father doesn't hurt us. I want him to stay, not the other one. I like him.'

I laid my hand on the boy's shoulder and felt him trembling. 'Did you see your old father leave? Did he say he was going away?'

The boy twisted the empty sack, frowning. 'He said he had to go and check the spring. But he never came home that night and then my new father came instead.'

'This spring?' I gestured towards the little archway near the entrance and the waterfall of ice spilling from its lip.

Sam shook his head. 'No one bothers with that one, except me. I don't reckon they know about it. Goes back straight into the earth, that one. Father had been checking all the ponds and streams and they were all frozen. He heard the holy well had stopped running, so he reckoned it might be the spring that feeds the well. It had never frozen before, but the river hadn't neither and now it had. So, he told me I had to hurry to the Abbey and tell them that the spring might be the cause of it, afore they went to the trouble of digging the well out.'

'What did your mother do when your father didn't come home?'

He thought for a moment. 'She waited same as always, and kept stirring the pot, so as his supper wouldn't spoil. Then when it got really late, she told me to go to bed and pretend I was asleep 'cause Father would be raging. But I fell asleep anyhow and he didn't come.'

'And the next day?'

He shrugged. 'She sent me out to look for him, case he'd had a fall, but I didn't find him. Next day, after I came back from my chores, my new father was there in bed, hurt his back. Mother said I was to swear he was my father, else the sheriff's men would come for him and the other father would come home and give me the worst leathering ever, her too.' He was shivering. 'I don't want him to come back,' he wailed, screwing his eyes up and shrinking away.

'He won't ever come back, Sam. I can promise you that.'

The boy tried to smile but his face was stiff with cold. The foxes had settled down to their bloody meal and I helped the lad replace the branches and bracken. He led me back to a path I recognised.

He grasped my arm. 'You'll not tell? Swear it?'

I didn't know if he meant me to keep the secret of the foxes or of Crowhurst. One of his secrets I could easily keep, but the other?

'On my mother's life, Sam.' He nodded, satisfied, then limped off in the direction of his own cottage.

I'd sworn on my mother's life, and I remembered with a pain I had not felt for years that I didn't even know her name. I could no longer picture her face, only her eyes, nothing else, as if they were all that remained of a vanishing phantasm. And I had no idea whether those eyes now lay somewhere under the frozen earth or if she still gazed upon it. I knew only that if she still lived, I was dead to her. I almost envied Sam.

*

THE HOUSE WAS SILENT, a tomb of ice and darkness. No torches burned on the walls of the courtyard; no lanterns glowed in the stables. I felt as if I had returned a hundred years too late and would find only the hungry ghosts wandering through decayed rooms and tumbled staircases. I put my hand to the door latch. I was by now well used to gauging the exact pressure needed to ease it open without a creak, but it was locked. I had never known the courtyard door to be locked before, for the servants used it all through the night to visit the jakes, tend animals or start the day's work long before dawn. I charmed the lock, of course, though it took longer than usual. My hands were so numb with cold, my fingers had turned to twigs. I was hugely relieved to discover that it had not been braced on the other side. I didn't relish the prospect of spending the dregs of the night huddled in the stables.

The passageway beyond lay in darkness, except for a single lantern at the far end which marked the foot of the stairs. If the kingfishers had multiplied or changed direction, I couldn't see them. Though I longed to curl up near a fire, I decided not to risk making for the servants' hall to snatch what sleep I might yet salvage. I'd be bound to wake someone and besides there would be little hope of getting near the hearth; every servant, cat and dog would be sleeping as close to the fire as they could squeeze.

I reached the top of the stairs and paced as softly as I could towards the gentlemen's room, where I could bed down outside their door.

'So, Pursglove, you've finally returned.'

I whipped round. It was too dark to see the face or even the form of the man standing at the end of the passageway, but I couldn't fail to recognise the tone in which Smith spat out my name, as if he had found himself chewing on a piece of filth.

'Come!'

As he led the way to the floor above, a second figure closed in behind me. In the insipid light of the single lantern that still burned on the upper staircase, I recognised the rotund form of Steward Brathwayt.

Smith strode into the library and Brathwayt followed me, closing the door behind us and leaning against it as if he thought I would try to flee. None of the candles had been lit and the only light came from the fire that had been revived in the hearth, the red and black shadows of the flames stirring restlessly over the walls, as if they were spectators in a courtroom, impatient for the interrogation to begin.

Smith lowered himself into his throne-like chair, which he had placed as close as was possible to the fire. Silhouetted against the blood-red glow in his black robes, he seemed, for an instant, to resemble the paintings of the Devil gloating over the dammed in hell.

His voice, when he finally spoke, was as low and measured as always, but heavy with fatigue. 'Where have you been?'

I was as exhausted as he was, but I couldn't afford to let my wits rest. 'I set off for the alehouse in Battle, but there was a disturbance before I could reach it – a chicken coop was raided and a search was made for the thief. There've been a good many raids. They thought the night-creeper was at work again.'

I saw his head jerk up. If he thought Erasmus was still close, he might not search further afield for a day or so at least. I sent up a silent plea to whichever saint or demon watched over fools and night-creepers that Erasmus had had the wit to put a good distance between himself and the town.

'And was it . . . the *night-creeper*?'

'The culprit was not caught,' I answered truthfully.

'We may safely assume the chickens were taken by a thief, whether a man, a stray hound or a fox hardly matters. It was an ordinary thief – not the night-creeper. For I think we both know he was occupied elsewhere this night.'

'That would seem to be the case, sir, if he was not engaged in his usual pursuits.'

Smith lifted his head and stared at me. The burning wood in the hearth crackled. The darkened room concealed the chaplain's expression like a black mask; only his eyes glittered in the firelight.

'This evening, some unnamed man prevented a friend of yours from being conveyed to a place of safety where he would have been cared for and protected for the rest of his life, and where he could do himself and no one else any harm. In assisting him to evade those trying to help him, that man has unleashed a creature who could destroy us all. The person who aided your friend no doubt considers himself a hero. He probably even thought that trick he performed with a lantern amusing. But we both know your friend is weak. He cannot control his own emotions or actions. He does not know how to survive out there in the world. Sooner or later, he will get himself into trouble. He will be arrested and when he is, he will talk, not just about Battle, but he will blurt out all he may have learned or overheard about the loyal Catholics and faithful priests who serve the Church across the land, even those who serve in other cities . . . in *Bristol*, for example. If a man turns a wounded wolf loose, and it savages a child, who is to blame for that death? The unreasoning beast or the man who unleashed him? The question is, did the man who released the wounded beast do so stupidly, through a misguided sense of friendship, or was it a cunning and calculated act of malice, knowing full well the destruction that would result?'

Smith paused, but if he was hoping I would be goaded into an answer he would be disappointed.

'I will not waste my breath asking you if you were out on the marshes tonight, Pursglove. You can equivocate better than any Jesuit. But I know our friend confided in you. I have made no secret of the fact that I did not trust you from the hour you arrived in Battle. Know this and be very certain of it, I will be watching you and I will not hesitate to act to protect Lady Magdalen or any of the souls in my care, if you give me even the slightest cause.'

Chapter Thirty-eight

THE MORNING SUN WAS as pale as the moon. Even the sky was blanched white, as if it too had been frozen. Everyone who stepped outside walked with their eyes screwed up against the blinding dazzle from roof and stone, twig and cobweb. Milk turned to ice in the pails before it could be carried from byre to dairy. If Crowhurst had succeeded in thawing the holy spring before his death, his work had long been undone, for boys and men were having to chip out every drop of water needed from the streams and melt them over the courtyard fires.

Steam and dense smoke covered the courtyard, which served my purpose well. I couldn't risk attempting another nocturnal expedition. Security in the house had doubled in the last two days. I was certain that Smith was having me watched day and night as he had threatened, and not just me, but every route in or out of the Abbey. The door to the courtyard was now not only locked at sundown, but braced too. The servants had been instructed to use pisspots, like the household, instead of going outside to relieve themselves after dark. I think Smith would even have had the dogs let loose at night, if the Master of Hounds hadn't protested that they'd freeze to death.

Arthur and the other men who were in the habit of slipping out to the alehouses in the evenings were in a foul mood, ranging around the servants' hall like caged bears, mollified only when one of the grooms of the chambers smuggled out the cards and dice reserved for guests so that they could spend the evening gambling in a quiet corner, away from the prying eyes of Steward Brathwayt.

As I reached the far side of the courtyard, I risked a glance behind me at the house. A solitary sheep is easy to spot in a field, but in a herd, even a wolf in a sheepskin stands a chance of passing unnoticed, and it would be hard to distinguish any man with everyone muffled up in several layers of bulky clothing. The pall of smoke and steam rolled across from the fires and only the faint outline of the building showed through, as insubstantial as a wraith. If they were watching from the house, I too had vanished.

Esther had said that when Lady Magdalen led a pilgrimage of the ladies, she always went first to Gray's well and then they walked on to say vespers at the spring that was the source of the well. That must be the one Crowhurst had gone to investigate the day he was killed. I was certain that Sam had not murdered his father, though he'd every cause to do so, and I also believed him when he said that he meant to do it as soon as he was strong enough to overpower Crowhurst. I knew what that kind of impotent rage felt like. When I was a boy there were nights when the thought of revenge was the only rope I could cling to that kept me from drowning in misery. But I had not killed Waldegrave – others yes, but not him. And Sam hadn't killed his tormentor. He could easily have lashed out in fury, but he wasn't capable of staging a death to look like an accident. I was sure now he didn't even realise that Crowhurst was dead.

Alys could have done it, but if she had, she must have had help. The man who now posed as Matthew Crowhurst seemed the most likely, if he was Alys's lover or her kin. But why had Yaxley colluded in the deception?

When I reached Gray's well, it was deserted. All attempts to get the water flowing had been abandoned. It was proving easier to cut ice from ponds and streams than from the well. The flowers brought as offerings had long since withered, but with their gilding of silver and ice-diamonds they had acquired new beauty, as if they had been plucked in a meadow that grew deep beneath the earth.

I'd heard the old dowager say that the path which led from the well to the spring was muddy and likely to be overgrown and covered with fallen branches. That suggested it went through a stretch of woodland. I picked my way to the ruined wall of the old church and followed it round, planning to start my search in the woodland opposite. But I had taken only a single pace away from the shelter of the wall when I smelled it – strong tobacco smoke, and there was something else, something fetid.

I drew back rapidly, taking cover behind the half-tumbled wall. As a field messenger, I'd quickly learned that the stench of a man is often the first warning you get before you hear or see him. If he was the minion sent to follow me, Smith should have chosen someone who didn't stink like a ferret. I listened as heavy boots crunched over frosted grass. But they were walking ahead of me, not behind.

I heard the click of a latch lifting and realised where I was. On the other side of that wall was the tool shed where we had stored Crowhurst's corpse. I was annoyed with myself. There was nothing sinister in someone from the manor going to that hut; they probably needed to fetch a spade or some other tool that was kept there. Except that Yaxley had told Smith no one had reason to go there in winter, and surely he would not have sent one of his own men in there, knowing that a body lay inside.

I edged around the stone wall, half expecting to hear a cry of alarm as an unsuspecting servant stumbled across the corpse. The door was closed, though I could hear movement inside, and moments later I heard it open again. Someone tramped away, moving around the far side of the hut and wall. I hurried forward, but they had already disappeared from view behind the Abbey ruins.

There were footprints in front of the door, and something else. Scattered sandy-red fragments stood out against the white frost like candle flames shining in the dark. I moved closer and crouched down – a few tiny clods of earth. Maybe old dry mud had fallen from whichever tool the man had collected.

I stepped inside, leaving the door ajar just enough to give me light. The storeroom was as I remembered it. Scythes and hay rakes gleamed in the shaft of light, their wooden shafts oiled, their metal blades coated in a thick layer of animal grease to keep them from rusting. It would plainly be more than his life was worth for any labourer to risk dumping an implement in here without having cleaned it more thoroughly than one of the serving dishes that graced the old dowager's table. Besides, I couldn't see any obvious gap where any tool might have been removed. Maybe whoever had come in here had stumbled across Crowhurst's corpse and retreated hastily in alarm.

The body still lay in the far corner, covered. I crouched and lifted the sack covering his face and that tell-tale broken nose. The skin had blacked a little more. The crystals of ice on his lashes, bushy brows and beard glinted in the winter sunlight slanting in from the half-open door. For a moment I thought his lips moved and his eyes opened, but it was only shadows darting across his face from the bare branches of the trees outside, swaying a little against the sun.

I pulled the sack back over the frozen corpse and rocked back on my heels, preparing to rise. Had I been standing I probably wouldn't have noticed them, but the fragments of dry earth stood out in relief as the edge of a shaft of low sunlight caught them. They were scattered on two or three of the worn flagstones, near the foot of the wall, in the opposite corner from where Crowhurst lay. A line of sandy-red soil marked the slim gap between two of the stones, partly covered by a heavy tar barrel. But scrape marks in the frozen green mould covering the stones showed that the barrel had recently been dragged aside, perhaps just minutes before. Wrapping my arms round the rim, I wrestled it inch by inch across the floor until both slabs of stone were exposed. One of them was rimmed all the way round by the narrow line of red earth. Someone had prised it up.

I glanced around until I spotted what I was sure I'd find: a mattock hanging among the other farm tools. The blade had been wiped clean of any dirt, but the metal was not glistening with grease like those on either side. The thin broad blade slid neatly down one side of the stone and I pushed on the long handle until the flag lifted high enough for me to wedge my boot beneath it, before finally heaving it up.

A hole had been hewn in the compacted earth beneath and a small sack lay at the bottom. I lifted it out. The contents clinked metallically, but the sound was muffled. A piece of sheepskin had been tucked around a small assortment of objects. I carefully unwrapped it. Two small reliquaries lay on the matted wool. One was in the form of a silver hand, two fingers extended in blessing. A tiny fragment of bone, magnified beneath a little crystal dome, was set into the palm. The other reliquary took the form of a brightly enamelled pendant depicting the face of a saint, with a scrap of cloth inside. They were surrounded by several other small metal objects, including a gold ring set with garnets and half a dozen ancient dirt-encrusted coins. The silver pieces were tarnished black, but small patches on each had been rubbed clean to reveal a hint of the precious metal beneath. All of the treasures looked centuries old – all, that is, except one. I picked it up, staring stupidly at what lay in my palm before I realised what I was holding.

Sunlight and shadow had been flickering constantly across the wall from the open door, and I'd been so absorbed in examining the contents of the sack that I didn't at first register that the shadow now looming over my shoulder was not moving. Even as that thought surfaced and I turned, it was already too late. I caught again that distinctive smell of tobacco and rotting meat, but before I could even raise an arm to defend myself, the searing pain of a blow exploded in my skull. A light brighter than the summer's sun blinded me and, with a roar like a huge wave breaking, darkness engulfed me. I felt myself spinning down and down, sinking through the cold earth into Hades itself.

Chapter Thirty-nine

I COULDN'T MOVE. I couldn't breathe. I couldn't see. I was being buried alive. I could hear dull thuds on wood, like clods of earth falling on a wooden coffin. I tried to yell, but no sound came out. I couldn't close my jaws; my mouth was crammed with what felt like small stones. I struggled to take a great gulping breath. Something hard shot down my throat, making me choke and cough so violently I thought my lungs would explode. Whatever was filling my mouth shot out, leaving me hacking and gasping. It was only then I realised I wasn't inside a box. I lay on my side, gasping and wheezing, trying to breathe slowly until the burning in my lungs eased. Lie still! Think!

My ankles were bound tightly, as were my wrists behind my back. A sack had been pulled down over my head, pinioning my upper arms. I pushed away the unpleasant thought that it might be the same one that had covered the face of Crowhurst's corpse. The ground beneath me was as cold as ice, leeching the heat through my clothes. I rocked on to my back and immediately regretted it. My head was swimming and thumping from the blow that had landed somewhere on the side. But I stayed there long enough to discover I was lying on stone, not frosted grass. I must be still inside the hut, then.

My teeth began to chatter as the cold seeped into me, but as I clenched my jaw, I felt something lodged in back of my mouth. I worked at the irritant with my tongue until it slid forward. It was small, smooth and hard – a bean. Dried beans had been stuffed into my mouth. My assailant intended me to die, like Bethia and Crowhurst. My coat had been stripped off, and my jerkin.

He was hoping the cold would finish me before I was found, like Crowhurst, and his wish might well be granted. It could be days or even weeks before anyone had cause to come into this hut. But Bethia hadn't died of the cold. Her throat had been cut. And I was lying there as helpless as a goat trussed and bound on a butcher's block.

The sound of another dull thump against wood filtered through the sack. I almost called out, but sense kicked in and I knew I couldn't risk it. It might be someone from the Abbey working nearby who could help, but equally it could be the killer and I couldn't risk him discovering that I had regained consciousness. If he intended to return and finish his task with a knife, I had to be ready for him, and I had no idea how much time I had left.

I rocked back on to my side, waiting a moment or two for the pain and nausea to subside, but I couldn't rest for long. I arched backwards, trying to reach my ankles with my bound hands. The ropes had been pulled so tight that my fingers scarcely had enough blood flowing in them to move, much less find the knot. I bent forward again, groping for the knife I always carried at my side and almost dislocating my shoulder as I strained for it. But, of course, it was gone.

I struggled once more to reach the rope about my feet and picked at it until my fingernails ripped. Finally, to my great relief, it began to give. If I could just free my legs and stand up, I could find the door and get out. Then I smelled it. Just a snatch at first, like a gust from a distant campfire. Smoke! No sunlight filtered through the loose weave of sacking, so I was sure the door had been pulled shut. I redoubled my efforts, contorting at an angle I hadn't managed since my youth, and finally the rope about my ankles slackened. I kicked it free, rolling on to my knees and staggering upright, struggling to balance on feet that felt like two lumps of dead, boneless flesh.

Even through the sack, the stench of smoke was growing stronger and now I could hear the crackle and snap of burning wood. Someone had set fire to one of the wooden walls of the hut. I lumbered forward, kicking out, feeling for the tar barrel I'd moved or the raised flagstone in the hope that the mattock would still be lying next to it. But either I was blundering in the wrong direction, or my assailant had removed all evidence of that hole and its hidden treasures.

Even though the sack was holding back the worst of the smoke, I was beginning to find it hard to breathe, but I stifled my coughing, in case the killer was listening outside for any signs of life. I could waste no more time searching the floor. I turned in the opposite direction from where I thought I could hear the crackle of flames and edged forward. With my arms pinioned by the sack and my hands still bound behind me, I braced myself for a collision with a scythe or the sharp tines of a hay rack hanging on the wall. But before I even reached the back wall, I stumbled over something on the floor. Unable to stop myself falling, all I could do was twist as I fell, so that my shoulder took the force of the impact. What felt like a hundred knives sliced into muscle and bone.

I was impaled and for a moment could do nothing as the blood ran hot down my back and arm. The slightest movement tore each wound still wider. Setting my jaw, I took a deep breath and dragged myself off, as each blade stabbed again into mangled flesh. I shuffled backwards until I could touch what I had fallen on. It was a threshing board, into which hundreds of razor-sharp flakes of flint had been hammered. Cursing at the pain and in the same breath blessing whichever angel or demon had tripped me, I rubbed the bonds around my wrists over the sharpened pieces of flint behind me, ignoring the hot spurts of blood that ran from the hundred slashes on my shoulder and arm each time I moved. The flints sliced through the rope as easily as a newly sharpened knife. As soon as my hands burst free, I dragged the sack off my head, but stayed crouching on the ground, my head throbbing, blood running over my hands as I tried to restore the feeling in them.

The storeroom was in darkness. Only a thin line of light near the floor marked where the door was, and that was forming and dissolving in the thickening smoke oozing in between the wooden boards of the wall. I was sweating. The heat was building inside the hut like a baker's oven but drops of water were showering on to my head. The rapid drumming I'd heard all around me was frost and ice that had formed inside the hut, now melting fast. But that wasn't that sound that sent my stomach churning. It was the crackle of burning wood, which was no longer coming from just one wall, but all around me and above my head. He had set a fire to engulf the hut and burn it to the ground.

I folded the sack and tied it over my mouth and nose, then crawled towards that thin line of light. I was almost upon it when I felt the scorching heat and realised that what I could see beneath the door was not sunlight, but fire. Flames were roaring up on the other side of the wooden wall. The stinging, acrid smoke of burning tar rolled in.

A pyre had been set against the door. I didn't doubt that if I pulled the door open, the whole blazing bonfire would tumble in on top of me and scatter across the floor, consuming anything it touched. I hadn't been able to find the tar barrel in the hut because it was out there, ablaze. I remembered the burning hut in the woods, the charred, blackened hand of that girl, the shattering explosion of the gunpowder. If those priests or that bastard of a steward had set this blaze, if they were standing out there as they had on that night, waiting for the flames to reach the powder . . .

I scrambled back, desperate to lay hands on an axe, even a spade, anything that I could use to break through one of the burning walls. But the heat was becoming unbearable. I was roasting alive. Forked tongues of flames were beginning to lick through the holes burned in the wood, vanishing and striking out again through the black smoke like a wall of snakes. I was choking. I could barely stand. I dropped flat to the flags, seeking the coldness of the stone, but they too were beginning to heat up. My lungs and eyes were burning in the tarry smoke. I'd lost all sense of whether I was moving towards the door or away from it. The floor was tilting wildly, like the deck of a pitching ship in a storm. Roaring filled my ears, and as if hell had burst open above me, one of the roof beams erupted into a blaze of scarlet flames. Every last wisp of breath was sucked from my lungs and I plunged into a bottomless pit of darkness.

Chapter Forty

A THUNDERCLAP BURST over my head. A blinding light split the darkness. The hut was collapsing into a ball of fire. I curled up, waiting for the blazing timbers to come crashing down on me, but I didn't feel them fall and for a moment wondered if I was already dead.

Something cold flicked across my chest and face. I tried to take a breath, but my throat was sealed. I rolled over, coughing and choking, fighting to suck down the icy air even as my burning lungs shrank from it. And only then did I grasp that it *was* icy and so was the ground beneath my face. I was lying on frosted grass. But I could still feel the heat, see the blazing light, hear the roar. Painfully, I turned my head. Flames were leaping into the sky from the heap of blazing timber, but I was not beneath them.

A cold hand flicked across my hair again, brushing off the sparks that drifted down. I squinted up. My eyeballs felt as if they had been skinned, every blink like brambles dragged over an open wound. I couldn't make sense of the blurred features of whoever was crouching over me, but his breathing sounded as rough and laboured as my own and he too was coughing.

'Pursglove? Can you sit?'

He seized me under the armpits and dragged me a few feet further back from the fire, propping me against a tree. I yelped as my lacerated shoulder thumped against the rough trunk.

'You're bleeding.' There was disgust in the voice, as if I had vomited on him. 'There is no sense in examining the wound out here. We'll see what damage you've done back at the Abbey. I sent a boy to fetch assistance, though it will be too late to salvage anything from that store. Lady Magdalen will be most vexed.'

'Master Smith?' I peered up, resisting the urge to rub my tormented eyes.

He stood up and I heard a crack above my head.

He broke an icicle in two and thrust half into my mouth. 'Suck that and hold your head still.' He rubbed the rest of the icicle over my lids, holding it against my skin until it melted and dripped into my eyes. 'If they have the wit to bring any water it will probably freeze before it gets here. So, this will have to suffice until we can get you into back to the house.'

I swallowed the last sliver of ice, letting it slide down my swollen throat. 'What happened? It was . . . a miracle . . . I got out,' I croaked.

'Shadrach, Meshach and Abednego may have had the miraculous intervention of an angel to deliver them from their fiery furnace, but I am afraid you, Daniel, had to make do with the offices of a mere priest. Though you should give thanks to the Blessed Virgin and the saints that I was on hand. A few minutes more and not even the Archangel Gabriel could have saved you.'

My vison was beginning to clear; Smith's eyes blazed out from a face that was blackened with tarry smoke, as my own must have been. Large patches of his coat and breeches hung in charred rags.

My head was swimming and spasms of violent hacking and retching repeatedly seized me as I struggled to make sense of what he was saying.

'What . . . what brought you . . . here?'

'I told you that after your absence the other night I would be watching you. It is my duty to protect Lady Magdalen and those souls in my charge. Did you think you would not be observed going off alone when you had no cause to leave the house? It was reported to me and I followed to see who you might be meeting.'

'The fire . . . did you start—'

'Don't be a fool, Pursglove. If I had set the fire, I would hardly have risked my own life to pull you out.' He coughed, pressing his gloved hand hard against his chest. I saw that too was almost burned through. 'Though perhaps I was the fool on this occasion. I should have left you to burn and rid us once and for all of the danger. If a hound cannot be trusted, better you kill it, before it turns and mauls you.'

'Then why . . . didn't you?' I wheezed.

He gave a mirthless laugh, his gaze resting for a long time on the blackened stones of the Abbey wall, which was all that still remained standing of the store, as if he was watching some scene from the past unfold, or perhaps it was the future he saw.

When he finally spoke, he was still not looking at me. 'I swore an oath that I would keep you alive,' he said softly. 'You have a powerful protector, Daniel, and they have other plans for you.'

'Who?' I demanded, pushing myself up so that he would be forced to look at me.

But if he had any intention of answering, I never discovered, for a group of men and boys came hurrying round the corner dragging a handcart, their shouts and bellows distracting both of us. Smith left me and marched across, snapping out orders before he had even reached them. Most he sent to drag the burning timbers apart and beat out the flames with the rakes, shovels and fire brooms they'd brought on the cart. They had also fetched a pile of wetted sacks, but those had frozen. Two of the men dragged the cart to where I was lying and helped me on to it. With no coat or jerkin, I was now shivering uncontrollably and was grateful for the blanket one threw around my shoulders. They set off back to the manor, with me jolting and rattling over every stone and frozen rut. I turned to look back. Smith was standing still among all the scurrying figures, staring into the dying flames, his face and charred clothes starkly black against the white landscape. But it was not him whose eyes I sought. It was the man who had set that fire, and I knew now who it was.

Chapter Forty-one

I HEARD HIS FOOTSTEPS approaching the workshop door and stepped back into the darkness behind it just as it opened. Holding a lantern before him, he lumbered in, kicking the door closed without bothering to turn. He passed so close to me, I thought I would smell that stench again, but like all those who had rushed to beat out the fire, the smoke from burning tar and timbers suffused his clothes and hair, overpowering all other odours. His heavy tread faltered as he caught sight of the object on the table. He picked it up and held it in the puddle of light. Then he emitted an almost animal cry and flung it against the wall, as though it was burning hot.

'Bethia was carrying that painted comb the night you killed her, wasn't she, Yaxley?'

His arms jerked out so wildly as he spun round that he almost smashed the lantern he was holding against the table, starting another blaze.

'What . . . what are you doing in here? You have no business coming here at this hour.'

He set the lantern down on the table and took a menacing step towards me. The light, cast upwards, made the knotted cords of his thick neck stand out more prominently than ever. My head still throbbed from the blow he'd inflicted earlier, and looking again at those muscled arms and shoulders, I was amazed it hadn't killed me outright.

I grasped the hilt of the knife I'd borrowed, sure he was preparing to land another punch with his meaty fist, but instead he stooped down, reaching into the shadows beside the table. When he straightened again, he was holding a sledgehammer. It would have taken anyone considerable strength to raise it, but he swung it upwards easily in both hands and took another pace towards me. Whether that lump of iron struck my skull or my shoulder, either way it was going to smash bones to splinters. I held the dagger out in front of me, jabbing it towards his guts, watching his eyes follow the blade. If I could taunt him into bringing the mallet down on the smaller target of my arm, rather than my head, I had some chance of dodging the blow.

The door behind us edged open. I didn't turn. The bailiff's gaze darted to whoever stood there – only briefly, but it was enough. I lunged at him, striking him with the hilt of the dagger beneath the elbow, so that his arm shot upwards and the massive weight of the hammer head tipped towards his shoulder. The momentum was enough to unbalance him and he crashed on to the ground, his head striking the wall as he went down. It didn't knock him out, but before he could recover himself, I was kneeling on his arm, the point of my dagger jabbing up under his chin.

Behind me, someone gave a cry of alarm. I fully expected whoever it was to try to drag me off, but instead I heard footsteps tearing across the courtyard towards the house. There was a yelp as their owner slipped on the icy flags, then after a moment they ran on.

Yaxley's free arm shot up, reaching for my throat. I rocked away from him, grinding his trapped arm beneath my knees, and pressed the knife-point into his neck until I saw blood running beneath his foxy beard.

'You should have made sure I was dead before you lit that fire, Yaxley, or did you mean me to burn alive? Did you want to hear me screaming from the flames? Did Bethia scream before you cut her? Did Crowhurst plead for his life?'

Footsteps were hastening back across the yard. Yaxley had heard them too. He called out, twisting and struggling so violently he almost impaled himself on the blade I was holding.

'Don't even twitch, Yaxley or I'll slice your throat open just like Bethia's.'

The footsteps quickened and burst through the door. Brathwayt, his chest heaving, ran towards us, but skidded to a stop when he saw the knife.

'Drop it, Pursglove!' He panted as if he was instructing a hound to relinquish a stolen chicken. 'I've men with me. You won't escape.' He beckoned frantically as if he thought they might slink off and leave him.

Arthur and Vincent, another of the yeoman waiters, hovered beside the door. Young Giles, who I assumed had raised the alarm, was peering around them from the safety of the courtyard. Arthur looked as if he'd rather dig out a cesspit with his bare hands than get involved in this. 'Best do as he says, Dannet. Don't want half the Abbey pitching in here.'

'Close the door, then, and stand in front of it,' I said. 'I don't want this bastard making a run for it.'

I reluctantly eased the blade away from Yaxley's throat, but kept a firm grip of it as I clambered to my feet. Brathwayt tried to grab me, but realising I was still holding the knife, backed away as if I had threatened him with it.

'Seize him!' he ordered.

But Arthur stepped between us. 'No call for that, Master Brathwayt. Dannet here came close to being roasted to death this morning. Bound to unsettle a man, that is. Hardly surprising he's a touch boiled-brained just now, but his blood will cool soon enough if you let him be. He'll not harm you, nor any of us, will you, brother?'

'He's harmed me!' Yaxley bellowed, lumbering to his feet. He raked up his beard, so that the blood could be clearly seen glistening on his neck.

'With good reason,' I said. 'Yaxley attempted to kill me this morning, and he's already murdered the woodward, Matthew Crowhurst, and Lady Katheryne's tiring maid, Bethia.'

342

Brathwayt, Arthur and Vincent exchanged the kind of glances which suggested they were in the presence of a dangerous lunatic who must be humoured.

'Matthew Crowhurst isn't dead, Pursglove.' Brathwayt said soothingly, as if he was speaking to his senile old grandfather. 'He was found alive and well, don't you remember?'

'The man living with Alys and Sam is not Crowhurst,' I told him.

The bailiff laughed. 'See, he's as mad as a bedlam beggar.'

There was a strangled squeak from behind Vincent, as if someone had started to speak and the sound had been smothered. Giles had evidently slipped in through the door before Arthur had closed it, and was now trying to melt into the shadows.

'Did you say something, lad?' Brathwayt asked him.

Giles stared hard at the floor, shaking his head.

'Matthew Crowhurst sold the vermin carcasses from his gibbet to your father, didn't he, Giles?' I said, quietly but firmly. 'You knew the old Crowhurst and you've seen the new one. They are not the same men, are they? Come now, speak the truth.'

'You tell him, boy,' Yaxley growled. 'Tell him he's talking out of his arse.'

Giles grabbed at the door latch and tried to lift it, but Arthur slammed the door shut again before he could get out. He seized the boy by the back of his jerkin and propelled him towards the steward, holding him there.

'When lads try to make a bolt for it, I always reckon there's something they're trying to hide, what say you, Master Brathwayt? You think on this, young Giles. Master Yaxley might hand you the bounty, but every penny you and your father earn comes from Lady Magdalen's purse. And if she was to learn that the lad working for her was a liar, I reckon she'd give orders his family wasn't to be paid so much as a single farthing ever again.'

The boy tried to break free, but Arthur shook Giles as a terrier might shake a rat, until he looked as if he might vomit.

''Course, I could flog the truth out of him, Master Brathwayt. There's a good ox whip in the stables, flay the bark off an oak tree, that would.'

'I advise you to tell us the truth, lad,' the steward said, 'unless you want a visit to the stables.'

Giles shot one desperate look back at the closed door, then screwed his eyes shut. 'Not Matthew,' he whispered.

'What are you mumbling about?' Brathwayt demanded. 'Speak up, lad. Are you saying the man living in the Crowhursts' cottage is not Matthew?'

The boy, his eyes still shut, slowly nodded his head.

'Then where the devil is Matthew? And who's that in his cottage?'

'Can't you tell the boy's a simpleton?' Yaxley said. 'And he's terrified by your threats. He'll saying anything to get out of here. He'd swear his father is a black cockerel, if it would make you let him go.'

'Is that right, lad?' Brathwayt growled.

Again, Giles nodded, though it was plain he was so terrified, he didn't really know what he was being asked.

'Even without the boy's testimony, there's one thing you already know, Master Brathwayt,' I said. 'That the maid, Bethia, is dead, murdered. You've seen her corpse.'

This did not seem like a good time to mention I also knew he'd helped to blow the girl's body to pieces. I needed him on my side.

Brathwayt turned to stare at me. 'How do you know she's dead?'

''Cause he's the one who killed her,' Yaxley said triumphantly. 'You all heard Pursglove threaten to cut my throat as he did Bethia's. So, he knew she's dead and how she died and that's proof enough for any magistrate. I reckon she found out he wasn't who he claims to be and he killed her to silence her.'

Arthur shook his head. 'That can't be right. Bethia ran off near a month before Dannet came on the scene.'

'But we don't know where she ran to,' Brathwayt said. 'Master Smith was convinced from the first that Pursglove was sent here deliberately to inveigle his way into the house, and it seems he was right. Some of the townspeople knew Bethia by sight and knew she worked here. Pursglove could have been in the area for weeks before he came to the Abbey gate. He's the kind of man a foolish young giglet like Bethia would be taken in by. He could have used her to learn all he could about the Abbey, then murdered her. It makes sense to me and it will to Master Smith too.'

'And I tied myself up inside that shed and set fire to it from the outside?'

'Who says you were tied up?' Yaxley said. 'I reckon you set that fire yourself and got caught inside when it took hold quicker than you meant it to.'

'He's marks on his wrists,' Arthur said. 'I saw them when I fetched him water to wash the soot and blood off.'

Yaxley shrugged. 'Could have made those himself.'

Brathwayt nodded thoughtfully. 'Master Smith says that he's known intelligencers who inflict manacle wounds on themselves, pretending they've been arrested, even tortured, to convince others to trust them.'

Arthur stepped forward and grabbed my wrist. Pushing up the sleeve and holding it out in the lantern light, he turned my arm over. 'Can't see how a man could have made those marks all by himself, without someone helping him, and none of us in the Abbey would have cause to do that. Those wounds are fresh, they are, and he's not set foot out of the Abbey these past two days. None of us have,' he added, with a baleful glance at the steward. 'So, there's none outside could have helped him.'

Brathwayt ignored his reproachful stare. 'Even if Pursglove was attacked and tied up, he has no proof Master Yaxley was involved. I understand from Master Smith that you admitted you didn't see who set the fire, since you claim to have been unconscious with a sack over your head at the time.'

'I smelled him.'

Yaxley laughed. 'Born in a kennel, were you?'

Arthur gave me a pitying look and his shoulders sagged. Loyal though he was, even he could not defend a friend who was plainly crazed.

Brathwayt shook his head. 'I know you can pick locks better than any thief who's ever swung at Tyburn, Pursglove, but are you really claiming you can tell one man from another by their smell?'

'I make no claim to that, but Master Yaxley has a distinctive smell at times, one that even an ordinary man like me can distinguish. Tobacco smoke, which I grant you nearly every man in Battle smells of, but also this.'

I lifted a stone bottle from the shelf, pulled out the stopper and thrust it under Brathwayt's nose. He recoiled, wrinkling his face in disgust.

'Oil of henbane,' he said. 'Stinks like rotting fish.'

'Every man describes it differently, but few can stand the smell. Arthur once told me that you didn't allow any servant to use it in the house. But a bailiff works mostly outside and men like him are plagued by rheumatism and backaches, made worse in the cold. That oil is what I smelled, just before I was hit.'

'You might smell the same on a dozen men, a hundred,' Yaxley jeered. 'You said it yourself: any man who works outside in all weathers suffers with fevered joints. Half the shire physic themselves with Devil's eye.'

'They're fools if they do, and if they weren't before, they will be after a few winters using that poison,' Brathwayt said, grimacing at the bottle. 'I've seen men fall into a frenzy and kill themselves or others, tormented into madness by the demons it conjures. The stink is not the only reason Lady Magdalen forbids it. It's witches' brew. It's . . .' He trailed off, staring at the bottle and frowning. I wondered if the same thought had suddenly occurred to us both.

The steward shook himself, as if dismissing whatever was troubling him. 'But he's right, Pursglove, any one of the outside servants or woodwards might have used the same oil, even some-one from the town. Many people appear to know how to come and go from the Abbey grounds without passing through the main gate,' he added, turning to fix Arthur with a pointed gaze.

Arthur assumed a nonchalant expression that deceived no one.

'And anyhow, why would I want to burn down my own tool store?' Yaxley demanded.

'Because I was inside it. You saw what I'd seen and you guessed I would realise who'd killed Bethia, and if her, then also Crowhurst. And I think you wanted to dispose of Crow-hurst's body, too, in case anyone should recognise him when he was finally buried.' I turned to Brathwayt. 'It was Crowhurst's corpse that was found frozen in the charcoal burner's hut, not a beggar's, and Crowhurst's body that was put in the tool shed to keep until the thaw.'

'Whether it was or wasn't, the man that Master Smith and I examined in the laundry had frozen to death. There was no suggestion he'd been murdered.'

'He may have died from the cold, but someone intended he should. I found the same marks on his wrists and ankles as were inflicted on me this morning. He had been bound up and left to freeze, and I found something else too. When I was tied up and left in that tool store to burn, dried beans were stuffed into my mouth. I found beans in Crowhurst's mouth as well, and in Bethia's throat.'

Brathwayt's head snapped up. 'There were beans in that pursuivant Benet's mouth when he was found. No one could understand that.'

'They put a pot of beans under Grandma's cot when she was dying,' Giles piped up. We all stared round in surprise; I'd half forgotten he was there. 'Then they ripped the feather pillow away, so she'd go quickly, for she was in such pain.'

'Why a pot of beans?' I asked.

It was Vincent who answered. 'For the ghosts of the dead, of course.'

Giles and Arthur nodded, but I must have still looked bemused, for Arthur added, 'If the spirit is torn from the body violently then it'll linger near the corpse and torment the man who did it harm. Have to give it a home, see, until it's ready to move on. If it goes into the beans, then it'll not haunt the living.'

'Then someone did do Benet harm,' Brathwayt said. 'I'm not saying we didn't all wish he'd come to a bad end before he could bring trouble to Lady Magdalen and the manor. But she would not have wanted him murdered.'

'So, you admit Benet was murdered,' I said. 'But even if I had been in these parts when he died, it's hardly likely that I would have killed a pursuivant if I'd been sent here as a spy for the same cause.'

'Are you accusing Master Yaxley of killing Benet too?' Brathwayt demanded.

'If beans were found on all three corpses . . . I discovered that a stone flag in that hut had been prised up and someone had excavated a hiding place beneath it. I found a sack down there containing two small reliquaries – one in the form of a silver hand, the other an enamelled pendant. I didn't have time to examine everything in the sack, but I did notice a ring set with garnets and some old coins. And this.' I bent to retrieve the wooden comb from the floor where Yaxley had flung it. 'I don't know where he got the other things in that sack, but I do know Lady Katheryne told me Bethia was carrying this the night she vanished.'

'And how do you know she didn't drop it, or sell it?' Yaxley said.

'To you?' I snapped.

'Anyone could have buried that in the hut,' the bailiff said. 'You heard Brathwayt, all of the servants and woodwards know that tool shed. Could have been any one of the townsfolk too.' He jerked his chin up defiantly, opening the cut I had made on his throat. Blood trickled down his skin, glistening in the lantern light.

'Arthur, would you look in that chest in the corner?' I said.

'I'll not allow any yeoman waiter to go poking around in my workroom!'

'Do as Pursglove asks,' Brathwayt said firmly, though he was not looking at Arthur, but directly at Yaxley, like a stag preparing for the rut.

'You've no authority over me, Brathwayt!' Yaxley bellowed. 'You get out of here right now and take your dribbling maggots with you.' He moved to block Arthur's way, his fist clenched, making it clear he was prepared to defend his territory by force if necessary.

'Dribbling maggots, are we?' Arthur said.

He darted around the other side of the table and heaved up the lid of the trunk. He dragged out two stuffed saddled packs. I'd glimpsed them before Yaxley had burst in on me, but I hadn't had the chance to search them. If they didn't contain what I'd wagered they would, I could expect no mercy from Yaxley, nor from Brathwayt either, if I'd made him look a fool.

Arthur unfastened the straps and began to heave the contents on to the floor. 'Well now, Master Yaxley. You thinking of taking a journey? You weren't going to leave us without saying good-bye, were you?'

He pulled out hastily packed clothes and all the other essentials any man might need if he was setting off on a long journey. One of the shirts fell to the flags with a clang. Yaxley tried to kick it aside, but Arthur snatched it out of his reach and unwrapped it. He tipped out the contents of the sack that lay inside, then held something up in the lantern light. It was the small silver reliquary in the form of a hand.

'That what you saw in the storeroom, was it, Dannet?'

'Pursglove put them in there! He was in here, ferreting about, when I came in and caught him. You said it yourself, Brathwayt, he can pick a lock as well as any thief.'

'How could I have taken them from the storeroom? Master Smith dragged me out unconscious and he will, I'm sure, be only too glad to affirm that I had no sack with me. I was examining them in that hut when I was struck and tied up, so only the man who attacked me could have removed them before the fire.'

Too late, I realised Yaxley was edging close to where the sledgehammer had fallen. I lunged for it, but Yaxley was closer. He seized the handle, swinging the hammer wildly from side to side as he ran for the door. We all jumped back, knowing a single blow from that heavy lump of iron could maim a man for life, if it didn't kill you. He reached the door and sprang the latch.

I don't know if Giles intended to bar the way or was simply scared out of his wits and was trying to escape into the yard. But without warning, the lad ducked down and ran like a hare, squeezing through the open door just in front of the bailiff. Yaxley tripped over the boy's leg and both of them crashed down on the frozen courtyard, half in and half out of the door. We rushed forward. I thrust my arm round the bailiff's throat, and the others helped me to drag him off the boy and hurl him back into the room. In the doorway, Giles lay still. Blood gushed up from the hole in his skull and poured over his face, steaming in the icy air. Splinters of white bone, brains and matted hair lay in a garnet-red pool on the sparkling white frost. The sledgehammer had fallen beside the boy, the iron head glistening wet in the lantern light.

'Where's it coming from?' Yaxley was peering down at the front of his blood-soaked coat, his fingers groping across his chest, as if he thought the blood must be his own.

We wordlessly stepped aside from the door and he stared past us. Then he gave an agonised cry, his eyes wide with horror.

'Not the boy . . . I'd never harm him . . . he ran straight into me . . . I never meant . . . he was like a son to me . . . I always saw they got extra, for his mother's sake . . . it'll break her heart . . . I never meant . . .'

'You may not have meant to kill him, but you did,' Brathwayt spat. 'You'd have killed any one of us if we'd given you half a chance, and you've slaughtered that innocent lad as surely as if you'd cut his throat. You'll hang for this, or worse.' He turned his back on the bailiff, and beckoned to the rest of us. 'Bring the poor lad inside. He doesn't deserve to be left in the yard like a dead pig. And find something to cover him with,' he said, wincing as his gaze fell again on the mess of bone, blood and brain.

The blood had stopped pumping from the wound, but even so a trail of it dripped over the flags as we carried him into the corner of the workroom and closed the door. Arthur snatched up some of the clothes he had earlier dragged from Yaxley's pack and used them to cover the boy, tenderly bunching a shirt and laying it beneath Giles's battered head as if he wanted to protect him from the cold, hard floor.

The violent sound of coughing and retching behind us made us spin round. Yaxley was steadying himself against the table, trying not to gag. A brown stone bottle fell from his hand and rolled across the ground. Even before I picked it up, I could smell the stench of rotten meat coming from it and knew it would be empty. I dropped it and covered the distance to Yaxley in two strides. I slapped him on the back to make him spew out what he had drunk. But he clamped his jaws tight, thrusting me away, and sank down into the chair.

'Quick, fetch a purge from the house!' I yelled. 'Some mustard water at least.'

But Yaxley grasped my arm and shook his head, then with a great effort swallowed hard and let out a breath. 'I'll not die a gallow's death . . . not dance for that braying mob of donkeys.'

The steward watched him, his expression nothing but contempt. 'I suppose we ought to send for Master Smith, so he can make his confession,' he said, without much conviction.

'No use . . . Smith won't absolve me . . .'

'He's right,' I said. 'Smith will never forgive self-murder.' I caught hold of Yaxley's shoulder. 'But you can tell us what happened to Bethia and Crowhurst. You can at least get those sins off your conscience.'

'And that pursuivant Benet,' Brathwayt added. 'For it's my betting you know something about that too.'

Yaxley pushed him away as he gagged and gulped, trying to keep the noxious oil down in his stomach.

I seized Yaxley's shoulder, pressing my face close to his, despite the foul stench of henbane on his breath. 'I won't threaten to hurt you, for we both know what you've drunk will put you beyond physical pain far sooner than you deserve. But I can ensure that your wretched carcass is exhibited in the market place, naked and mutilated, so that girls can giggle over your shrivelled little cods and boys can sling every piece of filth they can find at it, while the goodwives watch it rot day by day on their way to market. Or maybe you'd prefer us to feed your corpse as poisoned bait to the vermin you so carefully record and have them shit you out. So, let's start with Bethia, shall we? And talk fast – by my reckoning you haven't got long.'

Chapter Forty-two

YAXLEY DID NOT SURRENDER his secrets easily. It was only when his limbs began to burn and twitch that he finally comprehended the nightmare he was about to descend into. He must have been a powerful man all his life, and he seemed shocked as he felt the strength draining from his muscles. What might have taken a decade was happening in as many minutes; for the first time, he knew what it was to be weak and helpless.

'The holy spring. Got silted up in the summer. No men to spare . . . Lady Magdalen was taking some of her friends to the well. Relies on me to keep it flowing. Never let her down, never. I've brought up a coin or two in the past from time to time, when I've dug around, and a few old pins, same as in the well itself. People left them there years ago for luck. This time the spade hit something bigger. That silver hand.' He tried to point at the haul that Arthur had tipped from the sack, but the gesture was clumsy and uncontrolled, like that of a drunken man.

'Could see it was a reliquary. Some monk had buried that for safekeeping before old King Henry threw them out. Everyone in Battle knew the stories about the great reliquary of gold and jewels they had in the church.'

'Aye,' Arthur said. 'We've all heard that crock-o'gold tale. Remember I told you that one, Dannet? Old abbot sold it and everything else of value besides before Cromwell could lay his thieving hands on it.'

'But what if he didn't sell it?' Yaxley croaked. 'If they buried that hand, they could have buried all the Abbey treasure . . .

meant to come back for it when Cromwell and his dogs had forgotten about it.'

'So, you thought to strike it rich, did you?' Brathwayt sneered. 'Because I'll wager you weren't planning to hand over that golden reliquary to Lady Magdalen if you found it, any more than you gave her that silver hand there.'

'She's got wealth enough for a dozen lifetimes and it'll not be her that pays the price when they come for us, like they came for the old abbot and the monks in Henry's day. There's priests and others being smuggled in and out under the noses of the King's men. It can't last. We're being watched, and you know it, Brathwayt. Smith knows it, they all do. It's only a matter of time before one of the birds gets caught in the King's nets and starts cheeping. They've held off raiding this place because the old lady's got friends in high places. But she's failing, anyone with eyes can see that, and soon as she's dead, they'll pounce.'

Yaxley peered at the steward as if he could no longer see him clearly. He rubbed his eyes and gazed up again. His pupils had dilated so widely that the green of the eyes had vanished and only two black holes remained.

'They could send us all to the gallows and even if they don't, we'll be turned out on the road to beg for a crust, like the old monks were. You've no notion what that does to you. I've worked, man and boy, outside in all weathers – ice, flood and storm – while you and your soft-handed servants stand round the fires supping hot ale. Wet and cold eats into your bones. It cripples you. I didn't need to hear the seven whistlers to know this house is finished, and I wasn't going to wait for them to come for me. But I needed money, else how would I live at my age? That foreign bastard of a King has betrayed us all. Why should his men carry off the monks' treasure instead of me who's earned it?'

He broke off, staring fearfully up at the roof beams, shrinking from whatever he saw there. His fearful expression made us all peer upwards, but I could see nothing except a few spiders crawling in the shadows.

'But you didn't find the reliquary?' I prompted.

He dragged his gaze back, staring at his shaking hands, and tried to press them together, but they kept jerking away, as if they were no longer part of his body.

'Found a . . . few bits more.' His arm shot out again towards the sack. 'Hid them beneath the roots of the oak tree near the holy spring. Could only dig small patches of ground at a time. Woodward would have seen the ground was dug up, and her ladyship . . . when she came to the spring . . . misses nothing, that one.' Again his gaze had wandered and he was staring at something behind us.

It was starting to unnerve Brathwayt. 'I'm not interested in your treasures,' he snapped. 'What I want to know is, why you murdered that poor girl, Bethia. What harm did she ever do you?'

'Little whore . . . gives it up to any stable boy or scullion . . . even to one of those pious priests . . . heard her giggling about it with one of the maids . . . but she wouldn't give me the time of day . . . and I'm bailiff here . . . should have been grateful I even noticed her . . .' His words were beginning to slur a little. 'Thirsty!' He tried to rise from the chair, half turning towards the shelves behind him, but his legs would not obey him.

Arthur darted forward and after picking up a couple of bottles and sniffing the contents, brought the third back to the table. Yaxley made a wild grab for it, but Arthur held it out of reach. 'I might let you have a drop if you tell us what you did to Bethia.'

'Throat's burning. Can't speak.' His lips were indeed visibly sticking to his teeth, but Arthur refused to budge. 'If you can speak well enough to tell us your throat's afire you can tell us what happened to that girl.'

The bailiff scowled at him. 'She sang another song when I showed her that ring.'

'The gold one with the garnets, was that something else you dug from the spring?' I asked.

He nodded, his head lolling to one side. 'Sweet enough to me then, little whore . . . and after, when I told there'd be more . . . she was always in here . . . she was growing fond of me . . . I was going to take her with me when I left . . .'

His had been a lonely life, I realised, in spite of being surrounded by people, and for a moment he looked genuinely hurt. But perhaps it was just a spasm induced by the poison, for he pressed his hand to chest. 'Heart's pounding. Wine, need wine—'

'Save your breath for your tale,' Arthur said sternly.

The bailiff swayed in the chair and leaned forward over the table to steady himself. 'Had to find more gold to sell . . . have to keep two of us and she wouldn't stay if money ran out . . . wanted pretty things . . .'

Arthur had let the bottle rest on the table and now Yaxley flung himself across, snatching it before Arthur could drag it back. He couldn't grasp the stopper, so, almost weeping with frustration, he dashed the neck against the edge of the table and sucked desperately on the broken and jagged rim. Arthur let him drink, then pulled it from his grasp. Wine and blood trickled from Yaxley's mouth where the sharp edge had cut him, but he didn't seem to feel it.

'Tell me about Bethia, or I swear I'll screw your eyes out with this,' Arthur said, jabbing the broken bottle at Yaxley's face.

I was sure Arthur didn't have it in him to actually do it, but the fury in his voice told me he'd been fonder of Bethia than he had admitted to me, perhaps even to himself.

'Told me she had a . . . babe in her belly. Ladyship would turn her out . . . soon as she could no longer hide it. She wanted money to pay a woman in the village to rid her of it, and more besides. She'd been sneaking back from the town and seen me with Benet. Said if she lost her place, she'd go to the magistrate and tell them I killed the King's man . . . I told her, just a few more days, then we'd be rich . . . I'd take her to London, anywhere. I'd marry her . . . She laughed. She kept laughing . . . said the babe wasn't of my getting . . . she started searching, thought

I'd hidden the jewels in here, and all the time she was laughing. I knew . . . I knew then whatever I gave her . . . would never be enough . . . I'd never be safe . . .'

His gaze darted to the corner and he tried to rise, but fell back defeated. 'Foxes! See!'

For a moment I feared young Sam's pets had somehow found their way here, but there was nothing in the corner except a few empty snares.

'Can't you see their eyes? . . . Watching us. Have to kill them! Have to!'

'It's the henbane talking!' Brathwayt seized Yaxley's beard, dragging his head round until he was facing him. 'Look at me. You told Lady Magdalen that you had discovered the girl's body at night on your rounds. You persuaded her that Bethia had been carrying on with a married man from another village, who had more than likely killed her to cover up the affair.'

Yaxley flailed his arms like a drunken man, forcing Brathwayt to step back. 'Her ladyship wouldn't risk raising the cry of murder, not so soon after Benet.' His mouth contorted in a spasm. 'They buried her in the churchyard. Her ladyship was grateful. She thanked me . . . for my loyalty. She knew, you see. She knew what I'd done to protect them.'

'You fly-blown turd!' Arthur yelled, trying to seize Yaxley's thick neck. 'If the old lady even suspected what you'd done, she'd have woven the rope to hang you with her own hands.'

I dragged Arthur off Yaxley, but the bailiff seemed hardly to have noticed the attack. He was cowering from creatures only he could see that, judging by his terrified gaze, seemed to be climbing up the walls. He tried in vain to draw his legs up and was striking out wildly, babbling about stoats and weasels, and hedgepigs with blazing prickles swarming around him. His wits were going. If I didn't get the truth out of him quickly, he would take the secret to his grave.

'Yaxley, you said Bethia saw you with Benet and threatened to tell the magistrate that you'd killed him. Did you kill Benet?'

'Cecil's rat . . . been hanging around, watching the grounds, the spring . . . so I daren't dig . . . Word came from the innkeeper where he was staying . . . said Benet was leaving next day for London . . . He was excited, the innkeeper said, as if he'd found something. We all knew if he made his report . . . Abbey would be raided . . . But I'd never have killed him. Ordered to . . . had to do it. Him or me in that grave . . . that was the choice. Kill Benet . . . stop him going to London . . . Those were the orders . . .'

'Who?' I demanded. 'Who ordered you to kill Benet?'

He turned to look at the bottle of henbane lying on the floor, gesturing with a shaking hand towards it.

'If you think another swig of that is going to put you out of your misery quicker, you can forget it,' Arthur said. 'We'll not let you die yet, you bastard.'

Yaxley shook his head, gesturing towards the bottle again. 'Sp . . . Spero. Benet discovered who . . . Had to be silenced . . . Spero's orders.'

My heart began to pound as if I too had swallowed henbane. I grasped his head in both hands, lifting his face towards mine. 'Do you mean Benet discovered who Spero Pettingar is? That was what he'd found out, that was the information he was going to take to London?'

Slowly Yaxley nodded.

'Then he is here. Pettingar is here in Battle!' Blood was roaring through my veins like fire.

Yaxley shook his head. 'Not here . . . not Pettingar . . . Spero . . . Spero!'

I couldn't make sense of what he was saying. 'Then who is Spero? Who gave you the order to kill Benet?'

'Look, I don't know who the hell this Spero is, never heard of him,' Brathwayte said. 'Have you?' He glanced at Arthur and Vincent, who shrugged, their faces blank. 'But if he gave orders to kill Benet, he did us all a favour; that is one murder I won't hold against you, Yaxley. All I want to know is what happened to Matthew Crowhurst. I won't be taken for a fool; if that man in Crowhurst cottage is an imposter, as steward of this Abbey, I've a right to know.'

Yaxley and I both ignored him. Yaxley was gesturing frantically again at the bottle of henbane. He couldn't be hoping to drink more of it; it was empty, as we both knew. I snatched it up off the floor and thrust it into his hands. Arthur tried to grab it from him, but I shoved him away. Yaxley turned the bottle upside down and pushed it towards me. There on the base was a wax seal in the form of a wyvern, the same dragon-like creature I had seen on the medal in Yaxley's cash box.

Yaxley stabbed his finger repeatedly at it. 'Kill . . . Benet.'

Arthur peered over my elbow. 'That's the knucker, that is. Is he saying the knucker killed Benet?'

'Makes more sense than anything else I've heard in here this evening,' Vincent muttered.

Again, Yaxley gestured at the wax seal. 'Sp . . . Spero . . . Spero!'

His words were badly slurred, and the others shook their heads as if they couldn't make out what he was trying to say. But I was absolutely certain what I'd heard. That name was burned into me.

I grabbed the broken bottle of wine and poured the remains into a battered beaker that stood on the shelf. The inside was encrusted with a brown substance, but whatever it was it could hardly matter to Yaxley now.

'The poison is eating into his brain; soon he won't be able to understand anything we say, much less reply. Hold him still, Master Brathwayt.'

The steward steadied Yaxley's head while I held the beaker to his lips, and he gulped greedily.

'But what about Matthew Crowhurst?' Braithwaite repeated.

'I don't think he can get the words out,' I said. 'Suppose I tell you what I've worked out about Crowhurst's death, and he can nod if I'm right.'

The great black pupils gazed out, unblinking, from the flushed face and I felt as if I was looking into the eyes of a soul in hell. I set the beaker down, but his fingers groped towards it, his thirst so great that even a bottomless well could not quench it. I wasn't sure if he was even listening.

He stared at the hand reaching for the cup, then started shaking it violently, as if he was trying to fling it from his wrist. 'Spiders . . . can't get them off.' He clawed at one hand with the other. 'Spinning a web over my hand . . . Can't move . . . Can't . . .' Then he was watching his hand again, shaking his head, as if what he had seen had suddenly vanished.

'Yaxley, listen to me! You couldn't walk away from Battle while you still believed there was a fortune to be found beneath your feet. And I can understand you needed that money. If Battle is raided, no other noble house will risk taking on anyone who worked here.'

Arthur and Vincent exchanged anxious glances. I knew that thought must constantly be at the back of all of their minds.

'But overnight the ground froze solid. You could no more dig for treasure than the sexton could dig his graves, and even if you had managed it, the slightest disturbance of the soil would stand out like blood on a white sheet. You had no choice but to wait until the thaw set in. But you imagined yourself safe enough. You'd ensured that Benet never delivered his report, and no more pursuivants would come from London to replace him until the thaw, for they'd be likely to freeze to death on the journey. But then Crowhurst sent his son, Sam, to tell someone at the Abbey he thought he knew what was blocking the flow of water into the holy well. Who else would young Sam seek out and tell except you? You're the only person who ever visits their cottage, the only man he knows and trusts here. Sam told you his father was going to the spring. You knew if he found it blocked or frozen, he'd try to get the water flowing again. If that reliquary or some other thing of value was buried close by, there was every chance he might happen upon it before you did. So, you followed him. Did he find something, see something? Was that why you killed him?'

With great effort, Yaxley nodded. 'Old tree where I'd hidden them . . . exploded . . . frost. Matthew . . . dragged the branches off the spring . . . saw silver in the roots, glinting in the sun . . . stuffed it into his pocket.' Yaxley's words were so slurred we had to lean in close to follow them.

'So, you followed and knocked him out, fearing that when he had a chance to examine what he'd found, he might return and search for more as you had done. You dragged him to the charcoal burner's hut, where you knew no one would have reason to come for weeks. Stripped him, tied him up and let the cold do the rest. Then later you removed the bonds and to appease his ghost pushed beans into his mouth, as you had with Bethia and Benet.'

'Rat, huge rat, big as a man. Drowned it, didn't I, but it came back, back. Long yellow teeth, destroy everything. Have to stun them. Then drown them. But it's back. Can you hear it . . . gnawing through the walls? . . .' He turned, staring at the corner of the room, grabbing the empty bottle, which he seemed to be trying to hurl at the wall, but his hands were opening and balling in spasms and the bottle dropped from his fingers and shattered on the ground.

Brathwayt shook his head. 'We'll get no more sense from him now.' He looked at me. 'But what I don't understand is why he claimed this man living in the Crowhursts' cottage was Matthew. What was all that about?'

'I can't be sure, but from what little I managed to piece together from what young Sam told me, I think Yaxley knew that if Crowhurst was found and identified, people were bound to ask why a seasoned woodward had frozen to death on his own manor. Yaxley had half stripped him and if they'd examined him closely, they'd have seen what I did – the marks where he'd been bound. Lady Magdalen had swallowed the tale of the murdered girl, but, as Yaxley said, she's as sharp as a pin, and her suspicions were bound to be aroused if another servant was found murdered. So, he hatched a plan to arrange for a man to take Crowhurst's place, so that the search would be called off. A good job, a cottage, a dutiful wife – must have been a tempting prospect for a man who was down on his luck or maybe had reasons for wanting to hide where the sheriff's men were unlikely to think of looking for him.

'Sam was terrified of his father – he'd cruelly used both his wife and his son – and I imagine Alys was only too glad to see the back of him. She'd long been afraid that one day Crowhurst would push Sam too far and he'd kill his father and be hanged for it, that's if Crowhurst hadn't beaten the boy to death first. Yaxley probably persuaded Alys that if Crowhurst had vanished, it was only a matter of time before she would be forced to leave the woodward's cottage, and how would she and the boy survive then? But if she went along with the pretence, she'd still have a roof over her head and a man to provide for her, hopefully one who would treat them both better. Sam says that his mother told him the only way to stop Crowhurst coming back was to swear the imposter was his father. Yaxley was taking a gamble, though. Crowhurst didn't come to the Abbey to get his orders, but all the same, one of the servants might have seen him and realised it wasn't the same man, like poor Giles did. But Yaxley probably thought he'd be gone from Battle by then.'

We all glanced into the corner, where the dim outline of the dead boy lay beneath Yaxley's clothes.

Vincent coughed. 'One of the stable lads said he knew it weren't Matthew, but he reckoned Matthew must be wanted by the King's men and had been smuggled away.' He shrugged, mumbling to the floor. 'Wouldn't be the first time. Everyone knows how to fetter their tongues here; we've had practice enough.' Brathwayt glowered at him, but said nothing.

Yaxley shrieked. He was twisting in the chair, trying to draw his legs up and staring in horror at the floor. 'Water. The spring . . . coming up through the ground . . . full of blood. It's filling up

'. . . See, the creatures are waiting . . . stinging tail. I know its face, know its fangs. It's waiting . . . down there . . . under the blood.'

He tried to clamber up on to the seat, grabbing for the beams above his head. The chair toppled sideways and he crashed to the floor. His back arched like a drawn bow, straining so far it seemed his spine would crack. Then he started to convulse. His legs and arms drummed against the stone flags. Bubbles of blood burst from his clenched jaws and nostrils.

Arthur, Vincent and I rushed to try to hold him still. Brathwayt stared down dispassionately at the tormented figure, as if he were a pig being slaughtered for winter. Then the steward turned his head to gaze at the corner where young Giles lay. A scarlet stain had spread over Yaxley's shirt, which covered the boy's battered head. I wondered if Brathwayt would be the one who would take Giles's body back to his parents. Was he trying to find the right words to offer them? But words have never been invented that could ease such grief as they would know then.

After what seemed like hours, Yaxley suddenly went limp and lay still. His eyes were closed. Bloody froth soaked his beard. Arthur shook him, but he lay like a rag doll. His breathing came in rasps. As we stood watching him, it seemed so long between one sound and the next that we thought he had taken his last breath. Then another bout of convulsions seized him, and he arched and thrashed.

Arthur crossed himself. 'I'd almost swear to it that Matthew's dark spirit found Yaxley after all and possessed him to take vengeance. Either his, or the ghost of Benet. I'd not want to meet either of those demons on such a night as this.'

We witnessed three more fits; each time between them his breathing grew more tortured. We waited for the next breath, every man in the room holding his own, as if our breathing might snatch the air from him, until finally the breath we watched for never came. And outside in the frozen darkness a hound began to bay, then one by one every dog in the kennels joined in, howling into the night, as all around us the ice hissed and cracked.

Chapter Forty-three

THE CHAPEL WAS UNLIT except for the eternal flame that hung above the magnificent silver cross, shimmering in the sea of darkness, its five blood-red stones glowing like molten fire in the lamplight. The candles crowded beneath the saints had been trimmed but not yet lit, except one. A single candle burned before a painting of an aged woman swathed in widows' weeds, who gazed out sorrowfully from beneath the golden diadem that haloed her veiled grey head.

Katheryne stood before the painting and the same candle-light snaking over her own face made her look as ancient as the woman into whose eyes she stared. Her expression was bitter and hard beyond her years.

Her gaze flashed briefly in my direction as I walked towards her, but she did not move.

'Saint Monica, isn't it? If I remember my boyhood lessons, the patron saint of married women. Some might think it strange that you should offer your devotions through her and not your namesake.'

'Saint Catherine's patronage is cloistered women, or did you not pay attention to that particular lesson in your boyhood, Pursglove? As I told you, I have no intention of becoming one of those.'

'Because, as you told me, you have a lover.' I held out the painted comb. 'Is this the token Bethia was carrying to the tanner for you? The one Robert Tiploft was supposed to take to your lover in London to summon him to your rescue?'

She reached for the comb, but I held on to it, lifting it into the floating sphere of light, so that she could see it clearly. Her eyes widened and a dark stain flushed her cheeks.

'Where did you get it?'

'From Bethia's murderer.'

She jerked as if I had slapped her and swiftly turned her face away to stare back up at the weeping saint. When she finally spoke again, her voice was barely above a whisper. 'So, she is dead, then?' Her breath made the candle flame gutter, but it did not extinguish it.

As if the full weight of what I had told her had only just struck home, she suddenly whirled round to face me, her eyes wide with alarm.

'Who? Who killed her? Do they know what this means?' She gestured towards the comb.

'I am certain her murderer did not. Even though you said it was intended as a sign, it took me a while to discover its secret. What you told me was only a shadow of the truth. Roses for love, and thorns imprisoning a little cat, just as you described, but you did not tell me it was a spotted cat. This was not a message about *your* imprisonment that you were sending to your lover in London, was it, Lady Katheryne? In fact, I don't believe the message was intended for your lover at all.'

She lowered her chin, flashing up one of her wide-eyed innocent glances from beneath her lashes. 'What else would it be?'

'A wooden comb – an object anyone might carry, innocent enough to be overlooked in a search and not of sufficient value to tempt a thief. At first, I thought that the message might be the comb itself, some prearranged signal, or, as you wanted me to believe, that the riddle was contained in the painting. And that spotted cat – could it be a leopard? – peering out from the cage of thorns. That was indeed part of the code, but not the most significant part. And then I noticed something else, something that should have been invisible unless you knew how to look for it. It was your unfortunate maid who unwittingly revealed it. Tiny irregular indentations in the wood along the shaft of the comb and on certain of the comb's teeth. They looked as if they could have been made by the point of a sewing needle. So small and shallow, I would never have noticed them, except that a little blood had found its way on to the comb. I imagine her killer inadvertently smeared Bethia's blood on it when he was searching her corpse to retrieve a ring he had given her, or had her blood on his hands when he pocketed the comb. Later, he wiped the surface clean, but the blood had lodged and then dried in some of those tiny holes. Let me guess – the needle pricks on the shaft are coded letters, those on the teeth . . . perhaps a series of numbers, a date when a ship might drop anchor? And whoever had been intended to receive this cypher would have dabbed soot or ink on the wood to read the pattern.'

Katheryne had gone as pale and rigid as the statues of the saints around her. If she had been any other woman, I might have expected her to faint, but Katheryne was hewn from the same granite as her guardian, and she would no more surrender to a swooning fit than she would feign one, even if her life depended on it.

'Lady Magdalen's maid, Esther, drugged you the night the ship dropped anchor, either on Smith's orders or those of her mistress. After what you led me to believe, I thought they meant to render you helpless so they could quietly move you on board without a fight. But they never intended to do that, and I think you knew, or at the very least, suspected that you were not the "precious cargo". They gave you that sleeping draught to keep you from seeing who was. They do not trust you, Lady Katheryne. And they are wise not to do so.'

Her chin jerked up and her eyes blazed. I waited, hoping I had goaded her into speaking, but she had evidently been interrogated often enough by Smith and the old dowager to have learned how to hold her tongue. I felt a grudging admiration for her. I had been several years older than her before I learned to master my temper half as well.

'That ship did bring someone to England. It was the reason that the voyage was planned. That precious cargo, that valuable tapestry, had to be smuggled in from Brussels and it was someone who was central to furthering the Catholic cause here. A swallow returning to these shores. It was news of that swallow the priests were anxious should not be discovered when the man was murdered out on the salt marsh. But the last message young Giles brought to Smith concerned not one swallow, but three. I thought at first three birds were returning, but swallows fly in and out of England, and the other two were going out, the flight of those two birds hastily added. I thought one of them was you, but we both know that was never the intention. The second swallow proved instead to be that wretch Erasmus. He was a loose cannon that had to be firmly bolted down where he could do no harm. But the third?'

I held up the wooden comb again. 'That is what this cypher is about, isn't it? The spotted cat imprisoned in the cage who is never released. The baskets of food whisked up the back staircase long after everyone else has dined; the smell of burning wax in an unoccupied room; a slops pail emptied at the dead of night. Why keep a priest hidden even from his own brothers? Holt, Santi, Bray and Cobbe don't conceal themselves from the servants, because half the servants in the Abbey are hiding here in fear of their own liberty or lives. The priests among them are all prepared to flee or hide in the secret holes at the first sign of a raid, yet they move around openly inside the house, even attending Mass with your guardian's guests. Smith, and all of the priests, face death if they are caught. Surely this man who was hidden away had nothing worse to fear than them. So, why keep him hidden unless this priest was not a priest at all, but an imposter, one of Cecil's men or a priest that the old spymaster has turned?'

I gestured towards the candle burning in front of St Monica. 'Girls who want to get themselves a husband generally pray to Saint Anthony. Saint Monica is invoked by married women, and though I have not been forced to read the lives of the saints since

I was a boy, if I recall correctly, she has another patronage too – conversion. So, do you pray for your husband's conversion, Lady Katheryne, or for his life?'

'How—'

'The thimble you used to send me a message the first time we spoke. It was decorated with pomegranates and myrtle. Most in this household would take them to be the symbols of the Virgin Mary. Such signs might prove dangerous outside these walls, but in the circles in which your guardian moves, they are a badge of honour, and a sign of piety, except that the style in which these were inscribed suggested to me that the thimble was not given to you by anyone who shares Lady Magdalen's beliefs. In your husband's faith, love is not pledged with roses. His symbols of love, marriage and fertility are pomegranates and myrtle – Jewish symbols. Is that the hold they have over you? Did someone discover you had married a man whose faith alone would be enough to exile him, even see him executed? I take it he has not converted?'

'His parents fled to London to escape the Inquisition in Portugal. He was only a child; he remembers little of their life there, and here, they practise their faith in secret.'

'They are Marranos?'

She gave the briefest of nods. 'But they're no different from us,' she added defiantly, a spark of the old fire returning to her eyes. 'They attend the Protestant church as we are compelled to do, and then, in secret . . .' She swept her hand around the chapel. 'Isn't that exactly what we do? We are forced to live a lie, to be seen to utter heretical words and consume bread and wine that almost chokes us. The Marranos are forced to do as we do, and they curse silently every time they enter a church or listen to a Christian service.'

'*Shakets teshaktsenu* – Thou should loathe it.'

She stared at me, open-mouthed. 'You are one too?'

I smiled. 'No, not me. Though I will confess to muttering that particular curse a few times myself, and not just in a Protestant church.' I stared pointedly around. 'Smith doesn't trust me any more than he does you, but if it had ever crossed his mind I could be a Jew, I'd already be buried up to my neck in the salts, waiting for the next high tide. But I've lived in London long enough to count a few men, like your husband, as my friends and keep their secrets, as they have kept mine. You may see your husband's people as enduring the same misery and persecution as the recusants, but believe me, Lady Katheryne, no one in this house will love them for it. In Portugal and Spain, it's men like Smith who seek to burn Jews on the pyres of the Inquisition. I doubt that Smith would have any quarrel with the Inquisitors. Even in England, with the shadow of the same scaffold hanging over them both, a Catholic priest does not regard a Jew as his friend, much less his brother.'

'I know that,' she breathed. Her gaze darted towards the chapel door. 'The man who discovered our marriage swore he would not only inform my guardian, but denounce my husband, if I didn't do what he asked. That's why . . . why I was so afraid when the token wasn't delivered.'

'And why you tried to persuade me to become your messenger.'

Defiance flared again in her eyes. She had no intention of apologising for that, and I could hardly blame her. It was not simply her husband's life that would be forfeit, but hers as well. Ever since his enemies had succeeded in getting Elizabeth's physician, Roderigo Lopez, hanged, drawn and quartered for allegedly trying to poison the Queen, every Jew in England had been regarded as a heretic and traitor; a Jew with a popeling for a wife would be doubly so in the eyes of some. Catholics and Protestants across the land would for once be united in howling for their blood.

'Who was it who discovered your secret?'

She shook her head. 'I don't know.'

'But you told them about the man hidden in the Abbey?'

She would not meet my gaze. 'He wasn't hidden at first; he came to stay in the house like Father Santi and the others.

He said his name was Father Ratcliff and he needed a place of safety until he could escape to Europe. A few weeks later, some young men came here for instruction from Father Smith and to hear Mass, but shortly after they'd all returned to their homes, they were arrested. Even though they lived in different towns, the searchers seemed to know they were friends and what they had done for the faith, things they'd only shared with the priests here.'

'But you hadn't sent a message to London about them?'

She shook her head. 'He said his master wasn't interested in those sorts of visitors . . .' She hesitated, as if she had stopped herself from adding something more, then continued quickly. 'When Father Smith heard about the arrests, he became suspicious of everyone. He sent letters to check the stories of all the priests here. I heard Father Bray grumbling that Father Smith had questioned him for hours about where he studied and who his tutors were and his fellow students. When he's had a few glasses of wine, Father Bray is not . . .'

'. . . inclined to discretion?' I finished the sentence for her and she gave a half-smile.

'But I think Father Smith must have discovered something that led him to suspect that Father Ratcliff was not who he claimed to be.'

'You think he suspected him of being one of Robert Cecil's agents, and that's when he took him prisoner.'

Katheryne gnawed her lip. 'I've been thinking about that and I don't see how he could have, not if he was in the house. There are always people around. Ratcliff could have made himself heard. He could have been tied and gagged, I suppose, but they took him food, so if he could eat . . . he could call out. I think Father Smith must have convinced him somehow to stay hidden and told him that he would help him to escape abroad. Most of the servants thought he'd already left; that's what they were told, that he'd been smuggled away further north somewhere in England.'

'But if he was one of Cecil's men and Smith told him he was to be taken to Europe, he would have readily agreed, in fact he might have been trying to persuade Smith to arrange it, so that he could uncover the network – not just in England, but the one that stretches far across the sea.'

But Smith would never risk passing someone he suspected of being an agent down that chain. Ratcliff would not be allowed to reached the shores of France alive. Smith could not risk any more corpses turning up in these parts, especially if one of them was Cecil's man. But a man who vanishes into the sea can stay lost for ever. When the day comes that the sea gives up her dead, they say there will be many rising from those depths that not even the Devil knew were down there.

'You said that the man in London was not interested in those visitors who attended Mass here. So, who was it they wanted you to watch? Father Ratcliff? That was who the message on the comb was about, wasn't it? Were you instructed to warn them if he was in danger or was to be taken to a ship?'

Katheryne stared thoughtfully into the heart of the candle flame. 'No, Father Ratcliff didn't arrive until after I did. The man in the Wrestler Inn said the traitor was already here.'

'The traitor' – wouldn't Robert Cecil and his agents regard all those within this house as traitors? So just who was Katheryne's blackmailer, then? And whose cause had this particular traitor betrayed?

'You are sure the man who threatened you works for Robert Cecil? Could he instead be a King's man?'

Another of FitzAlan's men, like me, one who'd been tasked to discover exactly what the spy master was up to and what his agents knew.

'No, he is not a King's man!' Katheryne shook her head vehemently. 'It is someone who works *against* the King and Robert Cecil, someone who would see them both dead and the true faith restored to England.'

I stared at her, dumbfounded. 'But . . . but then why would he need you to inform on Battle Abbey? Everyone here champions that cause.'

Her gaze darted once more towards the door. 'Not everyone, Master Pursglove, not everyone.'

Chapter Forty-four

LONDON

DANIEL COULD NOT TELL how long the quarter of the body had been nailed up on Bishopsgate. It had not been there when he'd left London six weeks ago. The blackened, clawed fingers of the single arm hung down, as if it was trying to dig its own grave and burrow into the earth to escape the stares and mocking jests. Ribs, breastbone and vertebrae still gleamed white and stark through the mangled flesh of the severed neck and torso, and the blood that had dripped on to the ground below had frozen into a scarlet jewel, glittering on the icy flagstones. The birds had not stripped this lump of flesh from its bones. Rats had not gnawed it, nor maggots bred on it. It was frozen hard as granite and smelled as fresh as the side of pork the butcher's boy carried across his shoulders as he lumbered beneath the raised portcullis, cursing as he slipped on the puddle of bloody ice.

The severed heads skewered on the tall poles above the gate had been there long before the great freeze. Only newcomers, approaching the city walls for the first time, glanced up at them uneasily, suddenly realising that what they had taken from a distance to be a row of black ravens were the heads of men who had once laughed and loved as they had. 'Behold the head of a traitor.' But a traitor to whom?

Daniel had scarcely been aware of the bone-numbing miles he'd ridden to London, for in his head he was back in the bailiff's workshop, trying to recall every detail of what Yaxley had said, every glance, every clumsy gesture. If Yaxley's garbled words could be trusted, the Gunpowder Plot conspirator Spero Pettingar was no longer at Battle, if indeed he had ever been there – but his reach had extended that far and he had somehow learned that Benet had discovered his identity, maybe even his whereabouts too. And whoever he was, he had convinced Yaxley he was powerful enough to have him killed if he failed to stop Benet reaching London. But that did not mean Pettingar was a man of substance or standing. Even a thief like Skinner, whose haunt was the squalid ruins of Bristol Castle, could strike terror into his victims if he lurked in the shadows; even more so if he was a phantom without a face.

Had the bottle of deadly henbane been sent to Yaxley as a reward to ease his pain or as a death threat? It might also have been delivered as the means by which he should kill himself rather than be taken alive to the rack, if his attempt on Benet's life had gone wrong.

But there was something else nagging at Daniel. Yaxley had kept repeating the name *Spero*, but then he'd said *not Pettingar*. Was he simply trying to tell Daniel that Pettingar wasn't at Battle, or that Spero was using another name? The latter was hardly something Daniel needed to be told. Conspirators and priests alike changed their names more often than their linen; only a fool would do otherwise. He smiled wryly to himself: Pursglove was only the most recent of various names he'd adopted in his thirty years of life, and he doubted it would be the last.

But the wyvern seal – did that offer a clue as to Pettingar's new identity or was it simply a sign of his ambitions? The dragon-like creature had, in ancient times, been the battle standard of the English, proclaiming death to her enemies. Was it now breathing death to a Scottish heretic who'd usurped the Catholic throne of England?

The blast of a horn in the courtyard below wrenched Daniel's gaze from the gate and its grizzly trophies. A coach, pulled by four horses, was rumbling and creaking through the archway. The great hooves of the horses had been wrapped in sacking to stop them slipping in London's icy streets. Steam rose from their flanks and billows of white smoke from their nostrils as the coachman reigned them in. Daniel pulled his cloak tighter and leaned further out of the casement of the room he had rented. The courtyard of the Wrestler Inn had been almost deserted that morning, apart from a few stable lads and serving maids hurrying through, but the arrival of the coach had stirred up a maelstrom of activity, as if a wasps' nest had been smashed open and the insects were pouring out. Maids helped those inside the coach to descend and offered their arms to steady the women passengers while male servants caught the boxes and bags hurled down to them.

Ladders were brought for the passengers swathed in cloaks and blankets who had ridden on top of the coach, the unfortunate souls too poor or too tardy to have claimed seats inside. Several had been lashed on to their perches with ropes, in case their numbed hands lost their grip, and they were now too stiff to free themselves. All had to be helped down and were scarcely able to move their legs enough to totter past the stable lads who were trying to change the team of horses. One man had passed out and it took four of the servants to lower him to the ground. He lay unmoving on the frozen cobbles, his eyes closed, his skin almost as blue as the quartered traitor's flesh on the gate opposite. They carried him inside, but Daniel wondered if it might already be too late.

A man was picking his way across the courtyard towards the door of the inn. Daniel was sure he had not disembarked from the coach, but now he was mingling with those who had. A passenger for the next coach departing? Most of those passengers had arrived some time earlier and were already ensconced around the great fire, fortifying themselves with hot food and spiced wine against the bitter journey that awaited them, much to the gratification of the Wrestler's innkeeper. The coach had been expected both to arrive and depart several hours late, due to the treacherous conditions of the roads outside London, and that meant stranded passengers who would be obliged to spend more time and more money in his inn.

Did the man crossing the courtyard realise the coach would depart late? He half turned at the door, tilting his head up to examine the casements above. His face, like everyone who ventured out, was muffled up to his eyes, but as he moved, Daniel could see that his cloak was heavy, fur-lined, and not with anything light and cheap such as rabbit. The catch in the folds as it swung betrayed that there was a sword concealed beneath it. Such a man would surely not need to subject himself to the discomfort and inconvenience of riding in a public coach, when he might use a private one.

Robert Tiploft had left the comb with the innkeeper on the morning of the previous day. Daniel had not trailed him to London; there had been no need. He had ridden out ahead of the tanner and taken a modest room at the Wrestler overlooking the courtyard, knowing that if the large purse had done its work, Tiploft would deliver the package, however much he protested that this was the very last time. Like many in the land, the tanner had lost valuable business in the great freeze. Skins turned brittle and cracked instead of drying, tanning vats froze solid; he could not afford to refuse the money.

Daniel slipped from the room and hurried down a staircase that protested loudly at its ill usage by so many feet. The parlour was crowded. Through a thick fog of tobacco smoke and steaming clothes, men and women jostled to reach the blessed heat of the fire, yelling orders at the serving girls who squeezed between them, their faces flushed and shining with sweat as they raced between kitchen and customer with bowls of hot broth, caudles and stews.

Daniel peered around. All the passengers had unwrapped their faces and most pulled off their coats and blankets. Those who had just arrived were trying to thaw their fingers on beakers of hot ale and warm spiced cider, while regaling those about to set out with the horrors of their journey. The innkeeper was not among them, nor could Daniel see the lone stranger who had entered minutes before. He threaded through the crowd to the passageway beyond. A manservant came hurrying out of one of the doors, leaving it half open.

'I was looking for your master,' Daniel said.

The man jerked his head back at the door. 'In there, but your business had best wait. A fool of a groom sent for the physician for one of the passengers just arrived on the coach, but master says I'm to catch him afore he sets out and tell him not to trouble himself. Poor wretch in there is far beyond his help. And the master won't be best pleased if that moneygrubbing pissprophet charges him for visiting a corpse.' With another anxious glance behind him, the servant hurried out of the door, dragging on his coat as he ran.

As soon as he was gone, Daniel edged towards the small chamber normally reserved for those who wished to rest or dine apart from the crowds, and who were wealthy enough to pay for privacy. He avoided the partly opened door, positioning himself instead by the slender gap where the door hinged. A body lay on the table. The hand, which was all that was clearly visible through the doorjamb, was limp. The hairs on the back of it were white against the tanned skin, but the blue tinge of death was already apparent in the horny nails.

Coins clinked as if someone was weighing them in his palm. 'This is all he had in his purse and that'll not be enough to pay for his funeral.' That was the innkeeper's voice. 'If we can't find relatives willing to take charge of his corpse, it'll be a pauper's grave for him, that's if there's even space in the pit. Ever since the Thames froze, there's been more needing burying at the city's expense than when the plague comes calling.'

The drawl of a second, more educated, voice broke in. 'I suppose you have searched his bag for letters or papers that might identify his family?'

'He'd precious little in his bag except a change of linens; I reckon he was wearing every other garment he owned. And the only paper was a scrap with the address of a lawyer's chambers, and I'll wager a keg of my best sack our corpse was no lawyer. But if there's nothing else, sir, I'll bid you good day. I must need have words with the coachmen and their passengers before they disappear. One of them might have learned the old codger's name, before he was crows' pudding . . . But rest assured, I'll send word at once if the tanner returns . . . Oh, thank you, sir, much obliged.'

Daniel stepped rapidly back behind the opening door as the innkeeper emerged, peering at the coins he'd just been handed. He tucked them into the bag hidden beneath his jerkin before stepping out into the parlour. A ball of thick smoke rolled out into the passageway as he closed the door behind him. Before Daniel could move, a man emerged from the chamber, pulling the door shut. He froze and Daniel found himself staring into lizard-green eyes, widening with recognition and shock.

'So, Daniel, you are alive and in London.'

'Richard! Or am I to address you as Lord Fairfax now? I trust your gambling partner in the Three Pigeons recovered his earring, if not his ear.'

Richard's eyes flashed wide in surprise and he stared at Daniel, his jaw tightening, making the dagger-point of his close-cropped beard quiver like an arrow hitting its target. But he quickly recovered himself. 'You still have that firemark, I see. When my father threw you out into the gutter, I thought the next time I saw you I would be watching you mount a scaffold, as old Waldegrave predicted. But I hear you managed to talk your way out of the charge of sorcery by proving yourself guilty of deception and trickery, a common crossbiter. Even as a boy, if you found yourself in trouble you could always be relied upon to dig an even deeper hole for yourself with that tongue of yours; you never knew when to keep it kennelled.'

'While you always stayed silent and let others take the blame for your crimes. Is that what you did after your father's accident, the one that made you *Lord* Fairfax? I heard the stable boy who was blamed for that broken girth hanged himself. Did you persuade him to jump from that barrel or did you kick it from under him?'

'Slander is a serious offence, Daniel. It seems that you are missing your stinking companions, the Newgate rats. You are obviously anxious to return there, or perhaps I should spare the city the expense of your trial and settle the matter here and now.'

Though Daniel's gaze didn't stray from Richard's cold eyes, he saw the twitch of his shoulder that warned him Richard had grasped the hilt of his sword beneath his cloak. Daniel knew that he should walk away. A dagger was no match for a sword unless you had the element of surprise. But though he thought the years had taught him to master himself, he only had to hear that drawl, see those thin lips twist, to feel the rage boiling through his veins. He was itching for Richard to draw. *Just give me a reason.*

Without taking his eyes from Richard's face, Daniel gave a mocking bow. 'My apologies, *Lord* Fairfax. Of course, you were always a fastidious child: you wouldn't have kicked that barrel yourself. You never soiled your own hands when others could be made to wipe your arse clean.'

He heard the rasp as the steel blade slid swiftly from scabbard. But Richard's heavy cloak hampered him and Daniel's dagger was thrusting towards him before the point of the sword swung free.

The door to the parlour banged open and a serving maid hurried out in a billow of smoke, an empty flagon balanced on each hip. Daniel and Richard both jerked back, only narrowly avoiding skewering her between them. At the sight of the blades flashing up either side of her head, the maid screamed, throwing up her arms. The two flagons crashed to the flagstones and shattered. Daniel barely had time to sheathe his blade before the girl's shriek brought the innkeeper and several of his customers bursting through the doorway.

The innkeeper saw Richard's sword vanishing beneath his cloak and rounded on Daniel, whom he clearly thought must be the one who had given offence, but realising that he was a guest at the inn, the words died on his lips.

He cuffed the servant maid around the head. 'Clumsy wench! Two flagons broken; you think I've money to throw in the Thames? You get this mess cleared up.' He nodded at Richard and Daniel. 'You'll have to pardon her, sirs. Foundling, she is, and a more cack-handed goose you'll not find in the city.'

Richard tossed a couple of coins down on to the shards on the floor and made for the door, deliberately knocking against Daniel as he passed.

'They say the Devil's son has the Devil's luck,' he murmured. 'But you'd be well advised to take that coach out of London wherever it's going, because your luck has just run out, bastard!'

Chapter Forty-five

LONDON

THE BURNING COALS popped and shifted in the fire. On the deep feather mattress, Sir Christopher Veldon stirred, turned over and, opening his eyes, caught sight of the woman sitting by the hearth who was watching him through the gap in the sumptuously embroidered curtains hanging around his bed. A smile was playing around her vermilioned lips, as if something secretly amused her, a private jest she did not intend to share with anyone. It was an expression he often glimpsed on her face. She kept many secrets. He had no idea how long she'd been sitting there. But he guessed she had seen much of the sport that had just taken place behind his curtains. It entertained her to watch, that he knew.

The candlelight burnished her dark copper hair and deepened the cleavage between the soft mounds of her breasts, which swelled and sank with each measured breath, as if they were inviting him in. He felt a stirring between his legs and was pleasantly surprised by sensation. He wasn't amazed that this woman had coaxed his horn to rise – the mere sight of her could always arouse him – but he was gratified that he found himself ready to perform again so quickly. Not that he'd get the chance, of course.

He nudged the young man lying sprawled beside him, who yawned and slipped obligingly out of bed, pulling the curtains wide. He seemed not at all unnerved to see a woman sitting there. Naked, but seemingly oblivious to the chill of the room, the young man ambled over to the small table set near the fire, on which lay what was left of the platters of pastries and meats and a jug of purple wine. He downed a goblet of the wine in one draught and, standing with his bare backside to the woman, stuffed a slice of woodcock into his mouth with one hand, while scooping up a deer-tongue tart with the other. Only when the lady ran her leather-gloved fingers down the small of his back and over the tight round buttocks did a shiver run the length of his spine. He turned his head and gave her a lazy grin but did not move away.

They both watched the young man eat in silence, the firelight gleaming on the muscled torso, before a slap on his arse from that same leather-gloved hand told him he was dismissed. Without hurrying, he stooped to gather up the trail of his clothes from the floor, grabbed another tart from the platter as he passed, and slid through the door, pausing only to flash a disarming smile at the two remaining occupants of the room.

'I trust he gave satisfaction, Sir Christopher,' she said, laughter in her voice.

'Most comely and obliging, though he does not have your skills, m'lady.'

'I am surprised you still remember. I'd wager that your bed has rarely had time to cool since.'

'Nor has my passion for you, m'lady,' he offered gallantly. He flicked back the covers, patting the still warm and crumpled sheet beside him, and arched his brows in a mute invitation.

She laughed. 'When this matter is concluded, perhaps.'

'You have news?' His expression was suddenly serious.

She glanced behind her at the closed door, then moved to sit on the end of the bed, her voice lowered. 'I am told the package we were expecting has been safely delivered.'

'And safely contained?'

'Naturally,' she said. 'And we are keeping track of it.'

'And your hound, Daniel?'

'He's in London and will doubtless deliver his report to FitzAlan as soon as he is sent for, though I'll let him cool his heels for a few days before I tell FitzAlan where he is.'

'He rode back in this ice?' Veldon said with a frown. 'A trifle foolhardy, one might say.'

'Foolhardy he is not, but he is as stubborn as a rusty lock. Once he has set his mind to something, neither heaven nor hell will stop him. Besides, he is an excellent horseman. Some might say he was almost as skilful in the saddle as you, Sir Christopher.' She darted a teasing glance at him. 'He could certainly give young Carr a besting if he chose to, but that kind of glory just doesn't interest him. He refuses to be drawn into competition with any man.'

'That's precisely what troubles me.' Veldon pummelled his pillows into a more comfortable angle. 'Stubborn men are hard to persuade, and worse are men who claim to have no ambition for wealth or power. I don't trust them. They're curs without collars, nothing you can grab hold of and use to drag them where you want them to go. Are you really certain Daniel will do what is required of him when the time comes?'

'He will be convinced that is the only course of action open to him.' She glanced towards the shuttered windows, through which razor-thin blades of winter sunshine glimmered. 'I saw men netting wild ducks on my way here. They lured the birds with grain towards a funnel of willow, the mouth so wide the ducks thought it merely a gap between the scrub, then the dogs ran up behind to frighten the birds, which flapped along down the funnel that narrowed all the while until they spilled into the cage at the end.'

'From what I've learned of Daniel, I'd stake my life that not even you, with all your talents, could frighten such a man into a trap, m'lady.'

'You underestimate me, Sir Christopher. I know full well fear will never school him, but it is bait, not fear, that lures the ducks into that funnel. Daniel is, after all, still wanted for murder.'

Veldon nodded. 'And you are still sure FitzAlan doesn't know about that?'

'Not even his dear boyhood friend Richard knows it.'

383

This time Veldon laughed aloud. 'Oh, now that I can attest to, m'lady. Young Lord Fairfax would have used that juicy morsel to finish him long before, if he had.'

'Then trust me when I tell you, FitzAlan wouldn't have let him come within a hundred yards if he had any inkling.'

Veldon grunted. 'If Daniel killed a card-cheat in a tavern brawl or a cutpurse who attacked him on the road, I don't suppose it would trouble FitzAlan unduly. He'd surely expect that of any man.'

'But not cold-blooded murder. And our good Sovereign and his little beagle might even call what Daniel did an act of . . . *treason*.'

'And you, m'lady, what would you call it?'

'I'd call it a collar by which a cur may be dragged to where you want him to go.'

For the second time that afternoon, that secret smile Veldon knew so well played around Cimex's mouth. Slowly, oh so slowly, she peeled off one of her kid-gloves. Veldon took the cold hand in his own, raised to it his lips and kissed it.

Chapter Forty-six

LONDON

DANIEL KNEW HE WAS being followed. He had sensed the man trailing him almost as soon as he walked out of the courtyard of the Wrestler, catching the movement from the corner of his eye. Even on such a bitter afternoon, the city streets were crowded, but the way a man walks when he is occupied with his own business is quite different from a man who is concerned with someone else's. The figure was keeping pace with him, sliding between laden carts and the shop walls and drawing back into doorways and courtyards whenever Daniel paused.

Daniel kept to the centre of the street, dodging the horses and ignoring the curses of carters forced to slow as he weaved round them. His shadow could simply be a cutpurse who had decided that anyone with money enough to take a room at the Wrestler for several nights must have a purse worth the stealing. But if it was, the thief clearly wasn't well practised in his craft. They had passed a score of distracted men and women on that busy throughfare, any one of whom would have been a much easier and wealthier mark. That suggested a man who had more than the prize of a few coins on his mind.

Daniel watched an approaching wagon piled high with barrels, timing his steps so that he reached it just as it was passing the top of one of the side streets and, using it as cover, he slipped around it, forking right, left and right again, through a churchyard and a series of roads whose tall houses opened straight on to narrow pavements with no deep doorways or courtyards to provide cover for anyone still on his trail. He emerged on the wharf that ran along the bank of the Thames and made his way over to a rickety stall that had been erected in an open space in front of a warehouse. A birdlike woman, wearing a man's stained coat and an old felt hood tied round her head with a length of sacking, had built a fire where on most days of the year small boats would be unloading their cargoes and passengers would be jostling for one of the hundreds of wherries eager to carry them up or down the mighty river. But not a single boat moved on the river today. The Thames was frozen over, and the woman was doing a good trade selling hot spiced cider and roasted apples to those slipping and sliding across the ice between the city and Southwark. Daniel positioned himself close to the fire, from where he could study anyone emerging from the city streets on to the wharf.

'Hot codling to warm you, good sir?' the woman coaxed, wafting one temptingly towards him on a shovel. Her face was as soft and wrinkled as the roasting apples. 'If this freeze goes on, I'll be building my fire on the old river herself. Now, wouldn't that be something to remember on my deathbed? My grand-father swears when he was a boy the ice was so thick one year they roasted a whole ox on it. We always thought he was telling one of his parrot tales, but when you see a sight like that you get to thinking maybe the old man wasn't doting after all.'

She gestured towards a group of giggling women, their hair dyed in vivid hues of yellow and red, who were clinging to each other as they edged across the Thames towards the wharf.

'Bawds walking on water,' the apple-seller chuckled. 'I reckon the Archbishop would call that a miracle.'

The river had frozen into craggy waves and great slabs of ice rose out of it, like the stones of a ruined castle. Urchins had tied a rope to a length of ship's mast that stuck up through the frozen surface and were whirling round it, sliding on the ice and whooping with laughter whenever one of their playmates tumbled headlong or let go of the rope and spun away like a top. The great bridge that spanned the water and the buildings upon it were hung with sparkling icicles, as if all the houses were subtleties fashioned from marchpane and spun sugar. Even the severed heads of the traitors on the long spikes were encased in glittering white, so that they looked like the stone grotesques and gargoyles on some ornate cathedral. Great lumps of ice were jammed into the arches beneath the mighty bridge, trapping driftwood and all the rubbish that the Thames carried with it. The carcass of a cow was even wedged on top of one heap, frozen to the plug of ice.

Daniel had half turned to watch the activity on the frozen river. The low sun had cast his own dark shadow in front of him, but a second shadow was gliding over the frosted ground inches from his own. He whirled round, drawing his dagger in one fluid motion. A short, slight figure stood behind him, the face masked by a twist of cloth almost to the eyes and a hood pulled down low over his head. A fist was inching out towards Daniel, something grasped tightly in the gloved hand. Daniel slammed the hilt of his dagger down hard on the outstretched arm. His assailant squealed his pain. His fingers sprang open, and what he was holding tumbled to the ground. The apple-seller gave a cry of alarm. Daniel seized the man's wrist and twisted, so that he was forced to turn his back to Daniel as his arm was yanked up behind him. The point of Daniel's dagger jabbed beneath the man's ribcage, pricking his skin through the layers of clothes.

'Daniel, it's me! I mean no harm . . .' The voice was familiar, but for a moment Daniel couldn't think why.

'Show your face!' Daniel jerked the arm he was holding a little higher up the man's back, just enough to make it clear this was an order, not a request.

The man's free hand moved hesitantly to the cloth tied across his mouth and he tugged it down, revealing a wispy attempt at a beard and a face that looked even more gaunt and haunted than when Daniel had last seen it.

'Erasmus!'

The young acolyte nodded vigorously and dragged the cloth up again, though whether as defence against the biting cold or for fear of being recognised it was hard to tell. Daniel released him, but kept his knife drawn and covertly pointed towards the young man's belly as he turned.

'Did someone pay you to follow me?'

Erasmus looked bewildered. 'I . . . I found out you were staying at the inn, but I couldn't risk going there. I only wanted to slip something into your pocket. I wasn't going to speak to you. I thought you might not want to hear from me.'

His gaze dropped to the object which had been knocked from his hand. It was a small piece of folded paper, closed with a large blob of wax which had weighted it down, but as Erasmus retrieved it and handed to it Daniel, he noticed that no seal had been impressed on it.

'You want me to fetch one of the guards?' The woman held the iron shovel menacingly in front of her. She was looking from one man to the other as if she wasn't entirely sure which of the two she should brain with it.

Both Daniel and Erasmus shook their heads. Grabbing him once more by the arm, Daniel propelled Erasmus out of earshot, leaving the woman eying them both suspiciously.

Daniel made to snap the wax on the paper Erasmus had given him, but the young acolyte quickly put his hand over it.

'Not here. When you're alone. I wanted . . . I'm in your debt for helping me escape, and for . . . well, for keeping silent about that business in the town.'

Though he could see little of Erasmus's face, there was a desperate loneliness in his eyes.

'You haven't been tempted to try it again here?' Daniel asked, with a stab of concern.

Erasmus stared down at the boards of the wharf. 'I always wrestle with the temptation. It's a demon I cannot shake loose. But I have found other ways . . . A city like this has many dark secrets . . . hidden places . . . people with forbidden appetites.

The creatures of the night have a way of finding others like them . . .' He closed his hand over the paper and looked up at Daniel. 'I have nothing else to repay you with, but this. Do you remember the messenger from the ship, the one they found dead on the sands?'

'From Bristol, I remember.'

Erasmus frowned in surprise. 'I didn't realise you knew . . .'

'That much, but no more.'

'He was carrying papers for Father Smith. I glimpsed one of them. I couldn't take it, but I have written down what I remember of its contents. It means little to me, except that it concerns a name I heard Father Smith mention before, someone he was sure was known to you. Father Smith had been trying to find out about you. He had to be careful.'

Daniel nodded. Katheryne had said as much. *Father Smith became suspicious of everyone. He sent letters to check the stories of all the priests here.* But Daniel had expected no less from a man in Smith's position, even without Katheryne's confirmation. Whatever Smith had discovered about Daniel, though, it wasn't that he had been sent to Battle by FitzAlan. He would never have got out of there alive if Smith had found proof of that. Unless . . .

I swore an oath that I would keep you alive. You have a powerful protector, Daniel, and they have other plans for you.

Daniel had been staring down at the paper in his hands. Now he glanced up, a question already forming on his lips, but the place where Erasmus had been standing was empty. He stared around. A small crowd of laughing and chattering women and men had clambered up the steps from the river and were making for the apple-seller's fire, blocking any view of the street beyond the wharf. Erasmus was gone and it was pointless trying to follow him.

Daniel cracked the seal and unfolded the paper. The words were written in a scholar's hand, the letters starkly black in the sunlight.

'A man was found dead in Bristol. His corpse was dragged out of the river, but he did not die of drowning. You may know him as the Yena.'

A retort as loud as musket shot echoed across the Thames, followed by a rumble and a crash, as a slab of ice broke from the bridge. Shards of ice exploded outwards in a ball of white mist as it smashed down on the frozen river. But Daniel didn't even glance up. He was still staring at those black letters. There were so pitifully few to stand for a man's life and his death, yet how many words would ever be enough? He shivered as if a splinter of that falling ice had pierced his very soul.

Epilogue

SOMEWHERE IN THE darkened streets, a clock began to chime, and the old man lifted his quill from the paper and turned his head towards the sound, counting the hours – *six, seven, eight.* Not that he really needed to; over these past few weeks he'd learned exactly how long it took for these particular candles to burn down. Another hour before he could expect his visitor. Not too early: they wouldn't want to risk being seen by the apothecary or his apprentices working in the shop across the street. But not so late that a knock on the door or creak on the outside staircase might be heard by some goodwife tossing and turning in her bed.

The old man heaved himself up and took the single step to the hearth, adding just a little more coal to the fire, which should be giving off a good steady heat by the time his caller arrived, frozen to the marrow. He muttered a silent prayer of thanks. He would not have survived another winter in his old lodging with only a miserable brazier to keep him warm. That room had been four times as long as this, tucked up under the roof beams, large enough for all the books he had amassed, which to his great sorrow he'd been forced to abandon. This chamber above a gaunter's shop was tiny, space only for a truckle bed and a rickety table scarcely wider than a church Bible, but the room warmed easily. There were always blessings to be found if you searched diligently enough, the old man reflected.

Besides, what did he really need with those books now? He couldn't take them with him into his grave – if he was fortunate enough to be granted one. And soon now, he would have to move again; perhaps his visitor would even bring him word tonight. He sighed. Part of him, the part that was still young and full of fire, was impatient to be off. He had no way of knowing how many months or years he had left in this world and he wanted this deed done, wanted to die knowing his work was completed, that he'd accomplished something. But his bones ached and his knuckles were swollen and stiff. He was weary – tired of running, tired of hiding, tired of waiting in fear for them to come for him. If he was truthful, all he really longed for was to curl up in that bed and sleep like the beasts of the field, until spring brought an end to this ice. But even as he allowed that thought to enter his mind, he chided himself fiercely for his weakness, as he would once have lectured a lazy pupil. God's servants could not rest in this life if they wanted peace in the next.

The letter must be ready for his visitor to deliver. To be obliged to wait would be to put them both in danger. He rubbed his aching hands over the blaze, trying to force his fingers to obey him, then eased himself back on to the stool.

The old man dipped his quill in the black ink once more and added the final line. '*Serpens ni edat serpentem, draco non fiet*' – *Unless a serpent devours a serpent, it will not become a dragon.* Then, as he always did, he added his signature. It wasn't a sobriquet he'd chosen, but one that others had thrust upon him. But it was apt and it amused him. 'A foreseer of the future and devourer of the dead', that's how they thought of him, and he was not displeased.

Still smiling, he signed – '*The Yena*'.

Acknowledgements

This novel is the second in a new series set in Jacobean England, featuring Daniel Pursglove. I would like to express my enormous gratitude to Mari Evans, Managing Director of Headline, Frances Edwards, Commissioning Editor at Headline, and my agent, Victoria Hobbs, Director of A. M. Heath, for helping to conceive and shape the series, and for their continued encouragement and unfailing support. I'd especially like to thank my editor, Frances Edwards, for her untiring enthusiasm and for all her many ideas and suggestions, which always fire my imagination. My gratitude also to my copy-editor, Katie Green, who has so painstakingly checked the text and made many helpful and sensitive suggestions for improvements.

My thanks to all those at Headline who have worked on type-setting, proofreading, design, sales and publicity, especially Caitlin Raynor, Publicity Director, Headline and Tinder Press, and Jo Liddiard, Head of Marketing, Headline. A book is a team production and, as an author, I feel hugely privileged to be a small part of a very talented team.

This novel was written during the year of Covid-19 lockdown, which in many ways felt like the Great Frost of 1607, for the whole world seemed suspended, frozen in a perpetual winter. There can scarcely be any of us who have not suffered some kind of loss during this time, if not family members and friends, then employment, education, our health or precious moments that we could not share with those we love. But if we can learn anything from history, it is that our forebears endured some terrible times, but somehow the human spirit always emerged stronger for it, and the worst of times often became the catalyst for a giant leap forward and the dawn of a new and better age.

A book is a conversation between the author and the reader, a sharing of thoughts, imagination and experiences, a meeting of minds. So, finally, I'd like to say a huge thank-you to you, the reader of this novel, for your generosity in taking time to share this story with me.

Author's Note

The Great Frost of 1607–8 began on 5 December 1607 and lasted until 14 February 1608 in England, with many rivers freezing solid enough to walk on. The Thames was wider and shallower than it is now, so froze to a depth that meant people could light fires, roast meat and erect stalls on it. Although the winters had been getting colder, the extreme cold spell in 1607 was unexpected and so there was no official Frost Fair on the Thames, as there would be in later years. But some enterprising men and women did venture on to the ice to set up booths from which to trade that year, and that gave the city the idea of holding properly organised fairs on the ice during the subsequent winters.

Behind the Scenes of this Novel

There are many notable characters in history most of us are probably glad we never encountered, but others I would love to have met. As soon as I came across the redoubtable Lady Magdalen, Viscountess Montague, I found myself full of admiration for her spirit and the skilful way she managed to survive and keep her estates, when so many others lost everything, including their own lives. I was also fascinated by her personal moral code, for even when some of her own close relatives were plotting against the throne, she flatly refused to become embroiled in treason and yet walked that uneasy tightrope, choosing to shelter priests and others who undoubtedly had knowledge of, and in some cases direct involvement with, the Northern Rising Rebellion and the Gunpowder Treason plot.

Magdalen Dacre was born at Naworth Castle, Cumberland. Her parents came from two of the leading Catholic families, Dacre and Talbot. At thirteen she was sent as gentlewoman to the Countess of Bedford. At sixteen she joined Queen Mary's household and became the Queen's great friend and confidante. In 1554, when Mary married Felipe II of Spain, Magdalen was one of the bridal attendants. Magdalen was unusually tall and pretty, but was reported to be very religious, spending much of her time in prayer and wearing a coarse linen smock under her court clothes.

On 15 July 1558, Magdalen became the second wife to the widower Anthony Browne, 1st Viscount Montague, who was Master of the Horse to Mary's consort, Felipe II of Spain. Montague owned three estates, including Battle Abbey in Sussex, which his father had been granted by Henry VIII. Magdalen raised Montague's twin children from his first marriage, their mother having died in childbirth, and bore ten children of her own.

In February 1555, her husband went to Rome on Queen Mary's behalf to try to persuade Pope Julius III to actively back the restoration of Catholicism in England. In 1557, he joined the Privy Council. He was an executor of Queen Mary's will and chief mourner at her funeral. After Elizabeth became Queen in 1558, Montague publicly denounced proposals to elevate the status of the Protestant religion and was replaced on the Privy Council. Both Montague and Magdalen's brother attempted to circumnavigate the oath of allegiance by declaring it was their duty to support the Pope if he came in peace, but that they would support the Queen in the field if the Pope came in war.

In 1569, Viscount Montague, together with his son-in-law the Earl of Southampton, and Magdalen's brother, was implicated in the 'Rising of the North', a plot by Catholics to depose Elizabeth, but escaped punishment. In general, the Montagues were left alone, even though they had resident Catholic chaplains, all officially retired. They were not supporters of the Jesuit movement and one of their chaplains was a well-known anti-Jesuit. During Mary's reign they had founded two sumptuous chantry chapels, at Cowdray and at Battle. It was rumoured that even under Elizabeth and James, their chaplains celebrated Mass for as many as 120 people at Battle on occasion.

In 1586, Montague proved his loyalty to Elizabeth as one of the peers who tried Mary, Queen of Scots. In 1588, he prepared to defend England against the approaching Spanish Armada, raising a troop of cavalry. In August 1591, Elizabeth visited Montague at Cowdray House, his residence in West Sussex, where he entertained her lavishly for a week while hiding his Catholic priests and servants within the house throughout her visit.

But though he was favoured by Elizabeth, he was also kept under close watch, not least because his estates were so near to the coast, where foreign spies could easily come and go. In 1569, Archbishop Parker's commissioners reported that Battle Abbey was one of the places 'Marian' priests were kept. Marian priests were those who had been ordained during the reign of Catholic Queen Mary and were not punished by Elizabeth, provided they gave up the priesthood, in contrast to priests who were illegally ordained abroad during Elizabeth's reign and would be executed if caught in England. The following year there were claims that Sussex people were being turned away from the new religious practices by the 'long standing traditions' of Battle Abbey. Nevertheless, Queen Elizabeth continued to visit Montague.

The 1st Viscount Montague died suddenly in October 1592 and his widow, Magdalen, afterwards lived mainly in Battle Abbey until her death. Battle Abbey was said to contain a subterranean passage through which priests were smuggled into England and it would have been easy for her to move fugitives between her three properties. She even allowed a Catholic printing press to operate in one of her houses.

Under Elizabeth, Magdalen was only once accused of recusancy. Her house was searched only twice, and only one of the priests she was hiding was discovered and arrested.

But she always refused to aid treasonous plots, even those of another brother, Francis. And in 1597, when a messenger gave her a letter to be passed on to the Earl of Essex, Magdalen handed the messenger to the magistrate and also reported the incident to Lord Buckhurst, a Privy Councillor, sending her niece as a witness.

Guy Fawkes, who had been born into a wealthy Protestant family in Yorkshire, had entered the service of Magdalen's husband, the 1st Viscount, as a footman on his estate at Cowdray in West Sussex, shortly after leaving school. The Viscount was reported to have disliked him and he was soon dismissed. But Fawkes was subsequently employed by Montague's grandson Anthony-Maria Browne, 2nd Viscount Montague, and because of this association, the 2nd Viscount Montague was arrested and imprisoned in the Tower of London following the Gunpowder Plot in 1605. But since there was no evidence he knew about the plot, he was released. Strangely, in 1599, Lady Magdalen's house in Southwark had been searched for gunpowder on the strength of information given to the local justices. It wasn't found. But this was six years before the Gunpowder Plot.

In 1603, Richard Smith, a Catholic missionary and agitator who was 'Professor of Controversies' at the English College of St Gregory in Seville, was smuggled into England and hidden by Magdalen. He became her confessor. At the same time, the authorities under King James began to harass her for her recusancy, whereas under Elizabeth her 'crime' had been largely ignored. She particularly drew the attention of the notorious Catholic pursuivant Richard Topcliff, who claimed to have discovered a holy well in Battle Abbey grounds to which the women went 'as if on pilgrimage'.

This sudden attention from the authorities may have been in part because Smith encouraged Magdalen to view attending Anglican services to comply with the law as abhorrent. Before Smith's arrival, Lady Magdalen had attended services at St Mary's, the Anglican church, but the living was unique in that the Dean of Battle did not come under the jurisdiction of the local bishop and spent most of his time at Oxford University. In consequence, he didn't turn up to conduct services or even take communion himself for two years, so hardly anyone in Battle ever went to the parish church.

In 1607, the Privy Council announced that Lady Magdalen should not be sentenced for her refusal to attend services, because of her status, age and former fidelity to Queen Elizabeth, a decision which infuriated both Robert Cecil and King James. Lord Buckhurst's influence in the Privy Council probably helped to prevent her from being prosecuted for recusancy in 1607, but after his death, she was left without a protector.

Three men who tried to prove that Lady Magdalen's servants were priests in disguise all failed. Two she managed to get imprisoned on other charges, and the third, Master N. Benet, mysteriously fell into a pit at the end of the town and died. This was deemed to be 'suicide' and her chaplain, Richard Smith, records gleefully that as a result 'he was buried like a dog at the roadside'.

Magdalen herself died at Battle Abbey, Sussex, on 8 April 1608 at the age of seventy. Five priests came to her house the day before to say Masses for her. It wasn't until after her death that the recusancy commission actively pursued and punished her tenants and servants.

Battle Abbey is as intriguing as the Montague family and, like them, it harboured secrets which may never be uncovered. The monks of Battle Abbey owned 140 relics and an immensely valuable reliquary of gold and gems commissioned by Abbot Ralph (1107–1124). But in 1538, when the notorious Dr Richard Layton made an inventory for Cromwell, the reliquary was not listed, nor was anything of value. It was believed the monks had already sold the treasure, but suppose they had hidden it hoping that one day, when King Henry died, they might be allowed to return?

Night-creeping

I first encountered the practice of night-creeping many years ago, when I was working in Nigeria. There it was called night-running and involved individual adults or even whole families. Later, when I was working in Grimsby, Keith Gray, a Young Adult fiction author, told me about teenagers he'd known who had been night-creepers when he was growing up on the east coast of England. And as I began researching the phenomenon, I discovered that spates of night-running or night-creeping had occurred at various periods throughout the centuries in Britain and Europe, from Saxon times and probably even earlier.

Night-creeping is quite different from instances where an individual or a group deliberately terrorises a particular person or family in a hate crime, or attacks a household because they harbour a grudge against the victims. Night-creepers cannot easily control or rationalise what they do. They feel compelled to creep to houses or run through villages after dark, frightening a community by banging on doors and windows, dragging sticks over walls and fences, hissing and shrieking or doing anything to make a noise. They appear to be addicted to the adrenalin rush which comes from the danger of being caught, but also to the thrill of hearing the terror of those inside. They derive pleasure and power from living and working among their neighbours during the day, listening to them speculating about who might be doing this. In centuries past, victims of night-creepers often believed their cottages were being attacked by demons or evil spirits.

Night-creeping seems to be repeated in families and some addicts also believe they are possessed by a spirit which compels them to do it. One man interviewed in 2019, whose late father was also a night-creeper, thought he'd been infected by the desire when he stepped over a charm his father had buried near his threshold. Night-creepers report feeling sick and highly agitated if they are prevented from doing it or if they try to stop, and they are only able to rest each night after they've carried it out.

Glossary

BEARDED STAR – a comet, also referred to as a *blazing star* or *long-haired* star. In September and October of 1607, Halley's Comet was observed in the skies over England. Milton writes of a comet 'shaking pestilence and war' from its 'horrid hair', perhaps inspired by the knowledge that Halley's Comet had appeared in 1066, just before the Battle of Hastings. But King James, writing about another comet in 1618, said that although a comet was a portent of change, we couldn't presume to read God's mind and say it was an evil omen. It might be a good omen.

BLEAT – an old Sussex dialect word meaning bitterly cold weather or a cold, cutting wind.

BOILED BRAIN – an Elizabethan insult meaning a *hot-head*, a maniac, a fool who rushes in without thinking. Frequently applied to hot-blooded youths who might be too quick to draw a weapon or start a brawl.

BOUSY or BOWSY – *inebriated*. First used in the thirteenth century, deriving from a Dutch name for a type of drinking vessel. By the sixteenth century it had become a popular street term, meaning *drunk*. By the eighteenth century, the word had evolved to *boozy*.

BUCK TUBS – bed sheets and any garment worn next to the skin were made of linen, so that they could be washed and bleached regularly, and the wealthy might change their linen undergarments and shirts several times a day. A buck tub was about the size of a half-barrel raised on legs or on a stand with a tap or bung near the bottom and a shallow tub placed beneath. Linen clothes and sheets would be folded in the tub, separated by sticks so that when lye and water were poured in at the top they would run evenly through the layers. The cloth was then left to soak until the dirt had dissolved in the alkaline lye. This might have to be repeated several times before rinsing, with the linens being refolded between each soak. This process was known as *bucking*.

BUTTERED EGGS – the yolks from half a dozen eggs were separated from the whites, and beaten into a pint of cream which was then heated gently until it curdled. The mixture was suspended in a muslin cloth until all the whey had dripped out. The curds were beaten into rosewater and sugar, giving a sweet yellow 'butter'. The whites of the eggs were then added to another pint of cream and treated exactly as the yolks, producing a white 'butter'. The two were then eaten together.

CANTED – old Sussex dialect meaning *upset, tipped over* or *let fall*.

CROSSBITER – an archaic word for a trickster, sometimes applied to those who fleeced the gullible with the age-old three-cups trick, known then as *thimblerig*, or more elaborate scams such as faking the conjuring of spirits.

CROWS' PUDDING – was a euphemism for *dead*. 'Yield the crow a pudding' meant *to die*. The phrases were used from the sixteenth century in the same way as later euphemisms such as *kick the bucket, croak,* or *snuff it*.

DAISY WHEELS – believed to be an apotropaic mark to ward off evil spirits. The daisy wheel, or hexafoil, resembles a flower with six petals set inside a circle, with the point of each petal touching the circumference. They are found on ancient barns, on the beams of old houses, in churches and scratched on to gravestones. It was thought that evil spirits would be caught in the continuous lines like a net and would follow them in an endless cycle, never able to break free, because there is no end point.

DEATHWATCH – or *deadwatch*, a wood-burrowing beetle that infests old timbers. It was frequently heard making a rhythmic tapping or clicking in the night in houses or churches during the hours when people would keep a waking vigil over someone who was seriously ill or the newly dead; therefore the sound came to be thought of as a death omen.

FELO DE SE – 'felon of himself', that is, committing the crime of self-murder or suicide. From the mid-thirteenth century until 1961 in England and Wales, suicide or attempted suicide was a criminal offence if the person was considered 'sane' at the time of the act. In medieval or Tudor times, when a verdict of *felo de se* was returned on the deceased, the corpse was denied a Christian burial and would be buried at a crossroads outside the village or town, or on the northside of the church among the criminals, excommunicated and unbaptised, sometimes impaled with a wooden spike, or sprinkled with salt and weighted down with rocks so that the body could not be possessed by an evil spirit or demon and rise from the grave to cause mischief. Since it was technically an act of 'murder', up until 1822, all the possessions of the person who had committed suicide were forfeited to the Crown, often leaving a grieving family in penury, especially if the deceased owned the family house, land or business. The stigma and consequences of being found guilty of *felo de se* were so draconian that many coroners and juries returned the verdict that the deceased's balance of mind had been disturbed at the time, and therefore they were not sane and so not criminally liable for their actions. Up until 1961, anyone who attempted suicide but survived could be sentenced to prison, just as they could for attempted murder, unless they could prove they were 'insane' at the time.

'FY, FA, FUM! I SMELL THE BLOOD OF AN ENGLISHMAN' – this is an ancient rhyme, probably chanted centuries before it was written down. The playwright Thomas Nashe quotes it in his 1596 pamphlet, *Have with You to Saffron-Walden*, in which he shakes his head over men who spend hours arguing about what the words mean. In Shakespeare's play *King Lear* (c.1603 to 1606), Edgar, who is feigning madness as 'Poor Tom', repeats the rhyme when he appears to be babbling nonsense.

GAUNTER – a glove-maker, from the word *gauntlet*.

GAUNTLETS – (or *manacles*) were a method of torture, where the victim's hands were placed inside metal gauntlets or in manacles and tightly compressed by means of a lever. A chain was passed through rings on the gauntlets at the wrists and the prisoner was suspended by this chain so that his feet couldn't touch the ground and his full weight dangled from his wrists.

GIGLET – in the sixteenth and seventeenth centuries this was used to refer to a girl or woman whom the speaker considered to be lewd or wanton in the way she behaved or even dressed.

GILT – sixteenth- and seventeenth-century thieves' cant meaning someone who picks locks in order to burgle houses or steal the contents of chests. The origin is uncertain, but some have suggested that the term came about from the fact that the lock pickers were usually after items such as gold coins or gold jewellery.

HALCYONS – the birds commonly known today as *kingfishers*. Their ancient name *halcyon* comes from the Greek myth of Alcyone, daughter of Aeolus, god of the winds. Alcyone's husband, Ceyx, son of the Morning Star, perished at sea. His wife was so grief-stricken that she drowned herself. The gods took pity on them and turned the pair into kingfishers, so that they could be reunited. It was believed that kingfishers built a nest of fishbones which floated on the sea, into which they laid their eggs. For fourteen days in winter, when the halcyon was said to brood her eggs on the sea, her father, Aeolus, stilled the wind and waves. This period of unusually calm weather was known as the 'halcyon days'. It was thought to occur at the time of the winter solstice, 21 December, and start around 14 December, though later the phrase came to mean any period of happiness, peace and calm.

In times past, these unfortunate birds were thought to be able to predict the wind direction when killed and dried. Many Tudor and Stuart houses had a dead kingfisher hanging from the rafters inside the house as an internal weathervane and they were also used for this purpose on board ships. When they were hung up in the house, their feathers were said to renew their colour and iridescence every year. Kingfishers, if kept in a dry place, were thought never to decay and always smell sweet, so the carcasses of the birds were also stored in chests of clothes, sheets and blankets, as they were said to preserve them from moths and decay, and to give them a pleasant smell.

HENBANE – *Hyoscyamus niger*, also known as *hogbean*, *henbell* or *devil's eye*. It was used for the external treatment of chilblains, gout, rheumatism or arthritis, then called 'fevered joints'. In the Tudor and Stuart periods, arthritis was also referred to as 'sciatica' if it affected the hips, lower limbs or back. Henbane was applied to ease the pain and inflammation, either in the form of an oil, or by rubbing the skin with fresh leaves. Henbane has a very unpleasant stench, which different people describe variously as rotting fish, rotten potatoes, smelly socks or putrid meat, hence another of its names, *stinking nightshade*. It was linked to witchcraft, because even when used in ointments, it can cause nightmarish hallucinations, convulsions and temporary bouts of madness. When burned on a fire it was thought to conjure spirits of the dead. Henbane produces hyoscine, which, in 1910, was the poison with which the infamous Dr Crippen murdered his wife.

INVISIBLE INK – used by leading Jesuits and conspirators to send messages to each other. Father John Gerard, when imprisoned in the Tower, persuaded his gaoler to buy oranges for him to eat. Gerard carved little rosaries and crosses from the orange peel and wrapped them in paper on which he had written, in charcoal, innocent requests for his friends outside to pray for him. But he used the juice of the oranges to write invisible messages between the visible words, then paid the warden to deliver these harmless gifts. Orange juice, once heated, remains visible after it cools, so any recipient could see at once if the message had been intercepted and read by the enemy. But some secret notes were written in lemon juice, because unlike orange juice, it can be made visible by wetting it with water or by heating it, yet the writing vanishes again when dried or cooled. This was useful if the letter had first to be read by a friend with instructions to deliver it to another accomplice; the disadvantage was that you didn't know who else might have read it.

JAKES – the street term for a *lavatory* or *privy*, usually a public convenience or one used communally by several households or tavern customers.

KNUCKER – a Sussex water dragon: a huge serpent-like creature, similar to the Loch Ness Monster. The name is also given to the pools in Sussex in which the creatures were reputed to live, known as *knucker holes*. These were springs from which water continually flowed out, but which had no obvious source of water going in, and yet they never dried up or froze. They maintained a constant temperature in summer, and in winter gave off steam when the surrounding air was colder. The vapour was thought to be the breath or smoke of the water-dragon. Other places called knucker holes were sink holes where streams vanished underground. The legend attached to all knucker holes is that they are bottomless. *Knucker* or *nucker* comes from the Anglo-Saxon *nicor*, meaning *water monster*, a creature which appears in the saga of *Beowulf*.

KNUCKER'S MILK – beers were given many bizarre names in the sixteenth and seventeenth centuries, such as Father Whoreson, Viper's Blood or Cock a Leg, just as real ales are today. Every alewife or brewer produced their own beer or ale that had a different strength, consistency and flavour from those brewed by others. The names allowed customers to ensure they could ask for their favourite pint at fairs and markets where many different beers and ales might be on sale.

LEOPARDS – the nickname given to the bands of specially trained men who raided houses to arrest priests and uncover any signs of

Catholic observance. They were appointed, paid for and directed by the Privy Council, who issued a warrant ordering a specific house to be searched. The leopards would try to discover priest holes and hidden objects of devotion by knocking on walls to find hollow places, measuring rooms to see if dimensions inside and out tallied, tearing down panelling and plasterwork, ripping up floorboards and stairs, and vigorously questioning family and servants – sometimes for days on end, all the while eating and drinking at the householder's expense. To add insult to injury, the householder was charged a fee for having their property searched.

Catholic priests and others called the searchers 'leopards', because at this period 'leo-pards' were considered 'bastard' animals, 'unnatural' creatures that were not one of the species saved on Noah's Ark at the time of the flood. A leo-pard was believed to be the offspring of a lion's adulterous mating with a pard or panther, which, of course, defied God's command for animals to reproduce 'each according to his kind'. These beasts were thought to be ruthless killers who revelled in wanton bloodshed.

LIVERY – a term used to refer to a light meal left in a cupboard in a bedchamber in case the householder or guest should want something to eat between main meals or after retiring for the night. Since the last main meal of the day – supper – was served in the Great Hall at about 5 p.m., the adult members of the family or guests often needed a late-night snack, especially if they'd spent the evening gaming and drinking. *Livery* was also the term given to the evening's allowance of drink for each person.

MARRANOS – also known as *conversos* or *New Christians*, were Jews whose ancestors, originally from Spain and Portugal, had been forced on pain of death to convert to Christianity. Marranos was the name given to those New Christians who continued practising Judaism in secret, disguising the symbols of their faith in everyday objects, while outwardly attending church services and appearing to conform. Jews who fled to England and other European cities to escape the Inquisition were also pressured into converting in these countries too, in order to be permitted to work and function in a Christian society.

MATCHES – lengths of hemp cord soaked in a variety of chemicals. A 'quick match' burned between four and sixty centimetres (two to four inches) per minute. A 'slow match' would burn at the rate of thirty centimetres (one foot) per hour. The speed of the burn depended on the chemicals the hemp was soaked in.

MULBERRY TREES – the hardy black mulberry had flourished in England since at least Roman times. The fruit was used by the Anglo-Saxons to flavour a honey drink called *morat*. The leaves were used to treat burns, stop bleeding and as antidote to aconite poisoning and snake bites. The white mulberry is preferred by silkworms, but it thrives only in warm climates.

It is believed that King James opted for the black mulberry because he knew it would grow in the English climate, especially since the winters were turning noticeably colder. Between 1607 and 1609, he wrote letters calling on landowners to do their patriotic duty and plant mulberries to kick-start the English silk industry, charging them three farthings for one sapling, or six shillings for a hundred. But the project failed. Some historians believe this was because the silkworms refused to eat the black mulberry. Others think that the Jacobeans could not make the production of the leaves mesh with the life cycle of the silkworms in England, since the black mulberry buds late in the spring, long after any cold spell. Finally, some have argued it was the silkworms themselves that succumbed to the English climate during the bitterly cold years of the frost fairs.

NAVENS – a variety of turnip, generally chopped and added to mutton or other meat stews, as an alternative to carrots.

PINNANCE – a ship's tender. The small boat stored on a sea-going ship which was used to row men and provisions between the ship and shore, when a ship could not moor next to a wharf or quayside.

PISSPROPHET – a derogatory name for a physician, because physicians frequently based their diagnosis and prescription on a detailed examination of the urine of a patient. A physician would compare the colour of the urine to a wheel chart which might have as many as twenty different hues on it, also noting whether it was clear or cloudy and if the cloudiness settled on the bottom or near the surface. They also smelled and sometimes tasted it. Tests for the early stages of pregnancy could involve adding wine to see how it reacted or placing a pin into it to see if the pin rusted.

PURSUIVANT – in this context another name for *priest hunters*. They were individually appointed by the Privy Council and operated rather like bounty hunters in the Wild West, patiently tracking the wanted person until they were caught. They executed the arrest warrants for the Privy Council, who also appointed them to hunt down the writers of scurrilous plays and books, or anyone in hiding who was wanted for treason or heresy. Pursuivants were also required to furnish the proof which would lead to a conviction of the arrested person. So, unlike bounty hunters, pursuivants were also responsible for their prisoners, sometimes for weeks or months, until they were brought to trial, often employing torture to extract the necessary pre-trial confession. Sometimes they interrogated them in the Tower or Bridewell, but they could also set up their own private torture chambers. The pursuivant Richard Topcliff even devised his own terrible forms of torture, which he enthusiastically applied in the Tower.

QUINTAIN – a post with a revolving target set up for tilting exercises on horseback, on foot or even by boat. Many villages and towns had a quintain erected on the green. It consisted of a vertical post with a horizontal bar on top. On one end of the bar was a target, often in the form of a small shield. On the other end was a heavy sack of sand or a cask of water. The player had to run or ride at the target with pike, pole or similar weapon. If they missed, they'd be the object of derision. But if they hit the target, it would cause the weighted bar to spin round. The skill then lay in ducking or dodging away before they were struck forcibly from behind by the heavy sack or the cask of water, which, in the latter case, would drench them. It was a useful military training exercise for boys and men who might be pressed into service as pikemen, and throughout later centuries it remained a popular sport. Old quintains can still be found in some villages, such as Offham, Kent.

Quintains used by the nobility on horseback in the tilt worked on the same principle, except that instead of a bar, a life-size wooden figure was used, in the form of an enemy soldier or a classical character, such as an Ancient Greek hero. This figure would be mounted on a pole, holding a raised weapon in an outstretched arm. If the rider's lance did not strike it exactly in the centre, it would cause the figure to revolve. A skilled horseman would be able to ride clear and stay in the saddle. But the less experienced would be unseated, either by the momentum of the thrust of the heavy lance into empty air, or by being struck by the extended wooden arm and weapon of the spinning figure.

SALTS – Sussex dialect for *salt marsh*, an area of marshland that would be covered by the sea at high tide.

SEVEN WHISTLERS – the mournful cry of a flock of birds heard seven times was thought to warn of impending death and disaster, such as the collapse of a mine, a battle being lost, a storm at sea, or the fall of a great house. The birds are said to be lost souls come to warn the living and anyone who heard the cries and ignored them would soon join the ranks of the restless dead. The birds thought to be the whistlers varied around the country, but were all species which have a shrill whistling call, such as plovers, curlews, whimbrels or widgeon.

SEWER – pronounced 'sower', from the Anglo-French *asseour*, meaning a *seater*. This was the man who oversaw the very formal setting of the tables for a wealthy family and their guests and the elaborate ritual of the serving of the main meals. He supervised all the servants who waited in the Great Hall, ensuring that the ceremonies such as processing in with the meat and the art of carving and presenting dishes were enacted correctly. Rather like the maître d' in a top-class restaurant, this was a position of great respect within the household and in royal palaces the sewer was usually a nobleman of high rank or standing.

SHAW – old term for a *thicket*, or patch of dense woodland.

SKIMMINGTON – otherwise known as a *rough music* or a *charivari* or *shivaree*, in which a crowd collected after dark outside the house of someone they wanted to punish and made as much noise as possible by beating metal tools, pots and pans, shaking bird scarers or whirling bullroarers.

SKIRRETS – *Sium sisarum*, a hardy perennial root vegetable resembling a many-branched parsnip. The name comes from *skirwhit* or *skirwort*, meaning *white root*. They have a slightly peppery, sweet flavour, between carrot and parsnip, and their sweetness made them popular at a time when sugar was expensive. They were widely used both in savoury dishes and puddings, including skirret pie, bacon pottage, soups, stews, and with apples in sweet-battered fritters. Potatoes gradually replaced skirrets, which fell out of favour because their multiple long thin roots made them time-consuming to peel compared to a potato.

STOMACHY – Sussex dialect word describing a person who is proud, obstinate or difficult.

STONE-BOAT – a type of sledge that would be used at all seasons of the year to drag heavy loads such as rocks, wood, kegs and bales of hay over meadows, muddy fields, marshes, wet sand, heathland, or any terrain in which a wheeled cart or wagon would get stuck. Depending on the size of the stone-boat and the weight of the load, it might be pulled by people or by animals such as horses or oxen. Some had broad metal runners; others had a flat bottom of smooth planks that could slide over the ground and distribute the weight.

Being low to the ground, it also made it much easier to load and unload heavy objects in contrast to lifting them up on to a cart or wagon.

SWAGGERERS – gangs of young Englishmen who, particularly in London, amused themselves by hunting down and beating up Scotsmen who ventured out at night, often chasing them into alleys and courtyards where they could trap them. Swaggerers was the name the gangs called themselves. There were also packs of Swaggerers who specifically targeted the Scottish beggars in London, especially around Holborn. In retaliation, groups of Scotsmen would try to corner Englishmen and yank off the dangling earring which fashionable English men wore in one ear, carrying the valuable jewellery off as trophies. They usually ripped open the earlobe and, in some cases, sliced or tore off the whole ear in the process.

THIRTY-POUND KNIGHTS – this was one of the anti-Scots phrases that landed the playwrights George Chapman and Ben Johnson in prison when, along with John Marston, they wrote and published the play *Eastward Hoe* in 1605. It was a mocking reference to King James liberally bestowing knighthoods on the Scots in his retinue. It was said that any man, no matter what his birth, could buy a knighthood for thirty pounds. There was more than a grain of truth in this jibe, since James saw selling knighthoods as an easy way to raise much-needed revenue for his coffers. This practice naturally infuriated those hereditary knights who were descended from noble families and the men who had earned their knighthoods through bravery on the battlefield or other great feats.

TILLY-FALLY or TILLY-VALLY – something which is nonsense. It was also used as an exclamation.
    'I bet her husband murdered her.'
    'Tilly-fally! She's not dead. She's away visiting her sister.'

TURK – the mighty Ottoman Empire, which ruled the Middle East, Southern Europe, Greece, the Balkans and parts of North Africa, had been founded by the leader of the Turkish tribes, Osman I, in 1299, and though the Ottoman Empire in the sixteenth and seventeenth centuries encompassed many more ethnic groups than the once nomadic Turkmen, people in Western Europe still referred to men from the Ottoman Empire, particular the soldiers, as *Turks*. Christian Europe was continually fighting the Ottoman Empire for control of trade routes, and captured Christian soldiers and seamen were frequently enslaved and forced to row in the galleys until they were ransomed. Soldiers of the Ottoman Empire had a formidable reputation for fearlessness and fighting prowess, and therefore were often depicted alongside legendary warriors of Ancient Greece and Rome in pageants, mock battles and the tilts in England and Europe, representing the ultimate test of skill and courage.

TWITTEN – Sussex dialect meaning a narrow path between two walls or hedges or an alleyway between two houses, usually leading to a yard, a wider road or a piece of common land.

URCHIN – a *hedgehog*, also called a *hedgepig*. It was believed that every animal on land had a corresponding animal that lived in the watery kingdom of the sea. Porpoises, for example, were called *sea-swine*. The hedgehog's aquatic twin was the sea-urchin, so both were called urchins.

VERT – a French word meaning *green*, used in old Sussex dialect for a *field* or *pasture*. It can still be found, especially on old maps, as part of a field name, such as Long Vert or Upper Vert.

VOIDING BASKET or VOIDER – this was used to collect up all the dirty dishes from the Great Hall after the meals or from the bed-chambers where a livery, or light meal, had been served. To *void* a table meant to clear it as each course was finished and at the end of the meal.

WARD AND WATCH – citizens were obliged to help keep the peace and protect towns under the direction of the constable. Usually, a dozen or so men would patrol the streets in pairs. The day shift was known as *the ward* and the nightshift *the watch*. They were supposed to keep a lookout for thieves and muggers, break up fights and apprehend anyone who was drunk or causing trouble. How effective and diligent they were varied enormously from town to town, depending on the quality of the recruits and how willing individuals were to put themselves in danger.

WATCHERS – from 1591, all citizens, including innkeepers, were obliged to question any stranger they encountered about where they'd spent the past year, and if they weren't satisfied with the answer, they were to hand them over to officials. But watchers were men with local knowledge, recruited and *paid* by sheriffs, Lord Lieutenants and bishops to keep watch on the ports, harbours, coves and coastal roads of southern England for strangers being landed from ships or attempting to board them without being checked by customs officials. A single watcher, keeping an eye on a remote beach at night, would simply alert the sheriff's men if there was any unusual activity, but a group of watchers patrolling a road or harbour could legally seize a traveller and take him by force to an official to be questioned, if he seemed suspicious.

WITCH'S BRIDLE – used commonly in Scotland. The prisoner would be chained to the cell wall by means of an iron bridle with four sharp prongs that were forced into the mouth. Two spikes pressed against the tongue, the other two into the cheeks. This was often used as part of a regime to 'break' the victim by preventing them from sleeping for days at a time.

WYVERN – a type of dragon or winged serpent, but the wyvern has only two legs, whereas a dragon has four. In place of its back legs, the wyvern's body tapers into a serpent's tail with a diamond or arrow shape at the tip. A dragon or wyvern was the emblem on the battle standard English, probably last seen on the battlefield in 1066. The wyvern was the bringer of death and destruction, and in the Middle Ages it was thought they flew through the night sky, spreading plague and pestilence to both humans and livestock.

YENA – the old name for a group of animals which included the hyena, thought to be the offspring of dogs mating with cats. They were believed to live in tombs and dig up graves to feast on the dead, and they were said to be able to change at will from being male to female. If hunting dogs crossed the yena's shadow, the dogs would be unable to bark to alert the hunter. If a yena walked round an animal three times it could not move. The beast was said to carry a stone in its eye, also called a yena, which if placed under a human tongue would enable that person to foretell the future.

About the Author

KAREN MAITLAND is an historical novelist, lecturer and teacher of Creative Writing, with over twenty books to her name. She grew up in Malta, which inspired her passion for history, and travelled and worked all over the world before settling in the United Kingdom. She has a doctorate in psycholinguistics, and now lives on the edge of Dartmoor in Devon.